letting go
at 40

L.B. DUNBAR

www.lbdunbar.com

ROMANCE. FOR SEXY SILVER FOX LOVERS.

Letting Go at 40
Copyright © 2023 Laura Dunbar
L.B. Dunbar Writes, Ltd.
https://www.lbdunbar.com/

This is a work of fiction. Names, characters, places, and incidents are the product of the author's imagination or are used fictitiously, and any resemblance to any actual persons, living or dead, events, or locales is entirely coincidental.

The author acknowledges the trademarked status and trademark owners of various products referenced in this work of fiction, which have been used without permission. The publication/use of these trademarks is not authorized, associated with, or sponsored by the trademark owner.

Cover Design: Shannon Passmore/Shanoff Designs
Edits: Melissa Shank
Edits: Nicole McCurdy/Emerald Edits
Edits: Gemma Brocato
Proofread: Karen Fischer

Other Books by L.B. Dunbar

Scrooge-ish

Road Trips & Romance
Hauling Ashe
Merging Wright
Rhode Trip

Lakeside Cottage
Living at 40
Loving at 40
Learning at 40
Letting Go at 40

The Silver Foxes of Blue Ridge
Silver Brewer
Silver Player
Silver Mayor
Silver Biker

Silver Fox Former Rock Stars
After Care
Midlife Crisis
Restored Dreams
Second Chance
Wine&Dine

Collision novellas
Collide
Caught

Rom-com for the over 40
The Sex Education of M.E.

The Heart Collection
Speak from the Heart
Read with your Heart
Look with your Heart

L.B. DUNBAR

Fight from the Heart
View with your Heart

A Heart Collection Spin-off
The Heart Remembers

BOOKS IN OTHER AUTHOR WORLDS
Smartypants Romance (an imprint of Penny Reid)
Love in Due Time
Love in Deed
Love in a Pickle

The World of True North (an imprint of Sarina Bowen)
Cowboy
Studfinder

THE EARLY YEARS
The Legendary Rock Star Series
The Legend of Arturo King
The Story of Lansing Lotte
The Quest of Perkins Vale
The Truth of Tristan Lyons
The Trials of Guinevere DeGrance

Paradise Stories
Abel
Cain

The Island Duet
Redemption Island
Return to the Island

Modern Descendants – writing as elda lore
Hades
Solis
Heph

A Letter to Readers

Thank you for your patience. For those in my reader group, Loving L.B., you'll know the trials and tribulations I went through to write this book. I originally wrote Mason and Anna a story—87,000 words which is a complete novel. That story wasn't the right story for this couple, though, and my editor agreed. I could do better. They deserved better.

I'd posted that *Letting Go at 40* would publish in September 2022. By April, I panicked that it wouldn't happen. By June, I thought I could pull it together. Also by June, I accepted the defeat of not writing a good book. I've never had to cancel a pre-order. Not in forty-seven books. Not in eight years of publishing. The setback was personal. I'd failed.

I put off tackling Mason and Anna once more. Wrote another novel instead. Edited a novella as well. By August, I was freaking out again over this story.

In the spirit of *Letting Go at 40*, I had to get over myself.

There's truth in Ben's fictional tale. People die. We aren't immortal. And grief is one of the emotions the living must wrestle. I've had conversations with readers about Mason and Anna. Fear things would happen too soon. Desire for Mason's happily ever after. Concerns for Anna's grief. Readers loved Ben as much as I did.

I'm not professing I understand grief, especially the loss of a partner in marriage. I'm only telling a tale based on fictional characters and how they might realistically react when one is grieving, and another is longing. Guilt seems to go hand in hand. Guilt for living. Guilt for loving.

Honestly, Ben was such a great guy—fictional and all—and he realized that some hearts are meant to be loved and to love again. We live, love, lose and learn, he said, and those experiences cycle around and around, overlapping and intertwining, and giving us what we term as Life, capital L.

May your life be full. May your days be long and the years not short. Our hearts can break but they also mend.

May you love, learn lessons, accept loss, and live.

Thank you for reading Lakeside Cottage, the series, and falling in love with four friends (and one wayward brother).

I've loved them all.

Again and again, and again.

Hearts, L.B.

To be happy, you must let go of what's gone.
Be grateful for what remains.
Look forward to what is coming.
-- Unknown

8

Prologue

Present Day
September

On The Beach

[Mason]

As I stand on the shore of Lake Michigan, skipping rocks in the quiet morning hours, my heart is as full as my pocket. I've been down here on the hunt for heart-shaped rocks. Easy to spy when you aren't looking; difficult to find when you are.

I never imagined I'd be where I am. The place. The position I'm in. The edge of everything I ever wanted.

I had been cocky and confident at eighteen, I never thought I *wouldn't* get the girl. So many things had come effortlessly to me in my life, I hadn't considered that she wouldn't be the same. I thought she'd pick me.

I was wrong then.

She chose a better boy who turned into the best of men. They loved long and hard, and I'd give anything to have him back again.

We both lost someone two years ago. We both loved him.

However, I've been pining for her for twenty-five years. Mourning a different loss all this time. The perfect girl.

She might have only been grieving for two years, but her sorrow started the moment he was diagnosed. When the stopwatch started ticking, and there wasn't a race to be won but one to be lost at the end.

Besides, there isn't a structure for grief. No time limit or end date. Each person grieves in their own way.

In the peaceful minutes before the beach fills with friends and family, I stare out at a rock I skipped, hopping one, two, three, four times before dropping beneath the still-calm water.

Four summers.

Four directions.

Four friends. Zack, Logan, me, and Ben.

Staring up at the bright blue sky, the color nearly matches my lost friend's eyes. It isn't something guys might notice about one another, but Ben had the friendliest eyes. Laughter often in them; disappointment on occasion. Sadness and fear at the end.

If I could bring you back, man . . . The thought filters through my head, silently sent up to the heavens. While I was cock-sure and unflappable at eighteen, at forty-three I'm certain I do not have the power to return someone from the dead.

And Ben is dead.

The cold hard truth is my best friend died two years ago.

I didn't plan for things to happen as they have. I never in my wildest dreams suspected I'd ever be here, standing on her beach, a pocket full of heart-shaped rocks, and my heart on the line.

I saw her growing old with him. We'd all grow old together. A family of friends, full of faults but filled with love, always love.

But Ben is gone, his life cut short too soon. Anna will live out her still-young days with someone else.

I blink in the growing brightness of a new day. Or maybe I'm just overcome with emotion.

"Thank you, man," I whisper. *Thank you for trusting me with your care in the end. Thank you for believing in me when I didn't see it myself. Thank you for showing me the way when I was missing something, and I just didn't know what that something was.*

I'm more grateful than the spoiled eighteen-year-old I'd been when we met. More grateful than a man had a right to be, and I wouldn't give any of it back.

Not the friendship.

Not the love.

Not the trust.

Ben trusted me when I didn't trust myself. His dedication to our friendship was everything to me.

And now, the love I have from a good woman will match that everything.

I'll never mistake Ben's intentions, though. He didn't gift her to me.

But I'm getting ahead of myself.

As I stand on the beach on this particular morning, my thoughts flip backward over the course of the past few years. From the moment we turned forty, everything has changed for each one of us.

Logan fell in love with our best friend's younger sister and had babies.

Zack fell in love with the enemy; Anna's next door-neighbor.

Even Archer McCaryn returned and found love with Anna's single-mom friend.

The only ones left standing were Anna and me.

And the best way to recall our story is to start at the beginning, three years ago.

Chapter 1

3 Years Ago
August

The Reunion

[Mason]

I can do this. I can keep her out of my head.

This is my mantra as I pound on the sand beneath my feet and push my body along the shoreline, running as if I can outrun my thoughts.

Roughly twenty-two years have passed, and I still have to fight to ignore the feelings I have for her. I don't even want to think her name. I don't want to consider how shiny her dark hair remains or how smooth her skin still looks after all this time. I don't want to accept that despite having three children with someone else, her body still does it for me.

My dick aches.

I need to stop thinking about her.

My legs strain on the unsteady surface of early morning wet sand. My heart hammers. Ever since Ben called us to join him at his in-law's cottage I've been on edge. I shouldn't be here. I shouldn't be around them, but Ben was adamant. He wanted me here. He needed me.

Ben Kulis. One of my best friends; the truest of friends.

We've vacationed together in the past. There were years when all of us—Logan, Zack, Ben, and me—spent endless time together. Pre-relationships. Pre-marriage. Pre-children. At least for them. I've never been married and, while I have a child, that's a complicated story.

Legs pumping, I pummel the wet grains beneath my feet. The rhythm in my chest matches the *thump-thump-thump* of my heels. I will myself to tamp down my thoughts as I near the wooden staircase marking the climb to the house. A one-hundred-fifty step ascent leads up the bluff. The cottage, which is a humble term for such a grand house, overlooks

Lake Michigan. Lakeside is a sleepy area of million-dollar homes and family-inherited cottages.

I'd like to keep running but a lone figure sits in one of several Adirondack chairs on this private portion of beach and I slow my run. As I near Ben, he sits with his arms tucked beneath a beach towel covering his legs. A Michigan State sweatshirt that has seen better days covers his upper body. He's pulled the hood over his head and stares straight ahead at the slow ripple of the morning waves.

Cautiously, I approach him. My friend of twenty-plus years is different. While he's been smiling, he's forcing the curl of his lips. While he's been laughing, the sound doesn't brighten his eyes. We're here for two weeks and his body doesn't appear like he has the strength for two minutes of the façade he's working to upkeep.

Ben is a great guy. Blond hair, blue eyes, he has all-American boy written over him even at the ripe age of forty. But something about his present state suggests he's aged faster than the rest of us. A gorgeous wife, three amazing children, a steep mortgage and owning a small business can do that to a man. I wasn't jealous.

It's a lie I tell myself.

"Mason." My name comes out as if he was expecting me.

I'm the squeaky wheel in our cart of four best friends. The one who can't seem to settle down or grow up, depending on who you ask. The one who has had a multitude of women over the years but never the right one. And although I have a child, I'm a shit dad, according to most people, myself included, but it doesn't take away how fiercely I love my little girl. Ben knows my truths and I don't deserve his friendship.

"Hey man. What are you doing down here?"

Ben is nestled in like he's preparing for winter instead of a fine August morning where the day threatens to be warm despite the slight morning breeze.

"Just thinking thoughts." His tone is dull. "Take a seat."

I shake my head to decline. I'm sweating from the run and my heart races from pushing myself. But a glance at his expression has a new layer of perspiration developing. My insides are a riot of apprehension at the grave look on Ben's face. The dull undertone of his voice hints that whatever he is about to tell me will change everything. My chest heaves, but I can't seem to catch my breath. Is it exertion? Is it fear? Either way, I won't be able to sit still with the sudden anxiety coursing through my blood. I remain standing.

"I was going to grab some coffee before the chaos begins. What's up?" I tip my chin, trying to remain nonchalant which is the exact opposite of how I feel. It's as if my body knows before my head catches up that whatever Ben is about to tell me, I'm going to hate it.

Maybe he's finally wised up that I'm the worst friend ever.

I lust after—

"I'm dying."

The words were not what I was expecting. For half a second, I think Ben's joking but the grave expression on his face tells me this isn't a fucking trick.

My legs quake. My hands land on my hips without my control. I bend at the waist still certain I've heard him incorrectly.

The sudden thickness in my throat strangles my thoughts. "Excuse me?"

Ben focuses forward, eyes never leaving the water behind me. "I have pancreatic cancer. The prognosis is the inevitable."

Holy fuck. Just. Holy. Fuck. "Ben." My brain can't compute words. What can I say? What phrase would hold any meaning compared to what he's just told me? "Does Anna know?"

At the mention of his wife, Ben finally looks up at me.

Anna. His beautiful wife. An exceptional mother. A woman who treats friends like family, whether they deserve it or not. Ben's gaze answers my question. Of course she knows.

Since the moment they met as teenagers, they've been inseparable. Despite Ben being Anna's lawn boy and her with economic status off the charts. Despite him being from this small-town community and her growing up near Chicago. Despite this cottage being her family's second home. Ben made it his mission to make the quiet, shy, middle McCaryn fall in love with him.

I doubt it was a struggle for her. Ben is a great guy. He sees positive things in people they don't see in themselves. He saw something in me when we were young, and regardless of my internal betrayal, he's continued our friendship.

"When did you find out?" I'm not good with this stuff. Death in general makes me uneasy. Thinking about Ben being gone . . . the idea is unfathomable. We are too young for these kinds of conversations.

"I'd like to explain everything to everyone later. At the end of our visit."

Ben had requested our presence for two weeks at his wife's Lakeside home. She'd inherited the place along with her older brother and younger sister. Anna comes here the most.

Two weeks, Ben asked. Fun. Sun. Laughs. Nothing serious, although we've all had our downers. Logan divorced. Zack in a hell of a marriage. Me, the perpetual single guy who got the wrong kind of woman pregnant.

"But there's something I need to ask of you. Something that I need to say separate from everyone else present."

The clog in my throat thickens. Will he torture me for two weeks, making me wait out his request?

"Anything, man. Anything you want."

"I need you to watch over Anna when I'm gone."

"What?" I choke, then cough to cover the blunder. A sickening uncertainty fills my throat.

Ben meets my eyes again, holding firm despite the fragility apparent in his blue ones.

Dear God, kill me. I can't do this. This, of all things, is the one thing I can't do for him.

I'm going to be sick. My fingertips dig into my hips. I take a deep breath which only makes the nausea worse.

"She's going to miss me." Ben pauses. "She's going to need help with the kids. They'll need a man present, especially Calvin and Bryce." Ben has two sons, both in high school, and a middle-school aged daughter named Mila. "I know it's a lot to ask but I need you to step up and be who I know you are."

Despite my certainty that I'm not hearing him correctly, I nod as if I understand.

Anna has a brother, and as the kids' uncle, he should be their mentor, but he hasn't been around for years. I could mention our other friends—Logan Anders and Zack Weller. Surely they'd be better role models.

But I don't question anything.

Blindly, I continue nodding and stammer, "Of course. Whatever you need." I wave outward at him. "Whatever they need. Anna. The kids. Anything."

Exhaling, I try to gather my wits and focus. "But what about you? What's going on now? How . . ." *How long does he have?* I can't ask.

Oh God, not Ben. Of all people, not him.

Ben tips his head back, shifting the beach towel spread lengthwise over his legs. His arms remain tucked beneath the thin material, and he shivers as a breeze blows over us. He gazes upward. The height of the trees on the bluff shadow the beach in the early hours but soon the brilliance of another day will highlight the sand.

How many days does Ben have left?

"I don't think I have more than a year."

Tears prickle my eyes. My nose burns and flares. Holy fuck. Just *holy* fuck. This . . . this is too much.

Ben has stood by my side through everything. He's been the solid friend I never deserved and always needed. He shouldn't ask me to watch over his wife and kids, and yet, I would do anything he asked of me.

Any. Thing.

"But I don't want to talk about time yet." Ben's voice lowers. His head is still tipped back on the hard wood of the chair.

"Yeah, man. Okay. Whatever you want." I blink a few times. Swallow once more. The bile in my throat has settled into a brick of acid in my stomach.

This can't be happening. We are only forty. We have life to live and lessons to learn. We have love to keep giving our family of friends and our kids.

One of us should not be dying.

We should be grumbling about poor decisions, midlife, and what's next.

But there is no next for Ben.

And to honor his life, I'll do whatever he asks, even if I live the remainder of my days in a certain level of hell.

Perhaps I deserve it for these feelings I've had for some twenty-odd years.

I'm in love with his wife.

Chapter 2

3 Years Ago
August

The Reunion

[Anna]

From my perch on the landing, I watch Mason walk up to Ben on the beach. My husband woke early and slipped from our bed. Although I'm conscious of his movements, I wish I could read his thoughts.

He wanted to gather his friends for two weeks. Let them pretend they were young again, with excessive drinking and rigorous activities, both things Ben's body can't handle.

I could spend my morning pondering why this is happening as I've done since the day of his diagnosis. I could continue to curse God, and any other deity that wants in on my wrath. I could raise my middle finger, and then my fist, and scream at the heavens, and none of it would change the fact my husband is dying.

And he's down on the beach with one of his best friends, Mason Becker.

Without being in their presence, their conversation plays out in my head.

Ben is being altruistic. Mason is an ass.

I've known Mason Becker as long as I've known Ben. Both were young, fit, and fine in my late-teenage eyes, but while Mason was broody and distant, Ben was funny and sweet. He'd won me over with a smile, humor, and persistence. He kissed me one summer night when I was eighteen, and love blossomed for this shy virgin wanting desperately to be deflowered and bloom.

Ben had been all my firsts.

And he'd be my last.

I didn't care what he thought he knew of Mason.

From my position on the landing, marking a halfway point up the one-hundred and fifty step climb to my family's second home, I watch Mason react to Ben. With a certainty I shouldn't have, my head knows what Ben is asking. Mason's body language confirms my thoughts.

Within minutes, Mason is climbing the steps, leaving my husband alone on the beach. Ben will never again thunder up these wooden stairs the way Mason does.

Mason is fit. With model worthy looks, he's handsome to a fault. Artfully curled, brownish hair wraps over his head and kicks out along his nape. He has arresting blue eyes, and a smile that melts panties, although mine have always stayed intact. Too many of Mason's truths rest in my head.

However, Ben loves Mason. My husband has stayed loyal to a friendship that baffles me.

As Mason nears me, his head is lowered. The weight of his thoughts maybe keeping it downward. When he hits the landing, he startles when he sees me.

"Anna." He chokes on my name.

Mason and I don't really talk. He avoids me other than brief greetings or quiet partings. He never touches me. No welcoming hug. No goodbye kiss on the cheek. No physical contact ever. Not that I need it from him. If I were still a child, I'd worry about cooties from the number of women he's had in his bed. He's a sexual transmitted disease waiting to breakout.

My thoughts are unkind, and Ben would admonish me for thinking them, telling me I don't understand Mason. He'd be correct. I don't understand the man who stands before me with doe-like eyes, but a body tight like a hunter. With his shirt off, sweat glistens on his skin and his chest heaves from the exertion of climbing, or maybe it was his run, or perhaps whatever my husband said.

A man at forty shouldn't still have a body like he is twenty. His physical appeal has always rubbed me the wrong way. While I love my husband, I'm not blind. Mason is an incredibly good-looking man. A certain magnetism exudes from his toned form and edgy face. One look at that crooked smile of his and I can see why panties ignite and women fall into bed with him. My attraction to him has always bothered me.

"He told you, didn't he?" My voice is edgy, cutting to the quick. My skin feels sharp and prickly so the snark on my tongue shouldn't be any different.

Mason nods and grips the railing of the landing. He keeps his distance. One foot on the deck. The other foot poised on the stair below. His position suggests he might take off any moment, racing up the remainder of the stairs in an effort to get away from me.

"I won't need you."

"What?" Mason gapes. His fingers tighten on the railing, and he pitches forward at the waist as if I've punched him in his rock-hard abs.

"Whatever he asked of you, I can do myself." The words are harsh, aimed like the knife I've become, ready to slice at the world for what's happening to Ben. "I can handle this myself."

Turning my head away from Mason, I glare down at the quiet water, rippling against the sand. The lake is a lover's caress at this time of day, gently lapping along the beach, like a soft tongue along tender skin.

I don't want to lose Ben's touch.

I don't want to walk alone one day.

I don't want to release my heart.

My eyes close and I cross my arms over my chest as if shielding myself from the pain or perhaps holding myself together.

The sudden thud of feet on the plank landing warns me of Mason's approach. His whisper of my name has my lids flicking open before he reaches me.

"Don't." *Don't approach me. Don't offer me condolences I'm not ready to hear. Don't touch me.*

Mason stops short, as if he were able to hear my unspoken demands.

"I won't need you," I repeat. The words are a grizzled growl of contempt, unnecessary and unwarranted.

Mason's brows hitch. "But I'll do what he's asked. Whatever he needs from me."

Fuck Ben. Fuck Mason. Fuck life and death and everything in between.

Fuck my heart which is breaking when I've promised to keep myself together for these two weeks.

As I sit on one of two chairs allowing for rest from the climb up these stairs, I make another promise to the cursed universe.

I will never open my heart again.

I will never love like I loved Ben.

I will never let go.

Chapter 3

3 Years Ago
August

The Reunion

[Mason]

"Who put this here?" Anna asks Ben as he sits opposite her at the kitchen island.

It's been days since he told me about his condition, and I'm playing the fool, pretending among my friends that I don't know the life-altering news he shared with me. We've been in the sun, hit the bars, and played golf. Our time has been more about drinking beer and driving golf carts than keeping score.

"What is it?" Ben asks, rising and moving around the island while Anna fingers the item in her hand.

"It's a heart-shaped rock." Her voice lowers, curious, reverent even before she looks up at her husband.

Ben rubs a hand up her back. "Cute." His brush-off expresses his disinterest in the item.

Anna sheepishly looks up at him, adoring him with every gaze. "Is this from you?" Her dark eyes question him while I lift my coffee mug and briefly look away. Witnessing their love is difficult. Sometimes it's like a gut punch; other times I'm indifferent, steeling myself against what I don't have.

"Maybe one of the kids put it there," Ben suggests.

Anna quirks a brow, her expression saying she doesn't believe him. Cupping the roughly shaped heart in her palm, she brings it to her chest like a treasured gift. "Thank you," she whispers to Ben.

"Babe, it's not from me." He leans forward, pressing his lips to her cheek.

How will she survive without Ben? *I won't need you*, she snarled at me only days ago. I've never heard Anna's voice so edgy, so sharp. My skin is too thick for insults, but Anna's anger directed at me was like a knife to the chest. Her pain in losing Ben will test my own strength. I don't want to see her suffer. I don't want either of them to suffer.

With my gaze on the happy couple, Ben lifts his lids while his mouth lingers on his wife's cheek. He slowly pulls away, watching me.

Sometimes, it feels like my emotions are written on my face. The envy. The lust.

Ben's brows crease before he drags his gaze from me and speaks to Anna. "What do you think it means?"

Anna still holds the rock in her palm, caressing her fingers from her right hand over the flat surface and around the sculpted edges. Edges that have formed from weathering storms, shifting tides, and years of battering.

I can relate.

"Somebody loves me." She glances adoringly at Ben again, still disbelieving the rock came from anyone other than him.

"Hmm." Ben runs a hand up her back. "Who wouldn't love you?" He leans forward and presses another lingering kiss to her cheek, but his eyes shift to me again.

And once more, I sense him reading my mind.

She'll be his strength in the near future. He's the love of her life.

And I have a decision to make about my own role among them in the next year.

+ + +

When Ben finally announces his diagnosis and the purpose of our two-week visit, it's only a few days before our friend-time together concludes. Hearing him explain his prognosis to everyone else does not make it easier to hear.

My head remains lowered as Zack questions Ben about medical care and the sudden decision to move to Lakeside Cottage permanently.

"And I don't want the best medical care. I want the best life," Ben tacks this explanation on to something else he's been saying. His words are a muddle in my mind. "I want to spend my time in a place that makes me happy. I want to come home."

Best life. Makes me happy. Home.

Like an unending carousel, the phrases go round and round in my head.

Best life. Makes me happy. Home.

I don't have any of these things. Ben is about to lose all of them.

Logan speaks next. As my roommate freshman year, Logan was a goofy guy, with a big body and a larger heart. Women found him to be a teddy bear; the kind you cuddle, not have sex with. He asks Ben about the kids and their knowledge of his condition. My own thoughts leap to Lynlee, my three-year old daughter. By most standards, including my own, I'm a shit father. I've tried. God knows, I've tried to be better, but when you get involved with the wrong woman, she can make your life a living hell. She can also keep you from your own child.

"I want you to stick together as friends and help Anna if she needs it," Ben says, pulling my thoughts back to the moment. I stare at him, watching him with such intensity, as if willing him to live. As if I can telepathically remove the cancer from his body. I do not want him to die.

"Ben," Anna whispers beside him, and her warning tone is soft compared to the harsh statement she gave me.

I won't need you.

The message was received loud and clear, but Ben feels differently. He hasn't mentioned again his request for me specifically to watch over his family. He gives us all a blanket statement here, but his gaze shifts to me briefly after speaking.

"I wanted to spend one last time being us and acting as if we'd never grow old . . . together. I just wanted to hang out and forget." Ben is speaking to Logan, answering another question I haven't registered.

Forget, forget, forget becomes my new mantra. Although there is no forgetting this fucking news. This blasphemous curse on one of the best people I know. *Cancer, fuck you!*

My heart rate is rising as is the tension in the room. Voices are growing more intense. Logan turns on Autumn, Ben's younger sister, after having spent most of his nights secretly sleeping with her. We all know what they've been up to, though.

Zack, ever the serious one, and the lawyer in the group, is growing more agitated with the logistics of moving and medical care. "What's next?"

"We just live." Ben entwines his fingers with Anna's, bringing their joined hands to his lips and kissing them.

"Pretend nothing's wrong?" Zack's tone expresses his outrage. "How can you ignore this?"

"I'm not ignoring it. I'm just choosing to embrace what I have left before it literally eats me alive." Ben chuckles, but I fail to find any humor in his comment.

Abruptly, I stand and head to the bar area just off the kitchen. The space doubles as an outdoor entrance from the flagstone patio on the back of the house and a pathway to a den used by the kids. My hands shake as I scoop ice into a glass. The overly generous pour from a bottle of scotch glugs. The sound is an imitation of how quickly I plan to down this drink.

"Bring me one of those," Logan hollers, although he really shouldn't touch the hard stuff with his diabetes.

"Make it three," Zack adds.

I pour additional glasses after swallowing down my first drink. Tucking the bottle under my armpit, I collect four crystal containers. When I turn back toward the sitting area which is part of the large open concept kitchen, Ben is devouring his wife with a kiss that turns my dick semi-hard. This is not the time or the place to lust after her, but the response is a visceral need to expend the anxiety building inside me.

I need to go to town and find a woman to fuck. I'm the playboy in the group. No one will be surprised that I have a one-night stand. What would surprise them all is how empty I'd feel the morning after. The hollowness that fills me moments after a bad decision which always seems like a good choice right before it happens.

Anna pats Ben's chest and walks out of the room, and I circle the end of one couch. Two identical sofas fill the space, resting at a perfect ninety-degree angle from each other.

"I'll drink yours if you want," I say to Ben, handing him his glass.

"I'm counting on it," Ben mutters to the liquid inside the crystal. His words feel prophetic of deeper meaning.

I collapse back to the couch beside Zack and glare at the bottle I hold in one hand, balancing it on my thigh.

Glass half full or glass half empty?

Silence fills the air around us as I pour another drink for myself.

"This is stupid," I finally blurt. I chug my drink. I've lost count of what number I'm on for the day. "You want a better quality of life at the end of your time, so be it."

My eyes meet Ben's. Zack shifts beside me but I don't look away from our friend. The one who brought us all together.

Zack and I once argued over who knew Ben first. Was it me, the other lawn boy for Kulis Landscaping, or Zack, Anna's childhood friend?

The chicken or the egg? Which came first?

Inside my head, I'm a wizard of philosophy this evening. Or maybe I'm just getting drunk.

"If things get really bad, promise me you'll get medical attention. You won't just let yourself suffer in pain but do something to aid yourself. Do something to lessen it," Zack says to Ben.

He's been talking while I've been psychologic— . . . nope, philosophic . . . no, philosophizing. My tongue, pasty and thick, rolls over the difficult word although I haven't spoken it aloud.

"Maryjane for medicinal purposes. She's my kind of woman," I joke, lifting my glass. I could use a hit, or a woman named Maryjane. Either will do to drown out everything in my head.

Best life. Makes me happy. Home.

Because I'm feeling grandiose, or just plain full of myself this evening, I speak about something that's been weighing on my mind since Ben told me about his condition.

"Remember when we were young . . . er . . . younger, and we had a plan." I pause. "We were going to make our own business. No dads. No bosses. We'd be in charge. Logan would design houses. I'd build them. Benny would make them pretty outside, and Zack would make sure we stayed out of trouble. At least, legally."

Screw the Man. Fuck my dad. Weakly, I lift my glass with my silent thoughts in an empowering salute to screw over my father. In my younger years, I idolized the man only to one day realize he was nothing but a tyrant, not a parent.

I promised myself I'd be better than him.

I hadn't been.

What happened to that dream?

I hadn't realized I'd asked the question aloud until Ben says, "I married Anna."

"Yes, women. How fickle they can be," I mutter to the glass in my hand and down the rest of the scorching alcohol. My insides burn with a combination of anger at the universe and hatred for my father, the dream-stealer. I should be irritated by the truth in Ben's answer, but I'm not. Anna picked the better person. There never really was a choice, though. It's become a joke between Ben and me.

She would have picked me if I'd gotten to her first, I'd teased.

Ben often replied how he considered himself a lucky man. He sensed I might be right. If only I'd met her first . . .

"We were the four seasons," I mumble aloud. *Or was it the four amigos?* We couldn't have been The Three Musketeers, there are four of us. I twist the glass in my hand where a drizzle remains in the bottom and dances over the crystal.

"The four points," Ben corrects.

Ah yes. I was from Up North, as the lower half of Michigan calls the upper half which isn't the official Upper Peninsula. Ben was from the west side of the state. Zack was east for some reason, and Logan came from the south, in Indiana. Four points on a compass.

"Why didn't we do it?" The question is still legitimate. The answer is more than Ben marrying Anna. Why hadn't we formed our company?

What happened to those four young college men, scrappy and eager for life to begin, to take over the world, or at least forge our own path in it?

No one answers my question which isn't rhetorical.

"To Four Points," Logan says, lifting his glass

"To Four Points," I reply, raising my glass as well, smiling for some reason.

"To the future," Ben whispers.

"And the past," Zack adds. "And friendship."

We all drink in solidarity. Even Ben takes a small sip, before coughing like a frat boy after his first taste of alcohol. I reach for his glass and down the remainder.

Glass now empty.

While I might be filled with alcohol, I'm just as hollow as the morning after a one-night stand. Nothing is going to take away the burn of losing my friend.

Chapter 4

3 Years Ago
August

The Reunion

[Anna]

The day after Ben told his friends about his diagnosis, Mason leads the guys on an adventure. I'm not privy to where they are going or what they are doing. However, excitement fills Mason's voice when he tells Ben he has somewhere to take him. Mason even allows Zack's two young sons to go with them, calling it a guys' day out.

At least, I know they wouldn't be drinking or picking up women with rambunctious six-year-old twins in tow.

Then again, I wouldn't put it past Mason, the token single guy in the group.

Logan has been falling in love with Ben's younger sister during these two weeks and while I can't predict the outcome of their relationship, I envision a future for them. They think they are so sly, stealing kisses and sneaking off together.

I miss the days when Ben and I were so carefree. We'd kiss like we were the air each of us needed to breathe. Almost twenty years later, he still kisses me like that . . . on occasion.

Ben and I have a very healthy marriage. Our sex life is regular. Our communication is good. We're open to discussing anything, like the decision to move to Lakeside Cottage. The change will be major, and on the forefront of another life-altering moment.

At first, I worried about the kids, the boys especially. Calvin is a junior in high school and moving means giving up a lot for him. Bryce will be entering high school this fall, which he would have done in Chicago, but the move means a new-to-him community. However, I have faith he'll make friends easily. I don't worry half as much about Mila, my soon-to-be middle schooler, as she is resilient and even welcomes the adventure. I'm not certain she fully understands the gravity of her father's condition.

Still, the decision to relocate was made collectively, so after Ben returns from the guys' day out with news that he was going into business with Mason, Zack, and Logan, on the cusp of these other changes, I was not pleased. We argued, something we almost never do, although we weren't perfect as a couple.

On top of Ben's diagnosis, the decision to move, the potential of starting a new business while Ben was about to begin the battle of a lifetime, one more shocking thing got thrown into the scattered puzzle pieces.

"I'm staying," Mason announces as we stand on the driveway about to wish our friends safe travels to their perspective homes.

"What?" My question is an echo of Logan's who has just asked why Mason isn't packed and loading his sporty car.

I'm still reeling from the heated discussion with Ben last night. We should have been having sex. Instead, we fought over this new development and the last thing I want is Mason Becker lingering longer.

"Why?" Zack asks and I turn in his direction. Zack is one of my oldest friends. I've known him longer than I've known Ben and Mason as Zack grew up living in the house next door to Lakeside Cottage. Our mothers were childhood best friends. His older brother Noah was friends with my older brother Archer. Zack and I lined up in age while Amelia, my younger sister, was simply a tag along.

I like to take credit for Zack and Ben becoming friends.

Mason is another story.

"I'm the only one single. Ben's eventually going to need help. I can offer strength for things his boys shouldn't do, and Anna can't muster."

"Are you calling me weak?" I bark.

"You're the strongest woman we know." Ben tugs me closer as I stand under his arm, and he presses a kiss to my forehead. For some reason, the kiss feels patronizing. "But Mason has offered and . . . We'll talk."

The finality in his words is worse, condescending even.

There is no discussion.

I don't need Mason. I don't want him here. I can handle this, whatever the *this* may be.

While I'm steaming mad from this new revelation and Ben's dismissal, I hear something about Mason staying in the rooms over the garage. The cottage is actually a sprawling six-bedroom home, most of which have their own bathrooms, plus a main bedroom suite on the first floor, complete with a sitting area and bathroom. The house also has a three-car garage with a two-bedroom apartment above it. The garage is free standing and a dozen feet from the house with a private entrance to the apartment along the side of the building.

Living above our garage would cramp Mason's tramp-boy style. I will not watch Mason bring random women to the apartment. I don't need my kids to see that kind of behavior either.

When we were younger, Mason was a full-on womanizer. Girls willingly took off their panties with only a smile from him. He has these dimples that peek out, like he's a shy boy when he's a snake in disguise. Actually, a charming snake, like a cobra, ready to strike. I had to listen to his escapades all through college, and on several occasions, I witnessed the broken-hearted tears of girls who didn't understand the game.

Mason was never going to settle down. He wasn't a one-woman kind of guy. He was that guy who loved women in general and couldn't get his fill of them. He wasn't picky, either. Of course, that got him into trouble with one particular woman.

When we were in college, I began to think Mason resented me. He hated how often I was around, stating that I cramped their four-guys vibe. I was ruining his chances of scoring with girls. I'd argue I was present to protect my friends from making a big mistake.

The animosity between us grew from there.

Mason couldn't stand me. I didn't care for him.

How was it possible he was volunteering himself to stay in my home then?

After goodbyes and hugs, Logan leaves Lakeside with his daughter Lorna although my sister-in-law's heart is breaking. They've just had a two-week fling. Autumn is Ben's younger sister and a staple in our lives. We're going to need her even more once we move here.

Zack leaves with his two little ones, Trevor and Oliver, and I actually release a deep sigh of relief. I love children. I'm a teacher but those two are a handful.

As cars pull out of our driveway, I turn to Ben, with questions still weighing heavy on my mind. Did he not have faith in me to stand by his side and handle what the future might bring?

For better or worse. In sickness and in health.

My anger grows and I slip out from under Ben's arm and head straight to our bedroom. Ben and I have taken over the suite on the first floor. While I've inherited this house with my siblings after the unfortunate death of our parents, Ben and I are the ones to visit Lakeside Cottage the most. Making the executive decision to take over this room and claim the house for Ben's final year was easy. My brother Archer has been out of the family loop for years. My sister Amelia is focused on her career in Chicago. She'll visit but she doesn't want to live in Lakeside.

"What's wrong?" Ben's voice startles me as I hadn't heard him enter our room behind me.

I've picked up one of several heart shaped rocks that have appeared in the last two weeks. Despite the protest from Ben, I'm convinced the romantic gesture comes from him. With the first one in my palm, I stroke my thumb over the hard, flat surface. The movement soothes me. In this new development of Mason staying, I'm going to need all the calm and all the strength I can muster. I slip the comforting talisman into the pocket of my shorts and turn to Ben.

"Did you ask him to stay?" Does he really believe I won't handle what comes our way?

"Not in so many words. I told him I wanted him to look out for—"

"And I told you, I won't need help." I clarify, interrupting him with a hand in the air. "I don't need Mason."

Ben tilts his head, hands on his hips. He's already lost weight. His stunning blue eyes are less bright than they'd been even last month. The littlest things are what I'm noticing. Like how his kisses are both desperate but separating, as if every one of them is a goodbye. I'm not certain how I feel about them. Do I savor the denial in them? The hope we will live our forever as we vowed? Or am I disappointed in the slow disconnect of each one of them? The deep sorrow behind each kiss that *our forever* has a timestamp on it.

"Is the issue help, or is it Mason?" Ben's tone teases.

However, I'm not in a playful mood.

I met Mason the same summer I met Ben. They were both eighteen and worked for Kulis Landscaping, a local company owned by Ben's father. Ben and Mason cut the grass, pulled weeds, and raked leaves at Lakeside Cottage. The irony of the princess in the tower lusting over the yard worker was not lost on me.

Ben's history was simple. He came from a good family with a hardworking father. His mother worked in the company's office answering phones and handling the bookkeeping. Ben, and eventually Autumn, worked for the business as well.

Mason, on the other hand, came from money. His father owned a construction company in a relatively wealthy and touristy area of Michigan. Neither Mason nor his father, I suspect, ever touched a tool in their lives. They were general contractors, who supervised the building of condominiums and shopping centers. From what I'd gathered the summer we'd met Mason was popular in his hometown. He was spoiled and conceited, but devastatingly good looking.

He was the type of boy featured on a teen-heartthrob poster you hung on your wall. He was pretty to look at, but you didn't risk touching a boy out of your league. I wasn't his type anyway.

I never understood how Ben and Mason became friends. Mason was resentful of the summer job he had at Kulis Landscaping. Frank Kulis and Mason's dad were friends and Mr. Becker had hoped manual labor would teach Mason a lesson in humility.

Still, friendship bloomed between Ben and Mason. They were opposites in so many ways. Rich boy, poor boy. Large city, small town. Funny and sweet versus sexy and raunchy. Mason still acted like a twelve-year old adolescent was trapped in his body. However, the fine details of his stature suggested he was all man.

And all of that was neither here nor there at the moment.

I didn't want Mason staying. "I won't need him."

"I need him, then," Ben says, and every piece of anger in me shatters.

"Why?"

"Because I know it's going to get tough, and there will be things I don't want you to do." Ben sheepishly looks away from me. His pride is on the line.

"And Mason will do those things?" Mason will do all the intimate personal actions Ben will need as the disease debilitates his body? I doubted it.

"He will."

"How do you know?" I cock my hip and cross my arms over my belly.

"I just know." Ben holds his head higher. His eyes narrow at me. His decision is final.

I don't want it. I don't like it. But Mason is staying.

Chapter 5

2 Years, 9 Months Ago
November

Mason Stays

[Anna]

As much as I'd rebelled against Mason's moving into the garage apartment, he has not been what I'd expected. He's like the shadow permanently attached to you but only present during certain times of the day. His presence confuses me. His attention. His compassion. It's puzzling. This version of him isn't one I've seen before, or maybe I haven't recognized it in him.

Mason gives us space as a family when we need it and assistance when we ask for it, like carpools to the kids' activities and a live-in sitter when Ben and I travel back to Chicago for doctor visits. He orders food in on nights I haven't cooked and does laundry when I forget to check hampers. I work as a substitute teacher during the day to give myself something to do other than fixate on Ben's condition. I'd been a high school English teacher in Chicago, and I plan to take on a full-time position again.

But not yet.

In the quiet of a November evening, Ben has gone to bed early. He tires quicker with each passing day. His symptoms have been a slow drip now turning to a steady trickle. I'm afraid of the moment when it will be more.

Outside the windows, our surroundings are dark. Living on the lake, off a curvy shore-line road, there aren't streetlamps to illuminate the landscape. A single light highlights the driveway at night when Calvin works in town at an after-school job and Mason does whatever Mason does in the evenings.

Most nights he goes out. He doesn't bring women back to the garage apartment, that I know of. I'm certain Ben mentioned that type of behavior wouldn't be appreciated around our children.

I'm not a prude about sex and modern attitudes about it. Calvin has slept with a girl or two starting at the ripe age of sixteen, but he isn't traipsing them through the house. He does what kids do, I guess. Backseats of cars. On the beach in the dark. Maybe even in his room when we are out. I don't know and I never ask.

I feel displaced from my kids at times. My head is elsewhere. I'd never admit how I'm struggling. The move. The cancer. The uncertainty of our futures.

Tonight, I'm standing in the kitchen, lit only by a light over the sink, and I'm scrubbing the pots and pans left over from I can't remember when. A new heart-shaped rock has appeared next to the faucet. I find them in the strangest of places. On the surface of my nightstand. In the bathroom on the sink. Even on the end table closest to my spot on the couch. At times, I'm still convinced the small gesture is Ben's doing. Other times, I wonder if my deceased parents are sending me a message. Like a reminder from the grave. *You're stronger than you know.* Maybe it's them simply telling me they love me. Or maybe the universe is just playing some kind of joke on me.

With my thoughts circling, two arms extend over mine into the sudsy water. One hand removes the sponge in my hand. The other takes the pot out of my grasp. A subtle hip check forces me to the side.

"You don't need to do them," I argue, my tone rougher than it needed to be. We've had some particularly upsetting news earlier in the day.

Ben isn't responding to his treatments.

"I've got it," Mason says without looking over at me. I'm only inches away from him. With his shirt sleeves rolled above his elbows, his long, lean arms flex as he scrubs the pot. He's never struck me as a man who'd know how to wash dishes.

"I got it," I reply, pushing at his bicep, willing him to move out of my way and let me finish scrubbing the pot. "It's my house."

Mason doesn't budge. His firm, tall body stays in position. He rinses the pot and sets it aside before turning to face me. He leans his hip against the sink cabinet and stares at me with dark, molten eyes. He looks like a tiger ready to bounce.

I straighten my shoulders and lift my head. "My dishes. My house," I repeat, my voice rising. "My husband. My life." My voice cracks. *Dammit.* I place a hand on my upper chest. My shaking fingers spread out over my rapidly beating heart, as if I can keep all the cracks and fissures there from expanding, shattering. The only thing reminding me I'm alive and whole is the acceleration of that heartbeat.

Mine. Mine. Mine. I sound like a petulant child on the verge of having a tantrum. I'm ready to explode and it's a result of my once orderly life continuing to spiral out of control.

"My friend," Mason counters. His voice isn't stern but desperate, claiming his own possession over Ben. "I love him, too."

The admission causes both of our breaths to catch. Mine in surprise. His in relief.

He slams a hand against his firm chest. "Do you have any idea how hard that is for me to admit? Or how I even feel? I'm losing him, too."

Mason's voice cracks and his Adam's apple bobs. "The only person to ever understand me. Give me a chance. Stand by my side through every fuck up . . ." His throat constricts again and his voice breaks. "It isn't only your loss, Anna."

Tears are streaming down my face in quiet rivers. I don't speak. I don't fight back.

Within seconds, I'm in Mason's arms. He's hugging me and I'm clinging to him. For just a moment, I melt into his embrace, accepting his strength, feeling the frantic rhythm of his heart, and then I'm pushing him away.

We stare at one another again, breathing heavily as if we've run a marathon. As if we did something we shouldn't have done, which we didn't do.

It was only a hug.

"I'm sorry," I whisper. For touching him. For holding onto him. For not understanding him.

"Me too." He swipes a hand through his hair, mussing the natural wave of it. For the briefest second, I imagine it's what his hair looks like after a woman combs her fingers through it or clutches the locks as Mason kisses her senseless.

Just as quickly I shake away the thought.

"No, I'm sorry you're losing him. He loves you as well." We aren't talking about a romantic interest but a strange bromance. One where Ben understands Mason when others don't. And as Mason has just confessed, Ben has been the one to give Mason a chance, stand by his side, and accept who he is.

With my expression of Ben's feelings toward one of his oldest friends, Mason's eyes cloud.

"He sees what I haven't," I continue, voice wavering but knowing Mason needs to hear this. "Ben sees how good you are at your core." His dedication and devotion have been a trickle of surprise. Mason has been a better man than I'd thought possible.

Mason's head slowly lowers, like a puppy brought to task although he's done nothing wrong. In fact, Mason has done a lot right, and I haven't given his feelings enough thought.

With tears still trailing down my face and Mason's head bent, his forefinger and thumb rub against his eyes and pause at the bridge of his nose.

Something inside me cracks and I itch to reach for him again and offer him the comfort he needs. The compassion he deserves.

However, I'd be the wrong kind of woman for that, and with that thought, I quietly excuse myself and exit the kitchen.

+ + +

Earlier, I'd pushed Mason away. Not because Mason made me uncomfortable. There were plenty of things he said that were rude or crude, and I didn't approve of, but I didn't consider him a creep. He had a wild lifestyle; one I didn't need to grasp. It was his life. He could live it how he wished.

He *was* going to live while Ben might not see next summer.

And I could not grow too comfortable with Mason. I would not get attached to him.

But I was slowly accepting Mason was the brother Ben didn't have, even if his friendship with Zack and Logan was equally solid. There was just something different between Ben and Mason. Perhaps it's as he said: Ben gave Mason chances. Ben stood by Mason through thick and thin, and God knows, Mason's had some thick in his life. I didn't need to understand Ben and Mason's relationship. It was theirs.

Theirs, theirs, theirs . . .

Not mine, whispers through my head as I lie in bed, curled up beside Ben. He wants to move to a room upstairs. His argument is that he doesn't want this bedroom to hold memories of his last days but of our years together.

The late night talks. The connection through sex. The secrets married couples share.

With shaky fingers, I reach over to touch Ben's hair, damp from sleep and possibly the onset of another fever.

New tears spring to my eyes.

Shame comes from the comfort of an innocent hug. One shared between two grieving people before someone is actually lost. Every day, the Ben I know, the Ben I love, is slipping away from me.

I close my eyes under the pressure of guilt and grief, yet strangely still feel Mason's embrace. The strength of his arms. The beat of his heart. His scent which is distinctly clean, manly, and fresh compared to the sickness coming off Ben.

My beautiful Ben with his sweet smile, and once firm hands. A boy who bought me candy, gave me my first kiss, took my virginity—which I willingly gave to him—and then he stole my heart.

How will I ever let go of him?

Chapter 6

2 Years, 8 Months Ago
December

Before Christmas

[Mason]

Logan moved to Lakeside. He bought a house about half a mile from Lakeside Cottage. I couldn't be happier to have another friend nearby. I'm also thrilled because Logan was the last point in our compass to make the decision to start Four Points Construction.

The four of us will officially own our own business in the new year.

Ben's been a driving force in the push to move forward and resurrect this ancient plan.

With Logan's architectural skill and my construction knowledge, plus Ben's landscaping genius and Zack's real estate law expertise, we have all the areas covered. Ben might be our weakest link, but Kulis Landscaping has a local manager who is taking on the role Ben would play in our business.

Because of Ben's current state.

He's sick. Vomit. Diarrhea. It's literally shit everywhere. And seeing him so sick is killing me. I don't have the words to make him feel better or the strength to right the wrong of illness taking over his body.

"I'm sorry, man," Ben groans. He officially moved out of his bedroom with Anna. His argument was she wasn't getting proper sleep when she was working every day. Anna works as a substitute teacher and she wanted to quit rather than give up sleeping with Ben.

When Ben told me the excuse, in front of Anna, she and I traded glances. Anna might not have been sleeping well, but she didn't want Ben separated from her. Ben insisted, though.

With my arms around his back, I'm escorting him to his bed on the second floor. He collapses to the mattress, and I lift his thinning legs for him.

He mutters an apology again.

"Stop it," I order. "How many times have you helped my sorry ass when I've been drunk?" I laugh at the rhetorical question. Drinking was the name of the game in college. Drunk was my status most nights, but not drunk enough to not perform. To please a girl and have her please me. Sex, drugs, and rock 'n' roll might be a theme. For me, it was scotch, females, and any surface will do.

"You still drink too much," Ben mumbles, rolling to his side, tugging his knees to his chest. I draw a blanket over him and press down the sides, essentially tucking him in. His body grows frailer by the day.

Occasionally, I take a night off from nursemaid duty, giving Ben and Anna the privacy they need. A few months ago, I'd find the first available woman in town celebrating a girls' night out or maybe passing through on a fall weekend away. Lately, I don't have the energy to seek someone random. I hardly have the stamina to get myself off, but as my dick still works and I am a man, my hand is a steady companion.

"I'm still holding out for you to get some medicinal stuff for us." Ben and I haven't gotten high together since college. He wasn't much for pot when we were younger. He'd almost be comical in his current condition. Then again, the shit is legal in Michigan now, and I could easily get him a supply. "I bet you'd be cute if you were stoned."

"You got a crush on me?" Ben weakly smiles. His lips are cracked, and I reach for some balm, spreading the thick gel over his mouth. He's dehydrated.

"You know I crush on your wife," I tease. "She might have picked me."

This brings a larger smile to Ben's lips. Over the years the argument has changed from the cocksure college guy certain Anna would have chosen me to the hesitant belief she *might* have, but probably not.

"Lucky man I am that she didn't." Ben's eyes close while his smile fades. His cheeks are ruddy, as if he is feverish.

I pull up a chair and sit beside the bed. He hates feeling like people are watching him wither away.

Sometimes, I can't help myself, though. I stare at him, still questioning our friendship while there is nothing more solid in my life. My ego was inflated balls when I was young, but I wasn't so arrogant to dismiss the fact that Ben extended an olive branch first. When I had no one because my father dumped me in this small lake town, citing my need for an attitude adjustment and a lesson in humility, I didn't know a soul. Ben was one of the youngest workers at Kulis Landscaping where my father signed me up for a summer of manual labor, and that lesson he deemed I needed.

Ben was the one who asked me if I wanted to hang out with his friends. He didn't do it for any gain. Not the parties I had thrown back home. Not for the wealth I flashed with the car I had. *Dear Daddy took that away that summer.* Ben simply asked me to hang.

When Anna came into his life, we met Zack. Then we went to college and picked up Logan. Ben brought Logan into the fold as easily as he included me. Back in the early days, the four of us were inseparable. Ben was the glue. I stuck tight to him, forever grateful for his acceptance of me. He was the first person to see me as something more than a spoiled rich kid. He was a soulmate in friendship, or some shit like that.

The years passed. He married Anna, moved to Chicago, had children, and started a business. We still saw each other for important events but the events seemed to spread further and further apart. Logan and Zack's respective weddings. The birth of Logan's Lorna, and Zack's twins. The funeral for Ben's father and Anna's parents.

Three years ago, my daughter Lynlee was born. Ben is her godfather. Lynlee's mother, Samantha, picked some random friend-at-the-time to be Lynlee's godmother. Needless to say, Samantha and I are not together.

While I have visitation rights with my daughter, Samantha always has an excuse to keep my child from me or include herself in our time together. I didn't know my child well. She was quiet and shy, reserved even. I didn't trust Samantha as a mom, but I didn't have evidence to contradict her mothering skills. She wielded our child over me like a sword, threatening to separate us forever. What Samantha really wanted from me was money. Lynlee was only a means to ensure I paid. I constantly worried Samantha would split, and I'd never see Lynlee again.

"I can hear you thinking." Ben's voice is raspy while his eyes remain closed.

"It's nothing, man. Rest."

"Mason." Ben licks his lips. "Talk."

"Just more Samantha bullshit." The mother of my child is a wreck. In my thirties, I was still sowing my oats, sinking into anyone available. At thirty-six, I'd made an error in judgement with a woman high on life and a few other things. Despite condoms and the pill, the result of that night was Lynlee, my beautiful daughter.

At forty, I couldn't say I'd gained any insight about women, but I'd toned down the random hookups and one-night stands considerably in the last year.

Ben is silent and I think he's fallen asleep, so he startles me when he croaks, "And?"

I lower my head, not wanting to burden Ben with my issues. He has bigger concerns happening to him, like being fucking sick.

"Mason," he drones. He won't give up. This is Ben. He has some strange Spidey-senses when something is wrong.

"I think Samantha might be hurting Lynlee." I dig my fingers into my hair, clutching at the thickness against the back of my neck and holding it in this position.

Ben's lids flip open. "What?" His voice cracks around the question.

I reach for a water cup with a straw and hold it to Ben's lips.

"The problem is, I can't be certain, but Lynlee has marks on her sometimes. Ones I can't identify. When I confront Samantha, she says the bruises are just typical kid stuff." I'd made the unfortunate decision to trust Samantha, assuming maternal instinct was inherent to her, due to being female and all. What a bullshit thought. I should have known better. My own mother struggled with raising me. "I don't know how to ask Lynlee if Mommy hurts her."

I swallow around the disturbing thought and the bitter taste of calling Samantha Mommy. She isn't worthy of our child. I'm not worthy of Lynlee, either.

Ben stares at me with dull eyes that once sparked with every smile. "You need to get her."

Samantha and I agreed to mediation for custody. She couldn't afford a lawyer and I followed her lead. The issue has been . . . me. I don't trust that I'd do any better at parenting than Samantha.

"You know I'll never be a good dad." We didn't all have Frank Kulis as our father. I had Marcus Becker who turned out to be a son of a bitch.

"Don't do that," Ben whispers. "Don't compare yourself to him. You aren't like him."

I sigh and press back from the bed, hands on the edge of the mattress, arms tightly extended. "I'm not you, either."

I'm not condemning Ben or even putting myself down. It's just a statement of fact. Ben is a great dad. He's patient with his kids who are each struggling in their own way with this relocation, his condition, and the addition of me in their family, although I try to give them space as a unit.

Without remarking on my comparison to him, Ben adds, "You can do better, be better."

That's another thing about Ben. He always has faith in me. When I doubt myself, he's there to nudge me, assuring me I can be more than I am.

I shake my head. "I'm lost with my own kid." The admission is hard to say but Ben knows my truths. I've struggled from the beginning with my daughter.

How could I be certain the kid was mine? That was the first question I'd asked Samantha when she told me about the pregnancy. A paternity test later, and I had the proof.

The Big Man upstairs really had it out for me.

"Then find yourself," Ben says, addressing my confession. "Lynlee will lead you the rest of the way. No one knows how to be a parent. Your kids teach you everything. You're the student, learning from them. Each one will need something different."

Ben swallows as his voice strains. "Like Calvin will need to understand it isn't his job to be head of the family while at the same time, he is the oldest and the other two will look up to him. He's allowed to make mistakes. Admitting them will be the harder part."

I stare at Ben. What is he saying?

"And Bryce will always feel like the kid stuck in the middle. Unnoticed and underappreciated when he has the greatest of talents. Athletic and smart. What a gift. He needs to see they are both an asset and he should never let one disguise the other."

"Bryce will be great." Ben wants him to play football at our alma mater, Michigan State University. He's only a freshman in high school but I'm certain he'll earn a scholarship.

"And Mila." Ben swallows again but the strain in his voice sounds more like emotion than dryness. "Her mother might be queen, but she's my princess. Make her strong and independent like her mother has grown to be. Make her see she can do anything, like her Aunt Autumn." Ben chokes on his sister's name. "Let her know that being a woman is a gift, not a curse. Her body. Her mind. Her life."

"Ben," I whisper, slowly coming to terms with what he's saying. What he's asking of me.

"And get your girl. Spoil her." Ben's brows are pinched. "Tell her you love her every day. You can do this, Mason. I believe in you."

Ben knows my father never said those words to me. Not that he loved me. Not that he believed in me. His expression of affection: *You're just like me, son.* We were cut from the same cloth, according to him. His opinion was we crave women, different women. We aren't meant to be loyal to only one. Like he hadn't been faithful to my mother.

"You don't always think with your pecker, Becker," Ben teases while his lids close like they weigh too much to remain open.

"Are you suggesting I have a brain?" Like the scarecrow or some shit in *The Wizard of Oz*.

"I'm reminding you that you have a heart. Use it more often." Ben's voice drifts and his breathing grows steady but heavy. His treatments are merely experiments at this stage.

I don't want him to suffer.

He doesn't want to suffer.

And neither of us wants Anna to suffer.

Immediately, I close off my brain.

My heart isn't strong enough when it comes to thoughts of her.

+ + +

Once I'm confident Ben will sleep for a while without rushing to the toilet, I exit the room. In the dimness of the hallway, I nearly trip over Anna. With her back against the wall, just outside the doorway, her knees are pulled up to her chest, as if tucking herself into the shadows. She's wearing some kind of sleep shirt, that's long and pulled over her legs. The collar of the nightshirt is low, and with the stretching of the material, I have a clear view of her breasts.

I quickly look away. It's a visual I shouldn't see and won't be able to unsee once it's in my mind's eye. And the image of Anna's breasts would certainly be burned into my memory for eternity.

She looks tired as she looks up at me. Those dark eyes of hers are dull from lack of sleep.

"What are you doing out here?" I ask, curious why she's out of bed.

"I came to say goodnight to Ben." At times like this, when Ben's body acts out of his control, he demands Anna isn't near him. He doesn't want her cleaning up his shit.

"Were you listening to us?" The question comes out defensive and raw. Unfortunately, Anna is one of the people most judgmental of my relationship with Samantha and Lynlee. She's made similar assumptions to my original thought, that being motherly should be in Samantha's nature, but it isn't. Anna also doesn't understand why I haven't brought Lynlee around our friend-family.

She rolls her head against the wall, her eyes still focused on me with her head tipped back. Her hands are on the floor on either side of her hips. "I only heard you two quietly murmuring. I figured it was something intense. Or just guy-talk." She weakly smiles.

With a hand on the door trim, I slide down to the floor and place myself against the thin wall space between her and the doorway.

"I was telling Ben again how you would have picked me." The words tumble out before I think. Once upon a time, our ribbing was done openly in front of Anna, but after Ben told me that Anna found the joke offensive, we kept the jesting private, only between us.

Anna rolls her head against the wall again, craning to look at me beside her. She doesn't speak for a long while, only watches me. I don't look back at her face but observe my pinky finger twitching beside her hand braced on the floor. Her left hand is closest to mine, and my littlest finger hovers upward, eager to reach over for the rings on her finger. The ones that remind the world she belongs to another man. She isn't mine to touch.

A month or so back when we hugged in her kitchen was the first time I'd risked holding Anna in years, decades maybe. For all the times I've wanted to embrace her, I hadn't. One touch would break me. I wouldn't be able to let her go, like some reckless animal capturing its prey. Still, that night, I don't know who moved first. Was it her? Was it me? It hadn't mattered. For mere seconds, she clung to me, and I tightened my hold on her, not wanting to release her, needing her comfort, craving her warmth.

I hated myself.

My pinky pulls back in line with the rest of my fingers, and I lift my hand, swiping it through my hair.

"Whatcha got there?" Anna's hand covers something I can't see.

Her fingers scoop the item up and she flips her palm to show me. "It's one of my heart-shaped rocks."

I bite the inside of my cheek and nod once in understanding. She's convinced they come from Ben.

"I thought Ben could use the strength, so I was going to place it on the nightstand." Her thumb casually caresses the flat surface which looks almost polished to a shine. I haven't missed how she carries a rock with her and tucks her hand into her pocket when she's agitated or anxious.

"Ben's sleeping. You should probably go to—"

"It would have never mattered if I picked you," she interrupts me and closes her hand around the rock, placing her fist back on the floor while protectively holding the heart shape in her palm. "*He* picked you."

My head swivels in her direction. Her eyes are intense, focused on my face. I should look away from her, but I'm held in place by her words.

"What do you mean he picked me?"

"He wanted you as his friend. He wants you here. He picked you."

My thoughts flip back to my earlier memories of Ben inviting me to hang with him. Ben including me in parties and bonfires, introducing me to girls in the area. He didn't keep me from Anna. I simply thought she'd come to me. Girls always flocked to me. But not her. She went to him with his all-American smile and the good-guy gleam in his eyes. He was better for her than I'd ever be, but it never lessened my desire for her. Never lessened the magnetic pull despite everything I did to keep myself away from her.

"I'll never measure up to what he thinks of me." *You can do better, be better.* I swallow hard, the reality a difficult truth to digest. "I'd never have been good enough for you either."

"It's not a matter of being enough, Mason. It's just that you aren't . . ."

"Ben," I finish for her. Wholesome. Good. Perfect at so many things. I'll never be a man like that. I'm already tainted in so many ways. I've done things I can never take back. While Ben doesn't believe I'm like my father, on a spectrum, I don't line up with Ben either. I'm somewhere in the gray between the two extremes, and that doesn't feel any better.

I nod to express my understanding while Anna continues to watch me, head tipped to the side, resting against the wall at our backs. She'd never have wanted me—she didn't want me—and it was proven when she picked Ben. Although, there wasn't even a decision or choice to be made. Ben was her other half.

"Ben's sleeping. You should be too." Pressing off the floor, I stand upright and hold out a hand for her. To my surprise, she takes it with the same hand holding her heart-shaped rock. Her thin hand feels dainty inside my larger one. The flat surface of the heart in her palm melds into my skin, almost burning me with its coolness, imprinting on me. The sensation is a juxtaposition of my desire for her and my emotions for her husband. The softness of her fingers blends with the hardness of the stone and it's a reminder of what I've craved and what I can't have.

Her body language affirms my thoughts as she quickly pulls her hand from mine, taking the heart shape with her as if tugging my own heart from my chest.

Anna chose Ben.

And while Ben had chosen me for friendship, and I'd accepted that gift, I've always felt guilty for the sliver of truth in our jest.

I'd wanted *her* to pick me.

Chapter 7

2 Years Ago
July

Ben

[Mason]

The last six months have passed in a blur. I hadn't spent Christmas with Ben and his family, knowing deep in my heart it would be their last together. Instead, I'd gone home for two weeks in December. I'd met with my father and told him the fuck-you news. I quit Becker Construction.

What could have been my legacy I didn't want. The construction company was actually from my mother's side of the family. She was the one with wealth while my father had simply jumped into an existing business. No doubt he tripled it, but at what cost? He'd been unfaithful to my mother, drove her to day-time drinking, and alienated me, his only son. A child he hadn't wanted.

Once, the summer I was eighteen and working for Frank Kulis and his wife, Ruth, I caught the two of them kissing at Ben's house. I'd gone into the kitchen for some reason and froze, then took a giant step back. But I didn't walk away. Watching them kiss should have grossed me out as a teen, but it was the strangeness that held me in place. Frank and Ruth loved each other. They flirted and held hands, and in the moment, they were kissing like new lovers instead of people married for twenty years.

Watching them only solidified how much my own parents' marriage lacked warmth or emotion. My parents fought so much I didn't know why they stayed married, but I knew why they'd married in the first place. Me. *For the sake of child*, Marcus married my mother. What he'd really wanted was her wealth, local prestige, and the success he eventually built. I never wanted to be like them, blaming my child for the fault of adults who didn't understand love.

Quitting had been dramatic. I gave him the news, held up my phone, deleted his number, and told him never to contact me again. Then, I'd sent my mother to Florida with instructions to get a good lawyer.

Four Points Construction was born and slowly blooming.

Ben was fading.

When Ben had been too weak to attend a father-daughter dance in February with Mila, Uncle Mason played substitute.

When Calvin had wanted to give up baseball, I'd been the one to convince him to continue to play. *For his dad.* I attended all his games and livestreamed them to Ben at home.

I was stepping up for Ben's children, but I still rarely saw my own. Samantha played her games and Lynlee and I hardly had moments together. If Ben hadn't been so sick, he would have been disappointed in me.

Summer was here again.

Autumn and Logan were officially married, and she had a baby boy, whom they named Ben. No one missed the cruel irony that Ben was dying in the same hospital where his sister had given life. It was there when Ben made a final request. He wanted to go home to Lakeside Cottage.

Only a week or so after baby Ben's birth, the gang had gathered for his christening. Uncle Ben wasn't able to attend, so Zack recorded the ceremony. To my surprise, Logan asked me to be the godfather.

"There's no one I'd trust more."

I'm certain he trusted Ben more, but Ben wasn't going to be around to teach this new little guy the ropes of life. How to push Daddy's buttons and pull Mommy's chain and learn dirty words and get into trouble. That job always fell onto me. I especially loved riling up Zack's twin sons with double entendre words. Calvin and Bryce were old enough to appreciate sarcasm and an inappropriate joke. Mila and Lorna were still little princesses, but it didn't mean I didn't sneak them candy when moms said no or argued in favor of John Hughes movies when their moms said they were too young.

On this mid-July day, with all of us gathered for baby Ben's celebration, Ben asks us to take him to the beach. The request was out of the blue, and honestly, no one believed he should go down to the sand and sit in the heat. Thankfully, Anna was out with Autumn, and Mila, and Lorna, spending what Anna said was a much-needed day out for the new mother.

So without Anna's permission or her presence, we encouraged Bryce and Calvin to set up a canopy on the beach, while Zack and I took turns carrying Ben down the one-hundred and fifty steps to the water's edge. His body was merely a wisp in my arms. The load lighter than believable in a once-healthy forty year old man. I couldn't think about the frailty too much, or tears burned my eyes, and Ben didn't want tears.

Wrapped under a blanket and protected from the sun, Ben is quiet as we watch his teenage boys toss a ball and chase Zack's twins.

"That's the future of Four Points," I say, tipping my beer in the direction of the boys before glancing over at baby Ben. Maybe one day Lynlee will be among us. Maybe she'll be part of that future, but not today. Today is for the men in our friend-family.

"It's the cycle of life," Ben suddenly states, staring off at his sons. "You live and love, lose and learn, and then you start all over again."

"To the cycle," I state, holding up my beer and saluting Ben.

"To the future," Ben states, his eyes focused on his children.

"But also, to the past." Zack stares at our sick friend as he speaks.

"To friends forever," Logan adds, and I groan at how the statement sounds like he's a thirteen-year-old girl. The sentiment isn't lost on me, though, even when I try to lighten the mood by teasing him. Ben will always be a part of us, having shaped our lives by bringing us together in the past and forging our future with his investment in Four Points Construction.

"I've had the best life," Ben eventually says. "Because I lived every moment of it."

The beer on my tongue tastes like the sand at my toes. I swallow down the bitter brew and turn my head toward Ben who is staring at

Logan's baby boy. With a glance at Zack, I sense we are thinking the same thing.

This is the end.

Later that night, I spend a few minutes alone with Ben after Anna has ripped into me for allowing the guys to take Ben to the beach. Zack redirected Anna, taking her for a walk to cool down, while I helped Ben with his needs. It'd been a good day but the effort of it has crashed over Ben like a strong wave against an infant sea turtle.

With Ben tucked in, I ask what I've been afraid to ask.

"Why me, Benners?" I whisper to him as he lays quiet and still on his hospital bed. The one keeping him elevated.

Ben swallows hard, the motion a strain for him. "Why what?"

"Why are we friends?"

Ben slowly rolls his head on the pillow without opening his eyes. "Because you needed one. And so did I."

My throat clogs for the hundredth time this day. I roll my lips and lick them.

Ben read me correctly from the moment we met. He didn't see me as the wealthy kid throwing raging parties and pissing off my parents. He saw that I didn't have anyone genuine in my life and he chose himself to be that person. My person.

"You didn't ask me to stay," I say next, uncertain where I'm really going with my statement. Am I asking him a question? Like why didn't he ask? Do I want to know the answer?

"*Family* don't need to ask. They just show up for each other." Ben's hand flinches on the mattress and my eyes focus on the struggle of his movements. "I had faith you'd step up."

His arm continues to twitch, slowly vibrating against the bed, moving in my direction. I don't know what he wants but I have something for him.

I cup his hand with mine, pressing between us a flat, hard form. I close my hand over his, squeezing the solid item between his frail hand and the strength of my palm.

"Don't let go, Ben," I whisper, lifting our joined hands for my forehead and closing my eyes, sending up a silent prayer. I'm not ready to lose the one constant in my life, and yet, he's suffered enough.

It's time.

"I love you, man." My throat catches. The words scratch. I don't say them directly to anyone ever.

And as I press harder on the heart-shaped rock between our palms, I'm certain I'll never have the strength to say the words again. There won't be another person worthy enough to give those words meaning in my life.

I squeeze as if I can hold Ben in place while knowing I don't have the power to cheat death.

And within days, Ben leaves us with broken hearts but fuller lives because he lived his days with us.

He chose us.

Chapter 8

2 Years Ago
July

The Funeral

[Anna]

"Hello?" The click of the front door brings me out of my revery. I'd been standing at the kitchen island, wiping down a platter. *Circling, circling, circling*, the now dry porcelain. My thoughts have been elsewhere, however, I can't recall what I was thinking about.

"In here," I holler back, my voice lighter than I feel as I respond to my younger sister Amelia. She's here for the funeral.

As Amelia passes from the entryway to the kitchen, she struggles to offer me a smile as her lips quiver and her eyes glisten. After circling the island, I meet her halfway and she pulls me into a tight hug, petting my hair as if I'm the younger sibling. Like I haven't been taking care of her all our lives but she's here to comfort me. I melt into the welcome embrace. Guilt and relief are strange bedfellows, and the two collide inside me as I struggle to accept that the longest year of my life is over.

When we pull apart from one another, I skim my hands down her arms and catch her fingers, squeezing tight. Three years younger than me, you'd think we were a decade apart. Amelia has lighter brown hair than my dark tresses, plus she's thin and fashionable. She looks fantastic. However, my trained eye sees the exhaustion she's tried to hide with makeup. She lives and works in Chicago, preparing for world domination one day.

I'm so grateful for her presence. I only wish our brother Archer would make an appearance. The wayward son has disappeared from our lives. I'd always believed our father might have known where he was and what he was up to, but Dad never shared Archer's whereabouts with us.

"You look beautiful," I tell Amelia.

"You look exhausted. What can I do?" Amelia glances around my kitchen where casserole dishes have collected, and platters await the luncheon after the funeral tomorrow. The days blend together but the more I can keep myself busy planning, planning, planning, the less I fixate on the hole where my heart used to be.

"I'm all set. I have a caterer coming tomorrow and a cleaning service came yesterday." The hospice service worked quickly to remove all medical equipment. The room Ben was in has been sterilized and restored as a guest room. I keep the door closed, though.

Still holding Amelia's hands, the sound of bare feet enters the kitchen behind me.

"Mealworm," Mason cries out, yelling the nickname he'd given Amelia when we were all younger.

"I'm not that little girl anymore," Amelia warns. My sister has always had a huge crush on Mason and his bad boy ways.

"Hmm," Mason hums. "I can see that." I glance over my shoulder, catching him blatantly taking in my sister's curves. "But you still look good enough to eat."

I turn back to Amelia, who doesn't even blush at Mason's flirting. She holds herself poised and prepared for banter. "You can eat me anytime."

I'm the one turning five shades of red at the innuendo and the sudden sexual energy in the room.

"Whenever you're ready to dish, babe."

Glancing over my shoulder at Mason again, I catch the wink he's aimed at Amelia.

I hate that wink for some reason.

Mason has picked up a platter, holding it before him, like he's expecting my sister to jump up on it. She'll be his feast.

Turning away from Mason, I narrow my eyes at Amelia. "Ignore him." The command comes out gritty and harsh as I grind my teeth.

Amelia meets my gaze. "But he's too pretty to ignore."

Mason laughs behind me. His presence closes in at my back. He's become a shadow, following me, watching me, waiting for me to break, which I do only in the privacy of my room.

Amelia tugs free of my grasp and steps around me and into Mason's open arms. He tugs her close, hanging onto her a little longer than necessary, and pressing a kiss to her hair.

"I'm so sorry," she mutters to his chest.

"Me too," Mason mumbles back before gazing up at me, holding on to my face before I look away. I'll need to get used to these words. The next few days will be filled with condolences and apologies for something beyond anyone's control.

$+ + +$

As the funeral obligations wind down, exhaustion hits me hard. I check on the kids one final time as they hang out in the den, a designated kids' area in our home. Calvin and Bryce sit close on the couch, playing video games. They each have a friend lingering in silent support. Lorna and Mila are using colored pencils to fill in a flower print coloring sheet. Their collective comfort comes from being in close proximity to each other. I hug each of them extra tight before I'm led to my room by my sister.

At some point, I fall asleep with her arm over me. Amelia has been a solid comfort. Waking in the shared bed reminds me of when we were younger. When we'd crawl into this same bed when the suite belonged to our parents, and we were teens. We'd watch a movie with our mom on the television across from the bed on a dresser.

"What am I going to do?" I whisper to the room and Amelia shifts behind me.

"You're going to live. One day at a time."

I roll to my back and stare up at the ceiling. My eyes have been surprisingly dry today, but I doubt the tears have subsided for long. I notice someone has removed my shoes.

"I miss Mom." My throat thickens with a strong need for my mother.

"Daddy, too," Amelia says. "And Archer."

I held out small hope that Archer would magically appear for Ben's funeral, but he hadn't. His absence would make me angry if I had the strength to be mad.

Amelia and I remain quiet, each with our thoughts. The holes in our hearts are open wide today. So many missing pieces in the puzzle of our family.

"When did Mason get so hot?" Amelia finally asks and I turn my head in her direction, ignoring that she's laying where Ben once laid.

"What?"

"Mason Becker. He's always been hot but damn . . . In a suit, he's like chocolate mousse on cookie crumbles."

"What?" I repeat, brow pinching.

"Chocolate cake isn't a good enough metaphor for him. He's more decadent. More creamy. More melt on your tongue and explode in your mouth with goodness." Amelia closes her eyes and purrs.

I huff out a laugh. "How is this appropriate?"

Amelia's eyes open and she rolls her head to face me. "You can't meet a hot guy at a funeral?"

"You already know Mason," I remind her.

"And I'm saying I don't remember him like he is now. Suit porn." She fans her face with her hand, and I crack a smile.

Twisting her body, she rolls back to her side and stares at me. I don't admit I can't remember the last time something was melting in my mouth. Ben and I hadn't had sex for months before he passed, and it's the last thing I should be thinking about in the present.

My eyes well and Amelia blurs in my vision. She swipes at a tear that slips free.

"Of course, Mason will never think of me as anything other than Mealworm." She shivers at the nickname, reminding us both of turd-looking little bugs.

"Do you want him to think of you as more?" I ask, distracting myself as the tears slip down the side of my face to my ear.

"Could you imagine?" Amelia smiles slyly. "Come for me, Mealworm." She drops her voice, doing a poor impression of Mason. "That's it, baby mealworm."

I huff again.

"Just like that, Mealworm," Amelia continues, and my huff turns into a strangled giggle.

"Another one, Mealworm." Amelia pauses. "What a romantic. A book with that in it would sell off the shelf." Amelia spreads her hands like a banner. She's in marketing. "Imagine the branding. Mason eats Mealworm."

I snort.

Amelia chokes. "What was that sound?"

Within seconds, we dissolve into a fit of laughter while I try to rid my mind of images of Mason and my sister.

And suppress the endless tears.

+ + +

The days blur together as the end of July shifts to August. While our friends' group was just present for Ben's funeral, we will regather for the two-week vacation Ben demanded of his friends. He wanted them to reunite and reconnect annually in the first weeks of August.

Amelia has returned to Chicago. Mason remains, lingering in my periphery.

The night before Zack and his twin boys are set to arrive, I wake with a start as something brushes my hair over my ear.

I blink several times, attempting to clear my head and focus my bearings. I'd been dreaming. While I'd like to think the man in my dreams was Ben, I'm not certain he was. His stature wasn't right, and his hair color was off.

Staring into a pair of blue eyes, the wrong color blue, I realize where I am. I'm on the couch in the sitting area off the kitchen.

Mason is staring at me.

"Hey," he says in a voice quiet while rough.

Shifting my head, I glance over Mason's shoulder at the window above the other couch. Night has fallen.

"What time is it?"

"Time for bed, beautiful," Mason huskily whispers. "You fell asleep on the couch again."

For months, I've been falling asleep on the couch, not interested in climbing alone into my bed where I'll fight memories and struggle with dreams.

Shaking my head, I snuggle down into the cushions. "I'm comfortable here," I lie, tucking my hands under the throw pillow where my head rests.

"Anna," Mason softly admonishes, lifting his fingers and brushing through my hair again. My eyes close at the tenderness. My sister held me often while she was here. My children offer hugs, but their resilience has been surprising. Ben didn't want them to remember him in his final condition. He struggled with the desire to see them and the fear that he'd haunt them.

We are all grieving differently.

In many ways, I've grieved Ben long before he left this earth.

I shouldn't let Mason touch me, but the soft strokes soothe. With my eyes closed, I'm cognizant Mason is comforting me, but I don't care.

"Come on, Anna. Bed." His voice is quiet yet firm.

"I'm tired," I whimper. "So tired."

"You need rest, beautiful."

Beautiful. I don't feel beautiful. I feel worn down. The tears are exhausting. My head constantly aches. An itch of uncertainty exists beneath my skin.

"I don't want to go to bed." *Alone* whispers through my head.

"You aren't alone. I'm here for you," Mason says, his voice drifting, like I'm dreaming the words instead of hearing them.

I'm here for you.

Only I don't want him here, right?

I said I'd never need him.

I said I could handle everything on my own.

Suddenly, there's an arm under my knees and another under my neck, shifting me, lifting me. I squeak as my body elevates and then I'm hitched upward to readjust the position.

"What are you doing?" My voice cracks.

Mason doesn't answer. As he walks, I'm afraid he'll drop me, so I wrap an arm awkwardly over his shoulder, tugging myself upward against him. My nose presses into his skin, moist from the summer humidity. Sweet with a hint of masculine cologne and sunshine. Inhaling, I draw in a scent that isn't Ben's, but clean and refreshing. Alive.

We don't speak as he carries me to my bedroom on the first floor. Gently, Mason lays me on the bed and draws a light blanket over my legs and mid-section. He pushes back my hair again and my eyes close at the gesture. The touch is only comfort. He feels sorry for me.

Ben was so young.

She's too young to be a widow.

I'd heard the whispers at the funeral. Death does not discriminate based on age, though. Or character. Or goodness.

"Sleep," Mason whispers. His fingers tenderly stroke over my forehead, brushing back my hair. The crack of his knees tells me he squats beside the bed. "I'm right here." His touch is comforting, sweet even. In a way, I'm reminded of how my mother used to comb my hair with her fingers, coaxing me as an anxious child to rest.

Then something warm and firm presses against my forehead, lingering a second.

My eyes flip open as Mason pulls back, his face coming into focus. Our eyes lock.

He kissed me.

The gesture was soothing. A sweeping motion of comfort, like a gentle breeze blowing through beach grass on a warm day.

Mason's eyes shift. His gaze falls to where his fingers continue to work their magic, circling around my ear, dragging over my hair, soothing me, quieting me.

I might not have wanted Mason to stay when Ben first announced his diagnosis to his friends, but I'd pay a million dollars if I had it, to keep him stroking over my hair as he is.

I'm here for you.

Chapter 9

2 Years Ago
August

Second Reunion

[Mason]

Zack has arrived with his two little demons, who I actually get a kick out of. The older one by minutes, Trevor, is smart and a bit controlling. He's the alpha in their two-person twin-pack. Oliver is a follower, a little sweeter, and a touch sensitive but defensive of his brother.

If I believed in twin flames or souls separated at birth, I'd think Ben and I were like that, only complete opposites, reunited as friends to complement one another.

The house returns to chaos with friendly banter and quiet reminders of Ben's life. The goal of the next two weeks is to remember the good times. We don't need to reconnect as much as Ben initially intended because we are now in business with one another and speak often.

I've practically moved into the apartment above the garage with visits back to Traverse City every other weekend to see Lynlee. Visits that are almost always interrupted by some bullshit with Samantha. Some crisis that can't be avoided. Some need for funds like I'm a freaking ATM machine.

Lynlee is now four and full of fear. Death is a constant topic of discussion because of Ben.

Will I die? What if I get sick? Will she never see me again? What will Mommy do if I disappear?

I'm not certain there's any heartfelt concern on Samantha's part that I'll go away. Only a fear of losing out on the money I continue to give her, that she continues to waste on everything but our daughter.

The last time I visited, Lynlee had a burn mark on her inner arm. Samantha claims Lynlee bumped into her when she was holding a lit cigarette. I don't believe Samantha, but Lynlee backs up her mother's story.

I hate the position I'm in with Samantha.

One of the first nights during our reunion of sorts, we are gathered in the sitting area. Zack's boys are in bed. Mila and Lorna are up in Mila's room. Calvin and Bryce have been released to do what teen boys do on a summer night. Baby Ben is in his car seat, asleep.

Autumn breaks the momentary silence. "So, I have something for each of you."

Eyebrows lift while Logan strokes a hand up his wife's back.

"Before Ben passed away, he gave me an envelope for each of you," she continues.

"Jesus," I hiss, and immediately glance at Anna, who sits in an oversized chair.

Her face pales and she glares at her sister-in-law. "How did I not know about this?"

Autumn ignores Anna's outburst and continues. "He explained to me the four points needed to be recalibrated every year."

She carries on, explaining who represents each point of the compass, adding how there is an envelope for Anna's brother, Archer, the absentee McCaryn, which upsets Anna. Anna doesn't have a clue where her brother is or where he's been over the years, but apparently Autumn has a contact.

I watch Anna's face morph from irritation to confusion.

Autumn ignores the emotion rolling off Anna and addresses me. "Technically, you lived north but he's calling you West. Where the sun sets."

My hands shake as I take the envelope from Autumn.

Where the sun sets. If there is some prophecy in that statement, I'd take it to mean the end of a day. The end of a life. The end of our friendship.

Maybe Ben finally wised up to my feelings about his wife and his letter will tell me to fuck off. Exit their lives now that he isn't present.

"Ben suggested you open them on your own time but during these two weeks. In fact, he hoped that whatever you find on the page inside will begin during these two weeks. You have a year to fulfill his suggestion, which gives you until next summer when you meet back here. You can share your letters with each other, but he thought it best to make it a personal challenge."

I roll my eyes. "A personal challenge." Just what the fuck kind of game is this?

"There isn't one for me?" Anna questions, staring at the envelope remaining in Autumn's hand. "Archer isn't even here," Anna reiterates, her tone curt, her eyes searching her sister-in-law for some explanation.

"I think Ben hoped he might be."

Silence weighs heavy in the room. My eyes don't leave Anna.

Abruptly, she stands, visibly upset. "I'm going to bed." She storms off toward the hallway leading to her bedroom. Everything in me longs to follow her. I'll give her my letter. She can read for herself what Ben has to say.

Anna thought she had to face the rest of her life alone, but she doesn't. I was here for her. I'd done my diligence with Ben. The real struggle was going to be holding her together.

She'd need a friend, as Ben said he needed in me. *I* would be that friend.

"Well, what the fuck," I announce to the room ripping my envelope open and staring at the two words handwritten on stock paper. I blink, uncertain I've read them correctly. "Bastard."

I stand almost as abruptly as Anna and circle the couch heading to the barroom off the kitchen. Swiping a bottle off the counter, I press open the screen door and don't bother to hold it, to soften its return to the doorjamb. The slam punctuates the darkness, and then I'm thundering down the stairs to the beach, crumbling the parchment in my hands and upending the bottle, taking a swig directly from it.

Zack eventually finds me in an Adirondack chair on the dark beach and admits he isn't ready to open his envelope.

"Coward," I tease. Ben said I had a heart and I needed to use it more often. He forgot about that damn lion in *The Wizard of Oz*. I'm the one who is cowardly. Then again, it takes a brain to decipher Ben's meaning in his note and I don't have a clue what he's trying to say to me.

+ + +

"What are you doing?" Calvin comes into view as I slowly open my eyes to him. I'm drunk, but not drunk enough that two words on a piece of paper will stop haunting me.

"Sitting in the hallway." I state the obvious while avoiding the truth. I'm listening for Anna's tears. There are many nights I've sat here, outside her door, listening to the tortured sounds of her sobs. Every teardrop unlocks my heart, flooding it with a need to take her in my arms and comfort her. Hold her. Be here for her.

Calvin leans against the wall and slides down to the floor beside me. The bottle of scotch that I nabbed earlier rests between us. My head is tipped back. My wrists dangle over my bent knees. I should be concerned that he sees me in this condition, but he's grown up quickly in the past year. He's a young man whose childhood imploded when his father died. An unwarranted responsibility presses on his young shoulders to be the man of this family. I don't want him worrying about his mother and siblings. That's what I'm here to do.

"Think she'll ever stop crying?" Calvin asks, genuine concern and a dash of fear fill his voice. It can be frightening to hear your mother cry so much, so often.

I straighten my legs before me and roll my head against the wall at my back. "Eventually."

"Is this what they call a broken heart?" Calvin whispers.

For some reason, I snort. "More like a severed one."

"What do you mean?" Calvin's voice is louder, inquisitive.

"A broken heart is when you lose someone. Like a breakup or a loss of trust." I pause, listening for any noise behind the closed door. "But the sobs from your mom are the sound of her heart being ripped out. Two halves of a whole being separated." I pull my hands apart, dramatically imitating an explosion.

"That was graphic." Calvin snorts.

Maybe I'm a little drunker than I think.

Anna's tears are different from my mother's. My mother's wail was that of a heart shattered like a dropped vase. More elevated, like a piercing wound. She was painfully vocal when she learned of my father's infidelity. Then she became eerily silent, disappearing into a bottle.

My gaze drifts to the alcohol container beside me. Maybe I'm cut from the same cloth as her.

"But I get it," Calvin admits. Lowering his head, his voice drops. "I miss my dad, too."

With the admission, I reach out for Calvin, cupping the back of his neck and tugging him to my side. The kids have been incredible through everything. The transition of moving. The making of new friends. The loss of their father. They've known the outcome—Ben's passing was inevitable—and their quiet strength has been a blessing, but Anna and I have been vigilant about watching for signs of depression.

"You know you can talk to me about anything," I remind him before he pulls away from me.

He nods once while keeping his gaze toward the floor. "I talk to Keli about things."

My head shoots upward. "You got a girl?" How have I not heard of this?

"She lives in Chicago. We're only talking."

"Is that code for something else?" At forty-one, I pride myself on knowing all the latest lingo, but this sounds too simple.

"Nope. We just . . . talk. You know, like learn about each other."

"Did you kiss her?" I tease, leaning over to bump his shoulder with mine but realize we are too far apart from one another.

Calvin's face turns red. He looks so much like Anna in male form. A spitting image of what Archer looked like in his twenties.

"So, it is more than talking?"

Calvin softly chuckles. "A little bit. We met right before I learned about Dad." Calvin slowly lifts his head. "I didn't want to move. Was that selfish?"

Aw, man. "No. Not selfish at all. And you did move, so that was very selfless of you."

Calvin nods and returns to looking at his knees, bent toward his chest. "I want to go back," he whispers.

"Back in time?" I pop my head forward, wishing that could be an option in life and yet not wanting to turn back the clock. If I'd erase one thing it'd be Samantha but then I wouldn't have Lynlee.

"Back to Chicago. I'm only applying to colleges in Illinois."

"Oh." My head falls back to the wall. "Doesn't sound unreasonable. It's your life, Calvin. Your dad would want you to live it."

Calvin deeply sighs. "He wants everyone to live their lives, even Mom."

"She'll get there," I suggest, although I know nothing about grieving.

"He wants you to live yours, too. He appreciated you being here."

Slowly, I lift my head again, keeping my eyes on Calvin's profile. "You know there wasn't anywhere else I wanted to be this past year."

"Yeah, but you have your own life. Your own little girl."

I nod. "And for a blip of time, my life is here." *Let me worry about my little girl. I won't be here forever.* The thought has me turning my head toward the closed door, listening once more for wrenching sounds of Anna's grief. The thought of no longer being here makes me want to cry, if I were a crying kind of guy. Through everything with Ben, I've held myself together. Tears aren't my thing.

"You don't have to go," Calvin whispers, hesitation fills the words.

"I'll never leave you, bud. Never." I reach out and give his knee a squeeze. I'm not sick or dying, and until that day, I'll be by his side where I'm physically present or just a phone call away. "I'll always be around for whatever you need."

"Can I have a drink?" he nods at the bottle between us.

"Not on your life," I admonish.

"Worth a try." Calvin laughs.

While I'd have been the cool uncle in another life, probably letting an eighteen-year-old get drunk with me, I'm trying to be more responsible, more adult. More Ben. And he'd kill me if I let his underage son drink.

"How long do you sit here?" Calvin asks.

I tip my head back and close my eyes. "As long as it takes."

As long as it will take her to grieve and recover from the sever to her heart, I'll be here.

For her. For them.

Chapter 10

2 Years Ago
August

Second Reunion

[Anna]

The two weeks are passing in a haze of Ben memories. The jokes. The shenanigans. The good old days. And the weight of the future presses down on me. School will soon start and I'm returning to work in a full-time substitute position for a young woman on maternity leave. Calvin will be a senior and he's pushing all my buttons, establishing independence before I'm ready to let him go. Bryce is my quiet one and football will consume his time. Mila and I will be left to circle one another as my middle schooler pulls away from me.

And Mason is going to leave, as he should. He has a life and a daughter of his own.

Zack told me Mason disappeared the other night, saying he'd met someone in town and was going to see her again, and I accepted it's time for Mason to move forward. The idea of Mason with someone bothers me, though. *It shouldn't bother me.* But there's an itch beneath my skin at the thought of him randomly hooking up with a stranger. When did he find the time to meet someone?

Will I ever meet someone?

Ben and I occasionally joked about dating, usually after some exploit of Mason's. Ben would exaggeratedly shiver and graciously proclaim he was happy he wasn't dating in our current times. He was happy with me, and after years with such a good man, I couldn't fathom being with someone else. Still, I can admit, I'm lonely. I've missed Ben for months before he even left this earth and yet the finality of his passing was no easier even though we knew it would happen.

Sometime during these days together, Zack has formed an attachment to my next-door neighbor. Her name is River Nagle, and I'd, unfortunately, not met her because of the craziness of the last year. However, Zack has brought her around, including her in our chaotic dinners and a few of our days at the beach. My serious friend is almost blossoming before me into a new man. He's falling in love and doesn't know what to do with the emotion.

When I'm out of my head long enough to witness this change in one of my oldest friends, the process almost makes me sad. Not for Zack. I'm thrilled for him as he's freshly divorced and adjusting to being a single dad of two rambunctious boys. He needs someone stable and a bit carefree, which River certainly is, to balance him out. Or maybe keep him unbalanced. Either way, he's happier than I've seen him in years.

It's that happiness that rocks me.

I just want to be happy again.

I want the tears to stop flowing. I want to stop feeling this lethargy. I want to stop the hopelessness.

And for another night, everything crashes down on me. I'm crying again although I don't even know what I'm crying about. It's not a specific thing but perhaps everything. The guys and their good-time memories. Zack finding love with my neighbor. My kids, especially a recent fight with Calvin. Returning to work where I'll have the distraction and structure, but I'm not convinced I have the mental capacity to teach.

One night, I'm in my bedroom and a short knock sounds on the door. The room is dark. The hour is late. I hesitate for a moment, almost hoping whoever it is will go away. Then I reconsider, knowing it's probably one of the kids and they need me.

I slide out of bed with tears staining my cheeks and snot under my nose. I scrub a hand over my face and then run my fingers through my loose hair as I cross the room for the door. When I open it, the outline of a man stands just outside. His arms are stretched, fingers clutching at the doorjamb.

"Mason?"

"Anna," he whispers. Pain and anguish and something more laces my name.

"What are you doing out here?" My voice is raspy and hoarse from the tears.

"Why are you crying?"

The question sounds absurd. If anyone should know why I'm crying, it's Mason. He lost a friend, a confidant, a brother from another. Still, I shake my head. I don't know why the tears have fallen tonight. Looking up into his shadowed face, his blue eyes sparkle from the backlight of a lamp somewhere down the hallway. The tension in his arms almost vibrates as if he's ready to rip the wood trim off the casing around the doorframe. He steps forward, and without thought, I step back.

Mason enters, closing the door behind him and I lean my back against the wall. Our eyes lock in the darkness. The blinds are open. A natural glow dimly illuminates the space.

"What are you doing in here?" I nearly choke on the question. My heart hammers in my chest as my palms flatten on the wall. He's standing too close to me, and I'm surrounded in his scent. Expensive. Sensual. Alive.

His large hand lifts and he swipes a finger under my eye. Dragging it slower over my cheek, his hand curls and he cups the edge of my jaw. His thumb strokes my cheek next.

"When will you stop?" His voice remains low, patient, and curious. He isn't scolding me, telling me I must stop crying. He isn't upset, demanding the tears stop.

"I don't know." I rasp out the words, feeling the thickness in my throat again. My vision swims. I close my eyes as if shutting my lids will capture the sorrow and contain it. "I don't know if I ever will, but I want them to stop."

The thought saddens me even more. I want the tears to cease.

"They will," Mason whispers, his thumb smoothing over my cheek, brushing away each new droplet. "You're one of the strongest women I know. Solid as a rock."

My eyes flip open. Ben said something similar to me. The memory is foggy in my head. I inhale at the coincidence and the mention of stone. The heart-shaped rocks had continued to appear. Even after Ben was too sick to visit the beach. Even after his death. Maybe Ben is trying to reach me from the grave. But those thoughts need to stop.

Everything needs to stop.

The inhale of breath gives me a fresh whiff of Mason. He's crowding my space and yet I don't feel suffocated by him. I—

Our lips are touching before I can finish my thought.

At first, the connection is so soft, I almost think I imagined it.

I don't know why I'd imagine such a thing, but it doesn't matter in this moment.

Because a second brushing of lips occurs. A little firmer. A little longer.

My heart continues to hammer, nearly sprinting inside my chest. My hands are pressed into something soft and well-worn, and then my fingers curl into the fabric and squeeze.

The firm hand along my jaw turns into two hands cupping my face.

And my lips are pressed again with more intention, more purpose. I sip at the connection, pulling back but afraid to lose contact. My teeth nip at his lower lip before it can get away from me.

Then chaos ensues.

A tongue is rushing forward, tangling with mine as I open to accept the intrusion. My fingers are clutching at the softness of cotton beneath them and my body leans forward. My breasts ache, nipples sharp peaks beneath the thinness of my sleep shirt, and I meet the hard form of solid pecs.

A hand releases my jaw and strokes down my back, squeezing my ass and tugging me closer.

Our mouths continue to seek. Tongues. Lips. Teeth. The kiss grows more impassioned.

I release a portion of his shirt and reach for the back of his neck, fingers combing into hair thick and curled at his nape before clutching at him. Uncertain if I'm trying to pull him away or hold him in place, neither matters as the meeting of our mouths incrementally increases in eagerness. Desperate. Harder. Faster. As if we can chase whatever is happening between us.

My mind is vacant of all thought but his mouth against mine. His hand at my back holds me against him while the other hand on my face slides down my neck and over my chest. Then a firm palm squeezes one breast and I cry out into his mouth. He increases the pressure of his lips and hands, keeping me attached to him, swallowing the pleasure evoked by his palm kneading the swell that hasn't been touched in so long.

He tweaks my nipple, pinching it between his fingers before giving it a sharp tug. The sensation is unreal. A rush spreads through the center of my body, pooling between my thighs. The pulse jumps from a steady rhythm to a chaotic beat. I lift a leg, wrapping it over his hip and meeting the hard length of his excitement when he bends his knees, aligning our centers.

I grind forward. He presses back in response. We rock against one another.

Then his hand slips between my legs. Fingers coast over sensitive folds covered by silk pajamas. I reach for the waistband of his shorts, pushing at the edges. My fingers touch smooth skin and firm planes. A sharp V leading lower. The crispness of hidden hair. The solid shaft.

He pulls away, breathless. "Anna."

"Ben," I beg.

And we both freeze.

With my hand wrapped around his thick cock and his strong fingers between my legs, our eyes meet.

The blue inside the sparkle of his eyes is not the right shade.

"Mason," I whisper on a shaky breath.

"Anna." My name is a judge's gavel. A halt on everything we'd been doing.

What were we doing?

I was kissing Mason.

He was touching me.

I am holding his dick.

His fingers are against my most private place.

Instantly, we release one another. Mason steps back, hands in the air as if to surrender to the crime we've committed. My fingers fly to my lips, brushing over them, swiping at the evidence of what we'd done.

We kissed.

I don't blame him. I don't know who reached for who first. Or if either of us even reached. We drifted. We leaned. We melted together like chocolate swirled into a vanilla recipe.

And it shouldn't have been so delicious.

"Mason," I whimper his name, full of guilt and shame.

"Nope." His hands remain in the air before he swipes them both into his hair. I struggle to keep my gaze on his face and away from a peek at his manhood, still exposed and erect above the waistband of his shorts.

As if he read my thoughts, he reaches for his shorts and tugs them upright. I lose the battle with my eyes, as my gaze drops and I watch Mason adjust the long length, forming a firm wedge in his loose shorts.

"This never happened," I whisper to his dick. As if saying the words to this part of his anatomy could erase how he felt in my hands. How his mouth tastes. How his body heated mine.

I lift my eyes.

Mason meets my gaze with pinched brows and eyes that reflect a kaleidoscope of hurt and upset that quickly fades to blank and unreadable.

I'd called him Ben. "Oh God, Mason. I'm so—"

"Nope." A sharp finger points at me, willing me to stop talking. His hand trembles. His breathing ragged. He pauses and I hold my breath while he shakes his head. Then he's turning for the door, exiting my room, and I'm left in the dark.

With my bone-chilling disgrace . . . and the white-hot desire to orgasm.

Chapter 11

2 Years Ago
August

Second Reunion

[Mason]

"How do we do this?" I ask.

"I think we hold the card until we can't anymore, let it burn to nothing, then allow the wind to take the rest," Logan suggests as the three of us—Zack, Logan, and me—sit around a low burning fire down on the beach.

As we'd each received our notes from Ben with directives for our future, we decided to write Ben a response. Actually, Autumn might have suggested such a thing to Logan or maybe it was River, Anna's neighbor, who said something to Zack about reaching the spirit world by igniting a letter. She's kind of a free-spirit and he's been banging the babe next door for ten days until he fucked it up with her. It's written on his face how much he misses her.

But tonight is about Ben.

And because this is about Ben, I try not to think about how much I fucked up with Anna.

His wife.

Guilt was in her eyes. Shame was in her expression. But the honest truth is we would have slept together if she hadn't uttered Ben's name. His name stopped us both cold.

Because I was not him.

I would never be him.

However, desire burns inside me as I remember how her mouth melded with mine. The way her body molded against me, curving along my hard lines and bending into my deep grooves. The heat of her mouth.

The grip of her hands. If we had continued, the softness of her eager body would have been nothing the hardness of mine has ever experienced.

And something I should not think about happening again.

I'd kissed my best friend's wife.

As I stare into the fire before us, watching the edge of my note card burn, I have only one thought.

I'm going to hell.

Brimstone and flames are going to consume me when I die because of this one sin. My greatest sin. I kissed Anna . . . and I liked it. I liked it more than I ever expected, and I want it to happen again.

Nope. Not allowed that thought. Not one for now or later or ever.

Zack releases his note into the beach fire first, watching the flames devour the final corner of the cardstock. The concept is that whatever we've written will be carried into the universe and received by Ben. I want to call it voodoo but I'm not so convinced. Perhaps Ben already knows my guilt.

I drop the remainder of my card into the fire and watch the paper burn to ash.

I'm sorry.

I could have written something more profound, or I could have questioned what the hell his mission for me meant.

He'd only had two words for me. I only have two words for him. This isn't tit for tat, though. I messed up bigger than I ever have.

I gave in to the sadness in her eyes and the plea in her voice. *I want them to stop.* She wanted the tears to go away and all I could think about was how to distract her. How to take her mind off the pain. How to empty her thoughts of the loss.

Now, I've lost her.

Then again, I never had Anna.

Struggling to push the inner dialogue aside, I reach for the bottle of tequila near the foot of the Adirondack chair. Zack and I overindulged in this liquid-nemesis of ours last year when we learned about Ben's condition. I might have spilled a little too much truth after drinking more than my fair share of the Mexican serum. Zack had his own confession to make then.

He was getting divorced.

I lift the bottle in salute to our absent friend. "To friendship." Immediately, I take a deep swallow, allowing the bitter tequila to burn my throat and rip at my belly. I hand the bottle to Logan, not expecting him to drink but to at least follow the motion of honoring our friend with a toast.

"To family," Logan proudly states. His little family of Lorna and him has grown to include Autumn and baby Ben. I have no doubt more babies might be in their future.

Zack takes the bottle next. "To forever." He takes a hardy chug himself before releasing the bottle and puckering his lips at the sharpness. We should have brought limes to cut the taste, but we don't deserve comfort.

Tonight is about the friend we lost and the fate of the future.

I'm going to have to live with what I did.

And the guilty pleasure of finally kissing the woman of my dreams.

+ + +

This never happened. Anna meant every word as she ignored me for the remainder of our friends' visit.

On the day of departure for Zack, I step out of the garage apartment with my bag slung over my shoulder. Zack stands near his SUV parked on the driveway, wrangling his two boys inside it for the drive to their home outside Detroit.

I'd made some hard decisions last night and feel guilty that the boys aren't present this morning, but this isn't goodbye to them. It's a much-needed break for my own personal sanity and maybe some space Anna needs to figure out where she's going next. As for me, I might have finally gotten the wake-up call I need.

Anna will never be mine.

For some stupid reason, I glance at her as if she'll finally acknowledge me.

As if she'll accept what we did.

To my surprise, Anna is watching me. The expression on her face looks like panic. Is she worried I told the guys what happened? I wouldn't do that to her. To us. Zack and Logan's friendship means everything to me, and they forgive me for most of my fuckups, but this might be the exception. I wouldn't risk losing them.

I glance away first and open the trunk of my car, tossing my bag into the back. It's pathetic how little I kept here, commuting between the garage apartment and my townhome in Traverse City, roughly three hours away.

"Where are you going?" The anxiety I didn't want to see on Anna's face is expressed in her tone. Her voice hints at a tremble while her curiosity holds a demanding edge.

"I think it's time I leave, too." The words taste bitter on my tongue. I want to stay. I want to talk. We need to discuss how what happened is a natural reaction to two people hurting or grieving or something and desperate for comfort. Comfort that shouldn't come from each other. One of us needs to go and that person is me.

The air around us on the driveway seems to still. Zack is watching me with an intensity I can't address.

"What about Four Points?" Logan asks. He's given up the most to quit his job with an established architectural firm and move to Lakeside. Then again, the decision came from a desire to be with Autumn.

I pause, hand on the open hatch of my trunk. "Let's talk tomorrow." I glance at Logan, hoping he reads the need in my eyes. I need to get away from here. I need to separate myself from Anna before I do something stupid like beg her to talk to me, face this thing, maybe kiss me again.

No. No, no, no. I shake my head as Logan looks over at Zack before silently acknowledging me with a nod. *Tomorrow.*

I glance at Anna one more time and my resolve crumbles. I step up to her. My jaw ticks. I nearly bite my own tongue. My voice drops, hoping only she will hear the urgency in my words. "Ask me to stay and I will."

I hate the whining plea in my tone. *Let me in.* Let me be the one here for you.

Anna doesn't look at me. Something at the hem of her shirt is apparently more interesting.

"No." She nods slowly, once, then twice, as though she's coming to some kind of internal conclusion. She still refuses to look at me as she says, "You need to go."

The blow isn't as gut-wrenching as I thought. I didn't really expect her to say I should stay, right? She's grieving her husband, not wanting a romantic interlude. And honestly, I don't want a quick, grief-ridden fuck with her.

No, it's time to put Anna behind me. The Anna I've craved. The Anna I've lusted after.

I slip my hands into my pockets, and nod as well.

I don't like it, but I don't have to like it.

It's time for me to go.

Chapter 12

2 Years Ago
September

Mason Leaves

[Anna]

After the mayhem of the past thirteen months, September is like a door slammed shut to block out noise and chaos. My world becomes exceedingly quiet.

I return to teaching in a substitute position. Calvin and Bryce fall into their high school roles as a senior and a sophomore, and Mila begins sixth grade at the middle school. Logan's daughter Lorna is a year ahead of her, but it doesn't prevent the two girls from being best friends, and my home is a revolving door of Lorna and Mila here or the now-cousins spending time at Logan and Autumn's house half a mile up the road.

Either way, I'm often alone.

At forty-one, I didn't want widowhood to define me, but I didn't know how to be me without Ben, which actually scared me a little.

I'd spoken to a good friend of mine, Jenna Davis, about my fears. Back in the day, we'd been secondary education majors together at Michigan State University, and she'd become one of my best friends in college. We kept in touch over the years, sharing through social media the progression of our lives, but we also reached out when something more personal happened. She'd lost her husband in a tragic way a few years ago, and as I'd recently lost Ben, she attended his funeral. We talk a little more often now.

"As women, we're giant puzzles. Ben was . . . is a piece of you, but he isn't the whole you. You were married, yes. You also have children and a job. Friends and other family members." Jenna pauses on the phone.

She'd been a wild one in college and kept up her single-as-a-Pringle persona until well into her thirties. She reminded me in many ways of Mason. Then she'd met Ryan, and everything changed. Within months they were married with children and a mortgage.

"Life is full of adjustment periods, like our students transitioning back to school. A new set of classes and different combinations of kids within them. New teachers, too." She exhales. "I should be good at analogies as an English teacher but I'm finding I'm not expressing well what I want to say. The thing is . . . you're going through an adjustment period. And there is no definition of how to transition, only that it's a process of change. We all develop at our own speed and there is no rush."

Unfortunately, bitterness is seeping in about the changes in my life. The move from our home in Chicago. Giving up a teaching job that I'd loved. The pressure of substitute teaching.

Outside of widow, mother, teacher, friend, who the hell was Anna?

"Grieving is the same way, Anna. You'll grieve the rest of your life, but the issue is not letting that grief consume you. You are alive and Ben would want you to live your life." She pauses again, letting the hard truth sink in. "That's how we honor those we've lost."

I could say she knew where to place the proverbial knife in my chest, but her honesty is what I need. Too many people are sugarcoating Ben, like he's some mythological god when he was a man. A wonderful, beautiful, kind man who I loved with everything in me, and because he was human, he was also mortal.

My grandmother lived a long life with my grandfather, but he died when I was a teenager. When I was older, I remember her telling me how she allowed herself two weeks to wallow after his passing. Then one day she knew she had to get out of bed and move forward. One day at a time, she told me. She didn't want to miss out on what she still had by drowning in what she'd lost.

Ben is gone. The logic in my head knows he will never be coming back. The loneliness in my heart tells another story.

"I know," I whisper to Jenna, fighting tears. The struggle to hold them at bay has ebbed and flowed like a tide. Some days are rougher waters than others, but I am getting better. It isn't every day that I cry.

"By the way, did I mention I saw Mason Becker?" There is an unsettling cheer to Jenna's voice as she says his name.

Mason and I haven't had any contact since he left in August. It's been nearly six weeks of silence after more than a year of him living in my home as the third roommate. Ben was the first. My kids were collectively second and Uncle Mason had become a permanent structure in our lives. A shadow of sorts.

His leaving was a different kind of loss for all of us.

"Really?" I try to keep my voice steady. "Where?"

"At a bar in Traverse." Jenna chuckles. "Same old Mason. Think he'll ever grow up?"

Same old Mason meant getting drunk and hooking up with a random woman. The sickening thought pools together in my belly because I don't believe he is the same man he'd been before he shared a year of his life with us. He was different somehow. Or maybe it was just that the experience of losing Ben changed him like it had changed all of us. We each coped in our own way. For him, maybe it meant returning to old habits.

"You were at a bar?" A tease fills my throat, as I try to steer us away from Mason. Discussing him might lead to a confession I'd prefer to take to my grave.

"I had a date." Jenna sighs, exasperated. "I'm too old for this shit." Jenna is also forty-one and a single mother of two adorable little girls.

"God, I can't imagine dating." I used to cavalierly toss out those words, confident as a married woman I'd never have to tackle the uncertainty of dating. Now, my truth is I'm a widow. I'm essentially single and I literally cannot fathom ever being with another man.

But you kissed Mason.

I shake my head as if it will erase the reminder. I don't want to think about my lapse in judgement and loss of control. I shouldn't have let him kiss me.

However, the blame is not all on him. I kissed him in return. Pressing against his body. Clutching his shirt. Digging into his hair. Eventually touching his—

Immediately, I stop myself, willing myself to forget how he felt in my hands, but my fingers have a mind of their own and curl into a fist, feeling the invisible weight, the length, the strength like a ghost in my hand.

Ghost dick. I nearly laugh out loud at the thought and it's a good distraction, pulling me back to the present.

"Dating isn't something you need to think about right now," Jenna states. "You need to work on you first. Just be Anna."

"Is that just be comma Anna, like an interjection, or a complete statement, like just be Anna, to which I don't know who that is anymore?" My voice drops with anxiety in not knowing myself.

"You're a teacher, my friend. We are always learning. Reflective. Progressive. Transformative."

"You sound like an education manual." I laugh.

"God, who let me be a teacher, responsible for shaping the young minds of other people's children?" she jests. She's a great teacher, equally excellent in instruction and connections with kids.

"MSU did that." She'd even graduated with honors.

"I should demand a refund," she jokes.

"I'm sure all the kids you taught, and their parents, are grateful."

"If only taxpayer dollars reflected that gratitude." We both laugh, knowing this is a whole other conversation for another time.

"Alright, I gotta go. Rosie is too quiet upstairs which always means trouble." Jenna's youngest daughter is smart but a daredevil at the ripe age of two. Her four-year-old, Talia, is more of a worrywart.

"Hug those girls for me," I say, missing the days where I could easily hug my own crew. The hugs have come often in the past year, but the kids' rebound is happening faster than mine. They are slipping into routines, social activities, and friendships that don't involve me. Their growth is also part of my adjustment.

One thing I'm learning is I'm a creature of habit, and I don't particularly like change.

+ + +

My next-door neighbor, River, and I have developed a friendship, despite Zack having a summer fling with her. When River moved in, I hadn't had the time to properly meet her. Ben had been diagnosed already. Our move to Lakeside Cottage had been hasty and things went downhill rather quickly after Christmas. We'd always known Ben had roughly a year, but time sped up while being one of the longest years of my life. It wasn't until after his funeral that I finally introduced myself to my new neighbor.

She's currently a pediatric oncology nurse, and a woman who lost someone dear to her, so she understands my rollercoaster of emotions. As an outsider to our group, she is a welcomed friend for her objectivity. Every other word out of her mouth wasn't a reminder of Ben and it left me with the openness to *not* always discuss him. She listened when I want to talk, but she also distracted me, coaxing me into a variety of activities all intended to do one thing.

Reassess who I am.

One of the activities we partake in is Monday manicures and margaritas. Rudder's is a bit dark and dim but a bar off the radar of tourists and favored by many locals. And on Mondays, they have margarita specials. Most nights, our time out includes Autumn.

"Have you talked to Mason lately?" Autumn asks while her eyes are closed, and her feet are scrubbed. As a new mom, she loves these nights off while Logan watches baby Ben, which usually includes Lorna and Mila assisting as overeager helpers.

"I haven't," I admit sheepishly, not only for kissing him, but for not checking in on him. He'd been part of our lives for over twenty years as one of Ben's best friends. He'd also given up a year of his life to help Ben and he deserved more than a desperate kiss and then radio silence.

Ben would be disappointed in me for a number of reasons. Still, Mason hadn't reached out to me either.

"Mila told me he calls her or sends her text messages."

Autumn's knowledge bothers me. "When did she tell you that?"

She shrugs and opens her eyes to peer over at me from her chair beside mine. "She's shown me some of the funny memes he sends her."

He sends my daughter memes? "Are they appropriate?" I unfairly ask, protective of my daughter's age and Mason's history of immaturity, but also a bit upset that he hasn't messaged me.

With a cheerful huff, Autumn says, "As appropriate as you can be as Mason. Most of them are funny images of pop singers or actors with punny sayings. Or quotes to inspire her for school."

"Is Mila struggling in school?" Why am I asking my sister-in-law? And why does she know something I don't about my own child? Mason has been in contact with the kids but not me.

The holes in my chest widen with the guilt of acknowledging the disconnect I've had from my children's lives. I've been physically present but mentally checked out at times. I'm doing the best I can, struggling to push life forward because I can't live in the past. The past is dead.

"I don't think so. Mason is just checking in," Autumn adds, revealing more of his involvement and commitment to my children.

I tip back my head and stare up at the ceiling. Frustrated with myself, I accept I need to do better, be better.

"Has Mason contacted you?" River hesitantly asks. She's had her own issues with Zack since summer ended and he's returned to Detroit. I really want the two of them to work something out because I miss my childhood friend and he deserves the love River would bring to his life.

Rolling my head on the headrest, I glance over at River on my other side. "No." Sorrow fills my tone when I have no reason to be sad about Mason. Maybe it's more disappointment. In me. In him. He'd devoted all that time to Ben, but he'd also been helping me. Then again, he wasn't there for *me*. He was there for Ben. Ben asked him to stay for us. Mason's presence had been at Ben's request.

When Mason decided to leave, the sudden panic shouldn't have been there, but it was. Watching him exit the apartment with his bag over his shoulder, the rush of anxiety was a jolt to my heart. I didn't know how to be alone . . . how to be without him.

Did you want Mason to stay? River had asked me this question shortly after the guys left. While my head said he needed to go, another part of me wasn't as eager for him to leave. That thought makes me a terrible person. I kissed my husband's best friend only weeks after Ben's funeral. What kind of person does that make me?

Later, this question, along with three margaritas and a touch of melancholy at another night alone in my bed, has me holding my phone in hand.

I type out a question but don't hit send.

Why didn't Ben leave me a letter?

I stare at the words, a bit blurry in the text bubble. Mason's name dances as the contact at the top of the screen.

Why didn't Ben write me a letter? Why didn't he leave me a directive? Give me instructions on how I am to move forward without him.

You'll fall in love again, Ben had said to me months before he passed.

I'd been so angry.

Your heart is too big to belong only to me.

I hated his words.

My forefinger eagerly jabs the screen. Delete. Delete. Delete.

I was never going to love again. I shouldn't reach out to Mason. I shouldn't ask him something I'm certain he can't answer.

Holding up the phone, the screen glows in the darkness of my room. The last message from Mason is mundane and reminiscent of his presence shortly after the funeral.

Need me to grab milk at the store?

I hadn't answered him, and yet, I vividly remember him returning to the house with milk in hand. Setting the jug in my refrigerator, among all the casseroles from well-meaning friends. I had needed milk. I hadn't had to ask him to purchase it.

I sigh, frustrated with myself. Still harboring my guilt over kissing him.

This never happened.

But it did happen.

My phone lights up. The screen brightening with the presence of three little dots blinking. A message is being typed.

My heart races. My fingers sweat against the device in my palm. I actually hold my breath.

Then the three dots disappear, and the blank space under the last text remains.

Need me to grab milk at the store?

There are so many things I need, all of which can't be bought in a store. Most of which I'm afraid to admit to myself.

Because deep, deep, *deep* down inside, Mason had become important to me over the past thirteen months. A piece of me I can't shake loose, and I miss him. He's reaching out to the kids and sending them memes. He's checking in on them and offering them support.

And selfishly, I want my shadow back. It's foolish really. He'd been here for Ben, and it was a thought I needed to remember.

Mason was not mine.

He was Ben's.

Chapter 13

2 Years Ago
October

Almost Halloween

[Mason]

"Mason?" The female voice turns my head.

"Hey beautiful," I address Jenna Davis. Jenna was one of Anna's college friends and we hooked up one night, as college kids do. She lives in Elk Lake City, which is a small town about thirty minutes north of where I live in Traverse City. She's still a stunner with long toned legs and dark hair, and whenever I see her, I can't help but flirt with her.

"What are you doing here?" Her incredulous tone doesn't surprise me. The last place anyone would expect to find me is a pumpkin patch.

"I'm here with my daughter. This is Lynlee." I reach for her shoulder and Lynlee stiffens. She isn't afraid of me. Or at least, I don't think so. If Lynlee is suffering with Samantha, being skittish and uncertain of my touch is understandable. I just don't know what's happening with my little girl. Either way, I'm awkward showing her affection. Other dads walk around holding hands with their little ones, and I want that but making that happen doesn't come easily for us. Our relationship isn't strong as I only see her on Saturdays, and in the past fourteen months, I've had to miss some days.

"Hi." Jenna offers a quick friendly wave as she glances down at the straight dark hair and almond-colored eyes of my daughter. She looks so much like her mother while her temperament is the complete opposite.

"Those are my two. Over there." Jenna points only a few feet away from us where a little blond with riotous curls is trying to climb an oversized pumpkin and the second girl with rumpled brown hair cascading down her back looks like she's scolding her sister.

"Cute," I offer before looking back at Jenna. The dark brown locks of her older daughter matches her own. Jenna is tallish with curves in all the right places. She was wild like me in college but finally settled down with a decent guy, bought a house, and had kids. Seems the story of most women from my past. She's also a widow and this reminds me of Anna.

Jenna watches me a moment before tipping her head down, then back up. "I'm sorry again about Ben. I know you two were tight." She rubs a hand along my upper arm.

"Yeah. Cancer sucks." I squint, glancing over her shoulder. The urge to ask about Anna is a struggle and I lose the battle. "Have you spoken to Anna lately?"

Her brows lift. "Actually, we check in almost every week. She has a long year ahead of her. A year of firsts. First Thanksgiving without him. First Christmas." Jenna waves a dismissive hand. "She'll weather through, though. We all do somehow."

The little blond barges into Jenna's leg, drawing Jenna's attention downward as her knee jolts. Jenna lifts her daughter and presses a kiss to her cheek. "Right, Rosie?" She hitches the girl higher on her hip. "Anna is a warrior."

Rosie sticks her thumb into her mouth and ducks her head under her mother's jaw.

"Yeah, Anna's strong but I don't know how anyone. . ." I swallow. "Shit, I'm sorry."

Jenna lost her husband as well and I'd just inserted my foot in my mouth. She looks at me, offering a soft smile. "No worries." She presses another kiss to Rosie's round cheek before setting her back on the ground.

"I remember you guys always having a strong friend base and that's really important. So is family. While Anna's family is small, she has her kids to distract her. Plus, she's close to her sister who has been to visit."

"Amelia went to Lakeside?" It's rare that the youngest McCaryn comes home. She's busy kicking ass and taking names in Chicago working for some marketing firm.

"Anna just needed some girl time."

"Oh."

Jenna laughs. "Her sister even tried to hook her up on a date."

"What?" I choke on the idea of Anna with another man. "Isn't it a little soon?" Ben hasn't even been gone three months.

Jenna's laughter softens. "Amelia was only teasing. They went out for margaritas and Anna got hit on."

Of course she did. She's fucking beautiful. Didn't the asshole see her wedding ring? She's taken.

The thought brings me up short. Because she isn't really taken. Ben might be in her heart forever, but he isn't here anymore to keep assholes away from her. Assholes like me who took advantage of her one night.

Shit, I still hate myself for what we'd done. How far it almost went. Her mouth on mine. The curve of her body against me. I can still feel her phantom fingers around my cock. When I recall how she called me Ben, the sensation withers away. My heart shrivels a little more, knowing I'd never be him. Never be who she wants.

But that kiss haunts me. The way her mouth moved with mine—soft at first and then hungry for more. Her hands in my hair. Her fingers fisting me.

I shudder and take a deep breath.

"I haven't been south for a while," I admit, although I've had plenty of meetings with Logan and even Zack. Commuting three hours again, now for Four Points which we headquartered in Lakeside, is wearing on me. I love our new company and the strides we're making in forming a name for ourselves in environmentally-sound homebuilding. Even my vision for the company couldn't have predicted the way we've skyrocketed in demand.

If only Ben could see our success. He'd predicted how quickly we'd grow. He'd be so proud.

He'd equally be disappointed in me. He asked me to look after his wife after he was gone, not take advantage of her. I doubt he intended for me to kiss her. I haven't done a good job honoring his request to be there for her. Shame knots my gut.

"We should grab a drink," I offer to Jenna.

"Mason." She chuckles as she elongates my name. "I'm not going out with you."

I exhale awkwardly and swipe a hand through my hair. Teasingly, I ask Jenna out every time I see her. "Yeah, I didn't mean drink *drinks*. I meant, now. I could buy you a coffee. Maybe some apple cider for your girls."

"Oh." Jenna softly laughs and glances down at Rosie who is plastered to her leg. Her other daughter comes closer, struggling with a pumpkin that's too large for her little arms. Jenna takes the oversized gourd from her. "I should probably get Rosie home for a nap."

"No nap," the blond says around the thumb in her mouth.

Jenna shakes her head and smiles at her daughter before looking up at me. "It was great to see you again, Mason." She pauses watching me a second. "You should give Anna a call."

"Yeah, I've been meaning to." It's half-true. I should be calling Anna regularly, checking on her. I share memes and texts with the kids, but Anna and I have been on mute for months. I've developed a bad habit of looking at texts we'd traded in the past. One night, I'd seen three dots appear. Anticipation filled my chest, forcing me to hold my breath, like holding out hope that she was thinking of me. She was reaching out to me. She needed me.

Just as quickly the dots disappeared, and the screen dimmed.

Like an anxious teen, I typed out my own message, desperate to recapture her attention. What did she need from me? I'd do anything she asked but staying away from her was eating me up inside.

Instead, I hit delete on my message and tossed my phone aside.

I missed Ben but I'd come to terms with his passing. My strength came from the honor of caring for him in the end. He'd trusted me, like no one else had. As he always did. I think I did an okay job.

But I also missed Anna. We'd fallen into a routine. Maybe I only shadowed her, but she didn't push me away. We worked in tandem, tag-teaming for the kids, and seamlessly moving around one another like a well-oiled machine. Some reckless nights I even imagined our movements mimicked those of an old married couple. The ones where a wife moved left to put dishes in a dishwasher, while a husband moved right to place the salt back in the cabinet, like an unconscious dance.

I'd actually only ever witnessed Frank and Ruth Kulis move that way. Then Ben and Anna.

I was a fool to ever think I'd be part of something like that. Jenna's rejection didn't hurt me, but it was a reminder that I'll never be the guy someone settled down with. I wasn't the decent guy you could raise a few kids with. The cog in a gear you needed to make a clock tick or a mechanism function. I was the fun-guy, the one-night stand man.

"Great seeing you too, Jenna. Don't be a stranger." I nod at her girls and slip a hand around Lynlee again, tugging her closer to me. To my surprise, she leans into my leg, copying the way Rosie hugged Jenna's, and for a brief second, hope blooms for Lynlee and me.

A wild thought strikes. That one day I might be good enough for someone like Anna.

Then Lynlee pulls away from my leg and the bubble bursts.

+ + +

Seeing Jenna should have prompted me to call Anna, but I still put off the inevitable for a few weeks. The apology I owe her taunts me. My sin wasn't something I could discuss with someone else either, so I was stuck in this weird purgatory of wanting to contact Anna and not calling.

As for my confession to Ben, did he receive it? Did he forgive me?

My shame was a constant cycle, spinning out of control.

Taking the coward's way out, I asked Bryce about Anna when we were shooting texts back and forth one night.

Me: How's your mom?

Bryce: Good. Not crying so much anymore.

Me: Is she still crying often?

Guilt riddles at me again. I should be there for her. I promised Ben.

Bryce: Just every once in a while. Senior day was difficult. Calvin was honored for leadership.

Shit. How did I miss this? In a small town, kids can play more than one sport. Bryce loved football while Calvin excelled at baseball, but they each played the other sport as well.

I'd made it to a few games, keeping away from Anna where she sat with the other parents. Sometimes Logan and Zack would join me near the fence along the sidelines. I'd sneak off once the games were finished. I hadn't made it to senior day because Samantha pitched a fit about me taking Lynlee to Lakeside. She tossed out words like kidnapping and court. It wasn't like I asked for Lynlee overnight. Part of our agreement was my daughter didn't spend the night. But I was so sick of Samantha's bullshit.

Me: I'm sorry I missed it.

Bryce: No worries, man. Calvin understands.

Did he, though? He was only eighteen years old, at the end of one journey and on the verge of another. He'd be going to college next fall. Anna would be down one more family member, although Calvin could come home. She wasn't losing him forever.

Bryce: Think you might be here for Thanksgiving?

I hadn't thought much about the holidays for myself. Jenna's comments come back to me. Anna had a year of firsts before her. They all did, and I didn't want to be in the way.

Bryce: Mom's calling it a Friendsgiving. I don't think she understands the concept.

I chuckle as I type. **Why? Who is coming to dinner?**

Bryce: The usual. Aunt Autumn and Logan. Zack and River. Everyone will be here.

Everyone. Everyone else but me. The truth stings. I'd always been on the outside of that collective term, especially as people married and had kids.

The invitation wasn't exactly from Anna, but I needed to do better for the kids. Ben asked me to be present. He'd told me he didn't need to ask for more, like he hadn't officially asked me to stay and live with them that final year. In his words, he knew I'd be there. I'd step up for him.

I'd be there for Thanksgiving.

Me: If it's okay with your mom, I'll be there.
Bryce: It's okay with me, so be here. *Wink face emoji*

95

Chapter 14

2 Years Ago
November

Thanksgiving

[Anna]

"Mason?" My surprise couldn't be contained as I open the front door to find a sinfully gorgeous man wearing a bright blue suit standing there.

"Hey." Mason swipes nervously at his hair, detecting the shock in my tone. "Bryce didn't tell you?"

"Tell me what?" With my hand still on the doorknob, I cock a hip to the side. My middle child is the quiet one. He can also be sneaky at times.

"He invited me to dinner." Mason stares at me, expectantly, smoothing a hand down his tie.

"Of course." I shake my head, wiping away images of those same eyes staring into mine with trepidation after we— I cut off the reminder and skim a trembling hand down my hip, smoothing out my dress. "Of course. Come in. Happy Thanksgiving."

Stepping back, I wave at him to pass but he pauses before me, holding up a bouquet of fall flowers that I hadn't noticed he held at his side.

"Happy Thanksgiving, Anna." He leans forward, kissing my cheek. The kiss comes as a sudden surprise after years of him being careful not to touch me. And one night when things catapulted out of control.

With a sharp inhale at the sudden move, my nose fills with the crisp scent of him. Fresh. Expensive. Alive.

Confused by the subtle stirring inside me, I mumble my gratitude and take the flowers from him. I lift the fall arrangement to my nose, hoping to rid the scent of him whirling up more memories of how close we were, pressed together, fingers clenching, bodies grinding. The attempt at distraction is a failure.

Mason moves forward and a roar of his name is exclaimed. I had no idea he was coming. I should have extended an invitation to him myself. He deserved to be here. This was his family of friends.

"May-*son*." His name was emphasized by Logan.

"Mason?" Surprise rings in Zack's voice, matching my own shock.

"Well, well. Mason." The seductive tone of my sister purring his name does not settle well with me.

Hugs happen. Backs are clapped. And Mason falls into the chatter of our gathering, as he should. He works with these men. He's been friends with them for decades.

I'm the one with an issue here. When there isn't an issue. Because nothing happened.

Because of Mason's history with women, it seems easier for him to ignore the elephant in the room. Or me. I'm the elephant in a silky wrap dress.

Drinks are poured and the volume in the room increases. Knowing I can't sit still, or I'll think too much, I stand behind the large kitchen island, continuing to check on the turkey, double check the mash potato casserole, and begin making cornbread muffins.

"Watching him with a baby is making my ovaries weep." Amelia's voice turns my head and I catch a glimpse of Mason holding baby Ben. To my surprise, he looks comfortable holding a four-month-old, which I wouldn't have expected from him.

There have been too many things I haven't expected of Mason Becker.

"Stop ogling him." My face heats as I refocus on the bowl in my hand, spinning the metal container as I pummel the cornbread mixture with a spatula. Mason was rocking a suit jacket when he walked in but he's since removed the jacket, and rolled up his shirt sleeves, pressing them above his elbows.

My sister hums in appreciation. "Arm porn and baby holding is a lethal combination."

"You're objectifying him," I warn my sister.

"Mason doesn't mind if I objectify him." Amelia winks at me. She's a wannabe powerhouse with strong opinions about women and intelligence versus the female body as a climb-the-corporate-ladder tool. Still, she isn't shy about appreciating the male form.

"How would you like someone to objectify you?"

Amelia is feminism personified. She wants to break glass ceilings, open her own doors, and rule the world. I'm the opposite. When we were kids, I longed for someone to love me and someone I could love in return. He would take care of me, and I'd do the same for him. We'd have a nice house and raise our children. I wanted what my parents had, and I had it. Mostly.

"Please, let someone objectify me," Amelia drones, leaning her hip into the cabinet beside me. "I can't remember the last time I had sex."

I pause in whirling the spatula around the inside of the mixing bowl.

I can hardly remember sex. While I expected to retain the memories of Ben and I together indefinitely, there has been something lacking in reminiscing. I can't quite recall the feel of his hands on me. The way his mouth formed with mine. Or even how it felt to have him inside me.

The thought has me peeking over my shoulder one more time at the last person who did touch my body. The feel of his hands is like a ghost on my skin. The squeeze of my breast. The pressure between my thighs. The heat of his dick in my hand.

The spatula slips from the bowl, splattering cornbread mixture into the air and against the countertop.

"Whoa," Amelia cries out, reaching for a towel to wipe up the mess I've made. I glance down at myself, noticing I've splashed mix on the front of my dress.

"Shit." I tug the towel out of Amelia's hand and swipe at my dress. Of course, it's right between my breasts and I pull the top forward to rub the mess which only grows larger. For some reason, I glance over my shoulder once more, catching Mason looking in our direction.

Those deep blue eyes that are different, piercing and intent, hold heat like I've never seen.

My skin prickles. A slow pulse beats down low. I fight the sudden arousal, demanding my body to stop reacting to him.

He's simply looking toward the kitchen area.

But as I smooth the towel over my top, slowing in my attention to the spill at my chest, I can't seem to pull my gaze away from him. He lifts a beer bottle, taking his time to bring it to his pouty lips. His gaze doesn't leave my direction. His brown hair glows copper. The corner of his mouth curls upward as he places the lip of the bottle against his. One brow hitches as he tips back his beer. His Adam's apple bobs as he swallows.

"I just had an orgasm," my sister whispers beside me, and I quickly turn my head in her direction, tugging myself free from my own ogling of Mason. Amelia's bottom lip hangs open. Her fingers tug at the collar of her dress. Her eyes are trained forward, focused on something in the sitting area.

Or rather someone.

Amelia's gaze is locked in on Mason and when I glance back at him, I see he wasn't watching me.

He's admiring my sister.

$+++$

I might have closed the door to my bedroom a little too hard. Being that it's down the hallway from the kitchen, the sound resonates toward the party gathered in the open concept kitchen combination sitting area.

However, I needed a quick exit and a moment alone to collect myself.

I shouldn't have reacted to Mason and Amelia eyeing one another. She's a beautiful woman. Vibrant. Young. Or at least younger than me. Successful. Stylish. Worldly. While I'm successful in a different way— marriage and family—in comparison to my sister, there is no comparison.

And I hate that I'm comparing us, because I love my sister.

But I don't love the idea of Mason and Amelia together.

Hastily, I tug a new dress off a hanger in my closet. I've already removed the soiled dress and tossed it over the hamper for the dry cleaners.

As I stand before the closet, the door to my room opens. I jerk the new dress against my body like a shield.

"Haven't you heard of knocking?" I snap as I turn to find Mason standing within the room. His gaze lands on me, barely covered by the dress in my hands.

"I did knock," he states as he checks down the hall before shutting the door, closing us both inside the room.

"You shouldn't be in here." I step toward him and stop, still clutching the dress to my chest, hyperaware that I'm only wearing a bra and underwear before him.

"Is there a problem?" He keeps his eyes on mine. His shoulders are tight. Tension is visible along his neck.

"You're in my room," I remind him as if he isn't aware. He followed me.

"Do you want me to leave?"

"I need to get dressed."

"No, I mean, do you want me to leave the house? Do you not want me here?" The strain in his voice has the wind in my anger sail lowering a bit. He should be here. These are his people too. And I shouldn't be upset that he was watching my sister. He can flirt with whom he wants to. He can kiss whom he pleases. He can even fuck someone.

I just don't want it to be my sister.

My shoulders lower while my fingers squeeze tighter at the fabric pressed against my chest. "No. You should be here."

"But do you *want* me here?" We stand a foot apart but miles away from one another, so when he steps closer to me, he's too close. But I don't move back.

"It doesn't matter what I want, Mason."

He flinches at the directness of my tone, and his expression pinches, pained possibly. Thickness fills my throat. The kind choking off the truth of what I want. I do want him here. I want him shadowing me again. I want him looking at me, not Amelia.

Instead, I say, "I didn't mean to imply I don't want you here. You should be here. These are our friends. These are Ben's friends." The mention of my late husband causes Mason's head to snap back. Perhaps we need the reminder.

This was the bedroom I shared . . . with Ben.

This was the private space of our married life.

This is also the room where I kissed Mason.

My eyes drift to the space behind Mason. The expanse of wall that I'd stood against. The area where we fell into one another for a brief moment. A lapse in judgement, I remind myself, and draw my gaze away from the spot.

Only when I peer up at Mason, he's followed my glance, and is looking over his shoulder at the same location in my bedroom.

His head snaps back, turning to face me. "Ben asked me to watch out for you after he was gone. I haven't done a very good job."

Something in what he's said adds to my already existing irritation. "You don't need to watch out for me. You aren't beholden to Ben." I should argue that I don't need him, but the words somehow feel wrong.

"I gave Ben my word." Mason stares at me, our eyes connecting in a way they shouldn't. Are we both thinking of the same thing? His promise. My vows.

And yet we kissed. A kiss that was so much more than a kiss, and my body was ready to take it even further back then before my head got in the way.

I'd called him Ben.

However, my body recognized he wasn't Ben. The way Mason plucked at my breast. The way he lifted my leg. The way he kissed me was distinct. A good different when it was so, so bad.

"I won't be some obligation," I snark, attempting to adjust the dress clutched to my chest, but accepting that my dignity is lost. The arm over my chest isn't enough to cover my breasts. Tugging the material on my hip, only exposes more of my other hip, contained by boy-short underwear.

Mason's gaze falls to my hip and then leaps back to my face. He swallows hard, reminding me of him drinking that beer and Amelia claiming to orgasm.

"And don't hit on my sister."

Mason's brows hitch. His eyes widen as though surprised. "Mealworm?" The teenage nickname cracks in his throat.

"I saw you watching Amelia. She doesn't need a holiday fling."

Mason tightens his expression. His jaw ticks. His lips thin. "Maybe you need one."

"I . . ." My mouth falls open. "How dare you?" I'm still in mourning, as ancient as the term sounds. I'll never not be mourning.

Mason scrubs a hand down his face. The soft scratch of his palm over his scruffy jaw whispers between us.

"I'm sorry," I tell him.

He hangs his head. "I'm sorry . . ." He looks at me under hooded lids and his eyes are full of contrition. "I'm sorry for everything. I shouldn't have taken advantage. You were crying and I just wanted to distract"—he swallows hard again, cutting off his own apology—"I shouldn't have done that."

"Nothing happened," I state, convicted in word while not in my thought. I steady my voice, controlling the tone as best I can to wipe away the truth. Something did happen that night, that shouldn't have.

Mason nods once. "I'd still like your forgiveness. And I'd still like to be here."

"For the holiday?" Inside me, I panic. Will he only stay the day?

"For the promise." His gaze remains on me, locking me in place like prey under the spell of a predator. Although Mason isn't hunting.

"I was talking with Bryce earlier and I feel *chastised*." He coughs over the word. "I miss the kids."

The statement should sound strange from his lips and yet I understand what he means. He's spent a year of his life circling my children and they've missed him as well. When Ben was too sick to play games or watch movies or toss a ball, Mason did those things with my boys. When Ben couldn't go out in public, for fear of exposing himself to germs or a virus, Mason was the one who took Mila for ice cream, an occasional manicure, and the father-daughter dance.

"I'm not keeping them from you." My voice lowers with my own unsaid apology. I'm sorry he hasn't been present . . . for them. "But you don't need to feel like you *have* to be here."

We don't need you is on the tip of my tongue, yet again, I can't say the words. They won't be true. Calvin misses the camaraderie he'd built with Mason. Not quite father and son, but still man to growing man. Bryce misses the enthusiasm of Mason at his football games, although I've heard through the grapevine Mason has snuck in attendance and then disappeared before I ever saw him. Mila simply misses Mason's teasing and sense of humor, even if inappropriate at times.

As for me, I've missed Mason in my own way. Slowly, he slipped into roles played by Ben. Not replacing him, but a welcome addition to our family. A partner of sorts. Losing Ben was like losing a piece of me. Mason's absence has been like losing my shadow. Something I don't pay enough attention to when present but miss when gone.

"I want to be here. For them. For you." Mason waves out a hand at me. "And I wasn't flirting with Amelia. She's like the little sister I never had." He shivers as if the thought of them together repulses him.

I'm not so convinced Mason doesn't find Amelia attractive. She's gorgeous. "Well, Logan fell for Ben's little sister."

"And look how that turned out." Mason scoffs, shaking his head. "Marriage and babies, oh my. No thanks."

Our eyes catch at the teasing and a smile grows on his handsome face.

"Forgiven?" He arches a brow and tilts his head, exposing a damn dimple. Once again, I see how women easily drop their panties and fall into bed with him.

My panties will stay intact, though.

"Nothing to forgive." Nothing happened, I tell myself again, wanting to believe the lie while my skin prickles with the memory every single time I recall what we did. Mason watches my face and I school my expression in hopes not to give away my recall of that night.

"Shake on it." Mason holds out a hand and I glance down at his long fingers.

I will away more reminders of him touching me and tighten my hold on my dress. "Uhm." Looking up at him, recognition crosses his face. I'm still not fully dressed.

Mason licks his lower lip and bites at the corner. "Yeah. Sorry about that, too." He points at me and then hitches his thumb toward his shoulder. "I shouldn't have . . . I'm just going to . . . I'll give you a minute."

Awkward tension falls between us, and Mason turns toward the door. However, he pauses before he opens it. His gaze catches on something on my dresser.

"You still have all the heart rocks?" He looks at me. A collection in various sizes are scattered around the base of a lamp and piled in a small dish.

"I couldn't part with them." They remind me of Ben. The rocks stopped appearing shortly after his death. In the days following his passing, another one or two showed up, and I assumed they were little messages from the grave. Signs of strength and love. Silly to admit. However, I needed them. They were reminders that I would go on as he asked me.

Live every minute, Anna.

Mason pauses, staring at the collection on my dresser. Then his head swivels, and he glances once more at the wall where he cupped my face and kissed me senseless.

Nothing happened, whispers through my head, but when Mason looks back at me one more time, I'm aware of the lie I keep telling myself.

Because I'm afraid to admit something did happen.

Chapter 15

2 Years Ago
February

Galentine's Day

[Anna]

February is the month of love, and for the first time in my forty-one years, the shortest month of the year feels like the longest. Thankfully, the high school has a four-day weekend and I take a much needed mini-vacation to visit Amelia in Chicago. Her condo isn't big enough for my family of four, so each of the kids stay with old friends.

Calvin and I fought a few times last summer about some girl he was interested in, but I've decided to pick my battles with my oldest child before he graduates and heads off to college. He's spending his weekend with her at her parents' home. It isn't that I don't like the girl, but I don't want Calvin making decisions based on her. Then again, Ben and I did that. I attended Michigan State University for education when I could have gone to a college in Illinois instead, especially since I wanted to be certified in my home state. I chose MSU to be with Ben.

I don't regret that decision.

Since our awkward conversation at Thanksgiving, Mason and I have both made a better effort to text each other. The few words aren't conversations. Just a passing wish for a good day. Or a funny meme about construction work or teachers. The exchange is an attempt to fulfill promises to Ben. For Mason, it's obligation. For me, it's guilt. Ben would be disappointed in me for pushing away someone he loved.

"Happy Galentine's," Amelia cheers, holding up her margarita as we sit inside a popular Mexican restaurant. Joining us is a new friend of hers named Eva Nazar, who happens to hate Christmas. I've decided Valentine's Day is my new holiday nemesis.

"To gals without pals," Eva toasts and downs the entire margarita in one steady drink.

I stare at the thirtysomething as she sets her empty glass on the table.

"Well, gal, I needed that." She smacks her lips and heavily sighs. "But I need to get back to work." Eva works for Ashford's, an upscale department store in downtown Chicago.

"As I'm married to my job, I need to go make love to it." She snickers before standing. "Drink more for me."

Downing a margarita and returning to work would never be an option for me. I hardly have time to pee during my twenty-five-minute lunch break. The substitute teaching job I had in the fall turned into a full-time teaching position as the young woman who had a baby decided not to return to work. As I teach high schoolers, some days my teacher friends and I wish the water cooler held wine, though.

"So, this is your glamourous life," I tease my sister after Eva leaves. I hold up the margarita I'm drinking at three o'clock in the afternoon on a Friday.

"Please. There isn't much glamorous about my life. But these margaritas are going to be my *lover* for the evening." My sister rolls over the word before licking the salty rim of her glass.

"Please," I exaggerate back at her. "You must let me live vicariously through you."

Amelia slumps back in the booth and twirls the stem of her margarita glass. "Nothing too vicarious." She sighs. "The only thing wet in my life is this flute."

I sputter around the sip of margarita I've just taken. "Amelia," I chide. When did she get so crass?

She leans forward again and narrows her eyes. "I'm serious. I don't have time to get laid." Watching me, her face sobers. "Do you miss it?"

I stare at her, knowing what she's asking. In some ways, I should be offended at her blatant question. In other ways, I'm glad she asked because I need to talk to someone. While I've developed a strong friendship with River, and we've discussed aspects of grief, including the loss of sensual touch from another, I'm not always comfortable with her open approach to that conversation.

My sister is different.

"I don't think I could ever have random sex." My eyes lock on my sister for only a second before glancing away. I'm not judging. Her lifestyle is just different than mine. More complicated and complex in some ways. I'm used to Ben, being that he was my one and only for almost twenty-five years.

"No one says you have to do that." Amelia takes a sip of her margarita, watching me over the rim. "But have you considered dating?"

"It's too soon."

"Says who?"

I know all the arguments about grief and how individual the timetable is. I'll grieve forever for Ben, but there is a slippery slope to letting grief consume me. My grandmother's words come back to me often. Ben would not have wanted me to wallow away in his loss but live every day. Dating isn't exactly on the agenda yet, if ever, though.

"I don't think I'm ready."

"Don't you miss companionship?" she asks.

"Don't you?" I retort sharply. My sister hasn't had a boyfriend in years.

Amelia watches me. "We're different people, Anna. I'm good alone. You . . ." She pauses. "Not so much."

I stare at her over the table.

"Your nature is to nurture. You love . . . love."

"Why do I feel like that's a bad thing coming from you?"

"It's not," she defends, lifting her brows in surprise. "I'm jealous of that capacity."

My shoulders fall and I reach across the table for her wrist. "There's someone out there for you." Not that my sister needs to be completed by a man. That would be the last statement she'd make. But I believe in soulmates and Amelia has one somewhere.

"Well, he got lost somewhere on his way to me." She waves, dismissively ignoring my sentiment. "Typical male. Won't read a map. Won't ask for directions."

I laugh.

"I'm sure you have toys and all the playthings, but it's never the same as the real thing." Her voice drops on the last two words, innuendo clear.

I don't inform my sister that I don't, in fact, have toys or playthings. Ben and I were not like that. By most standards, Ben and I were rather vanilla. We didn't experiment much. We didn't mix up positions or locations or situations. Amelia doesn't need to know these things, though.

"Yes, but . . ." What can I do about it? I already said no random hookups.

"If you aren't comfortable with a stranger, you should be with someone you know."

"Who are you? And what have you done with my sister?" Where is all this coming from? Maybe Amelia is feeling her own loss during this commercialized holiday. She doesn't have a lover so she's projecting on me her desires, or lack there of, in her life.

"Just hear me out. Go out with a guy friend. Go home with him. Let him get frisky." Amelia rawrs, making a claw hand and scratching at the empty air before her.

I scoff. "I think the margaritas are going to your head."

"Hey, weren't you the one with the baby making plan for Autumn? Pick three guys. Let her sleep with each in order to become pregnant."

I did suggest those things. "But Autumn did not go through with that plan. I didn't know she only had one guy on her list." That guy was Logan and he's now her husband.

"Besides, all the guys I know are falling in love." Zack comes to mind as he moved in with River late last fall.

"What about Mason?"

"What about him?" I snap, glaring at Amelia as she takes another sip of her lime-infused drink. Her sip prompts me to take a deeper swallow of my own margarita. When I set the glass down, my younger sister continues to stare at me. "What?"

"You what?" she argues back, mocking my single word question.

"Why are you looking at me like that?"

"Why do you have that look on your face?"

I sigh. She's exasperating. "It's nothing."

"It is not nothing. You look like either you want to murder me for mentioning Mason or you're keeping a secret about him."

I glance away.

"Anna?"

I swallow hard, purse my lips, twist them side to side, and then peer back at Amelia. "I kissed Mason."

"You *what*?" This time the question is clear.

"It was a huge mistake and I told him we needed to pretend it never happened."

"Worst words ever," she exaggerates. "Not to mention, you can never pretend that nothing happened because something did happen."

I lower my head. "I'm a horrible person," I murmur to the tabletop, sliding my fingertips along the edge.

"No, you're not." Amelia pauses but I don't look up at her. The censure in her eyes will be more than I can witness. "When did this happen?"

Closing my eyes, visions of Mason kissing me return. Immediately, I open my eyes, not needing the reminder during my confession.

"A few weeks after Ben's funeral." My gaze remains on the table. I stare blindly at the fake woodgrain in the laminate surface.

Amelia exhales. "You know that that moment was a reaction to grief, right? Sometimes, we just need physical touch. Comfort. Sex is actually a natural response."

I place an elbow on the table and cup my forehead, hiding my eyes as best I can. "It still shouldn't have happened."

"How *did* it happen?"

"I'd been crying. Again." I emphasize. "Mason came to check on me in my bedroom." I glance at Amelia and then away again. I don't need to fill in the rest of the moment, but I whisper my final sin. "I called him Ben."

Amelia gasps. "Oh, Anna. What did Mason do?"

"We just stopped." It isn't the whole truth but enough of it. "And we never mentioned it again."

He apologized. I pretended.

To my surprise, Amelia snickers. Then she chuckles. Then she's outright laughing, bending at the waist and clutching her stomach.

"What the hell is so funny?"

"You." Amelia tries to gather herself, but she takes one look at me and bursts into laughter once more. "You're so good . . . that when you make one slip up, you act like the world is going to collapse on your head."

"It wasn't appropriate," I defend.

"Says who?" she repeats. "Who do you have to justify your actions to other than yourself?" Her laugh dies. Her glare focuses.

As guilt hits me, and an argument rolls over my tongue, I almost predict what Amelia will say next and I'm not wrong.

"Ben is gone, honey."

Yep. Truth is her counterargument.

"I know, but—"

"No, buts. It's your life, Anna. Your. Life." She narrows her eyes and stares pointedly at me. "Live it."

I'm trying, but kissing Mason was too soon.

My sister reads my mind. "There isn't a timetable. Too soon. Too late." She pauses, then tilts her head. "Actually, there is a timetable. It's the time in between."

She spreads her hands, palms facing each other. She shakes one hand. "There is the start." She shakes her opposite hand. "And the finish. In between is a journey called life and if anyone would have told you to make the most of every single day, it would have been Ben. That's the time that matters."

"But kissing his friend?"

"Not saying Ben would be pleased, if he were alive." Amelia pauses again, softening her expression while emphasizing her words. "But maybe someday. It could happen again." She shakes each hand, underscoring her visual. "Life is not a sprint. There are stops and starts, and even do-overs, if one is lucky. And always second chances."

"Second chances at what?" I've had amazing firsts. Marriage. Kids. Home. Work. I've done all I've wanted to do.

Amelia peers at me before lifting her margarita. "As it's Galentine's Day, *that* word is banned. But think about it. You never know." She hitches up one brow before finishing her margarita.

The word still isn't clear to me. I'm not in on the Gal Pal lingo as this night is another first.

The first time I haven't celebrated the holiday of love.

Chapter 16

2 Years Ago
February

Valentine's Day

[Mason]

Why didn't Ben leave me a letter?

The text from Anna comes in after midnight. She's away for the weekend, visiting her sister for some girl time. I'll be seeing her next weekend. The father-daughter dance has become an annual date with Mila, and I'll be attending again as I did last year when Ben couldn't go.

Calvin volunteered to take his sister, but Mila reminded him that it isn't brother-sister dance, which sounded all kinds of wrong to me. I kept my thoughts to myself. Calvin's efforts to take care of Mila is commendable, though. He's growing into a good man.

Mila asked me to be her date again because Lorna is going with Logan. The four of us will double-date as we did last year.

I don't know, sweetheart. I stare at the words and decide to delete the sweetheart before hitting send. In my head, I often add endearments to each text we share, which have been more frequent since our moment during Thanksgiving.

When no response comes from her, I have a question of my own. **Do you need a letter from him?**

Her reply is almost immediate. **I just want to know how to navigate without him.**

Oh man. The words aren't quite the sucker punch I expect, but I hate that she's melancholy. It's this fucking made-up holiday. Valentine's Day can suck it.

Typically, that's exactly what I'd have done to me on this greeting-card-company-bullshit-date. Sucking that is. Girls at the bar, whooping it up, hating on men, and then going home with a guy to prove their empowerment over one. Hey, I was an equal opportunity man. You want to celebrate being a winner, I won't mind you riding me for a score.

I wasn't like that anymore, though. I hadn't gotten laid in months and even that night was lackluster. I wasn't at my finest. And she wasn't the woman I wanted underneath me.

I wasn't allowed to think about the woman I wanted.

We were pretending we never touched.

Me: What do you need to navigate?

Anna: Between the start and the finish.

Me: What start and finish?

Anna: Birth and death.

Oh boy. **Me: That's philosophical for a Friday after midnight.**

Anna: I've been drinking.

The answer to every wayward thought. I chuckle to myself and respond.

Me: Maybe you should put down the glass and stop thinking.

Anna: Stop thinking. Good plan. I need to stop.

Funny how in my head, I can almost hear her voice slurring. She goes on weekly manicure and margarita outings with Autumn and River. After the first night, when Anna was drunk and had to be carried to her room by yours truly, I've learned through Zack that the evenings are typically tame.

Me: Are you thinking about more than just birth and death? I probably shouldn't be encouraging an inebriated woman into a drunk conversation, but I'm curious what else is actually on Anna's mind.

Anna: Yes. The in between.

Me: That's a lot of space.

I sit on the edge of my bed. I'd fallen asleep on the couch before the first text came through. With my phone on my chest, a movie played on my television, but I'd lost interest and nodded off. We've been working hard at Four Points, prepping for spring when construction season will hit full tilt.

Anna: Only one thing fills that space.

For some reason, my heart skitters. My lungs work harder. I stare at the device, hesitant to even ask what that one thing occupying her headspace could be.

Me: What?

I watch the three dots dancing for a long heartbeat.

Anna: You.

My breath catches. I want to toss the phone across the room. *Blasphemy*. She's drunk. This isn't a conversation or a confession. It's a stream of consciousness brought on by alcohol. And as much as I want more details as to what exactly she's thinking about me, I don't ask.

Me: Go to bed, Anna. Drink some water. Get some rest.

Anna: Still taking care of me.

The words stare back at me. I try. I try to take care of Anna as much as I devoted myself to Ben. However, my heart can only take so much.

Anna: You aren't obligated.

And this is my out. Anna has it in her head that she's an obligation instead of my friend. I want to be available to her because I care about her. Not just because Ben asked me to be there. Not just because he's gone.

I've always cared about her. I fucking love her and my heart wants to punch me in the face for such a thought.

Me: Night, sweetheart. I don't erase the endearment. I hit send and toss my phone to my nightstand then fall onto my back.

I should be too pissed off by her final comment to think deeper thoughts of her. I should ignore what happened one night as she's asked me to forget it. Instead, I close my eyes, pulling up the memory, and popping the button on my jeans. Sliding my hand into my pants, I curl my fist over my semi-quickly-turning-full-hard-on and squeeze.

Anna frustrates the hell out of me and taking it out on myself is a good way to loosen the tension.

Also, the only way I get off lately is by thinking of her.

+ + +

I should hate myself for whacking off to fantasies of Anna in my head, but I don't. Guilt eats at me for another reason.

As I lay in bed the following morning, I reach into the nightstand drawer and remove the cardstock paper.

Why didn't Ben leave me a letter? Anna had asked.

A better question is why did Ben leave me one? And what the hell does it mean?

Two words. Two simple words.

Let Go.

Twirling the note card between my fingers, I ponder a thought I've had each and every time I read the card.

What exactly should I let go of, Ben?

My bitterness toward my father.

My infatuation with his wife.

My failure as a dad.

I was supposed to have Lynlee as today is a Saturday. Instead, Samantha cited another bullshit excuse about having a girls' party to celebrate singlehood. Mothers and daughters only. I couldn't recall any friends of Samantha's with kids. She'd been friends-with-benefits with some guy from Elk Lake City before we met. He was a single dad and that's the only time I ever heard her mention someone with kids. She'd been pretty hung up on him, but he married someone else.

As for the bitterness toward my father, that ship sailed. Four Points was successful in its own right, building energy-efficient homes with sustainable products and systems. Constructing a house felt special compared to developing another bland commercial property. A home would be the result of a new build.

Thoughts like this made me think once more about Lynlee. I live in a townhome in Traverse City. I even pay Samantha's rent for an apartment, but I want a house of my own. Between my mortgage and the rent on Samantha's place, I could afford something bigger, with a yard, maybe a swing set or tree fort like Zack has for his twins. I want something permanent and set apart from a collection of homes strung in a line.

Deep down, I'd like to move to Lakeside. Logan moved there two winters ago. Zack moved last fall. Everyone important to me is in Lakeside.

Except Lynlee.

Let Go.

I stare at the words again.

Maybe Ben did mean my infatuation with his wife. The untold secret was always present in our private joke. Of course, I never spoke to a soul about my feelings until two summers' ago, after a little too much tequila with Zack. I shouldn't have ever mentioned how I felt because he watched me like a hawk after Ben passed. A hawk ready to swoop in and protect one of his oldest friends from a sly fox.

Maybe what Ben meant was I needed to let go of these consuming feelings of unworthiness. The squeaky wheel on the cart. The bad boy in the mix. Then again, someone has to hold the title, and I'm the last one standing as Zack and Logan have each fallen in love.

Love.

Fucking Valentine's Day. If I was in Lakeside, I know how I'd express the emotion and to whom I'd want to give it. Roses would be cliché. Violets wouldn't do.

But none of that matters as no one is in love with me.

I stare at the words.

Let Go.

Yeah, Benners. Maybe what I should be letting go of is the idea of love.

+ + +

The weekend after Anna's drunken text I arrive at Lakeside Cottage with a wrist corsage in hand.

Bryce opens the door and tells me Mila needs another minute. "That's actually some weird girl code to keep you waiting when she's been ready for almost an hour."

I check my watch. "Am I late?"

Logan and I made reservations for six o'clock at Driftwood, a popular restaurant in town. The three-hour commute from Traverse City to here was hell again. I really need to consider finding a local place so I'm not always crashing at Logan's or Zack's.

"Nah. I'm supposed to ask you if you'd like a drink." Bryce rolls his eyes. With his blond hair and blue eyes, he looks so much like his father. Even his exasperated expression is a replica of Ben's.

"Why the formality?"

"Fuck if I know," he mutters.

As a father, Ben would admonish his teenage son for his language. As I'm the playful uncle, I don't scold him.

"How are things?" I ask, following him into the kitchen. We had a long chat at Thanksgiving. As the middle child, he can sometimes feel left out. He told me how he understands that I have a life outside of their family, with Lynlee, but he felt abandoned when his dad died and then I left as well.

The admission hit me hard and I promised again to do better. Baseball season starts soon. Although Bryce's first love is football, he plays baseball as well.

"I made Varsity. Calvin isn't happy." Bryce shrugs. He's more athletic than Calvin, if there even is such a thing. "I also failed a chemistry test and Mom had a shitbrick."

"I had a brick because you went out the night before and didn't study."

When I turn to Anna, my breath hitches. Every damn time. Even in jeans and a sweatshirt. As if I haven't seen her over the years, changing as she had children, as she ages. She's so beautiful.

Directing my gaze to the girl standing next to her, I give her the compliments I want to give her mother. "Mila. You look beautiful." In a dress with a full skirt but Chuck's on her feet, she's a tomboy in feminine clothing. She tugs at the pile of fabric around her legs.

"Mom made me wear it."

Anna turns to her. "You picked it out."

Mila rolls her eyes, just like Bryce. Just like Ben. Her eyes are bright blue and friendly. She's a combination of Mom and Dad, but as she grows up, her features are more Anna. The angle of her cheekbone. The shape of her eyes. The smile on her mouth.

"For you." I hold out the corsage to Mila.

Anna nudges Mila, who rushes to the refrigerator. She produces a plastic container with a boutonniere inside. After I slip the corsage on Mila's wrist, she awkwardly holds the simple flower for me up to my jacket.

"Let me." Anna steps forward and takes the flower with two large pins in the wrapped stem from Mila. Curling my lapel in her hand, she fiddles with the flower and the pins.

"Don't stick me," I teasingly warn.

"I'd never hurt you."

We look at one another at the same time and our gazes lock for a second. My throat thickens and I inhale the sweet perfume she wears. Summer and freshness.

"We need a picture," Mila states.

Anna and I break away as if we've been caught doing something we shouldn't.

Bryce holds up his phone and we take the obligatory photos before he says, "Mom, get in the picture with them."

Anna nervously looks from me to Bryce and back.

"Come on, Mom," Mila encourages, and I hold my breath as Anna walks toward us, slipping her arm around Mila's shoulders. I drop my hand from Mila and place my hand on Anna's lower back. The touch isn't more than thirty seconds but instantly she feels familiar. Like a long-lost piece of me.

If only she felt that way in return.

I shake the thought and step back from both mother and daughter.

"Have fun," Anna says, tugging Mila in for a hug. She looks up at me and another tense gaze passes between us. We haven't spoken about her drunken texts.

Ignoring the tension, I reach out to Bryce, giving him a fist bump, and promise not to have Mila home too late, like it's an actual date.

"Make good choices," Bryce calls out as we exit the kitchen.

"For heaven's sake," Anna admonishes.

"What? Our babies are growing up so fast." Bryce mocks a sniffle and I chuckle to myself, uncertain if he means Mila or me.

Probably both.

Chapter 17

2 Years Ago
February

Valentine's Dance

[Anna]

When the front door opens, I immediately know Mason and Mila have returned. I unfold myself from the couch and head to the entryway where Mason is crouched down and Mila is giving him a hug while she stifles a yawn.

"Thanks again, Uncle Mason. I had so much fun."

"Anytime, baby."

He's sweet with Mila. It gives me hope he's sweet with his own daughter.

Mila releases Mason and I reach out, brushing a hand over her hair. "Did you have a good time?"

Mila nods, no longer stifling, but yawning wide. I chuckle and lean down to press a kiss to her forehead. "You can tell me all about it tomorrow."

My children don't need me to tuck them in anymore which is a stage I miss, so after a quick hug from Mila, she turns and trudges up the steps.

"Don't forget to brush your teeth." I holler after her before turning back to Mason. "She's not going to brush her teeth."

"Well, two sodas and a handful of cookies can't do too much damage, right?" He chuckles.

"Where's your bag?" I hadn't noticed him bring one in earlier.

He scratches the back of his neck. "I'm gonna stay in Autumn's old condo for the night. It's vacant."

My brows pinch and shoulders fall in unexplained disappointment. "Oh. You didn't have to do that. You could have stayed here."

Mason watches me a minute and his eyes look as if they see inside my chest. See my heart thudding from the letdown.

"Yeah, it's probably better I stay there. I need to head back to Traverse early."

I don't argue with him. "The commute must be getting old." Many of the meetings between Zack and Logan are handled by video conference but Mason comes to Lakeside at least once a week. The trips are normally here and back in a day or two at the most. He doesn't stay at the house, continuing to give us space as a family.

Sometimes that space is too empty, though.

"It's okay," he mutters, sounding tired.

"I'd offer you a glass of wine, but I don't want you nodding off as you drive to the condo."

Mason grins. "One glass won't hurt."

He follows me toward the kitchen. As we near the island that divides the sitting room from the cabinet space, I speak. "Thank you for taking Mila again. She really looks forward to this night. And I'm certain she had a good time."

"Me too." He nods as I hold up a bottle of Malbec which I already had open. I fill a glass for him and top off my own.

"Maybe one day you can bring Lynlee."

Mason freezes as he lifts his wineglass, pausing a second to look at me over the rim. "Yeah, maybe." He finishes lifting the glass and takes a large sip.

"You never talk about her." I don't know what I'm implying or even what I'm asking. Mason and I don't really talk. We text. Minimal, mundane messages.

Except for a week ago, when I drunk-texted him. Scrolling back through the conversation the following morning, my breath hitched at the confession I'd given him.

You. Too often he fills my thoughts.

"What do you want me to say?" Mason interrupts my reminiscing.

I shrug. "Anything. Tell me what she's like or what you do when you two are together."

"I don't get to see her as often as I'd like."

"Because of Four Points?" My brows pinch. He works too hard.

"Because Samantha is a bitch."

The venom in his tone surprises me and my eyes widen. "Why? What's going on?"

"It's nothing." He glances away before taking another big gulp from his wineglass.

"You can talk to me, you know?"

"What's there to say?" He heavily exhales, hesitantly eyeing me before speaking. "Samantha plays these head games with me. She constantly tries to insert herself into my time with Lynlee or makes an excuse why I can't have her on my day." He swipes fingers through his hair, mussing up the polished look he normally has.

I stare at him, completely floored. In the past, Ben had hinted that Samantha was a piece of work. He'd mentioned that Mason struggled in his connection with Lynlee, but I didn't realize Samantha might have been a huge cause in Mason's battles.

"I'm so sorry, Mason. I had no idea."

"Ben didn't tell you? I thought you two told each other everything." Frustration more than accusation fills his voice.

"He didn't tell me this. I'm sorry," I say once more. Again, I've misjudged him.

"We've been back to mediation a few times but nothing changes." He leans on the island, as if there is a heavy weight on his shoulders. He twirls the stem of his wineglass between his long fingers.

Reaching across the countertop, I place my hand on his. His head snaps up and our eyes meet again. "It's so unfair," I say.

Mason nods once. He glances down at where my hand covers his and I retract my touch, my palm too quickly cooling after the heat of his skin.

"So what kind of dances did you do tonight?" I tease, seeking something to break the tension. "An old school Macarena? The Cha-Cha Slide? A little dabbing?"

"I'll have you know I have smoother moves than all that."

"I bet you do." I shake my head as my lips curl.

"You know what they say about a man who can dance."

"What do *they* say?" I mock of the ambiguous and generic term.

"He's good in— Never mind."

I stare at Mason, completing the sentence on my own. *A man who can dance is said to be good in bed.* There's no doubt in my mind Mason is exceptional in that manner. The swagger, the confidence, the general air about him screams sensual and remarkable.

"I miss dancing," I whisper.

"Is that a euphemism?" Mason teasingly lifts a brow.

"No. Just that. I miss dancing."

Mason picks up his wineglass and swallows the last of his wine. Setting the glass back on the countertop, he stands and rounds the island.

"May I have this dance?" He holds out his hand, looking impeccable even after a night of school-gymnasium gyrations. His royal blue suit fits his slender but strong physique and accentuates the color of his eyes.

I glance down at myself, wearing a pair of pajama pants with notebooks on them and an oversized sweatshirt.

"I'm not exactly dressed for a ballroom."

"You're always beautiful, Anna."

The compliment catches me off guard, and my stupor gives Mason a moment to capture my hand and tug me to him. I catch myself against his firm, solid chest. His heart beats steadily under my palms.

He curls an arm around my lower back.

"There isn't any music," I whisper, my throat thick as I inhale the expensive scent of him.

"We don't need any." Mason sways right to left, his hips guiding mine to follow his lead. At first, we are inches apart but as we slowly spin, the distance closes.

Mason dips his head. His cheek is near enough I could rub mine against the tempting scruff along his jaw. His breath hits my neck and I tilt my head, telling myself it's to get more comfortable, but the real reason tickles my flesh. The stretch provides Mason more access to my skin. His nose brushes the column of my throat. The tip drags along the expanse of flesh, giving me chills.

His hand at my lower back fists into the fabric of my sweatshirt. The gentle pressure tugs me closer to him. While our opposite hands were cupped in a perfect pairing for standard dancing, he spins his palm against mine and spreads my fingers, entwining them together and lowering our arms between our chests.

The hand fisted in my sweatshirt releases and coasts up my spine until the heat of his palm cups the back of my neck. His fingers curl into the hair at my nape, holding my head tilted to the side, continuing to expose my skin to him.

I swallow hard as Mason shifts. His lips linger above my neck. There's a tender spot just above my shoulder. If he nips me . . . Who am I kidding? I don't want to resist. I want his lips there. I close my eyes in anticipation, in weakening, as I desire his bite. I want to feel his teeth dig into my skin and send me to my knees.

Instead, he steadily drags his mouth back and forth, hovering along the expanse of my neck, but never making contact.

"Beautiful," he whispers into my ear, and my body vibrates.

My nipples harden. A pulse beats frantically between my thighs. My fingers on his chest curl into his lapel. With my eyes still closed, I inhale, breathing him in. Aware that *him* is Mason.

I should stop this. I should push him away. But just for a moment, I'm lost in the solidness of his arms wrapped around me. The excitement of his mouth lingering over my flesh, teasing me, tempting me. I'm so turned on I might combust.

A soft kiss comes to my ear, and I freeze.

What am I doing?

Guilt slams into me again but I have no one to blame but myself. I was the one drowning in the moment.

Mason steps back as I stiffen. His fingers slip from my hair, taking their time to untangle from the thick mass. For a moment, the drag of his fingers down my back simulates the unzipping of a dress. One I'm not wearing but wish I was.

Our eyes lock on one another as he steps back, still holding my hand. Then he takes his time to untwine our fingers, pressing our palms together before he finally lets go. I hadn't realized how hard I'd been gripping his hand until his fingers release mine and they suddenly feel naked without his.

"I'm sorry," he whispers.

Shaking my head, I don't want him to apologize. For a reason I can't define, and I don't think I should try, I don't want him to regret this moment. Too much remorse lingers between us, and we need to move past it. But what does moving forward look like for us? I can't deny the guilt, but I also can't erase the slow-burning feelings I'm developing for this man.

Mason takes another step back, putting more space between us. The distance feels vast while it's not even a foot apart.

He scratches the back of his neck, flipping up the artful curls before smoothing them back down.

"You and Ben probably used to dance like this."

I tilt my head. "Like what?"

"Late nights in the kitchen." He purses his lips, twisting them, before glancing away from me.

"Actually, Ben and I never danced in the kitchen." Or late at night. Or at all. My voice is quiet with the admission. *Why didn't Ben and I ever dance in the kitchen?* I've heard of romantic moments like this, seen them in movies, too, but I had no experience with an impromptu moment of swaying without music.

Tonight's rhythm was only heartbeats and the meter of two people attracted to one another.

Two people who *shouldn't* be attracted to one another.

"Anna," he whispers, holding my eyes with his. A thousand questions fill my name.

"You should probably leave." The words are hardly more than a whisper. I want his next line to ask me if he can stay, but how would I answer him?

I wasn't ready to admit the truth.

"Thanks for the wine." His gratitude is louder. His tone a bit harder.

"Thank you for the dance." I meet his eyes. The shade is one I once considered wrong, but now see the coloring is just different.

Because Mason is so much more than who I thought he was.

Chapter 18

2 Years Ago
May

Birthdays

[Anna]

"Happy almost birthday, beautiful," Mason says into the phone, his voice chipper.

"Thanks. I think." I'll be forty-two in a matter of hours and where I am is not where I thought I'd be. Instead, I just feel older, worn down by the day to day of life. Kids. Work. Bills.

Calvin will start college in the fall. Thankfully, we had a college plan in place for him. Besides a small life insurance policy, I receive a dividend from Ben's initial investment in Four Points, which is generous but feels wrong at times as he isn't here, contributing to the overall company. Zack has assured me it's very fair and completely legal that I receive a payout.

Still, the house is a lot with taxes and upkeep. I wish Archer were present. I received a message from him last year that he'd be home in the summer. The timeframe could be any month this coming season. Or next year. Or maybe he meant last summer. I just don't have a clue where my brother is or where he's been, and I am still angry that Autumn had a way to contact him.

Anger described me best on my birthday.

"What will you do to celebrate?"

Being that tomorrow is a Tuesday night, I won't exactly go out and tear up the town. "Oh, you know. Just another frozen pizza and a glass of wine." The kids have practices—softball for Mila, baseball for the boys. No one will be home during the dinner hour.

"Yikes. That's . . . depressing," Mason teases.

"Tell me about it," I mumble as I lean back on the headboard in my bedroom. Reading was on my list of nightly activities, but even that felt depressing. I didn't want to read about fictional love lives and people getting it on.

"What would you have done in the past?"

He means with Ben. "Probably dinner. Maybe a movie. Come home and have sex." The final activity simply slips out.

"If you could do anything for your birthday this year, what would it be?" Mason asks as if I hadn't just exposed myself.

I sigh and close my eyes, pushing out of my head the impossible. "It doesn't feel right celebrating."

"Anna," Mason chastises. "You're allowed to live."

Silence falls between us, heavy and thick. He clears his throat eventually. "So, dinner?"

"Lou Malnetti's pizza."

"Deep dish with sausage, green peppers and onions." Mason repeats my order like a pro. Like he knows me. My mouth practically waters at the thought of cheese and spicy meat plus grilled vegetables in a deep-dish crust that melts on your tongue. "God, I miss Chicago."

"Hmm…sounds delicious. What kind of cake?"

"I'm partial to spice cake but you can't get that this time of year."

"Oh God, you're one of those pumpkin spice people," he teases.

"Oh God, you're one of those pumpkin spice haters," I jest in return. "I guess, I'd probably have white chocolate with raspberry swirl cheesecake. Like the kind at The Cheesecake Factory. Although pizza and cheesecake is not good for my waistline."

"Anna, I've told you before, you're fucking gorgeous."

The compliment has my belly fluttering.

"Now, tell me about the sex." Mason's tone is dead serious and aloof like a therapist.

"What sex?" I gasp.

"The sex you'd have on your birthday."

"Oh, God," I groan, chuckling at how ridiculous he is.

"Just talk me through it."

"I . . . That's dangerous." What do I even say? Ben and I would have sex. Just sex.

Mason chuckles. "Okay never mind. A movie and sex. There is always Netflix and a vibrator."

I shouldn't be shocked at how cavalier he is about my predicament. And as long as the admissions are already spewing from my mouth, I don't stop myself from what I say next. "I don't own a vibrator."

The heaviness that falls over the phone makes me wonder if Mason is still there. What feels like more than a minute, but was probably only seconds, passes before my name is a strangled sound through the device. "Anna."

I tip my head back against the headboard and stare up at the ceiling. "I shouldn't have said that. Thanks for calling and the—"

"Stop!" The sharpness of his command has my head popping upright. My breath hitches.

"Where are you right now?"

I hesitate before admitting more. "I'm in bed."

"Jesus," he hisses, and a rustling sound comes through the phone. "What are you wearing?"

Laughter rushes out of me as I choke on his name. "Mason."

"What? You deserve birthday sex, and if you can't have birthday sex, you definitely deserve birthday orgasms."

I struggle again with his abruptness and cough while dismissing what he's said. "It's not my birthday yet."

"Humor me," Mason teases.

"I don't . . . I should go." I squirm on the mattress, tugging on the blanket over my legs. The evenings are still cool, but the days are warming up. The breeze off the lake hints of summer.

"You don't touch yourself?" Mason sounds appalled and that's my cue to end this call.

"I really need to—"

"Let me talk you through it." His voice is low and intimate, asking permission while fully aware he would get it. He's going to tell me what to do with my body.

His name is a groan in my head, but I don't respond. My chest heaves. My breathing deepens. I curl my fingers into the blanket over my legs.

Can I really do this with him? I can't believe I'm considering it, but I can hear him breathing through the phone. His even breaths growing ragged. He whispers my name, and it sounds decadent, tempting even.

"You're in bed, right?" The question isn't seductive, but the depth of his voice is like the lap of his tongue over my prickling skin. "Lay back. Get comfortable."

"I don't think—"

"Don't think. Just lay back. Close your eyes. Take a breath." He inhales and exhales through the phone.

I almost giggle at his coaching, then I remind myself he can't see me. This will only be in my imagination. Another secret I keep to myself.

Following his directions, I scoot lower beneath the covers and close my eyes. I inhale and exhale in rhythm with him.

One final time I question what I'm about to do.

Then I picture Mason over me. His eyes. His mouth. His fingers.

"Run your palm over a breast. Feel the weight." He pauses, giving me a second to experiment with my own touch. "Your nipple is hard. Circle it with a fingertip. Go slow, draw out the pleasure."

I do as he says. My nipple tightens. Heaviness pulses between my thighs. My heart gallops.

"Do the same to your other breast," he commands, his tone growly. The ruggedness in the sound is like another long drag of his tongue over the peak of my nipple. "God, you have such amazing breasts."

His words cause my lids to flip open and I stare up at the ceiling. Why would he say such a thing? And why am I thrilled to hear those words from him?

"Come on, sweetheart." His encouragement comes as if he can see me hesitating. "Just listen to my voice." He hums, as if he's enjoying himself. "Pinch your nipple."

I do as he asks but then drag my hand down my stomach, eager to move on with this lesson. The movement blazes a trail of desire over my belly. My legs press together and my back arches.

"Mason," I whimper, needing more. Nearly begging for his permission to move to the next step.

His breath hitches. He groans as if excited himself. His voice deepens even more when he continues. "Draw your fingers downward. Slow." He pauses a beat. "Slip them into your underwear."

"I'm not wearing any," I admit breathlessly. I put on a pair of boxer-type shorts and skipped the underwear tonight.

"Fuck," he grinds into my ear, his voice desperate. "Touch yourself, baby." He hisses as if he can see me. As if he knows what I'm doing, and where and how. "Circle that sensitive spot. Feel the pleasure build."

For a few seconds, he doesn't speak as I do as he says, circling my clit and rubbing the swollen nub with my fingertips. Needily, I moan.

"Tell me how it feels." His voice drops, the command rough. The combination moves over my skin like a coarse fingertip.

As I've already thrown caution to the wind, I whisper, "I'm so wet."

Mason growls. "Imagine I'm touching you. My fingers want to fuck you." Strain fills his throat. "Fuck, Anna."

"Are you touching yourself?" The curious question bursts from me. Is he turned on by telling me what to do? I picture him holding himself, thick and long in his palm.

"Do you want me to be?" The breathlessness in his voice tells me all I need to know.

"Tell me what you're doing," I whisper. With my eyes closed, my imagination is in overdrive. My clit pulses as my fingers stroke. My libido is singing, hungry for the release.

"I'm cupping my cock and it's so fucking hard. Hard for you, sweetheart. You're kissing it, licking the length. And that mouth." His voice catches.

"My mouth what?" I preen, eager to know what he sees me doing to him.

"Focus, sweetheart. This is for you." He pauses. "Or does it help to think about my dick? Think about the tip at your entrance, swiping up and down against your clit?"

Yep, the thought of him teasing me, spreading me has my fingers rubbing faster. My legs spreading wider.

"You're ready, aren't you, baby? I could slip right into you, and you'd fucking come."

Oh God. I might have cried the phrase out loud, but I don't know as all I concentrate on is what he said. How hard he is and how long he'd be. And how wet I am and how wide my legs are spread. And how quickly he'd thrust into me, filling me.

I tip over the edge. Legs clamping together. Fingers stilling. My head is thrown back as I moan into the phone.

"Fuck, yes. Anna. Fuck. I'm coming too."

My lids open again, but in my mind's eye Mason is over me, entering me, going off inside me.

And as wrong as I want to tell myself this moment is, I haven't felt this right in a long time.

Alive while replete.

Sexy but exhausted.

Minutes pass as I catch my breath and listen to Mason breathing heavily through the phone.

"Many more birthdays, sweetheart." His whispery voice is both rugged and sated.

My vision is watery. "Thank you, Mason." Whether my gratitude is for the wishes or the orgasm, I can't be certain.

"And Anna." There's weight in my name as his voice deepens, becomes louder and firm. "There's no fucking way I'm pretending this never happened."

Then he hangs up.

+ + +

The evening of my birthday plays out as I predicted. The kids are all gone. I've decided to take a bath despite the early hour and skip dinner. I don't want to think about this day. My head hasn't been able to focus anyway after last night. The things Mason said. The things I did.

The doorbell rings, startling me as I'm turning for the hallway to my bedroom. I'm not expecting anyone, and I didn't order anything. Still, I check through the side panel window and open the front door on a rush.

"You ordered a pizza, ma'am?" The male voice is a horrible imitation of a Southern accent.

I swallow around the lump in my throat, caught between the most beautiful pizza delivery man before me in a suit and the emotion of him standing there with a box marked Lou Malnetti's.

"What are you doing here?" Laughter fills my voice as I stare at Mason on the stoop.

"Heard it's your birthday." He winks at me. "Special delivery." He holds up a plastic bag with The Cheesecake Factory written on it.

"Tell me you didn't drive to Chicago?" The round trip would be something like four hours from here and Mason lives three hours north of me on top of that.

"I didn't drive to Chicago." He shrugs, not offering any further explanation as he steps inside.

I follow him as he heads into the kitchen and sets the box and bag on the countertop.

"You should have what you want on your birthday."

Dinner. Cake. *Sex?* Our eyes hold, and I wonder if he's reading my thoughts. The things he said to me last night. The things I did to myself. I can feel the rush of red up my chest and along my throat.

Mason pulls a box wrapped in bright pink with a large black bow out of The Cheesecake Factory bag.

"You should open this later. On your own."

I tilt my head, before reading the card attached. *Celebrate every day.*

"Thank you," I whisper, staring at the bright package before looking up at him. "For everything."

"Anything for you." He smiles then quickly rounds the island to start my oven. Looking back at me, he takes in my attire. I'm still in my teacher dress minus shoes. "What were you about to do?"

"Take a bath, but you're here now . . ."

"Take the bath. The pizza will take an hour to bake. I have some phone calls to make. Take your time."

"You aren't leaving?" My throat catches on the possibility.

"And miss out on this celebration? Not a chance." He winks at me before tipping his head toward my room.

"Can I open this?" I reach for the package, pretty and pink.

"Uh . . . not yet. Later. After dinner."

The sheepish grin on his face and secrecy of the present has me curious but I follow his instructions. I leave the present on the counter and take a bath but I'm too anxious, fidgety actually, knowing he's in my kitchen making me a birthday pizza.

Mason will remove his suit coat, roll his sleeves above his elbows and look too sexy for his own good, so I decide to take extra care with myself, dressing in a casual summery dress while pulling my hair from the messy knot I had it in. I apply a fresh layer of lipstick in a light shade and comb my fingers through my hair. When I return to the kitchen, a glass of red wine awaits me on the counter.

Mason set the island and he points at a stool. "Sit."

When the pizza is ready, I moan at the deliciousness. Mason chuckles and the next hour passes with us sharing past birthdays from our childhoods.

"I wanted a dog. Instead, they gave me a car."

"You poor spoiled bastard," I tease.

Mason huffs. "Something like that." He reaches for his wine, polishing off his second glass.

"So, cake?" he asks.

"I'm so full." The truth hurts my stomach even more. He went through so much trouble to get both treats for me, but I can't eat another bite.

"Save it for the kids, then." He stands and takes our plates over to the sink.

"Leave those. I'll do them later."

He ignores me and rinses the dishes, setting them in the dishwasher before boxing up the remainder of the pizza.

"That isn't going to last long with two constantly hungry teens," I quip about Calvin and Bryce. "Mila should be home soon. Maybe she can sneak a piece before them."

"Maybe." Mason stares at me. "And on that note, I should probably leave."

"You aren't staying?" I don't know why I just assumed he'd spend the night.

He lowers his head a second, eyes aimed at the ground. "That's probably not a good idea." When he glances back up at me, his eyes are a deep mystifying blue.

"Okay," I whisper, taking his meaning. He doesn't want to make tonight longer than it's already been. He's already done so much.

"Present?" I point at the bright pink box that has been taunting me.

"Later," he repeats. "After I leave. And alone," he warns.

"So mysterious," I tease.

"Okay." Mason claps his hands. "One last thing." His tone serious, he rounds the island again and walks up to me. I spin on my stool to face him.

Only when his hands cup my face, my breathing ratchets upward. My heart begins to hammer. Then he's kissing me. It's only lips on lips. No tongue. No teeth. Just soft and sweet, tender and telling.

A birthday kiss.

A wish for many more.

And maybe more kisses.

Chapter 19

2 Years Ago
July

Ben's First Anniversary

[Anna]

I don't like to visit the cemetery.

In my head, I can't reconcile that Ben is there beside his father, Frank, who passed years ago from a heart attack. I don't like to look at the empty space next to Ben and the similarly empty plot on the other side of his father. Those areas are allocated for Ben's mother, Ruth, and me.

According to Ruth, we have a lot of living left to do before we join our men.

In the quiet of an evening, on the edge of the shore is where I prefer to seek him. In mid-July, the days are long, and the sun hangs in the sky, taking its sweet time to descend and close out another day. Another day without Ben.

A full year has passed.

In so many ways, Ben has been gone longer than the past three-hundred and sixty-five days. He wasn't the same man I fell in love with, or married, or shared my children by the time cancer claimed him. They say love shifts over the years. It changes and matures. Married couples adapt to new situations as they age together. Ben would have called bullshit. He would say the best stuff is what's in between the crust. The ooey-gooey goodness like the crème-filling of an Oreo or the warm, melty apples in a pie.

He also would have called me out for sitting here, feeling sorry for myself. He'd want me to enjoy all the cookies of life, not wallow in a pint of vanilla ice cream. And I wasn't even near the prime of my life when his life was cut short.

As the sun dips, I sit on an Adirondack chair on the beach, rubbing a heart-shaped rock between my fingers. The soothing talisman that will forever remind me of Ben. At the start of August, the guys will gather as they promised Ben. They will reunite as more than business partners but a family of friends, commemorating their best friend and their shared history. I'll need to mentally prepare myself for the shenanigans although the only one staying at the house for two weeks is Mason.

We still talk every few days. We never mention what happened the night before my birthday. Or how I officially graduated to the I-own-a-vibrator club. Heat flamed my face when I finally opened the little pink package from Mason. But I put his gift to good use after his innocent kiss charged through my body. He was one-hundred-percent correct. I couldn't pretend he wasn't affecting me because every time I touched myself, I thought of him. What he said. How he said it. The compliments. The encouragement. My imagination was no substitute for the reality of how he might feel but I justified my actions as everything was all in my head.

My imagination.

For the moment.

I didn't intend to act on anything with Mason while he might be the best person to discuss sex with. He had tons of experience. He'd also be a good person to discuss dating but that was the furthest thing from my mind tonight.

As I sit staring at the sun, spreading its warm glow while it lowers in the sky, I try to quiet my mind and bring my thoughts to Ben.

How am I doing? How badly am I fucking up?

Things just aren't the same without the balance of us as parents to our children. Then again, I have several single parent friends and they rock parenting. For my children, I put on a brave smile every morning and move through every day. They are my daily joy.

My mind drifts to the near future. Calvin will be headed to college. Bryce has his driver's license. Mila is changing into a young woman. A snapshot of the years flip through my mind until something catches the corner of my eye.

A tall, lone figure with slicked back hair that curls at his nape, crosses the sand. Dressed in khaki shorts slung low on his hips, and a faded concert T-shirt, he approaches me with his head bowed, face aimed at his bare feet in the sand.

"Mason?" I whisper into the wind.

As if he heard me, his head lifts. His gaze locks on me as he nears the set of wooden chairs.

"Is this seat taken?" He teasingly points at the seat beside me and then plops down before I answer.

"What are you doing here?" The question isn't accusation but wonder. Mason comes and goes from Lakeside, popping into baseball and softball games, or having dinner with the guys, but he doesn't randomly show at the house.

"I knew you might be here." He leans back in the chair and faces the water. The setting sun illuminates his strong features. His sharp nose. His pouty lips. The perfection of scruff on his jaw.

He slowly turns to me, eyes searching. "You doing okay today?"

I nod and glance away, chastising myself for admiring his features on today of all days.

Today marks one-year since my life changed irrevocably.

I repeat my earlier question. "What are you doing here?"

"Just thought you might want company." When I look back at him, he quickly glances away. "Or did you want to be alone?"

The honest answer is I've been alone long enough. But the truth is I wanted a few minutes with Ben in my head on this beach. We hold silent conversations in which I ask questions and he doesn't answer, but strangely, I feel him respond. A trick of the mind that the breeze is his reply to my thoughts.

"You didn't have to do that," I say, acknowledging Mason's desire to keep me company.

Mason looks over his shoulder at me and shrugs. "I wanted to be here for you."

"You wanted to be here because of Ben," I correct, tipping my head.

"Isn't that the same thing?"

"Is it?" I counter, observing him once more as he turns his face from me. Softly, I laugh. "Sometimes I'm not certain who loved him more. Me or you?"

"We loved him differently," Mason says, squinting out at the calming waters of the lake. "I loved him as a friend and brother. You loved him as a lover and partner."

"He was my best friend," I state, staring at Mason's profile.

"I want to be your friend, too." He turns to me as if I haven't clarified Ben's position in my life. Friend. Lover. Partner.

"You are my friend." However, my voice lacks conviction.

Mason rolls his head and narrows his eyes at me. "Sometimes, I don't feel like it."

I stare back at him. "You know, when we were in college, I thought you resented me."

"Resent you? How? Why?" He shifts in his seat. His long fingers clutch the armrest as his back presses into the opposite side of the chair.

I shrug. "I just thought you never wanted me around. *You told me you didn't want me around.* I was cramping the four-guys vibe and your desire to pick up random women."

Mason straightens his body and faces the water's edge. He leans forward and places his elbows on his thighs. "Is that what you really thought of me?" His head turns in my direction again.

"Actually, I thought you were the type of guy who would break my heart. That's why I would have never picked you, Mason." The confession isn't meant to hurt him, but he needs to know. I wouldn't have ever chosen him because my heart couldn't have handled someone like Mason.

"Tell me what you really thought." Hurt laces the sarcasm in his voice. His hands clasp between his knees and his head bows again, eyes focusing on his toes digging into the sand.

"I didn't know what to think about you back then." Thinking about Mason in college would have only led to trouble and I was so enthralled by the attention Ben paid me I wouldn't have needed to look for someone else. I wasn't tempted by thoughts of another.

"And what do you think of me now?" He slowly faces me.

"I still don't always know what to think, but I see that you are kind and loyal." He's fulfilling his promise to Ben. He feels obligated to me.

"What's missing?" He watches my face.

"What do you mean?"

"You said you don't always know what to think about me. What's missing that you don't know?"

"You never talk to me. You don't tell me about you. You ask about me, or the kids, or mention a build for Four Points, but you don't tell me about Mason. Or Lynlee. How things are with Samantha?"

Mason falls back in his seat and faces the sunset again. "There aren't things with Samantha."

This is exactly what I mean. Mason is vague with me. If we're friends, we need to talk. Not pretend. Not ignore. We need to discuss.

I sit back as well and stare at the water lapping lightly against the shore. I can't make Mason talk to me. I can't force him to open up. Maybe it's best that we just keep things on the surface. It'd be safer for me anyway.

"I made a mistake with Samantha," Mason starts, breaking into the silence between us. "I was reckless. Even with protection. She was high. I'd been drinking. It should have never happened."

I hold my breath, staying still, afraid a movement will make him stop talking.

He narrows his eyes. "I can't even remember the situation. Was it another disagreement with my dad? Only a lonely night? I was still lost in my thirties."

Mason rolls his head on the back of his chair and gazes at me. "Everyone was married. You and Ben had three kids. Logan had Lorna, and even though things were rocky with Chloe, he was married. Zack was with Jeanine, and even if she wasn't a prize, he had the twins. It was just me. Last man standing."

He turns to face the horizon once more. "I wasn't looking for marriage or kids, but it didn't mean I wanted to be the lone guy out there." Softly he chuckles. "And fucking Ben. He still included me in everything, never wanting me to feel left out." Mason turns to me again. "But even when I was included, I was always on the edge of you guys."

"Mason." His name is a whisper of guilt. I contributed to that isolation. We were always so standoffish. I didn't understand his relationship with Ben, and I still felt that resentment I was certain Mason had for me. I judged his waywardness with women. His party-set mind and carefree lifestyle. Maybe at times I was even jealous as I had Ben and three kids keeping me in place.

"Now, I'm forty-two years old with a kid I hardly know and a ball-and-chain I can't shake loose because she holds all the cards."

Samantha.

"We've been back to mediation, but it hasn't changed her." Mason looks back at the lowering sun. The streaks of fading yellow and orange bounce over his tan face. "Before Ben died, I told him how I was worried she was hurting Lynlee."

"Mason." I sit straighter and reach for his forearm, needing to touch him. Comfort him.

His gaze falls to where I hold him.

"What happened?" I ask.

With his gaze where my hand clutches on his warm skin, he speaks. "I've noticed burn marks. Samantha tells me her curling iron fell on Lynlee's shoulder. Or a cigarette ash hit her inner arm."

"What did you do?"

"I'm hardly alone with Lynlee, and if I question her in front of Samantha, she only looks at her mother for confirmation. It's like she's afraid to answer me. Afraid of me." Mason swipes a hand through his hair. "I have no idea what Samantha tells Lynlee about me, and I don't have hard evidence she's hurt my daughter."

He chokes. "I don't know what to fucking do. We promised no lawyers because she couldn't afford it and I just agreed with her." Mason looks up at me. "I gave Lynlee a cell phone, though. Told her to keep the phone a secret. There is only one number programmed into it. I told her to call me if anything happens."

Lynlee is five. Giving a child a cellphone at such a young age might not be an option for everyone, but in this case, I understood Mason's need for his daughter to communicate with him. Even at a young age, it's amazing the technology kids can learn and use.

"Mason, that's awful." Not the cellphone but the not knowing. The waiting for that one call you don't want to receive that says she's hurt or something worse. "As a teacher, I'm a mandated reporter. Suspicions of child abuse are no joke. There's a fine line. You can't coax kids into telling you anything. You have to report what you suspect, though. Your pediatrician probably told you there are clear distinctions between childhood bruises from an active kid and abuse."

Mason stares at me. "I've never been to a doctor visit. I just pay the medical bills when they come."

He turns away, shame filling his face as he tips back his head, gazing up at the sky, blinking a few times. "I'm a shit father."

"Don't say that about yourself."

He scoffs bitterly. "You sound like Ben."

"What did Ben say when you told him all this?"

"He told me to get my girl."

"And why didn't you?" There's accusation in my voice that has no place.

Mason levels his eyes on me.

"No." I shake my head. "You didn't go after Samantha because you were here?" I don't like the excuse. Ben would have been pissed at Mason for this feeble reason.

"I just couldn't handle one more thing."

On the tip of my tongue is a lecture about how we don't handle children. We love them, protect them, but Mason didn't have a guide for fatherhood. His father is a piece of shit from what Ben told me, and Mason's role models for parenting were his friends. He didn't allow them to mentor him, though.

Ben wouldn't have let this pass if he'd had the strength to intervene. He would have gone to Samantha himself and demanded Lynlee, although that might not have been legal.

"So, now what?" I ask. Mason needs to act now. No more excuses.

"Now, I wait. I take my every Saturday and hope nothing happens, but if it did . . ." Mason swallows hard. "I hope Lynlee trusts me enough to call me and I'll be there for her."

Deep within his eyes, I read the regret, the shame, and the sorrow.

I squeeze at his arm. "This makes us friends."

He chuckles without humor. "How does my sin make us friends?"

"Your honesty makes us friends." I release his arm but as my hand is slipping away, Mason captures it, curling his fingers into my palm before stretching them and sliding our fingers together. He keeps our joined hands on the armrest of his chair.

He doesn't speak again. He doesn't acknowledge he's holding my hand. He just stares out as the water softly laps the shore and the sun melts on the horizon, and we sit in silence. Each with our own thoughts.

His thumb eventually strokes over the back of my hand, and like the heart-shaped talisman in my other hand soothes me, Mason takes comfort from me.

Chapter 20

1 Year Ago
August

Third Reunion

[Mason]

As our friends' crew dedicates two weeks to a family reunion of sorts, upheaval ensues. The prodigal son—Archer McCaryn—returns and stakes his claim on his old apartment over the garage. However, Anna invited her college friend, Jenna, to come visit for these two weeks and she promised Jenna the garage apartment. And suddenly, Jenna and her two little girls are staying in the apartment with Archer as a roommate. It's a romantic comedy gone wrong if you ask me.

Which no one did.

I'm in the main house in a guest room on the second floor, itching at every turn because Anna and I are just too close in proximity. I should have stayed in the condo in town, but the point was to be as near to the guys as possible. The whole reuniting situation is just weird. Logan lives up the street and Zack is next door, a stark reminder that I'm always on the outs. But we promised Ben we'd gather at Lakeside Cottage for these two weeks, and with it being the first year after his passing, we don't want to dishonor his memory.

The kids are all included in whatever we do, which means planned activities revolve around nightly dinners and cookouts in backyards. Calvin and Bryce join some of the guy-shenanigans, like golf and boating. Mila and Lorna include Rosie and Talia in girl-time with crafts, princess movies, and home pedicures.

While all this chaos circulates, Anna and I orbit around each other but not with each other. As much as she said my honesty made us friends only a few weeks ago, we aren't talking. We're existing and I'm coming out of my skin, questioning every move. Are we distant because our friends are here or is there something deeper, something I'm missing? Does Anna not want Zack and Logan to know we're growing closer to one another or is all of us gathered together messing with her head, reminding her of Ben's absence?

One night, an adult-only evening is organized. We decide to go line-dancing at a local bar. I recall dancing with Anna in her kitchen and almost look forward to the group activity. People will pair off. Logan and Autumn. River and Zack. Archer will obviously need to be with Jenna as his sister would naturally couple up with me.

However, that is not how the outing goes. Anna's brother sits beside me. We don't have much to say to one another. He's been giving me the evil eye every time I talk to Jenna, flirting with the fact we have history from college, and we occasionally run into each other in Traverse City.

Little does he know, I'm watching his sister. The sway of her hips. The jut of her ass. The sound of her laughter as she enjoys herself, dancing with the other girls.

Or maybe he does know I'm lusting after Anna, catching me one too many times looking at her body moving with the upbeat rhythm of the country music.

When some guy gets too close to Jenna, Archer makes a scene and the two of them disappear. Anna watches them leave with confusion before she comes to our high-top table, taking the only available stool next to me.

As we sit through the remainder of the song and another fast-beat one, I hate the sudden frown on her face. Her body timidly hunches. Her position one of someone sulking.

Then a slow song comes on and the frown turns to a deep furrow of pain on her face. We silently watch as Logan brings Autumn into his chest and Zack leads River out to the dance floor, holding her back to his front and laying his hands over her swelling belly. Archer returns, tugging Jenna behind him, and the two of them take the floor as well.

My palms sweat as I rub them down my jean-clad thighs. "Would you like to dance?" I don't know why I'm so nervous, or my voice cracks. In an attempt to still my hands, I squeeze my kneecaps.

Anna stares out at the crowd and the coupling of our friends.

"I don't think so." Her brows pinch like she isn't sure of her answer. Does she think she's not allowed to dance? She isn't allowed laughter and a good time with friends? What about that night in her kitchen on her birthday?

"Why?" I ask, truly puzzled and put off by her answer. Why is she shutting me out these days with our friends present?

She lowers her gaze to the table and hastily swipes at a piece of loose and sweaty hair near her temple. "I don't want anyone to suspect anything."

"Is there something to suspect?" My tone is rough, angered even. We pretend that first kiss never happened. We act like phone sex wasn't a thing. *Nothing is going on between us.*

This is a lie I tell myself because the pull to her grows stronger with every conversation we share. Every honest moment and quiet stare. Every risky chance and soft touch.

"I'm just not ready to date," Anna defends, her voice rising over the music which might be slow but is loud. She sits up straighter and hits me with those warm brown eyes.

"No one's talking about dating. It's just a dance." My insides feel like a taut wire, ready to snap. Who the fuck said dating?

"Jenna keeps mentioning second chances. She's not pressuring me, just telling me it's okay to put myself out there. And River asked me to attend some grief group, hoping I'd meet people in similar situations." She air-quotes around the words. "Amelia will be coming for a visit because Archer is finally home, and she's going to push."

"Push what?" I stare at Anna, heart hammering.

"Dating."

I hold up both hands, still perplexed and panicking at the concept. "Anna, slow down. No one says you have to date." *Who the fuck would she date?*

"It's too soon." This conversation feels one-sided, like she's trying to convince herself more than tell me her position.

"Soon. Late. There isn't a timetable. It's when you're ready." *Is she ready?* Fuck, I don't want her dating. I don't want her thinking about dating, mainly because I don't want her thinking about some other guy. I want her thinking about me.

This makes us friends.

I might be friend-zoned, but I'm in a lane.

And I'll be damned if someone else thinks he's going to pass me.

+ + +

When the song ended, Anna said she'd like to leave and our party of eight agreed to go. Of course, everyone pairs off again as Logan and Zack each go home with their girls and Archer and Jenna head up to the apartment above the garage.

Leaving Anna and me to enter her home in silence. I follow her into the kitchen where a single light over the island illuminates the space. Reaching a boiling point, I can hardly contain myself when I say, "How long are we going to pretend, Anna?"

My voice carries and I have no idea if Bryce or Calvin are home while Mila is babysitting in Archer's apartment.

Anna freezes on the other side of the island. "Pretend what?" she asks, innocent and ignorant, as if she doesn't feel the attraction. The tremble in her voice gives her away.

I step up to the countertop and place my hands on it, stretching my arms to brace me upward. Hanging my head, I take a deep breath, attempting to control the disappointment before I share a difficult piece of me.

"I walked in on my father dick deep in his assistant when I was twenty-five."

Anna's breath catches but she has the grace not to interrupt me with sympathy.

"I thought he was the world. Despite his harsh words. Despite his hard lessons." I lift my head and glare at her, highlighted by the glow of the low lighting. "After that moment, something in me shattered. My parents never got along. I didn't understand their relationship. *For the sake of the child.*" I mock, knowing my parents married because of me. It was one reason I didn't marry Samantha. I didn't want to put Lynlee in the same position I'd been in between my parents. Plus, I didn't love Samantha, and she didn't love me. I don't know if my parents ever loved one another but my father proved he no longer cared about my mother or her feelings when he was fucking his assistant.

"At the time, my father told me I was like him." I narrow my eyes and slap at my chest. "I wasn't cut out for one woman in my life. Made from his mold, he told me. I'd never be happy settled down. Strapped with a kid." I choke over the confession and the words that cut me in my twenties. "And I believed him. I *pretended* I didn't see his indiscretion. Then my mother found out and fell apart."

The growing lump in my throat makes it hard to swallow. The agony in Mom's tears. The alcohol that took over her life.

"I was working in the family company. The business had been from *her* side. I was making strides. I had grandiose ideas that one day I'd take over *for her*. I should have quit. I should have returned to that dream that us guys discussed in college sooner, but I didn't break free. I fell into his words like I did as a kid."

Marcus Becker was a shit father. I'd learned from the best. Only I didn't want to make some of his mistakes. And I'd eventually disagreed with him on one thing. I could settle for one woman, and it wouldn't be settling. It would be more than I'd ever had in life, other than my friends, especially my friendship with Ben where I learned what a father should have looked like. How one should have acted.

"Mason." My name is full of pity as Anna pauses, her eyes wide, confused even. "I'm so sorry."

I'm certain she's wondering where all is this is going but I have a point.

"I fucked up in my thirties, Anna. I get it. Know it. *Own it.* But it doesn't mean I never wanted what all of you had." Still staring at her, I focus on her eyes, willing her to understand. "But I did learn a life lesson from dear old Dad when I was a teen. Dropped off in this sleepy lakeside town and expected to work landscaping when I'd hardly ever held scissors, for fuck's sake."

I don't break eye contact. "I learned I can't always get what I want." The wife. The kids. The happily-fucking-after.

Because I didn't get her, and I don't think I ever will.

"But I'm tired of pretending that's okay with me."

"Mason, I—"

The front door opens, abruptly interrupting us. Mila and Lorna come in after having babysat Rosie and Talia for the evening. Their laughter fills the void of an answer from Anna.

"Did you girls have fun?" Anna immediately shifts her expression, putting on false bravado to match their glowing smiles.

"Talia and Rosie are so cute." Lorna beams a smile at us. She's going to be a looker as she grows older, and Logan is going to have his hands full when she hits high school in a year.

"They're so sweet," Mila adds. "Did you know Rosie wants Uncle Archer to be her dad?" Mila laughs like it's the funniest thing she's ever heard, but Anna and I glance at one another.

What the hell is going on in that apartment?

"Well, Rosie doesn't remember her daddy. She was only a baby when . . ." Anna's voice fades. Jenna's husband was killed. The situation is still hard to believe.

"If Uncle Archer married Jenna, Rosie and Talia would be my cousins," Mila's voice is full of excitement at the possibility. "We need more girls in this family."

"Does that make them my cousins, too?" Lorna asks for clarification as Autumn is her stepmom, making Lorna officially part of Mila's family as a cousin.

"Other side of the family, honey," Anna says while still offering Lorna a smile. "But we're all family." She points in a circle including me in the visual.

"You'll never get me a new dad, right, Mom?"

The air is knocked out of my lungs and I'm certain Anna feels the same way. Her hand flies to her throat as she gasps.

"Why would you say such a thing?"

Mila shrugs. "Penny Redman got a new dad after her dad moved out."

"And Elizabeth Henley in my grade got a new dad when her parents divorced," Lorna adds.

"Uhm . . . well, those men didn't really replace their dads." Anna glances up at me before addressing the girls. "Their fathers are still their fathers."

"Penny says her mom says it takes a special man to be a dad. Any guy can be a father." Mila nods as she speaks like she's worldly and wise at almost thirteen. And who the fuck is this Penny girl?

"Well . . ." Anna looks at me again before facing the girls once more. "That's true. A man who has a child is a father. But a dad is someone who plays games with their kids." Anna reaches out and strokes Mila's hair, tucking it behind her ear. "He braids hair and paints nails, and takes bike rides, and goes to the zoo. And watches endless Disney movies and buys softball equipment. He cheers the loudest at games and goes to dances."

Anna's eyes well with tears which she fights to hold back. She doesn't look at me, but the weight of her words hits me in the chest. Am I only a father to Lynlee or am I a dad to her? Samantha would consider me a human cash register.

"And no one will ever replace your dad," Anna adds, blinking before swiping a wayward tear from her cheek.

Mila steps forward and wraps her arms around Anna's middle. "I know, Mom. You won't ever get married again, right?"

Anna glances at me, and then drops her head, placing a kiss on her daughter's hair. "That's right, honey."

My shoulders fall in utter defeat. I hang my head again and then lift it, swiping both hands over my face, feeling the roughness of my facial hair against my palms. The scratch is a papercut compared to the clawing pain running down my skin.

I have my answer to my earlier question.

Anna and I will be pretending there isn't a growing attraction between us for the rest of our lives, because I won't ever be Ben.

I can't replace him.

Don't want to replace him.

But I won't ever compare to the greatest dad. To Anna's lover and best friend and partner in life.

I'll never be good enough for her.

Chapter 21

1 Year Ago
August

Third Reunion

[Anna]

Going line-dancing as a group was a disaster. As a party of eight, it was evident who should be paired with whom, but I didn't want anyone suspecting anything about Mason and me. Attraction wavers between us but I just don't know how to act in front of our friends. It feels sacrilegious to publicly hint I have feelings for Mason as we mark the anniversary of Ben's passing. Maybe merely loneliness is attracting me to him. Maybe it's something more.

Our phone sex interlude was a montage on replay in my head, especially when I used the pink present he gave me on my birthday.

Then he kissed me, soft and sweet, wishing me more years ahead.

When he showed up on the night of Ben's anniversary, we crossed a new line—friends.

Only I don't know what that friendship should look like with others present. He'd been flirting with Jenna, and there'd been endless references to Mason's past. Two different women approached him when we were at the bar, rubbing in my face how easily Mason attracts women. Typically, he easily disappears with one as well.

Am I only another woman to him? One of Mason's multitudes? Was phone sex something he's done before? Does he gift other women vibrators? How often? To whom? My thoughts have been spinning in a way they have no business spiraling.

Then he laid out another nugget of his upbringing and a confession about his desire. How could Mason buy into the terrible things his father said to him? People always want to say teens are impressionable, but kids in their early twenties, fresh out of college and in their first real jobs, are just as persuadable. Especially a son worshipping a father, hoping to learn the family business and take it over one day, only to be told he's cut from the same cloth as his dad, which implies negative behavior toward women and lacking ideals about love.

When Mila and Lorna interrupted us, I was crushed. I needed to address Mason's angry tone and heightened emotions but Mila's comment about me never marrying again rocked me to the core. No one has spoken of marriage.

I simply panicked at the country bar.

Maybe because a part of me did want to dance with Mason. I wanted to laugh like Autumn did with Logan. And revel in a closeness River shared with Zack. Maybe I wanted to enjoy myself like Jenna did with Archer when they danced before we left the bar. Ben was dead but parts of me were tingling back to life.

And I just wanted to let go a little.

The thought still feels selfish.

I can't bring Ben back, but I don't know how to move forward.

I don't know how to be me.

One thing I knew without a doubt was I couldn't be another random woman to Mason. I couldn't be a mistake or a fling or a one-night stand. And for Mason, I was certain I was still a commitment he'd promised Ben. An obligation. I've convinced myself his birthday kiss was only empathy for a lonely woman turning forty-two. He was looking after me, but what did that mean? For how long? Eventually, he'd grow tired of watching over my family. He had his own to collect. Lynlee needed him.

He'd told me he wanted her here these two weeks, but Samantha refused such a long visit. Mason didn't even have overnight rights. He'd admitted this agreement was, in part, his fault. He didn't think he could take care of a baby. He didn't want to mess up.

While I might have agreed almost five years ago that Mason Becker could not handle the care and responsibility of a child, after his year with Ben, I see I'm wrong. Mason's doubts were unwarranted, but he'd fallen victim to them because he wasn't given a chance to be a father to an infant.

In addition to Mason's concerns about baby time, Samantha argued that Mason had an extensive nightlife of random hookups and one-night stands, and she didn't want her child exposed to such behavior. Despite the counterargument that Samantha had been a one-time decision, the mediator agreed. They'd revisit overnight stays when Lynlee was six.

I didn't want to believe Mason's behavior was still reckless but there was so much I didn't know about him outside of what he told me and his occasional presence in Lakeside. Did he date? He didn't mention anyone. If he hooked up with someone, he never said. There was countless opportunity for him to do as he pleased, though.

And he could do as he pleased.

He wasn't beholden to me. I didn't have dibs on him.

Still, the thought of him with another woman made me a little sick. And a lot jealous.

I was envious of everyone during these two weeks. Their love lives blossoming. Their independence blooming.

Ben believed in a life cycle for people, like the perennial life of plants. People live, love, lose, and learn. Sometimes several cycles happen at the same time. You learn as you develop love. Or you live through learning. He even believed we went through losses that also taught us lessons.

For me, I was stuck in the loss cycle, like a washing machine in perpetual spin. I didn't know how to stop the current swirling. I was angry that Ben wasn't present. I was upset by the friendship between the guys. I was covetous of their new business venture. They were living and loving and learning, and I was just . . . spiraling.

Sadly, Mason and I didn't have a moment alone to discuss what happened.

Then Archer pulled another disappearing act. The drama caused Jenna and the girls to move into the main house.

Once again, I'd felt entirely abandoned by my brother. We had been close as kids, but I didn't know my brother as an adult. Maybe I never knew him.

With thoughts like this, I retreat to my bedroom once Jenna is settled.

This past June, I'd changed the primary suite after the school year ended. Spring cleaning gets delayed to a June purge for teachers, and I'm often inspired to make changes when another school calendar ends. I'd repainted the room and bought a new bedroom set including a new bed with thick, white wooden posts on the four corners. The footboard columns stood mid-chest to me, and I gripped one for support, lowering my forehead to the swollen ball on the top and closing my eyes.

"Anna?" Mason's quiet call to me is both a welcome balm and a niggling contradiction. I want him to hold me. I fear he'll be another loss in my life.

"I'm fine," I whisper, lying to us both. With my eyes closed and my forehead plastered to the wooden pillar, I exhale. I don't feel so much like crying, as I do screaming.

"Is it Archer?" Mason stands close behind me. So close, yet so far away.

"I can't take anymore loss." The admission crackles through the room like summer lightning on the lake.

"My parents are gone. Ben is gone. Archer came back and already left. You're going to leave."

"Hey." Mason's firm hand slides up my spine and underneath my hair, cupping the back of my neck. "Logan. Zack. Me. We're all here. The kids are fine. Jenna will be good. No one else is going anywhere."

That was the thing. I didn't trust that Mason was here for the right reasons and as soon as he wised up, got bored, realized *I* wasn't enough, he'd be gone too.

The idea of his loss hits me in the chest, causing a deep ache behind my sternum and a cracking of my ribs. I didn't want to lose him. I didn't like the thought of him being out there, somewhere, but not within my grasp, not within my little bubble. It didn't feel fair to have these thoughts, to covet him for myself, but I also didn't want to give him up.

Friends? Deep down, Mason was so much more than a friend, but I couldn't put a label on what he meant to me.

I lift my head, certain a giant red mark is imprinted on my forehead, but I don't look back at Mason.

"I'm just . . ." I exhale, frustrated that I can't put into words how I feel. How losing him would be a loss I couldn't handle. He's a phone call away. He's an impromptu visit. He's standing behind me, offering me comfort and warmth as I panic.

My heart wouldn't recover if Mason disappeared, too.

"Relax," Mason murmurs, squeezing my neck. "Deep breath, okay?"

His strong fingers move down the column of my neck and dig into my shoulder. Then his other hand meets my opposite shoulder, and he squeezes at the mounting tension in my body. His skilled fingers press into the tight muscles and his thumbs knead just below my shoulders. His hands work down my arms, massaging away the stress, until my limbs are loose and relaxed at my sides.

"Do not turn around." His voice is firm, while low and gravelly, as his fingers brush the hem of my T-shirt. He pulls it up and over my head. I grip the bed post again for support. My skin pebbles with the cool breeze through the open window and a long, low exhale from Mason against my neck.

When his hands first touch my shoulder blades, I flinch.

"Easy," he murmurs as though speaking to a skittish animal.

"I just have all this . . ." I lower a hand and wave it around my belly. I feel caged, restless even. "Pent-up energy." Or frustration. Or anger or envy. Or fear. Again, screaming feels like a good option. A time bomb is ticking inside me, ready to explode.

Mason's thumbs dig into my shoulder blades as his fingers curl around my sides. The tips of his fingers are close to the edges of my breasts, and I close my eyes. My bra is hardly a barrier to his nearness.

What would it feel like to have his hands slip forward and cup my breasts?

The thought alone has my nipples hard, and I clutch harder on the bedpost before me.

We probably shouldn't be in my room—alone—again. He definitely shouldn't have his hands on me. But I crave his touch. The massage he's giving me and the calm he's infusing into my body is a soothing balm.

Unfortunately, with every press of his palms and squeeze of his fingers, my body winds up in a new way.

Mason's hands move down my sides, thumbs working along my vertebrae. Lower and lower he goes until he's at the base of my back. His thumbs dip into my shorts and rub my waist above my backside. With every movement of his hands, Mason exhales, long and deep. His breath brushing along my neck. The fine hairs there dance. My skin prickles further.

I tip my head to the side, relishing in the sound of his breathing, the feel of warm air along the column of my neck. With every knead of his fingers and resulting exhale, I'm hyperaware of Mason. Close. Comfort. Calm.

His thumbs continue to press into the top of my backside. My body reacts. I lean back.

"Anna," he warns, as my spine arches, my butt juts toward him.

My hands grasp the post tighter. Whether I'm using the wood as an anchor or an assistance to my desire, I can't be certain. Either way, I want more from Mason. More of his touch. More of his kisses.

With his hands at my hips, I reach down with shaky fingers and cover one of his wrists. Timidly, I tug his arm forward. His palm skims over my bare belly.

"Mason," I whisper. My eyes are closed but I'm keen to who is behind me. Who is touching me.

When his nose runs along the side of my neck, I'm aware this isn't in my head. This isn't a fantasy or my imagination.

Am I really doing this?

While I've argued with myself, stating I don't want to be another reckless woman to him, my current position suggests how reckless I am. My body is an out-of-control freight train, barreling toward broken tracks. Someone is going to get hurt. I have no doubt it's me.

Still, I press his hand lower, over the front of my shorts.

"Sweetheart," he groans, the sound as desperate as I feel. "What are you doing?" The question isn't really for inquisition. He knows where I've led him, and what I'm asking of him.

His mouth is just below the hollow behind my jaw, tickling, teasing. He drags the tip of his nose along the shell of my ear before lowering again, tracing along my neck, up and down. He exhales heavily at my ear, sending a shiver down my spine.

Tears fill my eyes, anticipating his rejection. I shouldn't be asking this of him.

Then Mason pops the catch on my shorts and lowers the zipper. His breath comes more ragged. The softness of the T-shirt he wore this evening swipes against my back.

"I'd never touch you unless you were mine, but I'll help you get what I think you need tonight." In a stealth move, Mason grips the back of my hand and lowers it into my shorts. My fingers quickly find my aching nub. With his fingertips behind my index and middle finger, he manipulates me, applying sweet pressure, moving in tight circles.

"That's it, sweetheart. Let go."

I arch again, seeking the hard length in his shorts. He juts his hips backward, keeping his lower region out of reach.

"All for you, sweetheart." He pauses a beat, running his nose along my neck again. "Do you use the gift I gave you? Does it help take off the edge?"

A hum is my only response.

His mouth is at my ear, the whisper a juxtaposition of warm air and a seductive tone. "I can smell you. Smell how turned on you are." He inhales, holding his breath. He's close enough to touch me, to find out for himself how slick I am with need.

What we are doing, how we are doing it, feels a thousand-times wrong, but I can't stop myself. I'm out of my head, drowning in the moment, soaking up the pressure that will detonate the tension inside me and give me sweet relief.

"Jesus, Anna. You have no idea how badly I want a touch. A taste. A chance."

My mind leaps to him on his knees before me, mouth wide, tongue eager.

"Oh God," I whimper, drawing closer and closer to the edge.

"I've got you, baby." His commanding whisper is both fierce and reassuring.

"Mason," I warn, as I rock against my fingers.

"I'm here, sweetheart. And I want you to drip over your fingers and coat mine. Give me something to think about at night, when I dream of you."

Does he fantasize about me? He wouldn't but . . .

"Come on, sweetheart. Let go." He nips me at that sensitive spot between my shoulder and neck and I detonate in sweet bliss. My legs stiffen. My hand stills. I lean forward, grasping the post before me while gasping for breath while the release washes over me.

Mason slowly lets go of my hand and grips my hip, holding me in place while my body trembles in pleasurable relief. My breathing is uneven. I just need a moment, I think.

Then, damn tears spill from my eyes, and I lower my head again to the ball on the top of the post. Confusion takes over. I'm not certain why I'm crying? Is it the endorphins? Or is there another reason for the salty mess sliding along my nose?

"Don't turn around," Mason warns again, softer, gentler. Does he sense how fragile I feel right now? My body continues to quiver, like I'm about to break into a million tiny pieces.

I'm relieved he doesn't want to look at me. I don't want him to see my tears.

His fingers snap the clasp of my bra, forcing it to open. I've been wearing it and my shorts the entire time. I catch the material against my chest as I hear him shuffling behind me. A hesitant glance over my shoulder gives me enough of a view to see Mason removing his tee.

"Arms up," he commands.

I release the bra pressed to my chest. My arms feel heavy again. My legs weak. The tears continue to stream down my cheeks.

Once I lift my arms, worn cotton flows down my head, cascading over my breasts, and falling to my thighs. Mason works beneath the hem to remove my shorts and I step out of them, holding onto the post before me once more. This time I know it's an anchor, attempting to hold me in place as a mixture of emotions bombard me.

Is it too soon to have feelings for Mason? I'm too young to be alone the remainder of my life.

Could Mason have genuine feelings for me? Or is he only fulfilling a promise?

Will he leave? When will he go? How will I handle more loss?

Mason's arms cradle my legs and I'm scooped up against his chest. He rounds my bed and lowers me to the mattress before pulling up the blanket. I swipe at my face, afraid to look at him. Ashamed of myself. When will the tears stop?

Another one leaks from my eye but he thumbs away the drop.

"It's okay, Anna. I'm right here."

But he's going to leave, eventually. He should leave. He said he's always wanted more with someone.

Despite my momentary release, my thoughts spiral again. I close my eyes to the truth. "I can't lose you next."

"Sweetheart." His quiet groan is a plea. Then a weight crawls over me and falls behind me on the bed. He wraps his arms around me and tugs my back against his chest. His mouth comes to my covered shoulder and lingers against his T-shirt. He surrounds me in scent and touch.

"No one else is leaving, Anna. Especially not me." He squeezes me tighter. "I'm not going anywhere. I'm here for as long as you need me."

Did I need him? I swore I never would. Oh, how my feelings have changed.

I very much want Mason in my life.

Chapter 22

1 Year Ago
August

Third Reunion

[Mason]

The evening after the shitstorm with Archer is our night to celebrate Ben.

Our bonfire ritual is set up much the same as the first time. We were supposed to write Ben another note in response to his request for each of us.

Zack's face holds a faint smile, proud of his accomplishments. He's completed his mission.

Logan, the lucky bastard, finished Ben's request for him before Ben actually passed away. He'd fallen in love with Ben's sister, and they became a family.

None of us know what Ben asked of Archer who was supposed to join us tonight. We'll never know now, as he's gone.

The situation with Archer is undoubtedly a clusterfuck. The heartbreak on Jenna's face says something definitely had happened in that garage apartment. The devastation in Anna tore me open.

As for me and another letter . . . I'm a failure. I still don't know what Ben intended with his message. I haven't done my best to take care of his family.

And I've touched his wife who I have no business touching.

Even though I told Anna I'd never touch her unless she was mine, there's no denying last night was sexy as fuck. My hand guiding hers. The sensual caress so close to where she needed me.

There isn't a doubt she needed to get out of her head and settle her thoughts.

I can't lose you next. The words were like her reaching into my chest and squeezing my heart.

Everything in me itched to approach her this morning. I'd held her most of the night, and while I should have slept, I didn't want to waste a minute of holding her in some unconscious state.

Instead, I've avoided her, rebuilding the wall that separates us in the presence of our friends.

There's one thing I'm certain of, though, I'm not letting Anna go.

This day has been long and filled with emotions. Archer's disappearance. Anna's fears. Anxious anticipation of this moment.

As Zack, Logan and I silently stare into the flames, the two of them burning their letters, the fire blurs in my vision.

"I fucking failed," I say aloud. A blank piece of cardstock taunts me, resting empty of words on the armrest of my chair.

"What do you mean?" Zack asks.

"I don't know what Ben wanted me to do. I don't know what his words meant. And I sure as fuck did not complete whatever he intended."

Without looking away from the wavering flame, I know Logan and Zack are both staring at me.

"You didn't fail," Logan scoffs.

"How do you know?" I snap, lashing out my frustration at someone who doesn't deserve it.

"You spent a year of your life living in Ben's house, wiping his ass, spoon feeding him ice chips, and playing housemaid to his family. You sure as hell didn't fail Ben." Logan surprises me with his accurate and abrupt assessment of what I'd done.

"I'm failing him now, though." I can't look up at my friends. "He asked me to watch out for his family. He asked me to be here for Anna. And the kids."

"You are here," Logan reiterates.

Swiping a hand down my face, I shake my head, back and forth, adamant in my failure. Zack and Logan have no idea what I've done. How I want more. How I long for what I shouldn't want.

Zack is watching me. I don't have to see the intensity of his gaze to know he's wishing he could dig into my head, read my thoughts. When he glances away, the invisible pressure on the side of my face lessens only the slightest bit.

"My card is blank," I admit, peering at the vacant paper, nagging at me with its emptiness. "I didn't write anything this year." I don't know what to say to my oldest friend. The best of men. My brother in soul and spirit.

"You didn't have to do it." Logan's voice lowers, as if I choose not to participate, like the decision was self-imposed instead of a complete lack of what to say. How to explain myself when even I don't understand what I should do.

I only knew how I shouldn't act but can't seem to help myself.

With every silent cry from Anna, I respond. Her sorrow. Her birthday. Her fears. Like this damn magnetic pull to her, to right her axis and balance her needs.

"Is this about Anna?" Zack asks.

"What about Anna?" Logan says next.

"Of course, it's about Anna." I fall back in my chair, shame in my admission, relief in my confession.

"What am I missing?" Logan asks.

I glance up at Zack who glares at me, knowing my truth. Then his eyes lower, allowing me to decide to confess.

"I'm in love with Anna." The second I admit the words, I rub the heels of my palms against my eyes, preparing myself for Logan's backlash. In frustration, my fingers slip into my hair, tugging the strands behind my nape.

"Tell me something I don't know," Logan scoffs. I stare at my friend, surprised, confused. Zack has turned his head in Logan's direction as well.

Logan straightens in his chair, hand on his kneecap while the other presses into the armrest. "What? I know you've always thought I was the dumb chump in the group. Good for a laugh. Lacking with the ladies, but

I have eyes. I've seen how you act or rather how you don't. Never touching her. Always watching her."

"I never thought you were a dumb chump." He's a fucking architect.

Logan huffs. "Dude, that's bullshit, but also not the point. I see you." He points two fingers at his eyes and then swivels his hand to point at me.

"I heard about her birthday," Logan admits. My face heats and it has nothing to do with the flames of the fire before us.

"And I heard she had a visitor on the anniversary of Ben's passing," Zack adds, his voice not condemning but concerned.

I scrub my forehead, elbow pressed into the armrest. "I shouldn't have these feelings. She's my best friend's wife." I'm practically screaming the words into the void around us.

"And he's dead," Zack adds, sympathy softening his tone. "You're not. And neither is Anna."

I risk looking at Zack, knowing that he and Anna have been lifelong friends.

"He'd never forgive me." I swallow hard, lowering my head. "And looking after her? This wasn't what he meant."

"Has something happened?" Logan asks, his voice hesitant while incredulous.

"Tell me you didn't fuck her." Bitterness rings in Zack's accusation.

My head pops up, and I narrow my eyes into slits at Zack, offended on Anna's behalf. "Never." The word is a threat and a confession. Fucking Anna isn't what I want. I've been with plenty of women in my life. Fucking around is all I've done. She is different. She's always been different.

Zack's shoulders relax. His head lifts. He nods once, both in apology and relief.

"She's allowed to live, though." Logan surprises both Zack and me and we look in tandem at him. He shrugs. "Dude, you think Ben wanted her to just sit around and pine over him. Ben loved life. He'd want Anna to live it to the fullest."

The words swirl around us, and I swear the flames nearly dance as if agreeing with Logan.

"Still, asking me to watch over her didn't mean he was giving her to me."

Zack is watching me again, tilting his head to the side a second. "Did you ever consider he might have been gifting *you* to her?"

"Gifting? What the fuck?" I pause.

"Because you just said you love her, dumbass." Logan laughs. "Who else is a man going to want to watch his wife than someone else who loves her?"

"Watch her," I clarify. "Not be with her."

Zack continues to observe me, taking a moment to process as he sometimes does. He never makes a rash decision. Always meticulous and a bit hardcore at times. Falling for River might have been one of the most spontaneous things he'd ever done. Out of character. Out of his element. And yet they fit together like pieces of a puzzle.

"Maybe it was more about her. Ben knew she had love to give and he wanted that love to go to someone who needed it most. Someone he trusted."

My brows pinch. Just what the hell was Zack saying? "Ben would not want me to be that man."

"Why not?" Logan asks.

"Man, you've got to let shit go," Zack mutters.

"What?" I lean forward in my chair, digging my elbows into my thighs as I focus on Zack. "What did you just say to me?"

Let go. That's precisely what Ben asked me to do.

"No one gets it more than me. Harboring old hurts. Holding onto the past. Freaking out about the future. Just let it go, Mason."

"Let go of what exactly?" I snap, as if I don't hear him loud and clear.

"All of it." Zack waves out. "Forgive yourself for whatever you need forgiving."

Zack breathes heavily. "And as for Anna. Hearts can't help what they want, who they love. If you love Anna, well, here's your chance."

"You know you sound a little like River with that hearts can't help who they love." Logan chuckles.

"And maybe she's onto something," Zack softens his voice, as he often does when referring to River. "Sometimes our hearts know things before our heads get the memo."

Zack glances at the fire, flames wavering in the breeze. He moved here to raise his boys with River. With love. They're even having a baby together.

Logan moved here as well, following my advice that you need to chase what you want in life.

Why was I the only one sitting still?

"I'm moving to Lakeside," I blurt, making the decision as I sit among my oldest friends.

"For Anna?" Zack's brows pinch in concern, returning us to the subject that has taken over tonight.

"For Anna. For the kids. For you guys." I pause, anxious while convicted. *Always on the outside, but I want in.* "For me. Everyone is here but me."

"What about Lynlee?" Logan questions. The guys only vaguely know my troubles with Samantha. How she's a bitch. I haven't opened up to them much about her manipulations over the years or my fears of fatherhood, but I need to do better. I need to let them in.

"I might need a lawyer. I want my daughter."

Mediation isn't working, and if Lynlee is being abused, physically or even mentally, I'm losing time. I want to raise her here among these men who are my family.

And near the woman who holds my heart.

Chapter 23

1 Year Ago
August

Third Reunion Over

[Anna]

When Jenna left to return to her home, misery and confusion filled my friend. We still have not heard from Archer and the number of holes in my heart grow. My parents. Ben. My brother. An overwhelming sense of loss takes over.

Mason suggests he stay a little longer, worried that something related to Archer could come back on me and the kids. Since the night he held me, a reinforced wall is built between us again. We exist among incidental chatter with tight tones and short answers. Still, deeper questions rest in his eyes when he looks at me. I'm certain mine don't disguise my confusion.

The entire two weeks has been a roller-coaster of emotions.

Reminders of Ben. Desire for Mason.

Despite the numerous times I denied any feelings for Mason when Jenna brought him up, and I dismissed all conversations about second chances, I can't pretend that something isn't happening between Mason and me. Something that goes beyond friendship.

I'm almost relieved our friends are returning to their respective homes. Life will return to our new normal. Our third reunion is officially over.

There are moments I miss from being married. The times when you climb into bed with your life-partner and talk about things that need to be discussed in the privacy of your room. However, I can't just invite Mason to my bedroom. Maybe tonight we can take a walk on the beach or sit on the landing and watch the sunset.

Our friends have hardly left when Mason and I return to the kitchen, and he gets a call.

"Hello," he hesitantly answers and then a heavy pause occurs. "Lynlee?"

His daughter's name in question has our eyes meeting. All thoughts of discussions about us leave my head. I step closer to him.

"Fuck," Mason growls as he drops the phone to the island counter and braces his hands on the top. The set of his shoulders pulls tight. His jaw tenses.

"What happened?" Any hesitation I've had to touch him is gone. I reach for his upper arm, needing him to look at me.

"I gave Lynlee a phone so she could call me if she needed me." Mason turns his head, looking at me over his shoulder. "Samantha found it."

He presses off the countertop and digs his fingers into his hair, tugging on the curls behind his neck. "She called me from the phone."

"What did she say?" This isn't good. I overheard Mason speaking with Zack earlier about an attorney before Zack crossed the yard for his place.

"She told me how dare I give Lynlee a phone. One with only one number in it. She warned me she was contacting the mediator." Mason releases his hair with a sharp pull. "It doesn't matter, though. I'm getting a lawyer. I want more."

My eyes widen with surprise and hope. "More time with Lynlee?"

"Yes." He turns, facing me full on. "I've got to get back to Traverse City."

A heavy pause falls between us as I nod.

"Look, I know we need to talk, but . . ."

"No, of course, you need to go." I stare up at him, his eyes another kaleidoscope of emotion. He doesn't want to leave. He feels obligated to stay as he'd told me he wasn't going anywhere, as he told the guys he was going to stay a little longer, but this is more important than him and me.

"Are you worried?" I swallow around the thickness in my throat. "That Samantha will do something?" Will she hurt the little girl we've never met? Or worse, will she steal her away from him?

Mason reaches for his phone. "I'll call a neighbor who I've asked to keep an eye on things." Once he presses the contact, he lifts the phone to his ear. "I'm so sorry," he mouths to me.

Shaking my head, I dismiss his apology "What can I do?" How do I help him?

Mason shakes his head as he brushes a hand down my arm, then he's speaking into the phone and walking around me.

With his retreating back to me, I shake. Within fifteen minutes, Mason is packed and I'm standing on the driveway as he throws his bag in the back of his car.

"Mason," I call out as he opens the driver's door, pausing to glance back at me. My arms cross over my chest, fighting the pull to step up to him, tug him to me. Tell him everything will be okay. *Ask him to come back to me.*

"Be careful." The words aren't enough.

"I'll call you," he says, dipping his head and ducking into his car.

Only he doesn't call.

Zack is the one who tells me Mason will be staying in Traverse City. He's fighting for full custody of his child.

+ + +

Within days of Mason's leaving, we take Calvin to college. The farewells are bittersweet as we stand on the beautiful campus. Pride swells as my child takes this next step in his life. Sorrow lingers that Ben isn't present to see Calvin at this stage. To watch our oldest son become a young man, eager for life to lead him where it will. Calvin wants to study criminal justice. My brother Archer is his new inspiration.

My chest pinches when I think of the absence of Mason. He was planning to drive with us, joining in the send-off of Calvin.

"I want you to have the best time," I tell my distracted son as we stand on the curb outside his dormitory. He's exhausted from carrying bins and assessing his room. We've been to a local superstore for groceries, hanging strips, and last-minute items he decided he needed to make his dorm room a haven.

Calvin nods once, brushing off my plea for him to enjoy himself. We've fought more than I like to admit in the past year as he's struggled with the death of his father and the decision of where to go to college.

"Dad would be so proud," I whisper, holding onto his upper arms, feeling the strength within them. He's gone from a goofy child to a grown man in a blink.

"Mom," he groans, swallowing hard as he lowers his head.

I promised myself I wouldn't bring up any sad topics today, but I still want him to know that Ben would be so happy for him.

"Okay. I love you," I say, holding back the tears. I'm excited for this new journey of his and I'm trying to keep my emotions out of it.

"Love you, too, Mom." He leans in and I take my cue to hug him and step away.

Calvin tugs Bryce in for a back-slapping embrace.

"Gonna miss you, man." My softer son hands out his feelings.

"Don't get into trouble," Calvin warns, pressing his brother back and leveling him with an eye like they share a secret.

Calvin turns to Mila next, folding her into his arms. Like a switch has been flipped, Mila bursts into tears, clutching at Calvin's shirt.

"Shit," he mutters, tugging her tighter to him. "Stay true to you, Meme." He leans down and presses a sweet kiss to the top of her head, using his childhood nickname for her.

"Stay true to you," she blubbers into his tee.

My own eyes well before I rub a hand down her back, signaling we need to step back or we're all going to be a mess on the pavement.

Calvin releases Mila and she wipes her nose with the back of her hand, then acts like she's going to rub it on his shirt. Wet laughter fills her when he jumps back.

"Alright," I softly command. "Car."

Mila opens the back door and Bryce rounds the car toward the driver's side. I reach for the passenger door handle, but a hand on my back makes me pause.

"Mom." Calvin's voice cracks. "One more," he asks, and I turn back to pull him to me, giving him one more tight squeeze like he'd ask of me when he was a child tucked in his bed, ready for sleep.

One more hug, he'd ask as a little boy.

One more hug, he's giving me as a man.

Chapter 24

11 Months Ago
October

Fall Surprise

[Anna]

Quickly time passes as August fades into September and September bleeds into October. Day by day, as my grandmother said. Calvin loves college but misses home. Bryce plays football. Mila and Lorna continue the revolving door between here and there, and I spend many nights alone.

Communication with Mason dwindles. Zack gives me updates. Mason's custody fight has turned from a battle to war as he secures an attorney. I've checked in with him, to be the friend he needs now, but his responses are vague.

Me: How are things with Lynlee?
Mason: We'll get there.

He's shutting down, and the hole in my heart allotted to him grows. I've missed him more than I want to admit.

Then, one beautiful mid-October day, my doorbell rings.

"Mason." I stare at him like he's a breath of fresh air, cool and crisp in the autumn afternoon struggling to let go of summer. He, on the other hand, looks exhausted but the timid smile he gives me lights up his face.

"I was in the neighborhood," he says as his hand shifts to someone small and trim, tucked against his leg.

The most beautiful wide-set eyes peer up at me.

Mason smooths a hand down her short, stick straight black hair. "Anna. This is Lynlee."

I smile wide as I crouch before her, extending my hand. "So nice to finally meet you, Lynlee."

She glances up at her father, waiting on his approval before she offers her hand to me. Mason nods. Her tiny fingers melt into my palm, and I cup my other hand over hers, holding onto her a little longer than I should. She's so beautiful, however, the wariness in her eyes says she's a little broken inside. Her gaze falls to where I hold her small hand inside both of mine. She doesn't flinch but she also doesn't return my grasp, almost as if she doesn't know how to respond to my touch.

Sweet child, I want to say to her. *I see you.*

"Come in," I say, remaining before her, eager to welcome them into my home.

Mason gently nudges Lynlee forward and I move to give them space to enter. "What are you doing around here?"

"We came to look at a house." The statement is tossed over Mason's shoulders as if it's the most casual thing to say to me. As if the thought doesn't make my heart flutter with possibilities.

"Are you moving to Lakeside?"

Mason glances down at Lynlee as they enter the kitchen and I follow. "Working on it."

I clasp a hand over my chest as if to contain the escalating patter inside. "That sounds . . . wonderful."

Mason meets my eyes, his brow arching. "Yeah?"

"Yeah." I offer him a soft smile. That hole in my heart, opened by him, wants to close.

"We stopped to see if we could have lunch with you." Mason glances down at Lynlee before looking up at me, hesitating. "But maybe I should have called first?"

"I'd love lunch," I admit, my voice rising a little too eagerly. I ask Lynlee, "What should we have?"

She gazes up at her father again, seeking something from Mason. Anxiety and confusion rests in her eyes.

"We could go out?" Mason looks at me, hopeful, but I'm already shaking my head. I want precious time with both of them.

"Tell me your favorite," I address Lynlee. *I'll make it happen.* If I have to run to a store and back, I'll make whatever she orders just to take the sadness out of this child's eyes for a few minutes.

"I like chicken nuggets." Her voice is quiet, lyrical even, but cautious. As if she's afraid to tell me what she'd like to eat. Afraid to open up to a stranger.

"I love chicken nuggets." My voice rises, overly enthusiastic. "What about apples? Do you like those? I have them, too."

She nods. "I like the yellow ones."

My stomach somersaults. "Those are my favorite, too." I clap my hands together, strangely excited to make chicken nuggets and apples for lunch.

Glancing up at Mason, he's watching me. A smile grows on his lush mouth, slow and a bit wicked even. That damn dimple of his makes an appearance. He's blindingly good looking.

But it's the words he mouths that stop my breath.

Thank you.

"Anything you need," I whisper back to him.

I once denied I'd need him, but now I want him to need me.

The next hour is spent in chatter—that is, my attempts to engage Lynlee in conversation while desperate to understand how things are progressing between Mason and Samantha. Does he have full custody? When is he moving? How does this effect Samantha?

"Let's take a walk," Mason eventually says once lunch is done.

The afternoon sky is a glorious blue. Fall is in the air, but summer is holding strong for one last whisper before giving in to a new season.

Once we hit the sand, Lynlee runs ahead giving Mason and I just enough space to openly talk.

"I have so many questions," I blurt, the excitement of his presence and meeting Lynlee still filling my heart.

"I don't have full custody but more visitation rights with overnights. I have to prove I'm present in Traverse City. No nightlife. No dates." Mason tips his head toward me. "Not that any of that is happening."

I put a pin in the dating comment. "What about a house here?"

"I'm moving forward in looking for a permanent place. Something more than the condo in town." Mason uses Autumn's old condo for his quick turnaround visits to Lakeside or the immediate area for Four Points projects. "But I can't move yet. It's an ongoing battle. Another reason I'm staying in Traverse City. I need to show involvement and accessibility. I even take Lynlee to and from kindergarten."

"I'm so sorry that it's taking so long, but I'm so happy you'll be moving here."

"Yeah?" He turns his head to me. Another boyish grin curls his lips.

I smile in return.

"So, what's been new for you? Nightlife? Dates?" He teases while his jaw ticks.

A strange disappointment washes over me at the jest. "You know that's not me."

Mason stops when something catches his eye and he bends to pick it up, smoothing a thumb over it before slipping it into his pocket. Then he reaches down for a beach stone and turns his body, flicking his wrist to toss the rock at the lake's surface.

Hop. Hop. Plop.

"I don't know that I'll ever be ready to date," I admit, letting the disappointment sink like a rock in my belly. The randomness of meeting someone new. The history that sits behind someone else. Mason is as good a person as any to discuss dating with, but the topic doesn't feel right with him. Maybe because if I'm going to date anyone, I'd like it to be him.

He retrieves another rock from near his toes and flips his wrist, flinging the rock toward the water.

Skip. Skip. Drop.

"What are you so afraid of?" he asks, squinting at the horizon.

I turn my head to look at his profile. The strong forehead. The bright eyes. The cliff of his jaw.

How I feel about you. The admission rests on the tip of my tongue but I don't open up. I can't tell him the truth. I don't think I can date because my heart is already leaning toward him.

"I don't know," I lie, as I turn to face the water.

"Maybe we should date," Mason teases. "A practice run for you." The suggestion is said through clenched teeth.

"I'm kind of complicated." A girlish giggle fills my throat and the heat that flushes over my skin has nothing to do with the warmth of the day. The moment would feel like we are flirting if it wasn't for the tension in his face and the bitterness in my mouth giving truth to the concept that he's only teasing me.

Mason has already done plenty to bring me out of my new shell. Phone sex. Birthday kisses. The night Archer disappeared.

We're walking along a dangerous ridge. One where I'm certain to topple over, while Mason isn't like that. He isn't going to fall in love with me.

"I don't think I'm the woman for you." Old defenses return. Mason was the kind of boy a girl like me couldn't handle. He had heartbreak written all over him in his twenties. I stare at his profile once more. Is heartbreak still etched in his skin at forty-something?

"Why not? What's wrong with me?" He turns to face me, propping his hands on his hips. "Why am I not good enough?"

"It's not you, it's me." I just said *I* wasn't the right person for him. I'm a widowed, single mother of three, with only a loose sense of my next steps in life.

"It's Ben," Mason states, turning his head and glancing out at the water again. His voice drops, frustration filling it. "Ben will always be between us. Holding you back."

"That's not true," I whisper. *But was it?* Was Ben the reason I couldn't move forward? Or was it me? Was I afraid to take a chance on something new and different? Someone like Mason? Or is it the fear of him breaking my heart?

I stare up at his hard-edged face. His expression is pinched . . . pained even. I've hurt him.

Skip. Skip. Drop. We symbolize those rocks hopping over the water's surface. Two steps forward. One plop into an abyss of guilt, shame, and secrecy.

My desire for him holds all three things in its arms.

"I don't need you to be Ben." My tone is edgier than it should be.

Mason turns his head, eyes narrowing on me. "What do you need from me then?"

My head drops. The intensity of his eyes is too much. "I don't know," I whisper again, watching as I dig my toe into the sand before glancing back up at him. "But I'm afraid of losing you."

He already knows this about my feelings.

"Why?" Mason steps forward. "Because we're friends?" He speaks the word like it's bitter on his tongue.

"Because I care about you," I admit, voice incredulous. Does he not see how I do care? "I've missed Ben so much, but I've missed you more." I swallow around the truth. I can't get Ben back but Mason . . . Mason is out there, doing God knows what, with whom, and now he has all this pressure to get his little girl.

There isn't space for me—the complicated friend—in his life.

"We've done things we shouldn't have done," I tell him, clutching a soft fist against my chest, caught between the guilty pleasure of the things we've done and a tiny hint of shame.

His head tips, questioning me, and I continue. "Talking to me like you have. Kissing me on my birthday. The night Archer left."

"Anna." Mason sighs, frustration filling his tone as he digs his fingers into his hair. "We're friends. That's what friends do. We're there for each other."

I flinch, eyes rapidly blinking. "Friends?" I choke on the word like my mouth is full of sand.

Friends? I don't have other friends who talk dirty to me, kiss me like he does, or even lead me through orgasms. What kind of *friends* does he have?

Then again, what other word did I expect him to say? What describes who we are to one another? Are we special friends? I don't even know what I'm thinking.

"You've just been so distant with all that's going on with Lynlee." Frustration fills my own voice, along with more guilt for wanting him when he has other priorities in his life.

Mason's shoulders fall. "I promise to do better."

"Stop making promises." I exhale. The threat of more obligation from him makes me feel sick.

Mason cups his forehead, digging his fingertips into his skin. Exasperation takes over his posture. "I'm doing the best I can."

"I know." I blow out a breath and glance away. He's done more than I ever expected from him. *For Ben.* For the kids.

For me, as his friend.

"It won't ever be enough, though, will it?" The quiet tone holds an eerie edge. "I'll never be enough."

"Mason, that's not true." I step toward him, reaching for him as Lynlee calls out to him.

"Dad." Her small voice booms on the vacant beach. She runs toward us, eager faced and grinning. It's the first time I've seen her openly smile. With her hand outstretched, she reaches us. "I found one."

Mason and I both look down at her open palm, held high and proud.

"Look," she says, but we're already staring and my breath catches.

"You're always looking for them, but I found one." Pride fills her voice at her treasure; however, I'm confused.

"It's a heart-shaped rock." My words come out strangled. My hand curls around my neck as if that will help me better understand.

"Daddy is always looking for them on our beach, but we never find them there. But I found one here, just lying in the sand." Her small voice still rings loud, excited by her find.

"I don't understand," I whisper, glancing up at Mason whose head remains lowered. His finger reaches out and strokes over the flat surface. The curved edges forming two humps while narrowing to a sharp point.

River is into nature and the symbolism of finding things within it. She once told me the heart-shaped rocks that appeared during Ben's dying could represent a sign from a loved one. An understanding that I was going through a tough time and a reminder to be strong. She also said they could mean to open my heart to new possibilities. The interpretation was really up to the receiver. Whatever I needed those hearts to be, they were.

When the rocks continued to appear even after Ben's death, I couldn't wrap my head around their meaning. Was Ben sending me messages from the grave? I didn't believe in such things.

Now I had an explanation.

Open my heart. New possibilities.

Mason? Had it been him all along?

Mason doesn't answer me but curls Lynlee's hands over the rock. "That's a precious find, baby girl. You keep this one. Keep it some place safe."

I slip my hand into my shorts, finding the heart-shaped rock I carry with me everywhere.

The one reminding me of Ben.

Because Ben gave them to me, right?

"You," I whisper again, staring at Mason. He refuses to meet my eyes.

"Think it's time to go, baby girl," Mason says, reaching under the arms of his little one and hiking her up to his hip. She wraps her arms around his neck and Mason finally looks at me.

"Thanks. For lunch. For today." He continues to stare while my thoughts flap around in my head.

The rocks were from him? For how long? From the beginning? Even after the end of Ben?

Why? How?

"Mason." My throat is rough but quiet on his name.

"I'll call you." He leans forward and kisses my cheek, like he didn't just rock my world.

Every pun intended.

Chapter 25

10 Months Ago
November

Friend-ly Phone Call

[Mason]

I didn't respond to Anna's inquisitive eyes after Lynlee found her treasure on the beach in mid-October. Instead, I went back to my staggering silence as I grappled with the adjustment of more Lynlee time in my life. I was enjoying every minute of my girl spending weekends and having overnights but my fears about Samantha were skyrocketing. She'd become more volatile. Her threats harsher. Lynlee was reserved every time she had to leave me, and quiet every time she returned to me. She wouldn't open up and I feared *how* Samantha was keeping Lynlee quiet.

In all this turmoil, I wanted to talk to Anna. Really talk. Ask her what to do. Ask her for advice. I was still so out of my element as a parent, but I couldn't bring Anna into this mess I'd made.

When she mentioned dating, I almost came out of my skin. Then I suggested we should date, and she shot me down. I shouldn't have been surprised. Our conversation led right to the reasons she couldn't be with me.

Ben. He'd always be there. A ghost between us.

I laugh to myself as I realize Ben told me I needed to let go and yet Anna was the one holding firm. To him.

Then, Lynlee exposed me and the heart-shaped rocks. I didn't want to talk about it then. How the rocks represented her to me. Strength. Perseverance. Love. They'd never been from Ben but a message from me that I believed in her. She would make it through the storm of Ben's passing. Her strength might appear in a new shape, but she'd be resilient and love again.

Only, I wanted that love aimed at me.

It wasn't going to happen but some nights I can't stop myself from taunting her.

"Do you ever think about it?" I ask her on the phone. My living room is dim. The light streaming through the blinds is minimal. The nights are so dark in winter.

Lynlee isn't here tonight, and the space feels especially quiet and vacant.

"Think about what?" Anna asks.

"That night."

"Which one?" Her cautious tone suggests she knows exactly which night I'm referring to.

"Any of them." I tip back my head exhaling before admitting the specific one I want to discuss. "The night we first kissed." The night she'd touched me.

Anna remains quiet.

Pure seduction and desire whisper through me. I want this woman so fucking much. "The night my hands roamed your body, sweetheart. Your breast in my palm. Your hand wrapped around my dick."

"Mason," she whispers, like I'm a secret. She can't tell anyone about me, but I linger in her thoughts.

"Ever think about what it'd be like? Just once, Anna. Just once, to let me touch you. Not just hover, but actually place my fingers where you need me. Rub that sweet spot. Dip inside you."

Her breath hitches. I don't have to see her to know she's turned on, but I want more than dirty talk through a device. I want to see her face as she climbs the hill of passion. I want to hear that catch at my ear when she reaches the top. I want to feel her body tighten while pliable under my hands as she rolls over the edge.

"Sometimes I wonder if we just gave in, if it would take away the ache," I admit to her, closing my eyes at the confession.

"What ache?" Her voice remains quiet though not ignorant.

"Don't you feel it?"

"Yeah." Her heavy exhale sends chills down my spine. I want her here. I want her straddled over me. Hands in my hair. Mouth on my throat.

"Just once, I want to slip inside you, sweetheart. Feel you around me." Wanting me. Begging for more. Then maybe I'd be rid of this stranglehold, this pull, this desire to have her. And I can walk away for once. I can let her go. We can be the friends she wants to be.

I choke on the lie I tell myself.

I don't want to be just friends with her.

And she doesn't want us to be anything else.

"Mason, we can't keep doing this."

"Doing what?"

"Winding each other up, only to walk away."

"What if I don't want to walk away?" What if I want to hold tight and never let go?

"Are you certain you aren't just feeling like I'm the one that got away?" She pauses. "Well, more like the one you never had."

She's so much more than that, but yes, at times, I do consider she's a quest I've never fulfilled and once I conquer the task, win her over, I'll be free of these chains around my heart.

Then I laugh, an evil, knowing guffaw at the way I try to fool myself.

When I don't answer her question, she adds, "We're too complicated."

She isn't saying no but she isn't saying yes. She isn't saying she wants me. She's afraid to lose me but she doesn't know what keeping me should look like.

"Who says we're complicated?"

"It would just be difficult with my kids. Our friends. Lynlee."

"Your kids love me," I quickly counter.

There is also the admission that most of our friends already know how I feel. I've no doubt Logan has talked to Autumn and Zack has told River. Jenna has hinted she knows something's up as well.

"And our relationship doesn't belong to our friends. It's ours."

"What relationship?" Her voice is a little stronger. No longer lush and low, sultry with need.

"Our friendship." The word feels all wrong. Anna is more than a friend. She's the closest thing I've ever had to commitment. I'm dedicated to her, *to us*, to the potential of what we could be if she'd only let me in.

"Yeah, friends." Her voice tightens and I shouldn't try to read into the drop in tone. I can't assume it's disappointment in the clarification of where we stand. Distance keeps us apart. She keeps us even further separated.

"I'm going on a date." The dart isn't one I intended to toss.

"Really? Anyone I know?" An edge lingers in the false lightness of her voice.

"Jenna." To my surprise, Jenna called me. I don't think she's over the damage Archer did to her heart, but she asked me out.

"What?" Anna's voice rises.

I shrug although she can't see me, acting as if the upset in her voice doesn't do strange things to my insides. Like cause my heart to beat faster and my dick to harden.

"She didn't mention it," Anna adds.

"Hmm. Maybe I'm supposed to be a secret." Which is just what I feel about Anna and me. We're a secret. We talk often but don't communicate. There's more between us. Maybe sex could be the solution. It's the only thing I know and yet I don't want *just* sex with her. I want more.

"Well, have fun." The fib in her voice shouldn't please me.

"I will," I lie in return, knowing Jenna won't be the one to give me what I want.

It's always been Anna who's held my heart.

Chapter 26

10 Months Ago
November

Goodbyes and Hellos

[Anna]

The day after Mason's call, I head to the beach despite the chill in the air. The firepit the guys used during their bonfire tribute to Ben is long gone. The Adirondack chairs have been stored away for the winter. The air is crisp and cold as I take a seat at the bottom of the stairs to the beach. In moments like this when I wander down here alone, I try to sense Ben's presence.

He used to be here.

Not that his memory is fading but his constant existence in my head is lessening.

I guess that means I'm moving on.

I've promised I'll never let go. He'll aways have a place in my heart. But as River once said, the heart is an amazing organ. And its capacity for love is limitless. No one is being replaced. I simply have room for more.

Room to love someone like Mason.

Though my hands are cold, I rub the heart-shaped talisman between my fingers.

"Forgive me," I whisper as if I need Ben's understanding. A breeze blows over me, and even in thick boots, jeans, and a fall jacket, I shiver. The response is only the weather, but I tease myself into believing Ben can hear me. He knows what I'm asking, and he knows why.

I promised to love him 'til death parted us.

Even death was never going to separate us from loving one another, but it would prevent us from living an eternity together.

Because I'm here. And Ben isn't.

As difficult as it is to admit, if he was alive and I was gone I wouldn't want Ben to travel the remainder of his life alone,. He was too good a man, too great a guy, and he'd deserve to share his spirit and energy with someone else.

I'm instantly jealous of something that will never exist, but quickly shake off the reality. Ben will never have another lover.

I will.

"I'll always love you," I say a little louder, feeling foolish while accepting I've done this in the past. I've spoken aloud as if Ben can hear me. Maybe he can. I blink to clear the sudden prickle behind my eyes.

Another breeze blows over me and I wrap my arms around my knees, clutching the heart shaped stone in my hand.

"You saw something in him, I didn't at first. He'd been your friend. He stood by your side, and he helped you when I didn't have the strength to do so myself." I swipe at the tear slipping down my nose. Slowly, my eyes and heart have opened to who Mason is. How he is good at his core. How he's devoted. How he's human. He made mistakes but he is willing to right them, and he works hard so they don't happen again. He's shown how greatly he could love. And **he had loved Ben.**

"But now I see him for who he is." I suck in air, willing away tears while a faint smile curls my lips thinking of Mason. "And I think you might understand."

Ben might have been the greatest love of my life, and I was so blessed. However, the idea of loving again was seeping into my heart, filling up some of the emptiness.

"In so many ways, I'll never let you go. But in order to live, I need to let someone else in."

The trees around me rustle. The wind remains gentle. If I take it all as a sign, it's tender empathy.

Then the breeze stops. The bare trees still. Even the lake feels like it's holding its breath, and there is nothing. No sense of Ben.

A finality rings in the silence.

"Goodbye, my love," I whisper but there's no response in the air. No sound from the winter-bare trees. Not even a speck of sand skitters over the beach.

Ben has let me go.

+ + +

"Mason?" I stare at him as he stands on my front stoop. It's almost midnight. "I thought tonight was your date."

Bitterness fills my voice at the thought of him with Jenna. As much as I love her, as much as I want her happy, the idea of her dating Mason did not settle well inside me.

"It was." Mason steps forward and I step back as he fills my space. He closes the front door, but I'm still frozen in the entryway, surprised by his appearance. Despite the late hour, he's dressed in a suit. I'd learned he and Jenna were attending a fundraiser together.

"Where are the kids?" Mason asks, crowding me in, towering over me until my back is to the front door.

"Bryce is at a friend's. Mila is spending the night with Lorna."

"Perfect," Mason mutters, eyes intense. His hands cup my face before I can question what's perfect. Ensnared by him, I don't speak as his mouth descends, taking its time to kiss me soft and sweet until I can't breathe. Until I can't keep this tame.

I fist the lapels of his jacket, tugging him closer to me. Our mouths move together, discovering one another. A rush of excitement ripples down my center.

Kissing Mason is different.

Kissing Mason is more.

I can no longer deny that I've wanted this moment. I've wanted his mouth on mine, taking from me what I've been desperate to give him.

As he tilts my head, the kiss deepens. Tongues seek. The touch is like a current to my center. I can't get close enough to Mason, pressing my body flush to his. And all the while, his hands continue to cup my face, fingers stroking at my jaw, keeping our mouths connected.

"Mason," I eventually groan. Nipples tingling. Center pulsing. I want to be closer and yet I don't want to break this kiss.

"Just kiss me, Anna." His mouth moves, taking a different angle. His lips sucking the swells as if he can memorize each curve and dip of my lips with the mold of his mouth. I've never been kissed like this. This consuming sensation threatening to swallow me whole if I'm not careful.

Mason said we should have sex. Get it out of our system. Maybe he feels it will sever the obligation he has to me. Maybe he knows I've been leaning in this direction for too long.

Gently, I press his shoulders. My head drowning in thought. My heart racing.

"What are you doing here? You had a date tonight." I remind him with acid on my well-kissed tongue.

"And there wasn't anyone else I wanted to kiss goodnight." He moves in for my mouth again. Kissing me whole. Kissing me replete. "There is only you, Anna. Only you for me."

His forehead tips against mine, and his hands remain on my face as if fighting the pull to lower and take more from me. Touch me in places I ache to be touched.

"Kiss me again," I whimper, still clutching his lapels, afraid to let him go. Afraid I'll melt into a puddle in my front hallway.

Mason complies, with a smile on his lips as they meet mine. Then he kisses me like I'm the breeze on a summer day and the warmth of fire in the winter.

And I accept I'm about to enter a new season in my life.

Chapter 27

9 Months Ago
December

Getting Caught

[Mason]

Knowing what I wanted in my life, I'd only intended to kiss Anna when I raced three hours to the southern part of the state.

If she didn't kiss me back, I promised myself I'd walk away. I wouldn't continue to push in a direction where the door was partially open but ready to close.

Instead, Anna kissed me with just as much passion as I hoped from her.

I didn't know about her sex life with Ben. He didn't talk about those things. I didn't need to know details, either. All I knew was a hidden fire existed in Anna. One not visible to the naked eye. One desperate to be lit. To flame. To burn.

And I wanted to be the match to start that blaze.

That night, my fingers hugged her jaw, wanting to move lower, willing to stay in place so I didn't break the spell of kissing her. Really kissing her.

Not a moment of sorrow. Not a birthday wish.

Just kissing. And more kissing.

Later, I'd gone to the condo in town to attempt sleep which never arrived. My heart raced. My dick ached. I suffered through the euphoria.

Within two weeks, River has a beautiful baby girl with a name as pure as hers. Lake Weller is born, and we all gather again to celebrate a new life in our circle of friends.

Anna is a proud stand-in aunt, hosting gatherings as she does to bring us together. With everyone present, Anna and I keep our distance when all I want is to pull her into my arms. The need to touch her makes me twitch.

"You okay, man?" Logan claps me on the shoulder while I'm holding Lake. "Babies make you nervous?" He teases as the expectant father of another little one. Autumn and Logan are making up for lost time. Years where she crushed on him. Months to get on the same page after they connected. They were meant to be together.

"I'm a chick magnet," I joke. "Girls love me. Right, Lake?" I press a kiss to the soft downy hair covering her sweet baby head.

Looking across the room, I catch Anna watching me, her eyes sparkling. I stand there wondering if she'd ever have other children, then kicking myself at the thought. We aren't too old, but her kids are in the teenage stage, and she'd likely not want to go in reverse. I'm miles behind with Lynlee, and I have too much to make up to her before I could consider bringing another child into the mix. I'm okay with where Anna and I are at in our parenthood journeys.

What I'm not okay with is the current space between us. The pull to be closer is almost unbearable and I'm coming out of my skin, ready to expose myself before our friends when I feel a tug at my elbow.

"Could I see you for a second?" Anna asks. I pass Lake to Logan, who fumbles the child as if he's forgotten how to hold a baby.

"Easy, man. Baby two is on the way. I wouldn't think you'd have fallen out of practice."

Logan chuckles. "Asshole. You only surprised me with the pass off." He lifts Lake and presses a kiss to her forehead. "Let's go find Daddy and tell him how Uncle Logan is the best."

Logan gives Anna a wink and stalks off looking for Zack, giving Anna the go-ahead to tug at my elbow and lead me down the hallway toward the bar off the kitchen. Only, she doesn't stop there. She pulls me down the hall to the den. The room is one-hundred percent kid-zone with gaming systems and shelves of board games. Plus, books for children and a cabinet with art supplies.

"What's going on?" I ask as Anna closes the door.

Her fingers twist together. She wrings her hands. Sheepishly, she looks at her feet before gazing back up at me, eyes alight with that fire that seems to scorch my skin.

"Kiss me."

A warm smile spreads my face as I step up to her, eager to honor her request. To give her the kiss I've been longing to give her since the moment I arrived. With every hesitant glance and caught look, I've wanted to pull her close and take what I desire. Still, I've understood her caution.

Her kids. Our friends. Would they understand? Would they appreciate the undeniable attraction between Anna and me?

None of that seems to matter as we stand here kissing like her house isn't full of people.

When the door suddenly opens, we jerk apart. Chests heaving. Hearts racing. Autumn stands with a hand on the doorknob.

"Just wanted to make sure you kids were playing nicely but I see you're getting along just fine." Her head tilts. Confusion is written in Ben's little sister's expression.

I glance at Anna, whose skin has paled. She steps toward Autumn. "I can explain."

Can she? Can she clarify what this is between us? Can she admit there *is* something between us?

"It's not what you think," she says.

The fire lit by desperate kisses douses to sizzled embers. My eyes catch on Autumn's a second, wanting to deny what Anna has said. It's *exactly* what Autumn thought. I was kissing Anna. Her widowed sister-in-law.

Autumn breaks eye contact with me and stares at Anna, soft, but hurt. However, her tone doesn't hold condemnation when she says, "Looked to me like you were kissing each other."

Anna hangs her head like an errant teen caught making out on the couch with her boyfriend when she should have been babysitting. Only I'm not her boyfriend and we hadn't made it to the couch.

Running my fingers through my hair, I tug at the back.

Autumn lays a hand on her growing belly and looks at me. "Do you mind giving Anna and me a minute?" Her voice softens as she gazes at me with the love of a younger sister and the caution of a friend.

"Take all the minutes," I quip, rushing past her without a glance back at Anna.

Anna who just shut that door that I was hoping was open just enough to let light out and me in.

Chapter 28

9 Months Ago
December

Letting Go

[Anna]

Tears fill my eyes.

Not only was my libido soaring but I'd been caught by my sister-in-law kissing her brother's best friend. A friend who was like a brother to Ben.

Closing my eyes, I will away the tears at the disappointment in the kiss ending and the upset at being caught kissing Mason.

"I don't know what to say," I admit once Mason storms out and Autumn closes the door.

"Then don't talk. Just listen." Autumn steps closer and takes my hand, tugging me toward the couch. We sit beside one another but I can't look at her even while she holds my hand in hers.

"I loved Ben," she begins. "He was the best brother anyone could ask for. He was kind, protective and included me even when I was a pain in the ass."

Weakly, I smile at the truth. Being four years younger than us, the guys didn't always love Autumn's inclusion, but Ben never wanted Autumn to feel left out.

"And I know you loved Ben," she continues.

I sigh at her declaration.

Autumn squeezes my fingers. "But Ben is gone. He isn't coming back. He'd want you to live, Anna."

"But with Mason?" Guilt has me opening my eyes and questioning my sister-in-law. A woman I consider one of my best friends.

"Why not with Mason?"

"Isn't it wrong in some way?"

"Does it feel wrong?" A gleam twinkles in Autumn's eyes. A grin grows on her face. "Because that kiss didn't look like anything wrong to me."

"It didn't feel wrong," I admit as heat covers my cheeks. Hesitantly glancing at Autumn, I quickly look away and add, "It felt good."

Unable to stop myself, I continue. "I feel alive when he touches me. I feel somehow . . ." I wave a hand around my torso. "Whole."

Mason is filling some of the voids inside me. My heart is riddled with holes but this, this emptiness inside, is slowly closing.

Autumn softly smiles. "I understand. I really do." Autumn had a series of long-term relationships. Most included living with a guy who took advantage of her kindness and left her footing the bills. She'd had a crush on Logan most of her life and when that crush was finally acted upon sparks flew.

"Can I offer some advice?"

I nod, eager to know what to do about all these feelings for Mason conflicting with how I think I should feel or behave or act.

"Stop thinking about Ben."

My head snaps upward and I stare at Autumn, eyes rapidly blinking. "I'll never stop."

"I don't mean stop loving him. Deep down inside, you'll always love him. But I mean stop *thinking* about him. His reaction to this. Or his feelings. Or even what Ben might think. This is your life, Anna. You need to think about you. How do you feel? What do you want?"

What did I want? I didn't have all the answers. But one thing I knew with growing certainty was I didn't want to *not* kiss Mason. I didn't want him to date other women. I wanted to explore whatever this was with him. Maybe he was a passing phase—like his need to have the girl he never had—but I didn't want the phase to pass without digging into it and learning more about myself, if nothing else.

"Just do me a favor," Autumn adds, reaching for my wrist and giving it a tender squeeze. "Be gentle with Mason's heart."

"I don't want to hurt him." My voice is soft, filled with the concern I might hurt him. And he might hurt me, but I don't think I'm able to stop the desire to discover more of who we are. "I wish I could explain what this is between us."

Autumn softly chuckles. "This is years of Mason pining for you. And maybe a little crush on your part."

"I never had a crush on Mason." Quick to defend myself, I dismiss Autumn's mention of Mason pining for me. I was never unfaithful to Ben in body or thought.

Autumn laughs a little fuller. "Come on, Anna. Have you seen Mason? Everyone's had a crush on him."

"But I never intended to act on it." The truth whittles away at me. Had I always been a little attracted to Mason on some level? Perhaps maybe physically. However, for years, I'd built a resistance based on how he acted toward me. Based on his history with other women. Based on his attitude and actions in general. But once I got to know him on a deeper level, once I saw his dedication to friendship in a new light, everything began to shift.

That's always how it happens when we trip. We don't see the crack in the sidewalk. We don't notice the ice on the pavement. And then, we are falling.

Mason slipped into the chasm in my heart. He tripped up all I'd known about him. He slicked over the rough patches and showed me he was something more.

"No one is going to accuse you of ever doing anything nefarious with Mason in the past. But the only direction you can look now is forward." Autumn squeezes my hand again. "Ben loved you, Anna. I love you. We both want you to be happy."

"Mason makes me happy." The truth is quiet while startling as I admit it aloud. When I think back on my days in the past year or more, the brightest moments include the times I'm talking to him or receive a text. The little things have been so big. His kindness. His patience.

"I can't define what we're doing." I swallow. "I don't think I'd be comfortable with everyone knowing until Mason and I know what we're doing. Does that make sense?" I tip my head toward the door, implying the rest of our friends. "It might be weird for them."

"I get it. I really do. But I don't know that I can keep this from Logan. However, I have a suspicion he won't be surprised to learn something *is* happening between you and Mason."

"Why? Has he said something?" My heart races, eager to know more. Anxious like a teenage girl wanting to know if her crush is reciprocated.

Mason has kissed a lot of women. He has experience in keeping his emotions separate from action. I'm not that type of woman. My actions are a reaction to emotion. I want him. I want him to kiss me and touch me because I feel things about him.

"I don't think you have anything to worry about where Mason is concerned. That's why I'm giving the warning to be kind to his heart. If you're using him, don't. We will find you another man to practice with."

"Practice?" I choke.

"Sex. That's where this is leading, right? Working up to having sex again." Autumn wiggles her eyebrows. The twinkle in her eyes mischievous. "Paybacks are hell, sister, and I owe you for that suggestion to make a list and sleep with three men in order to have a baby."

I laugh at the reminder. Logan was on the list. I'd had no idea Autumn wanted him to be the only man on it. Or that Logan would be willing to be the guy to give Autumn everything she wanted.

Now, Mason is the only guy on my list

+ + +

After a tight hug with Autumn, I swipe away a lingering tear and return to the gathering. Mason doesn't look at me but eventually saunters up beside me. Standing awkwardly side-by-side, he nudges my arm with his.

"Everything okay?" he asks, lifting a glass and eyeing the liquid within.

"I'm sorry," I turn to face him, giving him my full attention. "I panicked." I shrug, not feeling half as cavalier as my body language suggests.

I brush back strands of hair, tucking them behind my ear and hesitantly glance at our friends lingering in the sitting area before looking back at Mason.

"I shouldn't have said what I said." My gaze holds on his eyes. "Autumn knows it was exactly what she saw. I was kissing you." I glance once more to our friends and then back to Mason. "She knows I'll probably do it again."

After chatting with Autumn, I feel good, relieved even. Getting caught kissing Mason wasn't how I planned for anyone to find out about us. I don't think I'm ready for others to know, as I'd told Autumn. But I don't want Mason and I to stop the incredible magic that's happening between us.

The corner of Mason's mouth quirks up and he reaches forward, wrapping his arms around my head and tugging me to his chest. He presses a quick kiss to my head and then releases me.

Hours later, the house is quiet with the kids in their rooms. Everyone else has gone to their homes. Archer and Jenna are back with the girls, taking over the apartment above the garage again, and staying through the holidays.

I lay in my new bed, staring at the ceiling, torn between the desire to sneak up to Mason's room or continue the torture of denying the pulse between my thighs. The heat of need aches at my core. When there's no denying it anymore, I peel back the blanket, preparing to spring from bed and steal into Mason's bedroom. But the door to my bedroom slowly opens.

I don't startle but slowly sit upright. Mason stands in the doorway in sleep pants but no shirt. We hadn't spoken much the remainder of the day, acting as if nothing happened in the den. Pretending Autumn hadn't caught us.

But there's been no ignoring the energy sizzling between us. A crackling of something. We're either going to combust together or explode because of each other.

I'd rather not fight with him.

Mason closes the door behind him and comes to the edge of the bed. Without a word, our eyes connect. His nostrils flare. His chest heaves. He looks like a man who raced across miles to get to my room, not climbed down a flight of stairs.

"Mason," I whisper, confirming it's him when I know by the expensive scent who he is. Maybe his name is more a call. A siren's song pulling him to me.

As if responding, he crawls up the bed and over me, forcing me to fall back to the pillows. He hovers over me on all fours. Hands braced by my head. Knees on either side of my hips.

While the nights are cold in December, I wear only a nightdress to bed. One with thick straps and a vee at the breast. It falls to my knees and it's the perfect weight of fabric once I tuck myself into the layers of blankets on my bed. Tonight, I've been sweltering.

Mason rises over me, cupping my jaw in one hand, rubbing his thumb over my lips. Then his palm skims down my neck to my chest, and I'm an inferno.

"I swore I wouldn't touch you unless you were mine but I'm finding it harder and harder to stay away." He watches his hand blaze a trail down my skin. Palm pausing at the edge of my exposed cleavage. "Harder not to want to touch you. Taste you. Claim you."

"Oh God," I whimper. I want those things. I want his hands on me. His mouth on sensitive places.

"Tell me what you want, Anna."

"You," I whisper, knowing it's true.

"I need specifics. Kissing? Touching? Fucking?"

The directness of his last question brings my eyes to his. "Is that all we'd be to one another?" A one-night stand? Friends with benefits? Fuck buddies? The thought of any of those things doesn't settle well in my belly.

"Fucking you would never be enough. But I'm following your lead here. Your call with what we do."

"I don't want to hurt you."

"You won't."

The lie lingers between us. Mason is more sensitive than he wants others to believe. His love for Ben. His upset with Samantha. His disappointment in himself with Lynlee.

"I don't want you to hurt me," I timidly admit.

Mason's gaze leaps to meet my eyes. His hand returns to cup my chin. "I'll try not to."

It's the best he can offer and exactly what I want to hear.

"Kissing," I whisper, holding his gaze.

His lips are on mine before I finish the word. Heat blooms within me. His mouth is a winter fire on a dark night. He's everywhere with teeth and tongue. Nipping my lower lip and swiping into my mouth. We kiss, hungry and greedy, while he keeps space between our bodies. His chest hovers over mine but he isn't touching me. My nipples peak but they don't reach his naked skin.

With his hand on my jaw, his body is a fortress over mine. Pillars of strength, of reserve, as he doesn't lower to give me his weight.

Eventually, I can't take it anymore and my hips jut upward, seeking connection. Needing to feel a part of him. The part that's heavy and thick and long, and just inches too far away for me to caress where I need him most. My hands clutch at his biceps, hoping to weaken his position over me. When he doesn't budge, I slip my arms around him and press at his shoulder blades, smoothing down his back.

I turn my head, breaking from the kiss but Mason isn't deterred. He continues to kiss my cheek, my jaw, my neck. I'm not detained either. My hands wander the expanse of his back, feeling the muscles strain as he remains in the four-post position. Arms extended. Knees a cage.

Then my hands are at his backside, the firm globes unlike anything I've felt. The flannel material over them isn't allowing me close enough. Still, I squeeze, holding on as my hips buck once more, bringing my lower half up to meet the thickness jutting outward from the flimsy pants.

"Anna," Mason warns. His teeth graze my neck, scrapping at my skin, fueling the need in me.

"I need more," I admit.

Mason lowers, still balancing his weight off me but pressing his hardness where I'm soft. Where I'm wet and desperate. Where I'm warm and eager.

He presses upward, dragging himself across the area of me that's lusting for friction.

Mason's mouth returns to mine as he grinds against me. Hips shifting, thrusting his cock at my center. Teasing me with the motion of entering me.

With my feet planted on the bed, I respond by lifting toward him, rubbing myself against his firm length. My hands clutch at the tightness of his backside. The tension builds.

Once again, I break the kiss, peppering his neck with soft sips. He licks my neck, and I nip his shoulder.

"Anna," he grunts.

The silkiness of my nightie brushes against my hard nipples which are crushed under the strength of his chest. I hitch one leg over him, wrapping around him. Although we are fully clothed, I'm rushing toward the cliff. The precarious edge where I'll topple over and fly through the free fall.

"Fuck. Anna." He strains, pressing upward to balance on his arms over me again. The connection at our centers doesn't end. Mason grinds against me, pressing harder, wanting to go deeper. Wishing to be skin to skin and filling me.

The thought tips me over and I rise upward, wrapping my arms around his back as I bite his shoulder and fall.

The bliss isn't like anything I've experienced. Clutching at his sweaty skin, I hang on as I soar through an orgasm that has me seeing stars. My lower half clenches, the tension dragging on as Mason stills his body while one part of him pulses. His heart thunders. His cock jolts.

"Anna. Fuck," he groans as I feel him let go against me.

We're still covered by silk and flannel, but we might as well have been naked. If I saw stars with clothing between us, I can't imagine what I'd see if we were skin to skin.

He collapses over me and then twists to his side, taking me with him. "That wasn't what I intended to happen when I came down here." He softly chuckles, surprise in the sound as he holds me to him, pressing his lips to my forehead.

"That's exactly what I hoped would happen if you came down here," I admit.

Mason laughs a little harder. With the jostle of his body, the firmness of his chest rubs on mine. My body is still on edge. If he kisses me again. If he touches me. I'll be ready for more.

But maybe this is as far as we should go tonight, and slowly I regress into concern.

"Maybe this was too much?" Mason tightens his hold on me, as if he feels me slipping away.

"No." Adamantly shaking my head, I say, "This was perfect."

Chapter 29

9 Months Ago
December

The Morning After Effect

[Mason]

The next morning, I'm caught by Jenna sneaking out of Anna's room. What anyone else is doing up at this ungodly hour is beyond me. Why Jenna is in the main house is a mystery as well. The box of tea clutched to her chest when I startle her is my only answer.

"Um." Jenna holds her gaze upward, not risking a glance at my boxer briefs or the slight tent in them. There's no way to be discreet. I'm hard. Waking next to Anna didn't help.

Last night was a teenage fantasy come true. Who gets off fully clothed? Who comes in their pants like a randy teen? Apparently me.

I'd slipped from the bed last night but quickly returned in a fresh pair of underwear. I didn't trust Anna to be alone with her thoughts and I was correct in my assumption. She'd shut down. Not completely closed off but still struggling between her attraction to me and distracting ideas.

I didn't bring up Ben. I didn't want to discuss him after what we'd done.

In that damn romantic comedy *P.S. I Love You*, the Irish guy sleeps with the girl, and then they realize he'd been friends with her dead husband when they were kids. He offers to tell her about him after they had sex. I'm not that schmuck. I'm not bringing a past lover into bed with me.

"Good morning," Jenna mumbles to me, shaking the box of tea for further confirmation that her reason for being in the kitchen is a hot drink.

I run a hand through my hair, anxious that I've been caught but also a little relieved. I'm not going to be some damn secret. Anna and I aren't going to be friends with benefits or fuck buddies.

Not that I thought Anna would use me like that. I want more from her than just a roll in the sack.

Although I'd certainly repeat what happened last night in a heartbeat. Preferably without clothes next time.

I peer over my shoulder at the hallway for the main bedroom. "About that—"

"None of my business," Jenna immediately interjects.

"Yeah, I'd appreciate it if you don't say anything." I glance down at the floor.

"Not saying a word," Jenna says before exhaling. "But if I might say one thing . . ."

"Somehow, I figured you would." Jenna and I have become friends. Our date wasn't actually a date back in November but more like a friend helping a friend. Jenna didn't want to go alone to a school fundraiser. I'd donated to the night's silent auction and figured an appearance would be a good business move.

"Are you sure this is smart?" Jenna asks.

My shoulders slump. "I'm not a mistake." I fucking hate feeling like last night might have been one. In Anna's eyes. In her heart.

"I'm not saying you are. I'm asking about *you*. I don't want to see you hurt."

I don't want to hurt you, Anna had said to me.

I'd joked that she couldn't, but she could. She had the power to destroy me. To dispel the idea of love. To ruin any chance I'd give such a reckless emotion.

Still, I defend myself, holding up a shield as I dismissively snort. "How can I be hurt? I've had years to protect myself. Decades actually."

"Are you sure she isn't someone you want only because you haven't ever been able to have her?"

Funny Jenna says such a thing as Anna has mentioned the same idea.

I level a hard glare at Jenna. "Don't you think I've tried to tell myself that? Tried to convince myself that must be it. The reason I'm so attracted to her is because she isn't attracted to me, or because she's the only woman I haven't had."

I dig my fingers into my hair, holding the thickness at the top. Frustration fills me as Jenna reads my mind. I've had these exact thoughts. If I just fuck Anna, maybe it will get her out of my system.

Suddenly, I'm tugging my hands free of my hair, wanting to rip it from the roots.

Because I do not want to fuck Anna. I want to love her.

"I've tried everything I can to not think about her." I peer down the hallway, dark in the early hours of morning. "And it's never worked. Not another woman. Not too much booze. Not living away from here. Hell, not even having her under my feet, thinking I'd get sick of her."

"What are you doing then?"

"Nothing happened." I sigh, swallowing back the truth. "Nothing's happening."

Bitterness fills me again. I sound like Anna, denying that kiss yesterday afternoon to Autumn.

Where are Anna and I going? What are we doing?

"What will you do?" Jenna asks, concern in her voice. "Admit your feelings to her or keep fighting them?"

"Maybe that's a question for Anna." My response is sharp and unwarranted. But she's right. Am I going to admit how I feel or continue to fight my feelings? I don't have an answer for Jenna, so I shrug and turn away from Jenna, heading toward the front hall and the staircase leading to my guest room.

Every slap of my bare feet on the hardwood punctuates how I no longer want to be Anna's guest but a permanent addition to her life.

Chapter 30

9 Months Ago
December

The Morning After Miscommunication

[Anna]

Mason returned to my room after slipping out in the early hours of the morning. His entrance was more like a rush of energy than a subtle sneak.

I slowly sit up as he stands at the end of the bed, hands slipped into coat pockets. He's fully dressed in jeans, boots and a winter jacket. A bag hangs over his shoulder.

"I've got to go." He doesn't meet my concerned stare. His hair stands on end as if he's run his fingers through it repeatedly. "I got a call from Lynlee."

"Is everything alright?" Something is clearly wrong. Very, very wrong.

When he finally looks up at me, his eyes are haunted. His shoulders tense. I scramble from the covers and crawl across the mattress on my knees. Only when I reach for him, he steps back. I clutch the footboard, arms trembling from the sudden rejection.

"I'm not certain." His brows pinch as he returns his gaze to the floor avoiding meeting my eyes. "But I'm going to be gone a few days."

With that, he steps forward, air kisses my cheek and turns toward the door. He pauses before opening it, glancing back over his shoulder.

Nausea rushes in my belly. He's pulling away from me, shutting me out or maybe he's simply skipping out. Is this how it works? Was he counting the minutes until he could climb out of my bed? Was he holding out until the last second to leave?

"You're scaring me."

"You should know Jenna knows I was in here last night." He doesn't look for my reaction, but he pauses waiting on the denial that doesn't come. Our friends are going to find out, unless he doesn't want them to know.

Yesterday, I panicked.

Today, he's doing more than panicking. He's coldly walking away.

+ + +

Over the next three days, there have been intermittent messages stating how he can't explain everything over text, and he isn't in a position to talk. The not knowing is driving me mad.

Our family of friends is still gathered to celebrate River and Zack's baby, Lake, and now Archer has proposed to Jenna. I'm happy for my brother. So happy. But I can't help this niggling of sadness deep in my belly. I'm a lonely party of one in a gathering of love birds.

I haven't been able to stop my mind from racing with concern about Mason. Zack and Logan haven't been able to tell me anything either. They've each had hit and miss text messages and phone calls with Mason.

Suddenly, the front door shuts. I hadn't heard it open, and I hold my breath until Mason enters the room. His tall form fills the space. My heart and head are in conflict. On one hand, I'm so relieved he's standing here, like a breath of fresh air, looking like the dream he is. On the other hand, I can't seem to draw in enough oxygen. Anxiety fills me instead. Where has he been? Why hasn't he reached out to me? And what happened now with Samantha?

Let me in.

He immediately catches my eye across the room, as if I've spoken aloud. Those beautiful blues are filled with a mixture of emotion, but sadness is the most prominent. He looks like he's seen a ghost and the pallor of his skin is the same color as one. Darkness beneath his eyes is a stark hint that he's exhausted.

Movement happens behind Mason's thigh, and I squint at his long legs. His hand lowers and he reaches behind him for Lynlee. I'm immediately reminded of that day we spent together in October. Her quietness. Her soft smile. Her excitement finding a heart-shaped rock.

She's focusing on everything in the room and nothing in particular until those eyes meet mine.

I swallow at the intensity in them.

"Everyone, this is my daughter, Lynlee." She clings to Mason's leg.

Autumn is quick to stand but slow to approach the hesitant girl. River and Zack remain seated. Jenna and I trade gazes before I look at the other children in the room.

Trevor has his eyes laser-beamed onto the new girl. He'd previously been focused on Rosie, who is too young to notice the sudden shift of attention. Something nearly palpitates off the nine-year-old as he observes this newcomer. I don't think he feels threatened as much as curious. In awe, maybe. She's beautiful, even at six.

Oliver's head twists, his wild eyes full of confusion as he glances between his brother and Lynlee. Back and forth, back and forth. Then he gazes at Rosie. Conflict is written in his little expression. He's only one boy. How will he protect them all from the shenanigans of his alpha twin?

Finally, there's Talia, daggers in her eyes as her young ice-queen heart turns colder. She glares harder than normal at Trevor before staring at Lynlee. The girls are the same age. They're too young for the drama of love and the potential of dating, but if I had to write a book about their futures, how things would play out for the next generation of Lakeside Cottage, it isn't pretty.

It's still complicated among the adults, as Mason and I are now the only single people remaining among this crowd.

The last two standing in a sense.

If they only knew . . .

The other night comes to mind. The way he lingered over me, hovering like a heavy mist when all I wanted was to drown in the fog of him. Shivering, I suppress the urge to cross the room and pull Mason to me, tug him into my arms and settle the swirling emotions in his eyes.

"Where you been, man?" Zack's voice pulls me from my thoughts.

Mason combs his fingers through his hair, which looks like he's been doing it repeatedly for hours. "Later." His voice is hollow, distant even. He keeps his focus on Zack for a long moment, as if telling him things only Zack can understand.

Lynlee's equally haunted-looking, and I smooth the cushion beside me. Whatever is on her mind. Whatever haunts her heart. I want her to know I'm here for her. Glancing back at Mason and the haggard expression edged in his cheeks, I'm here for both of them.

Lynlee doesn't move, so I pat the space beside me, tipping my head in invitation for her to join me. In my other hand, I hold a small heart-shaped rock. The same one I've carried with me from the beginning. Lynlee's focus drops to the item in my hands and I hold it up between pinched fingers so she can get a better look at it.

The rock symbolizes so many things. Strength. Resistance. Perseverance. Love.

Eyes locked on the shape between my fingers, Lynlee slips away from Mason's thigh and approaches me. I hold out my hand, sensing something fragile within her.

My gaze leaps to Mason who is watching his daughter walk to me. His eyes meet mine and hold. When Lynlee finally stands before me, my attention falls to her.

"Hello, beautiful girl." Keeping quiet and low when I address her, her eyes remain on the heart-shape in my hand.

"Want to hold the rock?" I ask.

She looks directly at me, as if she's afraid to ask permission. As if she doesn't know what she wants. She's a child who looks a little like her spirit has been broken.

When she doesn't answer me, I hold out my palm, face up with the heart within it.

Take my heart, child.

She hesitates before reaching forward to run her finger over it.

"When you hold something like this in your hand, and rub at it, it's very soothing. Calming even. Some say we can draw strength from rocks." I glance at River. She's into new-age things, finding purpose in nature. "It makes us stronger . . . braver even."

Lynlee takes the rock from me and doesn't flinch when I grip her little hips and tug her onto the sofa beside me. As I lean back on the couch cushion, I ignore the stares of others in the room. No one knows Mason was here in October with Lynlee. Or showed up in July. Or surprised me in May.

He's been like my heart-shaped rock. A beautiful thing that I keep in my pocket, touching it to bring me comfort and peace. Only, I'm ready to share that soothing stability with others. I'm ready to share him . . . us.

Eventually, Lynlee leans against my arm and I glance up at Mason again, wondering what has him so frazzled, fried looking even.

He shakes his head when his gaze falls on Lynlee.

Later.

+ + +

"Samantha is dead. Overdose." Mason's words hit the room like a bomb.

Lynlee is upstairs in a guest bedroom. Archer took Rosie and Talia to the garage apartment. River went home earlier with Trevor and Oliver when baby Lake fell asleep. Baby Ben is sleeping in a pack-and-play in the formal living room. Everyone else lingers to hear Mason's tale.

Mason sits in the single overstuffed chair in the room. He holds a glass of dark liquid in his hands as he leans forward, elbows on his thighs. Zack sits closest to him on the nearby couch.

"The other morning, I'd missed a series of calls from Lynlee that Samantha hadn't woken up. That Lynlee couldn't get her to wake." Mason blows out a breath and meets my eyes. "I called a neighbor who had a key and told her to check on things."

His hollow stare holds on me as he explains his sudden absence.

The unspoken is he'd missed his daughter's calls because he'd been with me.

Guilt stabs me in the chest. Why hadn't he just told me?

"I didn't like Samantha, but I didn't want her dead." His voice cracks. The emotion isn't one of sorrow but disappointment. "I never trusted her. Didn't think she was good with Lynlee but this . . . this . . ."

He swipes a hand through his hair, then downs the remainder of the liquid in his glass.

"I knew she did drugs. She promised me she didn't do them around Lynlee." He huffs, suggesting Samantha had lied.

"Was it intentional?" Logan's voice is quiet as he asks.

Mason shakes his head. "Toxicology report says her blood alcohol was high, but it was the combination of drugs in her system that pushed her over. I don't think she planned to kill herself. She just wanted to get lost."

Mason glances at me. My chest aches. Has he done that in the past? Has he smoked too much, snorted too much, lost himself in others to dull his pain?

I don't like the idea of him hurting himself in this manner. He had Ben to talk to if things pained him. Did he not see that Zack and Logan were here for him as well? There were secrets I didn't know about Mason. Maybe Ben hadn't known them either.

"And Lynlee had been home?" Jenna asks, her voice high with concern.

"Samantha had hosted a holiday party. Said it would just be a few friends and their kids."

Mason tips his head back and stares at the ceiling. "How did I get myself involved in that woman's life?"

"A better question is what happens now with Lynlee?" Logan asks.

"You're her father. You have full custody," Zack explains and Mason's head snaps forward. He meets Zack's gaze.

"That's what I wanted, but not like this." Mason's voice is low, ragged.

"We know," Zack says, locking eyes with his friend.

The words necessary to comfort Mason escape me. Instead, I listen to the conversation around us but everything in me wants to wrap myself around Mason. Offer him the security he needs to know he's okay.

Lynlee is okay. They are going to survive this moment. I understand. He might not have loved Samantha. As he just said he didn't even like her, but the loss of someone imbedded so deeply into your life is profound. I'm living proof that life moves forward.

"How did things get so fucked up?" Mason asks Zack before lowering his head again. "Why am I always fucking up?"

"Don't do that," Zack says, reaching out and grabbing Mason's knee. "Don't take this on as your fault. She did this, not you."

A heavy silence falls around us, each of us lacking words.

"So, what's next?" Autumn finally asks, clutching hands with Logan as they sit beside me on a couch.

Mason looks around the room. "Once the funeral is over, we're moving. There's nothing left in Traverse City for us." His eyes shift to me and away. "I'd been planning on moving here for a while now but hadn't found a house yet. I really want a fresh start for Lynlee and me. To be closer to all of you."

"You can stay at the condo for now," Autumn suggests, speaking of her rental. The winter season is slow for tourism in this section of the state and Autumn doesn't currently have a full-time renter.

"You'll stay here," I finally speak up. "There's plenty of space in the house." The suggestion comes from two places. A need to help him. A desire to keep him close.

"I can't do that." His brows pinch at the prospect. "This is *your* home. Lynlee and I need our own space."

"Then the garage apartment." I fight the desperation in my tone as I glance at Jenna. The space above the garage belongs to Archer in our agreement about the Lakeside Cottage property.

Jenna nods. "You need to be near family."

Mason's head snaps up. He looks at Jenna before glancing between Logan and Zack, as if silently asking their advice or their permission.

"You know we want you closer, man," Logan adds.

"We'd be neighbors," Zack pushes, giving Mason a hopeful smile.

Mason gazes at me. "I can't intrude."

"You're not intruding," I assure him. He gave up a year of his life to live with us. Now, I want to return the favor. Offer him a refuge because the next year for Lynlee will be trying. "You're family, Mason. We'd love to have you here again."

I lower my voice and add, "I'd love you to stay."

"Only until I find us a place." Mason's throat bobs as he concedes. He licks his lips. His gaze drops to his lap where his fingers are clutching at the glass in his hand. "But if it's okay for now . . ."

"I'm sure." The confidence in my voice doesn't match the hammering of my heart. Because with Mason this close, there's no doubt where we are headed.

We aren't going to be the last two *standing* for much longer.

Chapter 31

8 Months Ago
January

A New Year

[Mason]

A funeral during the holidays sucks. The time passed in a blur. Samantha didn't have much family. Her so-called friends were minimal. Packing up Lynlee's belongings in their apartment didn't take much effort. The landlord would be responsible for cleaning the place. I put my townhome on the market and put most of my furniture into storage.

And suddenly, I was back above the garage at Lakeside Cottage. Only this time I had my little girl with me permanently.

The arrangement wasn't ideal. Lynlee was in for a bumpy transition. First, living with me full-time after losing her mother. Plus, leaving her home and moving into one that wasn't even mine. But I promised myself by summer we'd have a new place. One with a yard and a swing set and walking distance from the beach.

Lynlee loved the water which was currently frozen in spots because of the cold temperatures.

Still, if the weather was over thirty-two degrees, we bundled up and went down to the lake, provided there wasn't snow on the steps leading down to the shore.

Lynlee was quiet for weeks. Her shyness morphed into silence.

If I ever thought I loved Anna, I loved her even more for her devotion to my child. Without words, she often anticipated Lynlee's needs, including her in quiet activities like coloring or paint-by-number or some craft project I would never be able to manipulate. The two became peas in a pod while I watched and observed Anna be the amazing mom-figure she is.

As for me, Anna held my hand through the funeral. She never left my side, like a shadow, calculating my needs before I did. She didn't help us pack up in Traverse City, but she did help us unpack in the apartment, attempting to make Lynlee as comfortable as she could. Welcoming her and assuring Lynlee the bedroom with two beds was hers.

Christmas passed with too many presents for my little girl. Her newfound family spoiled her, making up for all the years they hadn't known her.

Zack and River bought her a bike since they bought new ones for the boys.

Logan and Autumn gave her a dollhouse.

Even Jenna and Archer gifted her a new doll.

However, the gift from Anna meant the most. It was a heart-shaped pendant made from a Petosky stone on a chain. Petosky stones are unique to the Great Lakes, found mostly on Michigan shores. The rock is recognizable for its sunburst impressions which are highlighted when the stone is wet or polished.

For strength and bravery, the card read.

Throughout our Christmas together, Lynlee would touch the stone at her throat or pull it forward on the chain to look at it.

My heart swelled three times that day, like the damn Grinch, only for different reasons.

I was absolutely in love with Anna.

And the only way I knew to express myself was by touching her, which didn't seem to be allowed. We stood close to one another. I might press a hand to her lower back. She might brush a palm down my arm. But holding her, kissing her, hadn't happened in the weeks since my move.

The tension was driving me mad.

+ + +

On New Year's Eve, we didn't make it to midnight in our party plans.

Was this a sign we were getting old?

Earlier we'd celebrated the coming year at Zack and River's home, but as kids started petering out, couples separated. Logan and Autumn went home with Baby Ben, Lorna and Mila. Anna followed me to the apartment as Lynlee dropped off when I carried her the short walk from next door.

Anna pulls down the covers on Lynlee's bed, and I lay down my sleepy girl before tugging off her shoes. Immediately, she curls to her side and tucks her knees to her chest. I brush back her dark hair and press a kiss to her temple, quietly telling her, I love her. The words come easier each time I say them.

Anna lovingly looks down at Lynlee as well before I nod for us to exit the room.

The garage apartment has two bedrooms with a living area and galley kitchen separating them. A bathroom is to the left of the small kitchen and closest to the larger bedroom which has a king-sized bed. In the living area, two well-worn red couches sit at right angles facing a flat screen television on a short stand.

"Want to stay?" I nervously ask as Anna heads to the door.

"Do you want me to?" She stops quick, turning to face me but cautious in asking.

"I wouldn't ask if I didn't." A smile eases onto my face and Anna responds in kind.

"It'd be nice not to go into the house alone, although I couldn't care less about it turning into a new year," she comments.

Her boys are both out tonight, much to Anna's dismay. She strictly told them to stay in place wherever they were going. Dark roads on a night like this are dangerous when *other* people have been celebrating too much.

"Not a fan of New Year's?" I tilt my head, wondering.

"I'm a teacher. The new year starts in August for me."

"Ah." I pause and tuck my hands into my back pockets. Why the fuck am I so nervous? "I never even thought about champagne, but I have wine."

"Wine sounds perfect."

Anna helps herself to a seat in the middle of one couch while I round it to the tight kitchen area, uncork a bottle of red wine, and pour us each a glass. Anna clicked on the television to the national celebration in New York City, however, the volume remains low on the set.

"What should we drink to?" she asks, surprising me as I hand her the glass and take a seat on the couch, sitting close to her.

"To a new year," I joke.

"How about just new beginnings?"

Everything in me wants to know what she wants to start.

"To new beginnings then." I clink my glass against hers and drink.

Anna sips hers and leans back on the couch. She glances around the room. "You know, I hardly came up here. This space was all Archer's until you." Her observation of the space stops on me.

"My home away from home," I jest.

"It's your home, Mason." Her brows lower, her head tipping to emphasize her words. "There's no rush for you to move."

"Not sick of me yet?" My voice teases while I'm holding my breath for her answer.

With her eyes directed at her glass, she shakes her head and takes another drink of her wine. When she finishes, she sets the glass on the table and turns toward me, bending her knee and placing her leg on the cushions. Her elbow rests on the back of the couch.

"You know, it's been a few weeks. You never talk about her." Her directness surprises me.

"Who? Samantha?"

Anna lifts a brow.

"What's there to say?"

"You weren't in love with her but how are you doing?"

I sigh as I slouch into the cushions at my back. "I just feel numb. Not empty like from Ben's death." I glance at her. "But just numb, like nothing. I don't feel any particular way."

I focus on her eyes. "Doesn't that make me a bad person?"

Anna swipes fingers through her long hair. She's dressed casually in jeans and a loose-fitting sweater. Cute ankle socks with pencils on them cover her feet, hidden when she was wearing booties earlier.

"I don't think it makes you bad, Mason. You had a relationship with this person, though. For good or bad."

"Seems like every relationship I've ever had has been negative." My father. My mother.

"Not your friendships," she reminds me.

"No, but my parents. Women." I tip my head back and stare up at the ceilings.

"You've never been in love?" Her voice softens, tiptoeing into a topic we probably shouldn't discuss.

"Only been one perfect woman in my life and she wouldn't ever be mine."

I feel the weight of Anna's stare on the side of my face and finally give into the pressure to roll my head and look at her.

"Mason," she whispers. "Why me?"

I can't say where or when or even how it happened. I just saw this shy teenage girl with deep set eyes and wanted her. Did I become a little obsessed when she didn't come to me? When she didn't become mine? Maybe. Did I resent her presence when she was all Ben could talk about and then she was always around, torturing me with her pure laugh and easy smile? Sure.

But was there a specific reason, an exact moment? I couldn't pinpoint it.

The attraction just happened.

"I don't really know. Maybe I just measure every woman up against you. How you open your heart easily to others."

"Except you," she murmurs.

My lips crook up on one side. "Except me." I stare at her. "Maybe it was the way you were with Ben. So loving. So affectionate. So easily his other half. And I just wanted that for me."

"But you never found it in someone?" Her question only clarifies.

"Call me jealous. Maybe envious. Thou shall not covet thy best friend's wife, and yet, I did." I'm laying my cards on the table. Confessing my sin.

"Maybe it's time for a new best friend."

I continue to stare at her, wondering what she means. "Who?"

"Me." Her lashes lower a little before her lids lift again, pinning me with those eyes that melt my insides and make my dick stiff.

"Friends," I whisper. Are we back to this?

"Or maybe we could just see where this leads?" Her arm falls to the back of the couch like she wants to touch me but I'm just out of reach.

"There's only one end goal for me with you, Anna." I want her as mine.

Her eyes leap to mine. She rolls her lips inward, as if she's contemplating what I'm saying. Then, she blows me out of the water. "I don't think I can continue to deny I have feelings for you."

Holding still, I don't even think I blink, not wanting to miss a hint of her meaning.

"But I need to be clear. I don't need you to be Ben."

"I can't," I murmur but she's already shaking her head.

"Ben is always going to be a part of me. A part of us. But what I need you to be is you. I just need you to be Mason."

Shifting forward, I set my glass on the low table and turn toward her.

"I need you to be the Mason Ben knew. The one I'm—" She stops herself short.

"The one you what?"

"The one who gives everything to those he loves." She didn't quite finish her previous statement, but this explanation is good enough.

"I'd give you anything," I whisper, reaching out to take her jaw in my palm.

Suddenly, the countdown sounds despite the lowered volume on the set.

Ten, nine . . .

"Anna," I whisper, leaning toward her.

Eight, seven . . .

"Kiss me," she whispers.

The remainder of the count is lost as my mouth is on hers within seconds and the new year begins with me kissing Anna.

Quickly, the kisses grow hungry. Anna climbs over me, straddling my lap, pressing her center against the hard length in my jeans, but it's not enough. My fingers are fisted in her hair at the nape of her neck and her hands hold the back of my head. Our bodies slowly grind against one another as my hand roams up her side, pressing into her to draw her closer.

"Do you have any idea what you do to me?" I murmur to her lips against mine. A slice of heaven on my tongue.

"You do the same to me. I can't explain it. I can't deny it either. I just have this need for you."

With Anna in my lap, I lower my hand to her ass and tug her closer, tighter.

"Do you use the toy I gave you for your birthday?" I tease thinking of the pink tickler and its vibrating speeds.

She smiles without answering and returns to kissing me.

"Who gave it to you, Anna?"

"You." She pulls back to look at me, eyes questioning.

My gaze holds on her eyes. "And who do you think of when you use it?" My voice is still strong. There is only one right answer.

"You," she whispers, sheepishly.

"Good girl." Clutching at her perfect ass with both hands, I tuck her tighter to me. Our mouths meet again, taking this kiss to frantic heights. I need to be inside her and the way she's rocking against me, she wants the same thing.

Before I know what I'm doing, I lean forward with my mouth still on Anna's and lay her on the square table in front of the couches. With her back on the surface, I flatten myself over her, thrusting against her center, simulating how I'd like to enter her, hard and fast.

Anna breaks the kiss, inhaling a deep breath like she's drowning in me. Suffocating in need. Her fingers tug my hair.

"Mason," she whimpers. "Maybe we should do it."

"What?" I nibble her neck, nipping up the slender column to her ear.

"Have sex."

I freeze. Teeth at her ear lobe. Hand just below her breast.

Releasing her ear, I pull back and stare down at her, spread out between wine glasses on a coffee table. My dick throbs, hard and furious against the heat of her center. Her legs are spread wide, one hitching over my thigh.

"When?" I question, voice croaking like a hormonal teen.

"Now."

"No."

"What?" she asks.

What? My dick echoes. Just what the fuck am I saying?

Slowly, I press off the coffee table and reach for her hand, tugging her upright so she sits on the table while I fall back to the couch. Rejection fills her eyes. She chews her lower lip.

"It's okay," she timidly says, her voice full of remorse.

"No, Anna." I scrub both hands down my cheeks. "Fuck, I'm messing this up." I exhale before cupping her face and holding her, so she looks at me, which she's doing everything to avoid.

"Of course, I want to have sex with you." I exhale again. "Just not like this. Not on a coffee table or with my kid in the next room."

This is Anna. My dream girl. It should be special and romantic.

"It's fine," she whispers, lids lowering so she still doesn't look directly at me even though I'm holding her face in my hands.

It's fine. Are there two worse words from a woman? It isn't fine and she's not understanding me.

"When we do this, it needs to be . . . right."

"And it's not right now?" Her voice trembles.

"It's—"

She abruptly stands, cutting off my thought and filling in my space as she's between my bent knees.

"I get it. It's fine," she repeats again, wringing out her hand before turning to step over my knee which cages her in. I catch her around the waist and tug her back to me, causing her to fall on my lap with her back to my chest.

"Anna. Just stop." I breathe in the scent of her hair, summery and fresh, taking a moment to calm my breathing while there's nothing I can do about the raging hard-on in my jeans. With my arms around her waist, I squeeze her tighter, digging my nose deeper into her hair. "We just need more time."

I need more time. This involves organization and planning. Your average date isn't going to do for such an occasion.

Anna is willingly saying yes to me, and I just said no because if I'm only getting one night with her, I want it to be perfect.

For her. For me.

"I'm not saying no to you. I just want it to be . . . special." I close my eyes hating how I sound like a virgin, saving myself for that one person. Being that Anna's the one person I've wanted for an eternity, I'm not far off in my assessment.

"Okay," she quietly whispers. Her head still remains forward, lowered toward her lap. I can't see her eyes. "When?"

"Soon."

My dick is still screaming at me. Soon should be now. This second. I'm so fucking hard and she's so fucking willing, but that's not how I want it to be.

I want Anna to be willing to open her heart to me, not just give me her body, and we aren't there yet.

"I promise, it will be so good," I whisper in her ear, nearly shivering with how incredible I'm certain it will feel to slip into her warm heat, lose myself in the depths of her.

To finally let go.

Chapter 32

8 Months Ago
January

A New Year Continued

[Anna]

He was rejecting me.

While I understood his reservation with Lynlee in the other room, my head could only wrap around the words from his mouth.

He didn't want to have sex with me.

At least, not now. Maybe soon. The caution in his tone suggested it might never happen.

I'd put myself out there, telling him I was ready, and he stomped on the brakes.

Mason is safe for me. I thought he'd understand my hesitations and limitations, but maybe that's just it. I've only been with one man. I'm certain I'd be the most boring lover. Pile on emotions, because sex was going to be emotional for me, and I'm a complication Mason doesn't need in his life.

He offers to walk me home, which is only across the driveway, but I don't want him leaving Lynlee. Instead, he kisses me long and tender at the top of the stairs, infusing the kiss with things I can't read into the mixed messages he's giving me.

Kissing. *Yes*.

Sex. *No*.

He watches me cross the distance to the front door. Without turning back to him, attempting to hold back the tears until I'm in my room, I enter my house to a commotion in my kitchen.

"Dude, chill," Calvin warns someone. He's home for winter break from college.

"I'm chill." The slurred response comes from Bryce. My seventeen-year-old son.

I rush to the kitchen where Bryce drapes over the island. While seated in a stool, his arm is extended and his head rests on the side of his arm. His eyes are closed. His body slack.

"Is he drunk?" I turn on Calvin who doesn't look surprised at my accusation.

"Where did you come from?" he asks, as if I'm the child and he's the parent. Admittedly, I'm wearing my winter coat and jeans, and it's evident I came from the front of the house not my room.

"I was at Mason's." I blow out a long breath, not feeling the need to explain myself to my eldest child. "What are you two doing home?"

I expressly asked them to stay planted somewhere, not wanting them out on a night like tonight when fools drink and drive. My head swivels from one son to the other.

"Are you drunk?" I snap at Calvin as the older one while both are still below the legal drinking age.

"Mom. I'm fine. I had two beers, but this idiot decided to do shots." He waves a hand at his brother.

"Isnot an idiot," Bryce mumbles.

"Why were *you* at Mason's?" Calvin asks me.

Bryce grunts. The snort dismissive, suggestive even.

"What does that sound mean?" With my blood pressure rising, and Mason's rejection still stinging, anger fills me that my seventeen-year-old is wasted and snorting at me with implication. Maybe it's more guilt eating at me that I shouldn't have asked Mason to have sex with me.

"Mason has a crush on you," Bryce singsongs, like a drunken sailor.

My gaze flits to Calvin, who glares back at me. "It's true."

"What?" I snap, not certain if I'm asking for clarification or simply responding like a teenager myself, using the word like a defense. *What?*

"We aren't talking about Mason and me. Why is your brother plastered?" I demand.

"Ryleigh has a crush on Calvin. She doesn't like me." Bryce's eyes are still closed. His voice warbling as he speaks like I didn't just ask a question.

"She does not. And it wouldn't matter. She's in high school," Calvin retorts as if he's so worldly and wise only six months out from high school himself.

"Does smatter," Bryce slurs. "She wants you." He whines the last word.

"This is stupid," Calvin huffs. "Dude, just chill."

"I'm chillin'. I'm a chill pill. I'm a little white dot melting on my tongue."

My head swivels to Calvin. "Is he implying he's on drugs?"

Calvin shakes his head. "He's not. He's just . . . yeah, he's wasted."

"Wasted all my love on you," Bryce sings, off key and rivaling Captain Jack Sparrow after a bottle of rum. "Unrequited love is the worst." He folds his arm, tucking his head into the crease, face down on the countertop like he's going to sleep hunched over the island.

"It's always the brother or the best friend," Bryce states, his voice almost clear before he's quiet again.

"What is he talking about?" I ask Calvin.

Calvin only shakes his head again and sighs. "It's nothing, Mom. Honestly. He likes this girl, Ryleigh. I was talking to her at the party. I'm not interested, though. I love Keli."

Oh God. I can't handle my boys falling in love.

"Mason loves Mom," Bryce mumbles into his arm.

"I think we should get him to bed," I state, hoping to ward off any more comments.

I step forward when Bryce wiggles his brows and suggestively says, "Think Mason took Mom to bed." My limbs and breath freeze momentarily. It doesn't last long, though.

"Bryce Matthew!" I snap, not liking the insinuation in his tone that Mason and I have had sex. Then again, I'm the one stinging from not having sex with Mason. *Which* my late-teenaged sons do not need to know.

"Uh-oh. She used both names. Am I in trouble?" Bryce lifts his head like it weighs more than his body. His eyes are still closed.

He has no idea the trouble he's in but the powerful hangover he's going to have tomorrow will serve as his punishment.

"Fuck. Dude." Calvin exhales before rounding the counter. He catches Bryce by the back of his collar and hauls him off the stool. "Time for bed."

Anger hovers over Calvin as he struggles to wrap his brother's arm over his shoulder and walk him to the front hall. I step up and slip my arm around Bryce's waist, doing little to support him as he's so heavy. My middle child already towers over me and outweighs his older brother.

As we battle up the staircase, Bryce's body goes limp, pressing down on us even more.

"Fuck, he is heavy," Calvin grumbles.

"Language," I snark without any bite. I'm grateful my son is helping me.

When we reach Bryce's room, I release my arm around him and Calvin lets his brother fall to the bed, face first. I turn his head, hoping he doesn't throw up.

"He's already puked a few times. I doubt there is much left in him. It's why we are home. We couldn't stay at the party when he was such a mess," Calvin explains, looking down at his brother sprawled out like a lumberjack and snoring like one as well.

"What happened?"

"A girl." Calvin says again with a shrug. Calvin remains in Bryce's room, staring over his brother. "What he said, Mom. He didn't mean it how it sounded."

"I'll deal with him tomorrow," I assure Calvin. Bryce and I are going to have a nice little heart-to-heart.

Calvin purses his lips and then pinches them between his fingers. The movement is something Ben would do when he contemplated something.

He releases his lips. "It's okay for you to move on, though." His voice is quiet, and he slips his hands into his pockets. "Dad wouldn't want you to be alone."

"Honey." I step over to him, pushing back his hair although he stands taller than me. In only six months, I swear he's grown taller, filled out more. He's a man, not a child, but he'll always be my little boy. "I'm not dating anyone."

"Don't think you need to date." Calvin shrugs. "You have Mason here."

"And what does that mean?" I drop my hand.

"I'm not blind. I see the way he looks at you."

"And how does he look at me?" My eyes dart over his face, holding my breath for his answer.

"Like Dad did. Like he loves you."

Our eyes meet while my brows pinch. "How would you feel about that?"

Calvin shrugs and turns toward his brother. "Like he said, it's always the brother or the best friend. I think I'd prefer you date someone we already know. Someone we like." Calvin turns back to me. "Well, love. We love Mason, too."

Calvin looks at me, searching my face. "The bigger question is how do *you* feel about him?"

"I . . . I care about him. A lot."

Calvin nods several times with short, tight dips of his head. "Don't use him, okay, Mom. We don't want to lose him, too."

"Calvin." I sigh, stung by his candor but understanding his words come from a place of compassion. "You won't lose him. And I don't plan to hurt him."

Calvin looks back at his brother. "No one ever plans to hurt someone."

Ah, the wisdom of nineteen.

"Maybe you should head to bed, too. Thanks for dealing with drunkboy here." I hitch a thumb at Bryce.

"That's what brothers do. We're here for each other, looking after one another, even if we don't live in bedrooms next door anymore."

Reaching for his scruffy face, I palm his jaw. "You're a good big brother."

"I try. It's what Dad wanted."

"He'd be proud."

"Not of that." Calvin tips his head at Bryce.

"We all have slip ups in life."

With my hand still on Calvin's face, he looks at me with candid eyes. "Don't let Mason be a slip up."

"I won't."

Or at least, I'll try my hardest not to.

Chapter 33

8 Months Ago
January

A New Beginning

[Mason]

The next morning, I hear about Bryce's incident. Anna is beside herself with worry, but I talk her down, reminding her he's a kid. He's going to test limits and cross boundaries.

Thank God Calvin was there, she'd said.

The day ahead of us is planned with board games and football watching. At one point, I observe Anna with Lynlee. They stand behind the kitchen island, heads bent close together as Anna shows Lynlee where to place finger foods on a giant charcuterie board. Lynlee giggles at something Anna says and Anna's grin is wide in response. The moment is picture perfect. Anna wraps her arm around Lynlee, tugging her into her side, perfectly symbolizing how she's embraced my child into her family. My heart is almost full with the image. The only tweak I'd add is me on Anna's other side, engulfing both my girls in a giant hug.

Anna's house fills with our friends, but it is nearly two in the afternoon before Bryce shows his face, looking a little worse for wear.

"Want a drink, Tito?" Logan teases and Bryce looks like he might puke on the spot. He takes one glance at the spread of food his mom has prepared and turns a sickly shade of green.

Holding his head as high as he might be able to, Bryce asks to speak to his mom for a second. To my surprise, he asks if I can join them.

For some reason, I glance at Calvin. He tips his head, suggesting I follow.

"What am I missing?" I mutter as I pass the eldest Kulis child.

"He owes you this," Calvin states, sounding strangely like his father in tone while looking more and more like his Uncle Archer.

Following Anna and Bryce into the dining room, I pause, feeling a little out of my element and a lot confused why I'm present.

"I'm sorry, Mom." Bryce hangs his head, eyes averted.

As Anna stands before me, her shoulders fall. A tightness about her melts away.

"Calvin told me I said some things that I shouldn't have said." Bryce quickly glances at me and looks away. "And I didn't mean them."

"What am I missing?" I ask again, this time to Bryce.

Bryce studies his toes. "I was drunk, and I said some things about you and Mom," he says weakly.

Instantly, I'm on edge on Anna's behalf. "Like what?" He can insult me all he wants, and I'd still love the fuck out of this kid, but disrespecting his mom is another story.

"I said . . ." Bryce swallows hard, looking up at me once and then turning his head. "I said I thought you had a crush on Mom. And how you wanted to take her to bed."

Hands coming to my hips, I tell him, "Not cool, Bryce." My teeth grit. If her kids don't approve, Anna is going to slam the door in my face. She'll deny her own happiness for them. It's just who she is.

Nothing has happened between us, though. Nothing more than hot kisses and an occasional orgasm which isn't a seventeen-year-old's business. Still, I want him to understand, sometimes you love who you love.

"I didn't mean any disrespect. To you or Mom." Bryce looks at his mother, eyes bloodshot with dark bags beneath them.

"I'd ask why you said them but I'm afraid your answer will be because you were drunk which is no excuse." Hurt fills Anna's tone. She's surprisingly calm.

Without thinking, I place a hand on her lower back and Bryce catches the movement.

"Sometimes there's truth in what drunk people say, though." Bryce glances at me and then back to his mom.

"Like what?" Anna asks Bryce, irritation growing in her voice.

Bryce looks at me, his gaze steady on mine. For a moment, I feel like I'm in an old Western film, where the two guys stare each other down, not wanting to pull the gun first, but knowing duty calls. Defend someone's honor.

"What if I did want to date your mother?" I ask.

"Mason!" Anna shrieks, turning on me, but I keep my focus on Bryce.

Man up, little boy. Tell me how you really feel.

My eyes narrow, warning him to be careful how he answers in front of his mother. He can tell me to my face to fuck off, but he should probably not use that language before his parent.

"If it means you'll be sticking around, I don't have a problem."

"Yeah?" His answer surprises me but then I'm reminded of the conversation we had that first Thanksgiving where Bryce told me how upset he was at my disappearance. How he felt like he'd suffered two losses, only I'd willingly left him.

I never intended to hurt him. I'd never leave if I have the chance to stay.

"I'm not going anywhere." I hold his gaze. This seventeen-year-old might actually understand I'm in love with his mom.

Well, shit.

"Does Calvin know?" I ask, having a private conversation with Bryce as we stare at one another.

"Know what?" Anna asks, turning on me again.

Bryce dips his head once before his mother turns back to him. "It's a reason he wanted me to apologize to both of you."

"Fair enough," I say as Anna's mouth is opening but it snaps shut when I continue. "We got an understanding, now? Man to man."

Bryce tips his head, while Anna looks between us. "What's going on?"

"I think so," Bryce says, his voice sheepish.

"You can come to me with questions." Or reservations. Or confusion. But somehow, I think he gets it. Needing to change the subject and check in with him on another topic, I ask, "How did things go with Ryleigh?"

"She flirted with Calvin."

"Damn. It's always the brother," I tease.

"Or the best friend?" Bryce tips up a brow, but his forehead furrows like the movement hurts his entire hungover head.

I make a fist and stab at my heart, but Bryce smiles at me, shaking his head.

"We good here," I point between Anna and Bryce, making certain those two are the ones who have apologized and forgiven.

Bryce looks at his mom again, eyes welling. Maybe a little in contrition. A little in pain. Hangovers suck at any age.

"Don't ever do that again," she warns.

Yeah, probably not a promise he can make her but maybe he can hold off until he's away at college, or better yet, over the legal drinking age.

When did I get so fatherly in my thoughts?

Bryce nods, dipping his head again, and Anna steps forward, bringing him in for a hug. Her son towers her in height and breadth, engulfing her like the giant bear he's going to be. Still, he holds on, letting me see how he's a giant *teddy* bear at heart.

When he's done hugging Anna, he surprises me by stepping over to me, bringing me into a hug as well.

"I'm sorry, man," he whispers to me.

"Hurts like hell, doesn't it," I murmur before pulling back.

"Loving someone you can't have?" The question stops me short, and I suck in air at the punch I feel to my gut.

"I meant a hangover, but yeah, maybe that, too." I glance over his shoulder to see Anna behind her son.

Because while he might approve of me dating his mom, it doesn't mean she's going to love me.

She wanted sex last night.

And one reason I said no is because I want to be more than a warm, willing body to her.

Chapter 34

7 Months Ago
February

Lover's Day

[Anna]

Despite how the New Year started, with Mason rejecting my suggestion to have sex, he's been attentive and affectionate. We spend every night making dinner together, him often insisting on purchasing groceries because I cook. However, he is there beside me, chopping or shredding, or just engaging in conversation about my day. Telling me about his. Lynlee is always present.

Sometimes I see her watching me and offer a small smile. I'm often rewarded with a timid smile in return. She talks more but not much. Mason put her in therapy. His instinct wasn't off although he responded a little late to his suspicions. Lynlee has finally opened up that her mother did purposefully mark her. My heart breaks for the child. A lot has happened for this little girl. The loss of her mother. Gaining her father. A new school. A temporary home.

Mason is still actively looking for a new house although there's no rush.

The more he melts back into our routine, the less I want him to leave.

Sometimes, I catch myself, wondering if it's the companionship I seek. The partnership I crave.

Then Mason kisses me and I know it's so much more.

We don't kiss in front of the kids, although he'll often press a kiss to my neck, just below my ear before leaving the house each night to take Lynlee to the apartment.

In the morning, he greets me in a similar manner when he joins me for coffee, and we get breakfast served and lunches made. Mason takes

Lynlee to kindergarten and Mila to the middle school while Bryce comes with me to the high school each day. Lynlee spends afternoons at either River's or Autumn's, and both eagerly agree she's a little helper with baby stuff even at six years old.

We've embraced this sweet child into all our homes and hearts, hoping one day she'll feel that love and accept us as family.

I don't want to replace her mom. Even if Samantha wasn't the best person, she was still Lynlee's mother, but I want this little girl to realize that not all moms act the way hers did. Most of all, that this mom—*me*—wasn't going anywhere.

I would always be here for her.

+ + +

On Valentine's Day, I'm a little surprised when Mason doesn't ask me out. Not that I needed to go out and celebrate the fabricated holiday, but it's still a special occasion for lovers.

Or were we only kissers?

We rubbed against one another and clung to each other when we had rare occasions to sneak into a dark hallway or down to the den, but we didn't do more.

The wait was a slow burn threatening to incinerate me.

Then I received the most gorgeous bouquet of flowers at the school. The display made a statement and a few coworkers and new teacher friends had questions.

I stumbled through surprised reactions and pleasing smiles. Some would favor a new man in my life. Others would question it.

I pulled up Autumn's advice. I had to stop thinking about Ben's reaction. I had to live for me, for what I wanted.

And I wanted Mason.

When I drove home with the bouquet, Bryce didn't even ask me who they came from. He just gave me a knowing smile.

Once home, I set the flowers on the kitchen island.

"Do you know where Mason is?" I ask Mila, who is sitting at the four-seat, round table in an alcove off the sitting area where she is doing her homework. The late afternoon sunlight is already gone in the depths of winter. Lynlee sits with Mila, working on a math game on a tablet. She's learning quickly despite a lack of parental instruction from Samantha in any form. She practices reading with either me or Mila or Mason nightly, and she's learning her addition and subtraction facts.

"I think he's in the den. He said he had to make a phone call."

I nod, although Mila isn't watching me, and head for the den.

Once inside, I step to Mason, slipping my arms around his chest, hugging him from behind, while he finishes his call. His hand smooths over my arm and his fingers slide between mine. When he finishes, he quickly turns to me.

"Thank you for—" His mouth is crushing mine before I complete my gratitude. Quickly, we heat from the striking of a match to a full-on inferno. My fingers grasp his shirt and his hands are in my hair, fisting it at the nape. Mason is rough while tender. Fierce and intense.

"I've been wanting to kiss you all day," he murmurs at my mouth. "How can I miss you so much each day?"

I don't know and I don't answer him, but I feel the same way.

With my fingers clutched in his dress shirt, and his hands fisted in my hair, his mouth returns to mine. Mason presses me backward until my back hits the wall of shelves. He bends at the knees to line us up and grinds against me.

"God, I want you," he mutters to me, lips never leaving mine.

I want him, too.

He pins me in place with the thickness in his pants, holding me pressed awkwardly against the shelving unit.

"I love your mouth." His gaze fixates on my lips, probably swollen and ripe from the eagerness of his kiss. Then he's back, thrusting his tongue into my mouth, sweeping over mine.

I rock my hips forward, desperate for more of him. Whimpering in need to strip our clothing and settle him between my thighs.

"I thought you said you weren't getting married again." A female voice squeaks.

Mason and I break apart. Stunned by the intrusion, his hand is still in my hair and I'm still holding his shirt. His lower half pins me in place but my leg wrapped around his hips falls.

Mila's voice was watery, matching the sudden tears in her eyes.

Mason releases me with a sharp drop of his hands and a giant step back. With my chest heaving, I reach for the shelf at my back, hanging onto a section that juts out to hold myself upright, struggling to collect my thoughts and calm my libido.

Shit.

"We aren't getting married. We're just . . ." *We're just what?* Kissing? Dry-humping? Winding each other up?

Mila remains frozen. With one hand on the doorknob, the other holds the door jamb and she glares at me with hatred.

For some reason, I glance at Mason. Maybe for support. Maybe for a clue as to how to handle this moment, only Mason is staring at me. His expression incredulous as well, as if he wasn't reciprocating my kisses.

I turn to my daughter.

"Mila." I panic and say, "It's nothing."

Mason sucks in a sharp breath but I don't glance at him. I follow my daughter who rushes from the room, thundering down the hall.

+ + +

Gently, I tap at her bedroom door. "Mila, let me in."

"What's going on?" Bryce steps into the hallway, and because my mortification can't grow any deeper, I tell him the truth.

"Mila caught me kissing Mason."

"Way to go, Mom," Bryce teases, staring at me with eyes that look like his father's. Guilt should hit me harder, but it just doesn't.

I'm not ashamed of kissing Mason.

Maybe a little thrown off because it wasn't how I wanted Mila to learn I was interested in Mason.

Maybe a little embarrassed that I was scaling a man in the den when Ben and I weren't really like that before our kids.

"You really think it's okay?" I question as if my seventeen-year-old has the wisdom to answer me.

"I say do what makes you happy." Bryce smiles at me before his expression sobers a little. "Dad would want that. You to be happy, that is."

"I know. But are you really okay with it being Mason?" Despite all their guy-code talk on New Year's Day, which I didn't understand in the least, I needed to know Bryce was good with me dating. Dating anyone, including Mason.

"Is it weird? A little bit." Bryce stares at me. "But your smile is finally back and I'm thinking that's because of Mason and Lynlee being here."

They are kind of a package deal, but then again, so am I. I have Mila and Bryce to consider most as they are both home with me.

And Bryce is right, my smile has been back. I've felt lighter, happier, having Mason and Lynlee in our lives. My life hasn't been anything like I thought it would be, but I'm glad they are here with us.

"So, any words of advice?" I tip my head at Mila's door.

Bryce steps forward and pounds on his sister's door. "Meme, open up." He uses her childhood nickname in a tone matching Ben's, and I'm startled by the likeness to his father in both his features and his voice.

The door slowly opens, and she sees me. Bryce catches the door before she can close it, and he presses it open further, his strength doubles hers.

"Don't be a brat."

"I'm not a brat," she states, sounding like one.

"Then talk to Mom."

This must be my opening to explain myself, although I don't wish to do it from the hallway. "May I come in?" My hope is showing her respect for her privacy will teach her to respect my decisions. Then again, she's twelve. Life lessons are hard when your dendrites detach, and your hormones wreak havoc.

Mila opens the door a little wider but steps into her room, tossing herself on her bed with her face to the wall.

I take a seat beside her, placing a hand on her lower back. "I'm sorry you saw what you saw, but I'm not sorry for kissing him."

"It's Uncle Mason," she groans. "Isn't there some rule about that?"

"He isn't a blood relative. He was your father's friend." I pause. "He's *my* friend."

Mila flips her head to look at me over her shoulder. "If you tell me he's your special friend, I'm going to puke."

"Excuse me?" I stammer. Who is this child and what possessed her to speak like that?

"Is he your boyfriend?" Disgust fills her voice.

"We're . . . friends."

"Friends who kiss?" Mila gags.

On one hand, I want to applaud my daughter's revulsion. Yes, don't kiss until you are much, much older. On the other hand, if she's talking special friends and vomiting at the thought, she's aware that people who like each other kiss.

"I guess so." I can't fight the smile despite the severity of this conversation. "One day, you'll understand."

"I understand now. You want to kiss him." Her face wrinkles up.

"Then if you understand now, I need you to act like a young woman and not a sulking child. People who like each other kiss each other."

"So, you like him? Like, *like* him like him?" Mila shifts again, twisting her body and sitting upright.

"Yes." The desire to smile once more is a battle I struggle against. I can't help the tingle inside but want to remain firm with Mila.

"Did you know Lorna has a crush on Bryce?" Mila shivers. "She thinks that because they are going to high school next year, he's going to fall in love with her."

I don't point out that Lorna is still young and will likely crush on many more boys.

Mila scoffs. "She's only going to be a freshman. Bryce will be a senior. Plus, we're like cousins now."

"Well, not blood related. Remember? Lorna is Logan's daughter with a different mom. But yes, still family."

"So, they shouldn't be together?"

Oh boy, this is getting complicated. "Well, between you and me, I think Lorna is a little young for Bryce. He's going to be focused on going to college and not interested in someone three years younger than him. But we don't want to hurt Lorna's feelings and tell her Bryce won't ever like her."

"But he won't."

"Actually, we don't know that. Only Bryce knows."

"Hey Bryce," Mila yells.

I cover her mouth. "I don't think this is really a discussion for you and Bryce. And I also don't think it's your business who Bryce or Lorna likes." I give her a warning glare. It isn't her place to decide who likes who or who dates who. "You wouldn't want people telling you who you can and cannot like."

"I don't like anyone." Mila sighs, falling back on her pillow and staring up at the ceiling.

I want to tell her to stay innocent and ignorant of boys until you are in your thirties. However, I chuckle to myself knowing that won't ever be a hard fast rule. I can't stop her from falling in love any more than I can stop myself.

Am I falling in love?

The question isn't one I can answer as I stare down at my frustrated child. One on the verge of being a young adult but not ready to cross that line yet. Next school year will be hard when Lorna is in high school, and Mila will still be in eighth grade. Sadly, I predict a separation in their friendship by age, school building, and boy interests.

"Lorna says that Autumn was in love with her dad when she was a kid. In love with her brother's best friend. So, she thinks it's okay to be in love with her best friend's brother. Since I'm her best friend and that brother is Bryce . . . just *ew*." Mila huffs, staring at the ceiling, still fixated on this issue. "I'm never going to fall in love with someone's brother."

I curl my lips inward, fighting another chuckle. She can't predict the future any better than me, but I'd wager she's going to fall for someone, and he might be someone's brother.

"I don't think you need to worry about that yet," I say, covering her kneecap and giving her a squeeze.

"But you're falling in love with Mason."

I can't keep up with the mind of a twelve-year-old girl, even if I once was one. I don't remember the circling thoughts and confusion about boys and love.

I just know, one day I fell in love.

That boy died when he was a man.

And I'm possibly falling in love again.

"We do like each other. A lot." Was I wrong to hold off on explaining how strongly I felt about Mason? It didn't feel right to declare my emotions to anyone but him first.

Mila nods, falling quiet for a long minute.

"Mila, do you understand?"

"Yeah, we're good." She rolls to her side on her bed, staring up at me. "You're not going anywhere, though, right? Like if you marry him, he'll live with us? Here?"

"Oh baby, where is all this coming from?"

"Remember I told you Penny got a new dad, and now her mom wants to live with him. And Penny's going to go live with her first dad. She has to go to a new school and move into another new house."

"Whoa, whoa, honey." I smooth her hair, brushing it back from her face. "We aren't going anywhere. We're staying right here. No new school. No new house."

Mila nods again, staring up at me. "Okay," she whispers. "After I finish my homework, can we have pizza for dinner? I heard Rosario's is making heart-shaped ones."

The reminder of Valentine's Day has me thinking of the flowers on the island counter and the man who kissed me breathless in the den.

"Heart-shaped pizza it is, my love." I lean down and hug her, knowing that a fabricated holiday for lovers will never top the love between a mother and her children.

Chapter 35

7 Months Ago
February

Girlfriend Day

[Mason]

The momentum of our kiss is lost after Mila interrupts us, although I don't blame Mila for the deflation in my chest. Anna's words popped that bubble.

It's nothing. How often am I going to hear that in reference to our kisses? How much longer will she say such a thing about us? About me?

Feeling as if I am nothing to her, despite the grateful kiss for the gorgeous flowers, I need a breather from all things Anna.

I send her a text.

Gonna take my best girl out for Valentine's Day. Maybe Mila needs some best girl time, too.

I don't expect to hear from Anna right away. She'd been upstairs for a bit before Bryce came down to tell me they were going to be awhile.

"Girl talk." He rolled his eyes and headed for the refrigerator.

Tonight's plan included pizza for the kids and then a late dinner for Anna and me, with steak and wine. I didn't think she'd want to go out, but we could celebrate in.

Then again, what were we celebrating? Some bullshit holiday proclaiming lovers appreciate one another? Shouldn't lovers do that every day?

However, Anna and I weren't officially lovers. We weren't officially anything.

It's nothing.

I was just a guest in her garage apartment. Deep down, I knew I meant more than that to Anna, but I still didn't know *what* I meant to her. Who was I to her?

Instead of thinking about Anna, I took Lynlee out.

Rosario's was chaos as they featured a special heart-shaped pizza for the night. Most of the customers were families, not couples on dates, and I did my best to engage my current date.

"Do you like your new school?" I prod.

Lynlee is a quiet child. Sometimes I blame myself as I just don't know what to say to her. Anna is so good at parenting.

Lynlee shrugs.

"Tell me about your teacher."

"She's pretty and I like when she reads stories and does different voices."

Offering her a smile, I say, "That is good. What's your favorite part of the day in school?"

She shrugs again as she draws pictures on the children's menu. I know she likes learning her letters and doing projects that help kids reinforce what a letter is and how they look.

"What are you drawing?"

"Today we learned about the letter V. The bottom of a heart is shaped like a V." Lynlee draws one to prove her point. "Miss Kelsey says that families mean love no matter what shape or size your family is."

Puzzled by this response, I ask, "What did she mean by no matter what size or shape?"

"Some families have a mommy and a daddy, but some families only have one. A mom or a dad. And some families have two mommies or two daddies. And some even have two mommies *and* two daddies."

Trying to calculate that out in my head, I assume the teacher means stepparents.

"And some people might live with grandparents, but no one in my class does. Although one girl lives with her aunt."

"Ah." I swallow a question I've been wanting to ask wondering how to ask. How would Lynlee feel about another mom?

"What would you think if Daddy ever married? If you had another mom."

Lynlee looks up at me, eyes wide. "I miss Mommy."

"I know, baby girl." I reach out for her hand and cover it. "And no one else will ever be your mom." *Thank God.* "But what if I married a woman? She'd be one of those two mommies that some of your friends have."

"I don't want two mommies, though," Lynlee admits as panic settles into her voice. Something in me wonders if her fear isn't so much me marrying but a repeat of the mother she had, even if she misses Samantha. Also, realizing I'm botching up what I'm trying to ask I decide to let it rest. Maybe I'll talk to Lynlee's therapist about this topic.

I glance down at the paper before Lynlee and notice she's drawn three people and working on a fourth.

"Who are you drawing?"

"That's you." She points at a stick figure with some crazy curly hair.

"And this is me." A shorter figure with straight hair that comes to the edge of the too-large head.

"And this is Anna." The image is proportionate to the copy of me but with long wavy hair.

Lynlee is in the middle of the picture, and Anna and I are apparently holding her hands.

"And who are you drawing next?"

"Mila will be here." Lynlee points to the person she's started next to Anna. "And Bryce will go over here." Lynlee taps at the empty space next to my stick person.

"Why there?" I'm only curious.

"Boys on one side. Girls on the other. It's how we line up to walk in the hallway."

She pauses concentrating on her drawing a second. "Love starts with the same letter as my name, Miss Kelsey told me, and love also has the letter V inside it. A heart in the word."

I can't seem to take my eyes off her drawing. "Anna has one more boy in her family. Remember Calvin? He has dark hair and went back to college."

Lynlee pauses a second. "We're all part of Anna's family."

The comment hits me hard and I sit back, blinking at my child. "Who told you that?"

"Anna. She said that even though my mommy isn't here anymore I can go to her for anything. She's family."

"Is that why you are drawing all of us together?" Lynlee has added Bryce with an extra-large head, making him bigger in size than me. He is as tall as I am and filling out in width, but he isn't that giant. Calvin is next and she's making him as big as Bryce.

Lynlee nods. "Families come in all shapes and sizes," she repeats what her teacher told her.

For the longest time, I just stare at the image, imagining us as a blended family. One full of love that starts with the same letter as Lynlee's name and includes the letter V which looks like a heart.

+ + +

Stirred by Lynlee's drawing, I sit on the couch in the garage apartment after she's in bed. The picture is displayed with pride on our refrigerator where Lynlee hung it with magnets Anna gave her.

Sipping from a glass of scotch, I note that I'm spending my Valentine's night in much the same way I did a year ago. Alone.

When a soft knock comes to the door of the apartment, I shouldn't be shocked, but I am surprised.

"May I come in?" Anna asks when I open the door.

I could snark that it's her home. The main house. The land. The apartment. This is her place. I'm a guest, but I bite my tongue and tip my head.

Anna enters, removes her coat and steps out of her boots. Guess she's staying a bit.

My head space is still clouded by Lynlee's words and Anna's earlier reaction. I drop back down to the couch and stare at the blank television set. Purposely avoiding turning on any lamps, I'd been sitting in the dimly-lit room.

"I'm sorry about earlier," Anna begins.

"It was nothing. Like you said." I reach for my glass and take another drink.

"Mason, you know I didn't mean that."

"Do I?" I turn to her. "Where do we stand, Anna? What are we doing with each other?"

"We're enjoying each other." She hesitates, not sounding convinced herself.

"Are you telling me or trying to convince yourself?"

Her back stiffens, forcing her to sit straighter on the other couch. We're four feet apart and miles away from one another.

"I like being with you," she admits. "My reaction to Mila walking in on us was just a reaction. I didn't know what to say at first."

The element of surprise had been the case with Mila's appearance and her outrage.

You said you weren't getting married again.

Out of the mouths of babes. How Mila jumped to marriage from a clandestine kiss is beyond me. But isn't that my end with Anna? I didn't want a fling with her.

Then there was Anna's response.

We aren't getting married. We're . . . Her pause seemed to say it all.

We're enjoying each other as she'd just said. The explanation sounds weak. Anna and I are clearly not on the same page.

"You could have said we are together. Dating." I stare at her.

Anna sighs. "Are we dating? I don't know a thing about modern dating. I take my cues from the kids who mention things like 'talking to someone' or 'hanging out with someone' but dating is a commitment that doesn't get said. And when it does, it's all official-like with words like will you be my girlfriend?" Anna wrinkles her nose. "Who really asks that?"

Priding myself on the modern lingo of dating, so I don't slip up and say something I shouldn't, I know exactly who asks questions like *will you be my girlfriend?* Kids. People under thirty act this way.

Of anyone I know, Anna should recognize commitment. She was married for almost twenty years. Plus, *I've* been here for her.

However, maybe she needs to hear it from me.

"Will you be my girlfriend?" There's an undertone of mockery in my question until a sweet flush rushes up Anna's skin. Her lids coyishly lower and she licks her lips.

My gut reaction says: I made her blush.

The palpitations in my heart say: I made her blush.

Anna did need to hear from me what I wanted and what she means to me.

Slowly, she stands and closes the distance between us. She steps between my knees and takes the glass from my hands, towering over me just a moment before slipping herself into the space between the low table and the couch before me.

With her hands on my chest, and her on her knees, she looks up at me, eyes wide and hopeful.

"Yes. I'd like to be considered your girlfriend."

Titling my head, I need clarification. "Are you a secret girlfriend?"

Anna lightly chuckles. "I think that cat is out of the bag, so to speak. I don't think I'll be running around telling everyone I have a boyfriend, but the kids know we are involved with each other."

"And how did that go over?" I already witnessed Mila's reaction.

"The boys approve. Mila will get there. She's twelve." Anna shakes her head, dismissive, like the age explains it all.

"I'm not going to survive Lynlee as a teenager."

"Yes, you will," Anna assures me, fingers toying with my shirt.

Will she still be my girlfriend in seven years when Lynlee hits her teens?

It isn't a question I ask because Anna's fingers are unbuttoning the bottom buttons of my shirt. Then she's pressing the material upward and lowering her head to press kisses to my abdomen. The muscles jump and flinch at the caress of her lips and soft suction from her mouth. Her tongue drags along my waistline while her fingers work at my belt.

"Anna." I comb through her hair. "What are you doing?"

"Now that I'm your girlfriend, I think we should take our relationship to a new level."

"Are we skipping some steps?" Are we hopping from make-out sessions to marriage?

"I was just thinking we could round a few bases."

With her long lap along my abs, my dick leaps in my pants. Who is this seductress and where has she come from?

With my belt unbuckled and my pants unzipped, Anna reaches for the waistband of my jeans, but I scoop forward and capture her lips. The kiss is hungry and needy. Sweeping into her mouth with my tongue, we tangle with apology and anticipation.

Anna is my girlfriend.

I don't even know what that means. Nothing will be different from what it's been, but still, there's a shift in her. In us.

Sliding my hands to her ass, I tug her upward and she's working on straddling me when I stand. She squeaks as her hands grip my shoulders and her legs wrap around my waist.

"What are you doing?" she chuckles before I press a quick kiss to her lips.

"Lynlee's in the next room. Let's take this to my room."

"Okay." There's a shakiness to her voice, in her acceptance.

I'm still not having sex with her. Not with apologies lingering and a new label between us. But there are other things I want to do to her and tonight we need some make-up time.

Once we enter my bedroom, I sit on the edge of the bed with Anna straddling over me. Our mouths connect, desperate and eager for more. When I slide my hands up Anna's sides, she pulls back and slips off my lap.

"Where are you going, beautiful?"

"I like when you call me that," she whispers as she stands before me, spreading my knees to place her body between my legs.

"You are incredible to look at." With my palms on her belly, I push her sweater upward and press kisses to her stomach like she did to mine in the living room.

"I don't always feel beautiful," she whispers.

My head snaps upward. While my fingers remain curled into her sweater and exposing her skin to me, I watch as her hand moves to her stomach, fingers spreading to cover her flesh.

"Why not?" Puzzled, I can't imagine why she wouldn't feel attractive.

"I'm not . . ." She glances to the side.

I take her chin in my fingers. "Not what?"

"Young. Thin. Without marks of bearing children." The words come out in a frustrated rush.

"Are you kidding me?" I snap. "You're fucking gorgeous. I love that you had kids. It's made you stunning in a new way." I release her chin and run a fingertip over her belly. "I love every mark and line." My voice drops, awed at the wonders of motherhood.

"Your heart is astonishing. Your intelligence sexy and your compassion mesmerizing. You're beautiful in so many ways, shapes and forms, Anna. Do not think for one second that I'm not tempted by the full package of you." I pause from tracing her stomach and look directly into her eyes. "You're a gift I never expected to receive.".

Her breath hitches. "But I'm not like other—"

"Just stop," I growl, reaching up for her chin again. "Stop right there before you piss me off."

"But—"

"Anna. Get on your knees. I'm going to show you what you do for me."

She drops to her knees with a thud, and my dick jumps at how quickly she responded to my command. Reaching for the back of my collar, I tug my dress shirt over my head, putting my bare chest on display. Anna's hands immediately stroke my skin, but I catch her wrists, setting her arms to her sides.

"Not yet, sweetheart." I lower my pants, taking down my briefs to expose how hard she makes me, how badly I want her. "This is what you do to me. This is all for you. You make me crave you. You drive me mad." Leaning back on one arm, I grip my dick and stroke upward once on the heavy length.

Anna kneels upward and pushes my hand away, wrapping her own fingers around my length and squeezing.

"That's right, sweetheart. Don't be afraid to grip me harder." I cover her hand with mine, guiding her to be rougher with me. Her eyes spark, empowerment filling them. Need building. She licks her lips and I groan.

Leaning forward, she kisses the tip of my dick and my hips buck, wanting more. Her tongue hesitantly comes out, licking around the crown. My hand combs back her hair again, not wanting to miss a moment of watching her enjoy my cock.

"Don't tease me, beautiful. Take what you want from me." With that, Anna opens and draws me deep into the warmth of her mouth. My own lips fall open, but I stay silent, stunned at the pleasure, the heat, the heaven of being inside Anna's sweet mouth. She sucks hard and long, dragging her lips to the tip before opening wide again and taking me to the back of her throat.

"Fuck, baby." I groan, eyes closing at the attention this woman lays on me. The suction. The draw. Her mouth seems starving, and I'm thrilled she's hungry for me.

For this first time, I'll be too quick. Too much build up. Too much time has passed.

"Anna, if you don't like—" I catch my breath as her teeth drag along my length with just the right amount of pressure. "I'm going to come down that pretty throat unless you pull back."

The comment spears her onward, taking me harder, deeper, faster. Her head bobs. Her mouth salivates and then I'm pulsing into her, holding her hair back and staring at the marvel of Anna on her knees before me.

I'm hardly finished when I scoop my hands under her arms and pull her off me. Lifting her upward, I toss her to her back on the bed and shift positions with her. I'm on my knees at the side of the bed, fumbling with her jeans and tugging them off her legs.

My palms skim up her ankles, over her shins and cup her kneecaps. Then I'm spreading her legs wide and pulling her to the edge of the bed. Anna pops up on her elbows, eyes wild and watching me as I press kisses to her inner thighs, working my way higher until my nose runs over the slip of fabric covering her.

"Heaven," I whisper to her before pressing a kiss to her covered center. I glance up at her face, meeting her eyes. God, I love this woman, but we aren't there yet. We aren't tossing out emotions, but we have labels on who we are.

She is mine.

And I can finally taste her.

Wasting no time, I remove her underwear, keeping my eyes on hers, before bowing between her legs. Still glancing up at her, my tongue comes forward and I swipe the wet seam of her.

Her eyes rolls closed and her head tips back. "Mason," she moans.

"That's me, baby. I'm going to take care of you." I'm going to love you. I'm going to show you how beautiful you are.

With my tongue, I lap her folds until her soft pleas beg for more. Then I latch onto her clit and suck hard, savoring her essence and drinking in each sigh of desire from her. My fingers join the moment, dipping into her heat, drenched in her warmth. Her legs spread wider. Her heels come to my shoulders, and she falls to her back on the bed, writhing while digging her fingers into my hair, tugging at the curls.

"Oh God. Mason. It's been . . . Never like this . . ." The stammering goes on as her body responds to me, dripping with the tell of how turned on she is, how much she wants this, how much she wants me.

With a hitch of her breath, I know she's close, and I slide two fingers into her, opening her up for me while my tongue and mouth continue to work that point of pleasure.

She's so sweet. So wet. So eager for more.

And when I nip her clit, she breaks. Legs snap together, holding my head between her thighs. Her fingers curl into my hair, tugging at the ends, keeping me in place as I take every drop, and sigh, and cry of my name, until her legs fall open and her fingers loosen.

"Oh God," she murmurs as I look at her, finding her blinking, not with tears but with wonder. She shifts to glance at me, still between her spread knees, blowing warm air at her sensitive center. "That was incredible."

"Yeah?" I tease, witnessing a glow on her face and smile slowly curl her lips.

"Yeah."

"Might need to do that again."

She softly chuckles, rolling her head on the bed, staring up at the ceiling. "Might be ready sooner than you think."

"Oh yeah?" I exhale, forcing my breath to meet her pretty pink swollen flesh.

"Yeah." She laughs, sheepish but not shy.

And I want her to know again how beautiful she is to me, so I start the process all over again with tongue and lips and fingers.

Chapter 36

7 Months Ago
February

Father-Daughter Ritual

[Mason]

When I enter the house, a week after Valentine's Day, Anna is surprised to see me dressed in a suit with Lynlee beside me.

"What's going on?" She anxiously chuckles, taking in my attire before smiling down at Lynlee. "You look beautiful," she says to my girl.

Lynlee is wearing a puffy yellow princess dress, per her specifications, which was nearly impossible to find in the middle of winter. When Anna twirls her finger for Lynlee to show her everything, my daughter spins in a circle. Removing her winter jacket like a superstar model, she shows off for Anna who claps her hands together. "Spectacular."

Lynlee smiles a rare full smile at Anna.

"I'm here for Mila. The father-daughter dance."

Anna looks up at me. "I didn't think you two were going. *Mila* said you weren't going." Her face reads both puzzled and concerned.

"We're going." I'd bought the tickets for the annual fundraiser a while back, intending to take Mila *and* Lynlee.

Anna steps back in the entry way and calls up the staircase. "Mila, Mason is here for you."

A door opens upstairs, and soft feet cross the floor before Mila leans over the railing. "I told you I wasn't going." She pouts as she glares at her mother, not giving me a second look. Mila has been suspiciously not around the past week.

"I don't know why she's acting like this." Anna turns to me, eyes concerned.

Seems Mila is holding a grudge over me kissing her mother.

"Do you have other plans?" I ask Mila, staring up at her as she grips the railing half a flight above me.

"She doesn't," Anna mutters beside me before staring pointedly at her youngest child.

"Mind if we chat for a second?"

Anna turns back to me at the sound of my voice, and I tip my head toward Mila.

She shakes her head, eyes full of concern before she holds out a hand for Lynlee. "Let's go take your picture in that beautiful dress."

As they walk toward the kitchen, I take the stairs two at a time before stopping a few steps lower than Mila. We're eye level when I ask, "What's going on?"

"I don't want to go." Her tone is defiant but her lower lip trembles.

"Why not?"

"I just don't." Mila crosses her arms, again defensive but the slump of her shoulders suggests something otherwise.

"Talk to me, sweetheart."

Mila turns her head to the side and then turns back, giving me a look that mirrors Ben's. "You kissed my mom."

"I know." I exhale. "I won't apologize for that, though, Mila. I like your mom. A lot." I love her but I don't think confessing my emotions to Mila before Anna is on board the love train is a good idea. "You'll get that when you're older," I add.

"Everyone says that to me, like I don't understand. I'm twelve. Not a child." Her voice suggests she's very much still a kid, but I'll play along.

"Okay, as a grown up then, tell me what's wrong with kissing your mom and why you really don't want to go to the dance?" I'm not letting her off the hook with a lame excuse of she doesn't want to attend. We've enjoyed the past two years, and Lorna and Logan are going again.

"It's a *father*-daughter dance. You aren't my dad," she whispers, gaze lowered to her feet where her toe is trying to dig into the wooden stair. "And you have Lynlee."

Is she jealous of my daughter? And what about what she said regarding Ben?

"You're right. I'm not your dad."

Mila's head pops up.

"Your dad was a great man. I can never be him." No matter how hard I tried, if I tried, I'd never be Ben. "I'll never be half the man he was." I exhale, releasing the frustration and the honesty. "And I'm not certain I'll even be a good dad to Lynlee."

Mila's eyes widen. Her mouth falls open but then clamps shut.

"So, here's the deal. I need help. Because you had a great dad and I'm trying to learn how to be at least a good one. And since you're grown up, you could teach me. You could give me pointers and advice, and check in on me, see how I'm doing. For Lynlee. Being that she's a girl and you're . . . a young lady, and I want to be a good girl dad."

Mila's face turns a sweet pink, and she avoids my gaze again.

"I'd really like you to go to the dance with us. You can roll your eyes with Lynlee when I do something stupid and scowl at me if I embarrass both of you." I pause, before offering her more truth. "I didn't have a great dad myself, Mila. Your dad was my example of good parenting and fatherhood. He was trying to teach me how to be better when he passed away. Now, the people I count on to continue his lessons are you and Bryce and Calvin."

Mila sniffs and swipes at the side of her nose where a tear softly streams. Another tear leaks from her other eye.

"What do you say, kiddo?" I cough. "I mean, young lady."

With a wet chuckle, she says, "I'll go if you don't call me young lady."

"You got it, teen spirit." Mila rolls her eyes and I smile. "There's my girl." She laughs a little harder and I hold out my hand. "Deal?"

Mila stares at the hand a second and then surprises me by tossing her arms around me, nearly knocking me down the stairs in surprise. But I catch her, like I always will when she leaps, and hug her hard.

"I just miss him," Mila mutters into my neck.

"I know, baby. Me too."

I miss Ben every day and if I could bring him back, restore him to life to save them all from heartbreak, I'd smash my own heart to do it for them.

+ + +

Mila asks me to give her a few minutes and she races up the stairs to her room to change. I swipe two hands down my face, scrubbing off the conversation. As I descend the staircase, Anna stands near the bottom, just off to the side of the banister.

"Were you listening?" I ask.

"I didn't mean to." She shrugs in a manner so similar to her daughter. Or maybe it's that Mila is a miniature of Anna.

"How'd I do?" I tip my head toward the upper landing.

"You were perfect," Anna whispers. Her own eyes glisten but she fights back the tears. She steps up to me and slips her arms around my waist, and I hug her as tight as I hugged her daughter.

I'm here to take care of all my girls.

As we stand there hugging, the front door shoots open and Calvin rushes in.

"I made it," he blurts, eyeing his mother still standing in my embrace. He's wearing a tie and a dress shirt with nice pants and a leather jacket over the ensemble.

"Calvin, honey, what are you doing here?" Anna asks, stepping toward him.

"Mila told me she wasn't going to the dance." He pauses, eyeing me standing there, dressed myself in a suit, minus a tie. "But you're here." A question of curiosity lingers in his voice.

"I'm here." For Mila. For him. For Bryce who is absent. And for Anna.

"Did you come home to take Mila to the dance?" Anna's brows lift in surprise as her hands rub up Calvin's arms.

"I did. I didn't want her not going. I know it's father-daughter, but I figured a big brother could stand in." Calvin glances at me again, a puzzled expression still on his face. "Unless you *are* taking her."

"How about if we all go? You, Mila, Lynlee, and me."

"Is that what a double date is?" Mila asks as she walks down the stairs, and we all turn. She's changed into a deep blue dress and tucked her hair up in a twist. It still looks like a messy bun with strands hanging out here and there, but that's a look.

"Mila." Anna exhales. "You look beautiful."

Mila nears the base of the staircase wearing black Chucks and I smile to myself. She has a style all her own and I'm proud of her. She's a good kid who's testing the waters of being a teenager and I'll have a lot to learn from her as I raise Lynlee.

"So, double date?" Mila asks, hitching a brow. Like a light switch flipped, she's a new person in her dress and a smile.

Will I survive a teenage daughter?

I look to Calvin, who nods. "You look pretty, Meme." He winks at her.

"I almost forgot." I step toward the hall table where I set the corsage and open the package. "For your wrist."

Mila cautiously removes the flowers as if they're precious gems and not a few tea roses on elastic.

"I didn't get you a flower." Mila glances up at me, before guiltily looking at her mother.

"I can help with that," Anna offers and tips her head, so we follow her to the kitchen. The Valentine flowers from a week ago have dwindled down to a few still holding onto their luster. Anna pulls two flowers from the vase, snips off the long stems and rustled around in a drawer before pulling out a few pins.

"Someone sent you flowers?" Calvin asks.

"Mason gave them to me for Valentine's Day." Anna works at securing a flower to her son's shirt while Calvin glances down at her and then looks at me.

Our gazes hold a second before he says, "Smooth move." He turns to his mother. "That was nice."

"It *was* nice," she says, stepping over to me and holding my lapel to attach the impromptu boutonniere. Her eyes meet mine and she offers me a timid smile. I want to cup her face and kiss her senseless, but we have an audience and I already feel all eyes on us.

"Okay. Pictures," Anna announces, stepping away from me after one last look, and swiping her hand down my chest, which causes my heart to hammer and another part of me to spring to life.

We gather and pose in various combinations. Anna's home is filled with pictures of her kids throughout the years with her and Ben. I especially like one of the five of them, laughing at something while they should have collectively been looking at the camera. It's a good reminder of them as a family. A moment only they remember and freezes a moment that caused their laughter. Like a private family joke.

One I'll never share with them.

I'd like to make my own memories. A family of different shapes and sizes like Lynlee mentioned only a week ago.

Some days I think we'll get there.

Other times I'm still not certain.

Mila's behavior tonight is an example of the rocky road still before us. A highway I need to navigate or reluctantly take an off-ramp. Only, I have no plans to exit this journey.

"You okay?" Anna's voice breaks into my thoughts as Mila retrieves her jacket and Calvin helps Lynlee back into hers.

"Yeah, I'm good."

"You sure?" Anna's brows hitch and she bites her lower lip.

Using my thumb to tug that mouth I want to kiss free from her teeth, I nod. "Definitely."

I won't be making any detours. I only have one destination with this woman.

"Save me a dance in the kitchen later?" I lean closer to her, inhaling her scent.

"Definitely," she repeats my word, fighting a large grin.

And I realize I'm already making new memories with her. For us.

Chapter 37

4 Months Ago
May

First Date

[Anna]

February blew into March with an all-out blizzard and by the end of the month I'd had enough of winter. The kids and I went to visit Ruth, Ben's mother, in Florida during our spring break. Mason took Lynlee to his mother's place in another part of Florida.

April escaped me as sporting practices ramped up and the end of the school year began. Bryce plays baseball. Mila has softball, and Lynlee is in dance classes and swimming lessons.

"We need to go out," Mason says one night in May, anxiously digging his fingers into his hair.

"I'd love to go out, but Mila has practice." I'm team mom this year.

Mason groans. "This weekend?"

"Jenna is coming to visit." In addition to everything else, after my brother proposed to Jenna, he asked me to help them plan their wedding. They are getting married this coming August at Lakeside Cottage. The romantic in my brother wanted them to take their vows where their love began. Somehow, I've become the wedding coordinator.

Mason steps up to me as I stand between the kitchen island and the sink cabinet. He cups my face, kissing me hard and long.

"We need time for us." He stares at me, pleading with me. An anxious excitement fills his eyes. "And it's your birthday in a few days."

We've spent months of me sneaking into his bedroom above the garage after long days of work and shuffling around kid activities. I'm not complaining about the private attention Mason gives my body, but I wouldn't mind an actual date where I can feel like an adult with a life outside of only the kids around us.

I'm happy where our relationship stands but I also feel like we are in a holding pattern. There isn't a rush for more, but we seem stuck in a stagnant pause. Mason is affectionate. We kiss often. We touch and taste when we are alone, but we haven't had sex.

I'm starting to think we never will.

Mason and I work well together—a team—reminding me of the days when Ben was sick, but I wouldn't mind us feeling more like a couple.

A date sounds wonderful.

"Friday?" I question.

"Friday." His answer is punctuated with another searing kiss.

+ + +

When Friday arrives, Mason takes Lynlee to Logan's so Lorna can babysit. Mila is there as well, and the older girls plan a sleepover. With an empty house, it's tempting to want to stay in and ask Mason to ravish me, but his excitement about a date didn't go unnoticed.

He wants to woo me.

When he returns from dropping off Lynlee, I meet him on the front stoop like it's a first date. In many ways, it is.

Mason exits his SUV and stumbles when he looks at me. "You're breathtaking."

I'm wearing a strapless dress with a loose skirt below the waist. I haven't worn something like this in a long, long time and I'm surprised this dress still fits. I'm a little breathless in it, but I didn't want to dress in my typical teacher attire or mom clothes. Tonight feels special.

"You look rather yummy yourself."

Wearing a white linen shirt and navy-blue linen pants with flip-flops, Mason is casual beach night out personified. His hair has that perfect yet wayward curl to it and his facial scruff is trimmed around his mouth. A tinge of red creeps over his cheeks at my compliment.

He glances down at my feet and smiles. I'm wearing flat sandals, matching the relaxed look of his footwear. The temperature is warming up with some days actually hot. The evenings can still be cool but pleasant and this night hints that summer is around the corner.

Mason opens the passenger door for me and holds out a hand. He stops me just short of entering the vehicle. "I just want to say thank you, in case I forget later."

My brows pinch. "Thank you? For what?"

"For going out with me."

His name is a soft caress on my lips. He almost appears . . . nervous.

"I'm honored." I don't want to even imagine the number of women he's gone out with in the past or the types of dates he's been on, but I am flattered by how much he wants to do this tonight.

He gives me a quick kiss and then lightly presses my lower back to help me into the SUV.

When we arrive at the marina in town, I'm a little surprised. He doesn't own a boat, but he guides me down a dock and boards a small cruiser.

"Whose is this?" I ask as he reaches for me, grips my hips and lifts me.

"A friend's."

I scoff at the vagueness of his answer, but Mason is already settling in behind the steering wheel and starting the engine. The boat isn't a speedboat or a classic wooden one. In my limited boat knowledge, it's simply a boat with space for sleeping and a kitchenette below deck. The bow is long and flat over the cabin. Behind the captain's bench is a sitting area.

Mason pats the bench seat, and I climb up next to him. He navigates out of the marina and across the open water of the lake. We don't talk as he pilots us at a top speed across the flat, early evening water. The sun will start setting soon. The moon is predicted to be full tonight. The air is chilly at this speed, but I snuggle next to Mason, wrapping my arms around him as we streak over the lake.

The wind whips through my hair. So much for the loose curls I attempted. Eventually, I gather the wild strains into a ponytail. Mason reaches over and wraps the collected hair around his fist, giving it a playful tug.

"About twenty minutes and we'll be there."

"Where?" I shout over the roar of the engine.

Mason only smiles.

When Mason slows the boat, and we pull into a small cove, he checks some dials and cuts the engine, dropping the anchor.

"Where are we?" I ask, unfamiliar with this particular area while it looks like a typical Michigan shoreline. One marked by soft, rippling lake water, a curtain of green trees in various shades, and a lazy sun dropping in the sky.

My skin hums. The color of everything seems brighter, the textures more defined.

"Nowhere special," Mason states. His twinkling eyes hint his words are clearly a lie.

"*What* are we doing here?" Curiosity has the best of me. I didn't bring a bathing suit although the lake temperature would still be extremely cold, and at this time of night, nearly freezing.

"Having a picnic."

Mason presses at my hip so I'll slide off the bench seat. He drops below deck but quickly returns with a picnic basket and a blanket.

"Let me take this up front first and then I'll come back for you." He kicks off his flip flops and easily climbs up on the narrow ledge between the windshield and the front of the boat. He flicks the blanket outward, spreading it flat, and sets the basket down then returns for me.

Holding out his hand, he helps me upward after I kick off my sandals. He points out where to grab to traipse the thin edge to the bow of the boat. Guiding me with a hand on my hip, we reach the deck, and Mason sits. I follow.

The air is crisp with the slightest of chill but my skin is on fire. I don't think I've ever been in a more romantic setting, and I've definitely never had an evening picnic on a boat.

Mason pulls a bottle of wine from the basket, already opened, and pours each of us a glass.

He holds up his. "To first dates and fresh starts."

"I like that." I smile before lifting the glass and taking a sip. "This is good."

"Michigan wine. Nothing like it." He sips as well, and we sit in comfortable silence for a moment. The lull of the boat is relaxing. The quiet around us calming.

"What is this place?"

"There's a sandbar beneath us. It's a destination for boaters, but apparently, not tonight." Mason chuckles as he looks around us.

"So you hadn't planned for us to be in seclusion."

"No plan. Just hope." He eyes me over the rim of his glass as he takes another sip of wine.

"What do you hope for?" My voice lowers as if someone else might hear my question.

"Lots of things." He arches a brow as I watch him.

I chuckle as I prompt him to explain. "Like . . ."

"I hope you enjoy the night."

"So far, it's lovely."

"You're lovely." He takes another drink of his wine as he casually leans on one elbow, holding his upper body upright while his long legs stretch before him, crossing at the ankles. He watches me.

"This feels . . . romantic for a first date." The wine. The picnic. The sunset.

"I want to impress you."

I smile. "I'm impressed." With him and how different he is than I'd originally thought. With how far he's come with his child. With how supportive he's been of me.

"Tell me something you've never told anyone," I challenge.

Mason tips his head, eyeing me over his shoulder. "Seeing as you know my biggest secret . . . the night we first kissed—"

"Mason," I warn, not wanting to bring up things we haven't ever discussed and shouldn't really. It was a moment of weakness at a difficult time.

"The truth is, I didn't want to stop that night."

I lower my eyes, staring at my glass of wine. "It wasn't appropriate," I state, thinking back to the passion and shame of that night.

"It wasn't good timing," Mason clarifies. "And I shouldn't have taken advantage of the situation."

I clear my throat. "You didn't take advantage of me." I was just as guilty that night. Just as needy.

"This isn't really first date conversation," I say, uncomfortable with the building tension and the reminders of that evening. How I'm still mortified that I'd called him Ben.

Mason softly chuckles. "I wouldn't know what first date conversation is."

"You've been on first dates," I tease. Hasn't he? He's dated. I'm certain he has.

But Mason stares at me and understanding becomes clear. This is why tonight is so important to him. He hasn't had first dates or at least not many over the years. He's met random women in bars and gone home with them, but he didn't date them.

"I don't know what's first date material either." I've only had one first date, and that night led to the ultimate commitment. I married the man twenty years ago.

Mason looks down at the wine glass in his hands. "Let's agree that we've made some missteps, but we're past that now." He glances up at me, hopeful that we've moved on from that night almost two years ago.

"I would hope so." I smile, knowing we are now. He lives in the garage apartment. We share incredible stolen moments of intimacy and almost all our days collaborating together with our children.

"To letting go," I raise my glass in a second toast and Mason straightens, his glass still lowered to his leg.

"What?" he whispers.

"Let go?" I question, lowering my voice as well.

Without responding to my toast, Mason sets his glass aside and takes mine from me. Then he tips up my chin and kisses me long and slow. Soft sips and teasing laps. No tongue or teeth or eagerness. He's kissing me like he wants to memorize my mouth, imprint it on his forever.

Strangely, I feel the same way.

When he pulls back, his blue eyes gleam. The color I once thought was wrong feels right, blanketing me in the comfort the shade represents.

Mason shifts, pulling out items for our meal. I'm surprised to find an entire charcuterie board, artfully arranged with meats and cheeses, fruits and olives, which leads us to a discussion about olives. I like the black ones. He likes kalamata.

There's an ease to being with Mason because we have known one another for twenty-five years, but there is also so much I don't know about him.

I've told my kids over the years that not knowing someone is what dating is for. It's the time to learn about someone, develop feelings, or not, about another person. It's also the time to experiment. Like trying a person on to see if he or she fits you.

Mason fits me.

We agree to disagree on which olives are better until he slips one in my mouth. I hesitantly chew, disliking the flavor but Mason is quick to rescue me, his mouth distracting me from the lingering taste.

After a generous sip of wine once we stop kissing, Mason moves the charcuterie board to the side, and I scoot closer to him. He lies back on the deck, and I tuck into his side.

One thing I've missed in our nights together is we don't spend the night together. We make out like randy teens and end up in his bedroom, touching and tasting, learning about one another, but I don't linger. Once we finish, he holds me until I'm sleepy and realize I need to go home. Other nights, time is our constraint. We know we only have an hour with my kids gone and Lynlee in bed, so we rush to cross a line. One building throughout the day.

With Mason, I've discovered many things about myself and sex.

I've always been pleased with it, but Mason is an entirely new level of satisfaction. The things he does to me. The way I react. Those years of experience and the multitude of women he's been with give him an advantage over me. He's a master and I'm a mere student.

"I can feel you thinking," Mason murmurs, turning to place a kiss on my forehead. With my head on his shoulder and my arm over his chest, I'm as close as I can get to him.

But I'd like to be closer.

"I'm impressed," I repeat as I said earlier. Mason shifts so I look up at him. "With everything you've done for me and the kids. With Ben." I swallow around the mention of him. "With the way you are with Lynlee."

Mason's brows pinch.

"With tonight. This moment. You. I'm impressed."

"Anna," he whispers, twisting his body so we face one another, resting on our sides. His finger skims the edge of my face, brushing back hair that's come loose from my ponytail. He leans forward and kisses me, soft and tender. Like a whisper of the wind or grains of sand scattering over the beach, the touch is nothing more than subtle sips. When he pulls back, he traces down my nose and around my eyes. Over my lips and along my chin.

Memorizing me again. Memorializing this moment.

I don't want to forget a single second myself.

And this night, this moment, feels monumental.

"Mason." I swallow hard, then plunge on. "Make love to me."

Chapter 38

4 Months Ago
May

Birthday Presents

[Mason]

Make love to me.

I'd promised myself I'd be good. I wouldn't push or do anything other than kiss her, maybe taste her, but hearing her say this . . .

Pressing on her shoulder, I guide her to her back, peppering her face with more kisses. I move over her chin and along her neck, blazing a trail of kisses to her bare shoulder. Once there, I roll her again, so I can kiss her upper back until I reach the zipper of her dress.

She wore this strapless dress that plumps up her breasts and has given me a delicious view of her skin. Taking my time, I unzip the dress, kissing along her spine as each vertebra is exposed. She isn't wearing a bra. Pushing open the material, I rub my hand along her back a few times and she shivers.

"Cold?" I whisper, catching her eyes.

"Nervous," she admits.

"I'd never hurt you, sweetheart."

"I know." Her gaze holds on mine, willing me to take her acceptance. She knows.

"Your body is everything." She is everything to me.

She timidly smiles at me. The side of her face rests on the blanket and I roll her to her back once more, tugging the dress down to expose her to me.

Her nipples are hard pebbles in the cool evening air. Her breasts are plump swells that I've sucked on and nipped. We've been naked before but tonight feels different.

Raw. Exposing. Real.

This is it. I'm finally going to make love to Anna.

And I'm a nervous wreck. I don't know how to go slow. I don't know how to be gentle when I simply want to ravish her, take her, imprint myself inside her.

Still, I take my time, brushing my fingertips along her collarbone and down the center of her body, swirling around her heavy breasts before pinching the nipples.

Anna arches her back, watching me until the pleasure takes over and her lids lower. I lean forward, hungry to taste her skin and nip at those peaked nubs. Her fingers dig into my hair, holding me in place as I pay attention to one and then the other breast. Marking her with eager suction and tender bites.

I move down her body as I often have, heading for where she's sweet and ripe, always ready for my mouth and tongue. Anna is innocent but learning, craving. She's admitted when she hasn't done something before. She's enjoyed what I've done to her. The touches. The kisses. The way I do them.

Tonight, I'm learning a lesson in patience.

I blow on her center, hearing her whimper but moving onward over her body. Kissing her thighs, moving between them, but then lowering down her body to run my tongue along the back of her knees, nibble at her calves and kiss her ankles. When I run my thumb up the arch of her foot, her leg flinches.

"That tickles," she moans but it's opened her legs wider and I remove her underwear.

This moment is heaven. Anna spread out on a blanket in the cool evening air. The sun setting. The quiet around us. She's everything I've wanted and more than I hoped for.

Kneeling back, I tug off my shirt before dipping between her thighs, paying her homage where I've done it not nearly enough. My tongue swirls. My fingers dip. Anna moves in rhythm with me until she's close to the edge.

I pull back and she hisses. "Please."

"I'm coming for you, baby." I dip my fingers beneath my waistband, shoving my pants down along with my boxer briefs. When I pull a condom from my pocket, Anna lifts her head.

"Condoms. Right." Her head falls back, and she stares up at the sky.

I climb over her, gently gripping her chin. "Look at me. I haven't been with anyone in over a year and even before then it was rare."

Anna nods but a tear slips from her eye.

"You're the only person I want, Anna. The only one." Period. She's it for me.

I lean forward and kiss her while my thumb swipes away the tear. When she's kissing me back, we've moved on from the awkward moment.

I pull back and cover myself. Bracing on one arm, I hold myself in my other hand, rubbing my heavy dick back and forth through folds already slick with need. Anna's legs spread. One lifts to wrap over my hip.

"Please. Mason. Please." Begging me isn't necessary. I'm going to give this to her and take it for me.

As my tip crests her entrance, and I glide into her heat, I'm a fool for ever thinking I'd be able to fuck Anna out of my system. As I slide to the hilt, buried as deep as I can get, I pause. The need to orgasm is strong and fast. My skin tingles. My balls tighten. I could blow with one thrust.

Only, I savor the moment, staring down at Anna as she stares up at me, adjusting to my size, to the feel of me inside her. With a slow breath, I revel in the connectedness. This is more than just joining two bodies. This is Anna and me. Together. Finally.

"Good?" I whisper, knowing I'll withdraw if panic sets in. If this isn't what she wants after all. But God, I hope to experience her more.

"Perfect," she whispers in return, nodding for emphasis. With her hands skimming my back, she tucks her body, lifting her head and seeking my lips. We kiss and kiss and kiss, until Anna's hips flex and my cock pulses.

"Anna," I groan against her mouth.

"Move," she moans. "Let go."

I pull back and glide forward. Back and forth a few times, stretching her, prepping her, until her head tips back and her hips start to rock underneath me.

Then I can't hold back. I'm thrusting faster, surging harder, seeking deeper to make my mark on her.

Anna's hands clutch my ass, digging her nails into the firm flesh, holding me inside her. Bracing myself on one arm, I slip a hand between us, stroking over that sacred spot.

Anna's eyes open, catching on mine. "What are you doing?" The question is breathless, curious.

"I want you to come around me."

"I—" Her breath catches, thoughts scattering as my fingers stroke and my dick thrusts. I brace myself higher over her, watching her body respond to my touch with both fingers and cock. Watching myself disappear into her body. Watching her come alive because of me.

When I look up, Anna is staring back. Her breathing shallow. Her hips dancing.

"That's it, baby. Let go."

Anna's gaze leaps to my eyes and we stare at one another until she breaks first. Rolling her head to the side, her lids lower as euphoria takes over. Her hips are wild and her moans desperate. I pinch her clit, and she softly cries out as she squeezes me. Tightening her body while clutching me inside her, I move faster, slipping to my knees and lifting her lower body over my thighs.

"Need more," I tell her. "Need all of you."

"I'm right here," she moans, still releasing over me. "I'm yours."

The words spur me onward, hammering into her until I'm ready to break myself. Then I pull out.

"Mason?" she questions, concern in her eyes.

"Not done with you. Not even close." I flip her to her stomach and then tug her hips upward. I don't ask if she's ever done it like this. I don't care who was first. I just want to make a lasting impression upon her now.

I slam into her, and she squeaks, fingers twisting in the blanket beneath her. On her knees, her arms stretch before her, and I rock back and forth, enthralled by her position, enraptured by her willingness.

"Do you like this?"

"I love it," she moans.

"Touch yourself."

She hesitates as I pummel in and out. Then her fingers are stroking her clit, and occasionally brushing against me as I move within her. The sensation is unreal, and I call out her name as I still inside her and break loose.

Anna groans as well, losing herself around me as we come together like a perfectly timed dance.

Or a long overdue moment.

I've never wanted anyone the way I've wanted this woman.

And I know I'm never going to want someone else after this night.

Chapter 39

4 Months Ago
May

Turning 43

[Anna]

With our skin clammy from the exertion and the chill of the sun setting, Mason slips free from me after minutes of deep breathing and soft kisses.

"We should jump in the lake to clean up." Mason collapses to his side beside me then falls to his back, hand flattened on his chest.

"I didn't bring a suit." I'm still on my belly, heart hammering, thoughts racing.

I just had sex with Mason Becker.

And I liked it. I liked it so much.

"Does it really matter?" His head rolls to face me and a boyish grin curls his lips. He looks lighter, happier even, than I've ever seen him. Mason is good looking on an average day but after sex, he's nearly blindingly handsome.

Softly, my lips lift, understanding what he's saying. He was just inside my body. Not to mention, we just made love on the deck of a boat where anyone venturing into this cove could see us.

Do I need a suit to cover myself? "I guess not." I lick my lips and admit, "I've never been skinny dipping, though."

"Really?" Mason shifts to his side, his entire body facing me. Without a thought, he removes the condom, then sits up to slip it back into the foil packet.

"Good girl, remember?" I joke about myself when he falls back to his side. Ben and I did spontaneous things, but we were never *that* spontaneous.

"Then let's go." Mason sits up again and slaps my backside, before hopping up to stand in all his naked glory. Me, I take my time to roll over, dismissing a little ache down low and the pressure from being on my knees.

Did we really do what we did? That wasn't a dream?

As I press myself upward, Mason holds out a hand. When I place my fingers in his palm, he tugs me the rest of the way. The force he uses, pulls me against his body and skin slaps skin.

"Are you sore?" His voice is tender, matching his touch as he smooths back my hair and removes the ponytail holder from the back of my head.

"No," I admit. I feel surprisingly good. Better than good. Still, my hand lowers to cover my belly as I often have when with him. And just like he always does, he tugs my arm free.

"You're beautiful," he tells me.

Typically, I'd be self-conscious standing bare naked on a boat on a lake despite the apparent seclusion. But I feel . . . beautiful.

"You're perfect, too," I whisper to him, eyes lowering to his firm chest.

Mason hums. "I want you again, but I need a minute." He glances over at the lake. "Dipping in there might cause me to need even more than a minute."

I laugh as I stare at the water, softly lapping against the side of the boat. "I'm nervous. I bet it's cold."

"Only way to know for sure." Suddenly, Mason's arms are around me, hoisting me a few inches off my feet.

"You wouldn't," I yell.

"Oh, I would." His voice fills with laughter as his fingers slip through mine on one hand. "I'll never let go, Anna."

The whisper at my ear is a promise in several ways.

Then he counts to three as I relax into his body, and we jump.

Together.

+ + +

After plunging into the water and breaking the surface, I let out a scream. The lake is take-your-breath-away freezing. I'm not certain I can tread water, I'm instantly that cold.

Mason is there, though, holding onto me and tugging me back toward the boat.

"Fuck it's cold." He laughs as he tosses his head, forcing his hair to whip away from his forehead. He looks youthful and carefree.

As we reach the back ledge of the boat, Mason grips my hips and hoists me awkwardly upward until I can tug myself the remainder of the way. He gracefully pulls himself upward and stands on the back deck.

He's quick to step into the sitting area and climb the side of the boat for the blanket we used earlier. He wraps it around me and then descends below deck in search of towels.

When he comes back to me, he's wearing a towel around his hips and hands me one which I wrap around my middle. He slips the blanket back over my shoulders and rubs at my hair with the extra towel.

Eventually, I pull free of his attention and finger comb my own locks while he disappears again only to return with a bottle of scotch.

"To warm us up." He holds the bottle higher before taking a sip directly from the container.

Mason hands me the bottle, and I take a timid sip. I'm not a hard alcohol person. He sits on the bench seat and pats the space beside him. I sit as well, and he wraps his arm over my shoulders.

"The sun is almost gone," I whisper, afraid to break the spell around us. Only a sliver of golden yellow marks the horizon. The sky is a ripple of muted pinks and dull orange. The lake is a perfect deep blue like Mason's eyes.

"Another day," Mason replies, his voice just as quiet as mine.

Another day. How different I feel. More than a year ago, the thought of making it through a day was filled with dread. Back then, my goal was simply day-by-day and step-by-step. At some point, I passed from anger and bitterness into quiet acceptance.

I shift, looking at Mason in profile. When did I cross the line to peace?

When a wave of cool air brushes over the boat, I shiver and tuck the blanket tighter around me. Mason still holds the scotch in his hand, and he takes another pull from it.

The motion focuses me on his mouth, his lips. Mason is an incredible kisser and touching his mouth with mine makes my blood heat. My body ripples with excitement every time he kisses me, and I'm almost ashamed of the immediate desire that rises within me. Almost.

Instead, I stand and climb over him. His gaze falls to my eyes, questioning me as I awkwardly straddle him with the blanket around my shoulders and towel around my middle.

"Whatcha doing, sweetheart?"

"Just need to be closer to you." I tuck against his chest, placing my ear on the center, listening to the strength of his heartbeat.

Mason is alive. He's here. He's present. And he isn't going anywhere. These are reminders I tell myself as the boat lulls me and his heat warms my skin.

Mason kisses the top of my head, lingering there as we quietly sit, watching the sun slowly disappear. He takes another pull from the bottle then mutters, "Can think of a way to be closer."

I chuckle against him. Lifting my head, I look up and his eyes say it all.

Mason likes sex. He's good at it. And he's introduced me to a side of myself I didn't know existed.

I'm enjoying the newer Anna.

And now is the time to act on her again.

I slip from Mason's lap, and he tugs the towel around his waist free. With the bottle in his hand, he spreads his arms. "Take what you need from me, baby. Make me yours."

He's already hard, but still, I reach for him, making a tight fist around his firm length, squeezing, tugging, feeling the weight, and marveling in the fact I do this to him.

"Climb on my lap. Put me back inside that lush body."

My skin heats, certain my face has turned red, but his words spur me on. Mason often talks this way to me, giving me the power to take what I want while he's demanding I do things.

On your knees, Anna.

Suck me, sweetheart.

Touch yourself, baby.

Things I want but still love his command, because I know I'm the one really in control. If I ever said no, he'd stop. I haven't turned him down yet, and with this thick length in my hand, I do as he asks.

I lose the wet towel wrapped around my body but keep the blanket draped over my shoulders. Then I climb his lap, and straddle his legs, pressing my center against his hard shaft. I rock back and forth a few times, spreading myself over him.

"Fuck, Anna. This body." One hand skims up my side, molding to my shape like a sculptor admiring his art. Then he's squeezing one breast and dipping his mouth to the other, licking my nipple. The tips are already tight and peaked from the cold water and cool air, and his mouth is a fiery contrast. Excitement burns within me.

"Slide my dick inside you, baby. Take what's yours."

Jesus. His words send a ripple through my body like the sudden rush of a river, and I slide up his length, balancing on the tip, before lowering over him, drawing him into me.

"Fuck." He groans, eyes closing a second as I still and adjust to the fullness. When he first entered me earlier, the sensation was overwhelming. The connection. The exposure. The intimacy. I'd forgotten how good this feels.

With my fingers digging into his hair, Mason tips his head back and I glide up and down his length, finding a rhythm of friction that quickly turns my simmer to a boiling need.

"That's it, sweetheart. Fuck me."

His crass words have my eyes snapping to his.

"The things you do to me. My body. My heart." He slaps at his chest. "You could shatter me, but fuck do I want to be broken by you."

I stare at him as I ride him harder, hands landing on his shoulders.

He could break me as well. I haven't felt anything like this. This freedom. This control. This power. I don't want it to end yet the build comes, stacking up brick by brick until I know the wall will tumble.

"I . . ." My breath hitches. "It's going to . . ." I'm going to crash and crumble and enjoy the topple. Because I fall. I fall hard and deep, digging my nails into his shoulders and riding him faster than I've ever done.

"There's my girl," Mason proudly grunts as I hammer over him, drawing him tighter inside me as I let go.

Then, a shaky wall starts building again.

"Mason?" His name is confusion. He's brought me to orgasm more than once in a night but this . . . I never come twice with penetration. Still, I climb, and I claw, and the tension creeps up my center again.

"Fuck. Anna. Fuck my cock like that, sweetness."

My arm slips around his shoulder, and I cling to him as I grunt and moan, tossing my body up and down over his until his fingers find that sensitive nub. My breath catches and I silently scream as I break over him once more.

Only, Mason grabs my hips, moving me with the bucking of his hips until he stills, pulsing inside me, filling me.

Our eyes catch. He isn't wearing a condom this time. His breathing seems to heighten as realization hits him, but he doesn't stop. He juts and jolts within me as I ride out the unraveling of me around him. Then he's capturing my mouth and kissing me hard, holding onto the moment before reality hits.

Suddenly, I'm crying silent tears. When the salty liquid hits my lips, I pull back, hanging my head.

"Hey," Mason whispers, tipping up my chin. "What's this?"

"We didn't use a condom and I'm not on the pill."

"Anna." My name is a tender caress as his fingers brush back my still wet hair. "I'm clean, baby. Okay? You're safe with me."

Safe from pregnancy? I'm forty-two. Then it hits me. Today is my birthday. I'm forty-three.

And more tears flow. The fear of another child isn't really the issue. I'm just overwhelmed. This night. This day. Mason.

He's kissing my chin and my jaw. My cheeks and my closed eyes. "It's okay, baby. Talk to me."

Instead, I kiss him, keeping it slow and soft. Eventually, Mason pulls back, pressing his forehead to mine. "Too much?"

Maybe that's just the thing, none of it was too much. It was everything I'd been waiting for, more than I should ask for, and afraid *what's next* is settling in.

"Did you mean it?" he asks, his voice quiet, directed at my lips with our heads still together. "Earlier, you said you were mine."

Did I mean it? I hate that I pause but then I nod. "I'm yours as long as you're mine."

"Anything for you, sweetheart."

Then he's kissing me again, sealing us together.

Chapter 40

4 Months Ago
May

Turning Points

[Anna]

Mason drops me off at my front door like it's a regular date. He kisses me long and slow, taking his time not to miss a curve or corner of my mouth.

"Night, beautiful," he finally says with a kiss to the tip of my nose. He waits until I enter the house and close the door before he crosses the driveway to the garage.

My hair is still wet but tucked into a messy bun at the back of my neck. Bryce is obviously home, as evidenced by the pile of dirty dishes in the sink. That kid can eat.

I chuckle as I head down the dark hallway to my bedroom, but there I pause just inside the door.

I stare at the bed.

Ben did not pass away in this bedroom. He asked to be moved upstairs, claiming he'd have a better view above the tree line surrounding the lake. The excuse was lame, but Ben was weak, and I didn't wish to argue with him. He took a guest room in the corner, that overlooks River's backyard from one window and the lake through the back.

The room has been cleaned and painted and restored to a guest bedroom with a new look.

Despite the updates to my own room, it still feels like a room I shared with Ben.

And I'm tired of sleeping alone in it.

Suddenly, I miss my parents. This was their room first, filled with the antique furniture they loved. Those pieces were replaced with more modern items that Ben and I preferred. Now the room is feminine and sweet, but a masculine mist still lingers. Although Ben is gone, I can't shake what this room represents.

Turning back, I head down the hallway and climb the stairs to the second floor, staring at the open doors of some rooms. Noting the closed doors of others. Mila's room with a bathroom. Calvin and Bryce's rooms with a Jack-and-Jill bathroom between them. The former main bedroom that had once been my parents' when they first bought the place. The room has gone through many transitions.

Amelia and I shared the space in our teens. The boys had the room as children as it was more of a bunk space with three twin beds. Once we moved here, Bryce and Calvin each took a room of their own as this was our new permanent residence, not a vacation destination or weekend getaway spot.

Stepping into the room at the end of the hallway, I pause and fumble for my phone in my bag. I hadn't even set down my purse in my bedroom.

"Hey," Amelia groggily says through the phone. Did I wake her on a Friday night? It's not even ten and she's an hour behind me. As the sun set the lake grew inky and Mason didn't want to pilot the boat in the dark, so we headed back to the marina. He didn't ask me to join him in the apartment. He didn't ask if he could come into the house.

Maybe we both needed a minute to understand what happened between us.

"What's going on?" Amelia breaks into my thoughts.

"I've been thinking." I continue to stare into the room with three twins, recalling the layout when Amelia and I were children. A large double bed. A small sitting area.

"Sounds dangerous." Amelia chuckles. A rustling sound follows.

"Did I wake you?"

"Uhm . . . no." She laughs.

Again, I consider the time difference. "Something else I interrupted?"

"Negative there as well." I don't press for more and Amelia asks, "So what are you thinking about?"

"I need a change." I turn in a small circle, remembering how Amelia and I climbed into bed when we were younger. Giggling about boys. Sharing our thoughts. Expressing concerns about an unknown future.

"Like what?" Her voice is cautious and curious.

"I think I'm going to move."

"Out of Lakeside Cottage?" Amelia gasps. "Are you coming back to Chicago?"

The thought crossed my mind once or twice when Ben first passed. Returning to our old neighborhood. Getting back my former teaching job. Then I reconsidered. I didn't want to make another move. Plus, Ben wanted us here, and at first, I didn't want to feel like I was leaving him behind if we went back to Chicago.

In all honesty, this is my home, though. My family has too many shared memories in this place. I don't think I could ever leave Lakeside Cottage and live anywhere else.

"No, not leaving. Just moving bedrooms. Is that weird?" I pause as I cross the room and take a seat on the edge of a bed. "It's probably weird."

"Should it be weird?"

"I don't know. That's why I'm asking you." I huff feeling the ache of my thighs and a pinch someplace else.

Mason.

"What's going on with you?" Her curiosity turns to concern.

"I slept with Mason." My eyes close as I fall back on the bed and brace for Amelia's wrath. She had a crush on him. She's defended him. However, she also knows that we've spent enormous amounts of time together, and we've done a few physical things, like kissing and touching.

"Well, hallelujah and praise Jesus and oh my God, give me all the details."

I laugh with relief. "I am not telling you about it."

"I had sex with a stranger. I'll tell you about that," she teases. At least I think she's teasing.

"Us McCaryn girls are a bunch of sluts," I joke.

Amelia guffaws. "No, we aren't. We're modern women in our forties, enjoying life and taking what we want from it."

Curling to my side on the bed, I tuck up my knees. "Huh. I'm a mother of three, and a widow."

That shouldn't make me un-sex-able, but I still can't believe what Mason and I did. I'd practically begged him to make love to me and then he rocked my world, doing to me things I'd never done, making me feel in ways I've never felt.

"You're more than a mother and a widow, Anna. Your children are individual human beings and do not define you. As for being a widow, that's not a definition of you either." Amelia sighs. "You're a woman who has desires. Wants and needs, and they deserve to be met. As long as no one is hurt, you should seek whatever brings you joy."

"Do you think I'll hurt him?" I pause a second. "Will he hurt me?" What if I am just the woman he never had? Now, he's had me. Did I disappoint or satisfy him? Why am I questioning myself?

"You might hurt him, and he might hurt you, but no one ever enters a relationship with thoughts of heartache. You can't think like that, or you'll never be in a relationship."

Says the woman who hasn't been in a committed relationship for years.

"Look, I get it. You're sensitive. Romantic. You're really falling for him and don't know what to do with all those feelings because you've only been through this once before."

Ben.

"It's okay not to have all the answers tonight or tomorrow or even next week. You like him, right?"

"Yeah," I whisper, a smile curls my lips, happiness ringing in my tone.

"And he likes you." There isn't a question or doubt in her voice.

"Yeah," I agree even quieter.

"Then there isn't an issue." Amelia pauses. "Unless his dick is tiny, which I refuse to believe about him."

"Amelia!" I shriek, falling to my back again and dropping my legs off the side of the bed. I scoff and decide we need a subject change. "So who is this stranger of yours?"

"Just what the name implies. A stranger. Someone I don't know and probably won't ever see again."

"How do you know?"

"Because the city has three million people and if I divide it unfairly down the middle of men and women, I still have a one in one and a half million chance of seeing him again."

"Did he have a big dick?" I burst into riotous giggles after asking. I don't really want to know.

"You *are* a secret slut, aren't you?" Amelia teases back.

"Ha ha." I mock.

"Seriously, just enjoy Mason. Don't overthink. For once in your life, just let go a little."

Her words remind me of Mason's expression when I made a toast about letting go. Even when I repeated myself, his face was almost . . . pained. Then he kissed me, and my thoughts scattered.

"I'm trying," I reply to her.

"Good. Now, back to details. Length? Height? And rank?"

"You're impossible."

"These are important features. Inches. Thickness. And on a scale of one to ten—"

"Good night, Amelia."

"You called me, remember?"

I chuckle. "I did. And I'm going to move to Mom and Dad's old room on the second floor."

"Really?"

I sit up and gaze around the room again, envisioning the changes I'll make. "Definitely. How about the room downstairs becomes yours permanently? You'd have privacy with the bathroom, office, sitting area and bed space. Then maybe you'd come visit more often." I might sound a bit like a henpecking mother, wanting her child to come home more often, but I really do want Amelia to take a break from the fast pace of her life and visit me here at the house. Lakeside Cottage belongs to her as well as Archer and me.

"You know I don't need an entire suite for me."

"I know. But I kind of took over as Archer likes to remind me and he has the garage apartment as his share of the property." We each own Lakeside Cottage. Archer accused me of commandeering the place, but he'd been missing when our parents passed and didn't have a say. Amelia had been too busy to care what I did with the house.

"Except Mason lives there."

"For now." The words taste bitter. I don't want him to leave but he can't live above my garage forever. He's been looking sporadically for homes as that's part of his business and sometimes he shows me prospects, but he hasn't found a place in the immediate area, which is what he wants. Homes rarely go on sale here as they are often passed down through families. Logan got his house when someone died, and the family didn't want the place.

"Think he'll move soon?"

"I don't know." The thought makes my heart thud erratically.

"There is no rush for anything. Not him to move. Or you to make decisions."

I exhale and sit up straighter. "No, I've decided. I need to move out of that lonely bedroom."

"Maybe move Mason into your bed?" Amelia teases but I chew on my lip.

Could we live together? I don't think I like that option. Plus, we each have kids and I don't want to turn into Penny-something's mother, trading out men, living with them and having my kids call them dad. Then again, I'm not Penny's mother and I'd never ask my children to call another man their dad.

Mason would never ask that, either.

I lower my voice. "I don't think we're there yet."

"Again . . . no rush, Anna. You have time ahead of you."

I want to believe her, but we both know time can be cut short.

"Thanks for taking my call," I whisper.

"Of course, big sister. But next time, I want details. Let's forget length and girth. It's the motion of the ocean that's important, not the size of the mast."

"Oh my God. Good night, Mealworm."

Amelia chuckles. "Now you sound like Mason. This must be serious." She makes kissing noises through the phone like when we were teenagers. "Good night, you."

"Night."

When we hang up, I feel lighter, determined to make a change.

Still giddy from earlier, I think of Mason. Yeah, I like him. His mast and his motions.

Chapter 41

2 Months Ago
July

Bedrooms and Bumbling Things Up

[Mason]

After our date in May, Anna becomes insatiable. Not that I'm complaining.

She has summers off. With the boys at work, Mila at a friend's house, and Lynlee attending summer camp art classes, I come home for an impromptu lunch date that leads to us ending up in my bedroom.

Breathlessly, we lay beside each other. Chests heaving. Hearts galloping.

"Holy shit," I mutter, on my back. Anna giggles. Our position hadn't been anything unusual. Anna's quite adventurous and allows me to experiment on her body, teasing, testing her. She's always willing but this time, something was different.

Intense. Intimate. Incredible.

We've been like this for nearly two months, the longest I've ever been with a woman. I don't want our situation to ever end. In fact, I've been waiting so long for Anna I want to take the next step.

"Let's move in together," I blurt as my heart rate lowers and I stare at Anna laying on her stomach. Her hair is removed from its previous ponytail and sprawls over her shoulder. Her eyes glitter as she gazes back at me.

She giggles again, girlish, sweet. "We practically are living together."

I get what she means. We share meals and groceries. Do laundry and take care of household needs. We spend time with the kids, playing games and attending activities. But I want a little more for us. Her and me, exclusively.

"I know," I say, shuffling to sit upright and leaning against the headboard. Anna shifts to her side, watching me.

"But . . ." I swallow hard. "Don't you want more than sneaking up into this bedroom?"

Anna props herself up, taking the bedsheet with her, covering her chest. "What do you mean?"

"Why don't we ever have sex in your bedroom?" Anna moved out of the bedroom she shared with Ben. The week-long project took place in June after the school year ended. She painted the largest bedroom and bathroom on the second floor, moved furniture and bought new linens. She even did further updates to the main bedroom on the first floor.

Yet, I haven't been in Anna's bed.

In my dreams, I've taken Anna on every surface of the house. In reality, our moments have been confined to her sneaking up to my bedroom above the garage or impassioned moments in her first-floor powder room.

I haven't taken her on the kitchen counter or the sitting room sofa. Not the living room floor or the dining room table.

And I'm tired of it.

I want more from our relationship than all these stolen moments. Sure, we make dinner and hang out. We watch movies and have lunch. We even make a production of Saturday morning breakfasts, but there's something beneath the surface missing . . . for me.

I'm in a position I never, ever expected to be in. Cancer sucks, for sure. Anna grieved long before Ben passed. She had a year of firsts without him. Then a second year, wading through her new normal. While digging deep for patience and compassion, I've weathered all the milestones along with her, but now I feel like I'm in a holding pattern.

We're barreling toward Archer and Jenna's wedding. I want to know what the future holds for Anna and me.

"What are we doing? Where are we headed?"

Anna blinks several times, staring at me like she hasn't seen me before. "What do you mean what are we doing?"

"Stop parroting me," I snap, losing the stranglehold on my patience. Digging my fingers into my hair, holding it at the base of my neck, I realize I'm losing a grip *on us.*

"Where do you want us headed?" Anna's voice softens.

"Where do *you* see us?" I counter, staring at her as her eyes lower. She can't even look at me. "Is there an us?"

Her head snaps up, eyes wide with hurt. She glances around us. The rumpled bed sheets. My naked chest. She sits straighter, tugging the sheet up to her throat.

"Don't do that. Don't hide. We need to talk about this."

"I don't know what to say." Her voice weak.

"Do you see a future for us?" What the fuck are we doing then? She isn't some fuck buddy to me, but maybe I'm just some kind of transition for her . . . or boy toy . . . or I don't know what. *For a good time, call Mason.* I've heard it before.

"Why aren't we more open about us?"

"Open?" She echoes me again, like she doesn't understand the word. "Our friends know we are together. Our kids, too. We're dating."

I groan. "Why aren't you spending the night with me?"

She stares at me. Even confused, she takes my breath away, but I need to breathe. I need to know we have a future. I want what Logan and Autumn have, and Zack and River. Even Archer, as much as we haven't always gotten along. I'll own that I'm envious of the commitment he's about to make with Jenna.

For the first time in my life, I want forever. I want all the hours in a day and all the nights in a week. I want months and years with this woman.

Not sneaking into bathrooms or stealing moments in my bedroom.

"We just don't do that." Anna lowers her head, clutching the sheet at her throat.

"But why not?" I release my hair and slap at my sheet-covered thigh before shifting to cup her cheek. I repeat myself when I say, "We should move in together."

Anna's eyes shift away from my gaze. "I don't think I'm ready for that."

Not ready? It's been two fucking years.

Anna pulls back from my touch, and I lower my hand to the sheet between us, clenching the material in my fist.

"Anna, you mentioned letting go when we had our first date. You know what the irony of that statement is . . . Ben said the same thing to me."

Her breath hitches and shaky fingers cover her lips.

"His note to me . . . the ones he wrote to the guys. He had two words for me. Let go." I stare up at her. "This is me letting go, Anna. I want forever with you."

Anna's head is already shaking. Tears fill her eyes. She's slowly slipping backward, removing herself from the bed. "Why would you bring Ben into this?"

"What?" *Fuck!* "That's not what I'm doing. This isn't about Ben. This is about you and me."

My fingers tighten in the sheet, as I watch Anna scramble for her clothing. She picks up her shorts, clutching the small material to her chest.

"There isn't a you and me, is there?" My voice drops, my tone brusque. "There's never going to be a you and me, is there?"

Anna quickly glances at me. With silent tears, slowly trickling down her cheek I have my answer.

"This was just sex, wasn't it?" My voice hardens.

Anna leans down to grab her tank top, adding it to her meager attempts to cover herself. "No," she whispers, choking on the word.

Fuck, I can't watch her cry, and least of all because of me, but this had to be said. We need to talk about the future. *If* there's a future.

"This isn't enough for me." If I strike first, she can't hit me where it will hurt most. When she tells me it isn't sex, but it isn't more. When she says we're friends, like it's a dirty word. There's no doubt Anna cares about me, and she loves my kid, but us—Anna and me—she doesn't love that idea.

My heart clenches, tightening my entire chest. Fuck, this hurts. This hurts so much. My throat burns and I blink to clear the sting behind my eyes.

Ask me to stay and I will. What a goddamn fool I've been to think I'd ever be enough. That she'd ever want me to stay in her house, in her heart, making a life together.

With her clothes collected, she's made it to the bedroom door. Her supple ass on display. Her short, firm legs. Her sexy spine I kissed along only moments ago.

"I found a house," I blurt.

Anna's head snaps back and she spins to face me. "I didn't know you were still looking for one."

"I've always been looking." The search has been limited. I found issue with every location because I didn't want to leave. Another house wouldn't have Anna.

Ask me to stay and I will. Now, I know I should leave.

"You don't have to move." Her voice is weak; her words not enough.

She's standing across the room from me instead of talking to me, clutching her clothes like a one-night stand trying to sneak free of my bedroom. As I stare at the woman of my dreams, I realize our time together might have been just that. A dream. A fantasy that came to fruition due to tragedy. I can't turn back time, but I can change the future, and that future is either with Anna because she wants me by her side, in her bed and her heart.

Or without her.

My heart implodes, chest clamping tighter.

Self-preservation strikes again.

"I think it's time I go." I lower my head, unable to look at her. "Lynlee and I can't continue to live in a borrowed apartment. The goal has always been to make a home for my daughter. Give her a house with a yard. Get her a swing set." Fill all the spaces with love.

She deserves it. Dammit, I deserve it.

"I've fucked up long enough as a parent. And I'm done fucking around with my life."

"What are you saying?" Anna chokes on the question but she can't be that ignorant.

"I'm moving out." I look up, bold and direct, catching those soggy brown eyes.

We stare at one another for a long, hard minute. She doesn't respond to what I've said, but a sob breaks free. The sound is a final clamp on my chest, piercing my heart, shattering me.

Then, she nods once and exits my room, shutting the door behind her.

I fall back to the pillows, staring up at the ceiling. Both my hands scrub down my face, questioning what just happened. Wondering what I've done.

I just broke up with Anna.

Chapter 42

2 Months Ago
July

Ben's Second Anniversary

[Anna]

It takes me a few minutes to collect myself. My fingers shake so badly I can hardly dress. I trip over sliding my leg through my shorts. My tank top gets caught on my breasts. All I can think about is fleeing this apartment.

Let Go.

Why would he mention Ben?

The smallest reprieve is that Mason doesn't exit the bedroom. I snatch my phone off the low table between the couches and rush out the apartment door, closing the door with a soft click before pressing myself against it. Taking a few deep breaths in the bright sunshine, I tip my head back and close my eyes. Silent tears trickle down my cheeks.

One minute we were basking in the afterglow of some incredible sex. The next I was giggling about moving in together until I realized Mason was serious. I want us living together. One roof. One house. One family.

My head was spinning. From there, everything spiraled.

The future. Us.

What did I want?

Was what we had enough? I hadn't thought about it. In the months since we started having sex, Mason has been on my mind constantly. Not that he hadn't been before that time, but sex had upped the ante. I couldn't stop thinking of him. The way he touched me. The way he held me. The way he made me feel so incredibly alive. And whole.

I'm moving out.

How could this be happening? My biggest fear has come to fruition. Mason would leave. He'd grow tired of his warped idea of obligation to Ben and get sick of me. He wanted more from me, but didn't he see he had all I had to give?

I thought we were in a good place. *What the hell just happened?*

I stumble down the steps along the side of the building. My feet feel heavy. My heart weighing me down.

Is this just sex?

How could he ask me such a thing? He means so much more to me. How can he not see it, feel it? He's all I think about and all I want near me.

Suddenly, my phone vibrates in my hand, startling me so much I juggle the device before righting it and answering.

"Hello?" My voice cracks.

"Anna?" My sister giggles. "Am I interrupting something?" Her voice drops, salacious and scandalized.

"No. I . . ." The lump in my throat makes it hard to speak.

"What's wrong?" Amelia's instant concern has the tears leaking faster. I fumble with the front door of the house and slam it shut without a glance behind me. Racing to the stairs, I take them two at a time.

"I think Mason just broke up with me." My cry is jagged, like my heart has just been cut out of my chest.

"Oh, honey."

I enter my bedroom and shut the door, locking myself inside in a familiar position. Hiding my heartbreak. With my back to the door, I slide down the barrier and sit on the floor, head tipped back.

Quickly, I relay how we'd just had sex, and then he was questioning our relationship.

"He said he wanted us to move in together. I thought he was joking." But did I really think that? Would it be a joke to Mason? He'd know it wasn't a joke to me. However, he also knows I'm not really the living-together type. I'd want a more binding commitment, something Mason wouldn't ever want.

Hell, he hasn't even said he loves me.

"Does he want you to move into a new house with him?" Amelia is quiet for a moment. "It would make sense. The cottage holds a lot of memories."

This house does hold memories, but it contains more than the history of Ben and me. My parents lived here. I've moved my children here. And here is where Mason and I finally connected with one another.

"I don't even know. But he found a house. He's moving out." I sob. "I thought everything was okay with us. What am I missing?" While I'd been married to one man for nearly two decades, it didn't mean I was an expert in relationships. I knew Ben. I don't know what Mason is thinking.

"What exactly did he say?"

I tell her about questioning us, our future and then asking me if this was only sex.

"Mason does not believe what you are doing is only sex," Amelia interrupts me, voice firm with conviction.

"How can you know?"

"He loves you." She exhales, confident in her opinion.

"He mentioned Ben."

She gasps. "He didn't."

"He told me about Ben's letter." I pause. "The one he wrote Mason before he died."

"What did it say?" The curiosity in Amelia's tone would be almost comical if this were a funny situation, which it's not.

"Let go. Two small words."

Amelia is quiet a long time while I silently cry into the phone.

"How did Mason use them?" she eventually asks. "How did Mason use Ben's words with you?"

"He said this was him letting go. He wants forever with me."

Amelia sighs. "Anna. Honey. That's your answer. Mason loves you." She softly chuckles. "He just told you he did."

"But why bring up Ben?" I whisper.

Amelia pauses a beat. "This isn't about Ben. Or is it? Mason's telling you he wants forever. He's put his heart on the line, Anna. Maybe this is about you. Are you still holding onto something?"

I shake my head, recalling that late fall evening on the beach last year. Ben is gone. Well and truly gone. I don't feel his presence. I don't sense messages from some place beyond now that I know the truth about the heart-shaped rocks.

Mason. Mason was my rock.

"I think I fucked up," I whisper to my sister.

"I doubt it. Just talk to Mason. Let go yourself. Tell him how you feel."

How did I feel? I don't say the words aloud, but my sister answers me.

"You love him, right? You don't want to lose him. You want him in your life." Amelia sighs. "You're getting a second chance to love, Anna. Take it."

Her tone is nearly a plea, coaxing me to give in. To let go.

Was I holding back? Had I been too comfortable where we are? I could use the excuse of time, but I didn't need more time to consider how I felt or what I wanted.

I wanted Mason.

"Thank you," I whisper to her, hastily swiping at my damp face. "I didn't mean to dump all that on you. You called me. What did you need?"

"Well." She softly chuckles. "This feels a bit prophetic, but I was calling to check on you."

"Check on me?" I run a finger under my nose. I really need a tissue.

"For today."

Today? Amelia's silence forces me to recall the date. How could I have forgotten? The kids and I had a long talk two nights ago. We planned to go to the cemetery this evening and then do something just the four of us tonight.

Of course, I hadn't forgotten. Not completely.

"Oh my God." My voice shakes as new tears spill from my eyes.

"Are you okay?" Amelia means to soothe.

"I don't know if I'll ever be okay." If I thought Mason asking me to live with him was a joke, now the day felt like a sick prank from the universe.

"Is Archer's wedding going to be difficult for you?" Amelia and I have already talked about our brother's upcoming nuptials. How he deserves a happily-ever-after and so does Jenna.

"It's okay to be happy for them but still be sad," Amelia reminds me, her voice still low as if soothing a child.

"I'm so jealous," I whisper. Envious of their joy and love. Sad at my loss of Ben. Even sadder that I'm losing Mason. "Does that make me a bad person?"

"Not bad, just human. Don't give up on Mason, though. Any relationship is new for Mason. You're his first love."

I snort.

"I'm serious. Mason loves you. I'm certain of it. Hell, we're all certain of it. And it sounds like he's just eager to start a future."

Amelia's words are a good reminder. Mason and I are both new to what we are experiencing. I don't want to lose him, and he needs to know that. However, I can't ask him to stay if he's determined to go.

"What do I do?" I ask in a watery voice.

"Decide what you want and then don't give up until you have it."

Says the woman who hasn't ever fought for a man.

Then again, I've never had to do this before either. It's time to make a new choice.

I pick Mason.

Chapter 43

1 Month Ago
August

Wedding Rehearsal

[Anna]

Unfortunately, Mason avoids the house for the next week.

The plan was for Archer and Jenna to take over the garage apartment with Rosie and Talia. Mason and Lynlee would relocate to the main house for the ten days Archer and Jenna are present. Autumn and Ben's mother, Ruth, will be staying in the house as well. Additional guests are staying at Bluebird Hollow Inn where the reception will be held. Archer and Jenna have mutual friends from Elk Lake City where Archer moved into Jenna's home.

However, I had no idea if Mason and Lynlee would stay as planned until the last minute, when they walk in with Ruth Kulis in tow. Mason picked Ruth up at the airport.

"Hello family," Ben's mother calls out and Mila rushes toward her only grandparent. The two embrace and it's a brief reminder of all Ben will miss. The continuing relationship of his children with Ruth. She's had her own struggles, dealing with the fact she is outliving her son. Still, Ruth has a similar philosophy to Ben.

Be grateful for the days you have and what remains in your life.

Embraces are shared and Ruth's presence is a welcome distraction from the tension between Mason and me. A week has been too long for the stilted texts we've shared about pickups, summer-day activities, and the wedding preparations.

"The most handsome man picked me up at the airport and look who I found in the backseat?" Ruth reaches out for Lynlee and tugs her to her side as if she hasn't already just spent an hour in the car with her. "Isn't she the most beautiful gift?"

Ruth presses a kiss to Lynlee's head, still squeezing her little form. My gaze leaps to Mason before dropping back to Lynlee.

"Yes. She is one of the greatest gifts."

I seek Mason again, willing him to read how much I consider him a gift as well. One I don't want to lose. We desperately need to talk but the wedding is going to take precedence.

When the door opens again with the booming sound of Archer calling out, "Is that Ruthie?" chaos ensues in my home. My brother hadn't known Ruth like the rest of us, but he was present when I first started dating Ben. Archer was around through the birth of my children, encountering Ruth at momentous occasions like christenings and birthdays, and then suddenly, he was just gone. It's no surprise, then, when Ruth bursts into tears at seeing the prodigal son returned.

"Oh, my goodness. The men are getting handsomer and handsomer." Ruth hugs Archer like a long-lost son. Maybe his presence triggers her loss. Archer had been gone for more than a decade but now he's back. Her son will never walk in the door again.

If Ruth feels this way, though, her smile and happy tears don't give her away. She's just as eager to meet Rosie and Talia and see Jenna again. Her enthusiasm only adds to the joyous occasion we'll celebrate in a few days.

Still, I continue to seek Mason in the group, willing him to look at me. Begging him to give me that look.

The one Jenna once described as a look that meant I was his everything.

Because he's everything to me.

I love him.

"There she is." Logan's loud voice breaks into my revelry next. Autumn and crew follow as Logan calls out while hugging Ruth, "Mama K, I missed you."

Everyone was close to Ben's mother.

Glancing over at Mason once more, my heart patters. I've missed him. And it wasn't just the sex. I missed the friendly banter and steady companionship. I miss the subtle touches, like a constant reminder he was here for me. I miss the way he'd just stare at me, like he couldn't believe I was real. Then he'd kiss me, and I'd forget myself. I'd forget everything but him and me.

Why wasn't he sleeping in my bed, holding me all night? I've been so lonely without his presence every day, but the nights have been the hardest. That's when my mind wanders and I just want to curl into his chest, breathe in his sharp scent and hear his heartbeat.

To know he's here, alive, and mine.

$+++$

My sister arrives two days later. She'll be staying in her new sister-suite as we jokingly call the refreshed bedroom on the main floor. I want her to feel welcome at Lakeside Cottage whenever she wants and I'm hoping by designating a specific space for her, she'll visit more often. Even if she's busy, the drive is only two hours from Chicago, and I'd love more long weekends with her.

As we stand in my kitchen, the house is chaos. I'm hosting the rehearsal dinner. The meal is catered, and we've been fortunate to set up tables outside in the side yard. It's a beautiful August evening.

Jenna and Archer's wedding party includes two of her friends from Elk Lake City, Tricia Ramirez and Britton Scott, along with Amelia and me. Archer has asked Tricia's husband Leon to be his best man as the two have formed a fast friendship. He also has Noah and Zack standing up with him and a former associate named Braxton Hawes.

"Hello, lovey," the burly man greets me, instantly giving away he's from England. His voice is nearly as deep as Archer's. Their statures match in height and shoulder span, suggesting that he's had experiences similar to Archer's past. I've only heard his name in passing but it's Amelia's reaction to him that has me puzzled.

"Hello, dove," he greets her, a wide, sheepish grin forming on his face. However, Amelia is stiff and reserved as she extends a hand.

"Amelia McCaryn. Sister of the groom." Her voice is tight. Her posture rigid.

"Braxton Hawes," he greets her. The corner of his mouth curls higher as his voice drops. He holds her hand despite her attempt to pull back. "Nice to meet you."

After dropping her hand, Archer claps Braxton on the back and leads him around the room for more introductions.

"What the hell was that?" I ask, speaking out of the side of my mouth.

"What was what?" Amelia mutters, watching Braxton walk away. He's thicker than Mason, less polished in his dark gray pants and a silvery dress shirt, but his backside is very fine. And Amelia is staring at it.

"Do you know him?"

Amelia sighs before dragging her gaze away from him. "I don't."

Does she want to know him? We're interrupted when more people arrive and my questions about Amelia and Braxton disappear.

Mason comes down the stairs with Lynlee beside him. He looks amazing in his famous blue suit. The one accentuating his eyes.

"Hey." His voice is quiet as he tips his head at me. "What can I do to help?" He's already been a silent assistant, helping Archer set up tables and arrange tablecloths. Earlier, they cleared off the stone patio for the official rehearsal. They've already laid the kindling for a bonfire on the beach after the meal tonight.

"I think we're good." I glance around the kitchen where hot serving trays are set on the island.

Then I look at Mason and our eyes hold. We have so much to say to one another. The news of his house-finding has spread among us, and questioning gazes have fallen on me with every announcement.

I don't want him to go, but before I can speak with him, my elbow is cupped.

"Hey, love." I turn at the sound of Braxton's rough timbre. "You're needed outside."

Glancing back at Mason, he's already walking away from us, heading toward the bar, and ignoring me once more.

Chapter 44

1 Month Ago
August

Wedding Rehearsal

[Mason]

"What the fuck is wrong with you?" Logan mutters as he stands beside me. We both face out the glass door that overlooks the stone patio where the wedding party is being arranged in a semi-circle around Archer and Jenna.

The setting is perfect, but I'm in the shittiest mood.

I want to be in Archer's position, marrying the woman of my dreams.

Instead, I told her I was moving out when I still haven't signed the official contract for the house. Normally places go fast in this area. I like the house well enough, but there's been a missing component in every place.

Anna wouldn't be there.

For the last week, I've been arguing that the distance might do us some good.

I want forever with you.

After all this time, how can she not see it? How does she not feel it? I'm in love with her. I've been in love with her for ages.

And a damn wedding is the last place I want to be when I'm losing the woman I hoped would one day be my wife.

I wanted to ask Anna to marry me when everything turned in the opposite direction.

When I don't answer Logan, he says, "Hard to imagine Archer is getting married."

"Hard to imagine," I mutter, lifting my glass and taking a gulp of the scotch I poured. It's going to be a long night. A long few days. It's been a helluva week.

Logan turns back to me. "What is your problem?"

"What a schmuck." I nod toward the glass, watching as Braxton shifts Anna to a different standing spot in the wedding party arrangement.

"Down, lover boy." Logan chuckles and I realize I might have growled with my thoughts.

"This sucks."

"A wedding?" Logan asks. "Or pushing away your girl?"

Anna is close to Autumn. Autumn tells Logan everything. Is that what Anna told Autumn? That I pushed her away. Is that what I did by admitting how I feel, what I want?

Logan might understand my position. He panicked and nearly lost Autumn when they first got together. His groveling included upending his entire life, which was due for a change anyway.

"Do you really want your own house?" Logan looks around. "Do you really want to move away from her?"

My gaze remains on Anna. "Don't really have a choice. We aren't going in the direction I want." I take another sip of my drink, realizing if I don't slow my pace I'm going to be drunk before dinner.

"What direction is that?"

I turn back toward him unable to answer.

"Four points on a compass, man."

Logan points out at Zack who is part of the wedding party. "East." He points to himself. "South."

Then his gaze falls on me. "West." He pauses a second. "We all know Archer isn't north. Not really. Ben was our true north. And he pointed you at her." Logan waves his finger back out toward the yard at the beautiful woman wearing a yellow dress that's fitted at the top and hangs loose and flowing down to her knees. I hadn't noticed at first but the color matches what Lynlee is wearing.

"Don't be stupid. Everything you've ever wanted is right there." He jabs at the glass.

"And she doesn't want me. Not like I want her," I snap, turning on him.

"How do you know? Have you asked her? Have you told her how you feel?" Logan stares at me. "I'm not the guy who had all the moves with women. That was all you. But I still like to think I know a thing or two about them. They need to *hear* how you feel."

"I told her," I mumble, glancing down at my glass which is empty.

"She isn't someone you make moves on. You *love* her," Logan continues as if I hadn't said a thing.

I thought I'd been doing that—showing Anna, proving to her how I feel, what I want.

"Be smooth with words, man. Time to use three little ones that mean a lot." Logan tips his head toward the yard.

I gaze back at Anna. Hadn't I already said I loved her by telling her I wanted forever? What if I tell her I love her, and she doesn't feel the same way? What if she can't? We have chemistry, and the attraction is undeniable, but loving me is a different wheelhouse. Telling her I love her is a risk I'm not certain I can take.

Braxton touches Anna again, and innocent or not, I step forward as if I can walk through the glass barrier.

"For a man afraid to say he loves her, you look ready to make a scene." Logan chuckles and pats my back. "I'd suggest you let it all hang out there. Just let go and tell her how you feel."

The words are a taunting whisper in Ben's voice.

Let go.

+ + +

"That Braxton is a funny chap." Logan chuckles as he slaps my shoulder and falls into the seat beside me.

We sit in one of the furthest tables from the McCaryn clan which includes Archer and Jenna, Amelia, and Anna, and that fucking funny chap Braxton.

"What? Are you British now?" Zack laughs from the other side of me.

"Didn't you notice his accent?" Logan chuffs.

"I'd like to chap his ass," I mutter, lifting my third drink. Fuck that accent. Why do women find it so endearing? If he calls someone lovey or dove one more time—

"Chap his ass? Turning over a new leaf?" Logan huffs, hitching a brow at me, and clutching my shoulder, jostling me. He gives me a knowing glare. "Done with women?"

"Fuck you." I brush off his touch.

"Easy." Zack narrows his eyes at me, but my gaze is fixated on Braxton.

"Tally ho, ya ho." *Oops.* I might have said that a little too loud.

Braxton lifts his head. As Anna sits beside him, she glances up and across the yard, spearing me with those eyes. The dark daggers I've ignored for almost a full week.

"Chill," Zack grits but I'm over this evening. Over watching some other guy touch her and tease her and make her smile.

Isn't that what's going to happen if you don't tell her how you feel?

Someone else is going to realize she's a catch. Swim in and hook her. Fucking hell. Now I'm thinking in fishing metaphors.

Without excusing myself, I stand and head inside the house making a beeline for the bar. As I stand before the counter, preparing to make myself another drink, a hand cups my elbow and tugs me toward the den.

"What the . . ."

Anna pinches me through my button-down which is rolled to my elbows. I removed my suit coat after the second drink. It's warm.

Anna's heels tap on the tile floor before she pushes open the door to the den and we both stumble inside. She closes the door behind me, and I spin to face her.

"What are you doing?" Her voice is hushed even though there isn't anyone near. Everyone else is outside where the party has finished dinner and people linger before we head down the beach stairs for the bonfire.

"What am I doing? What are *you* doing?!" I echo and flick my hand upward.

Anna shifts, jutting out one hip while her arms cross over her middle. Her head tilts.

"Oh, come on, Anna. Don't play innocent with me. I see you with Braxton."

Her face pinkens and she chokes. "Braxton? He's just . . . flirty. It's nothing."

"Nothing?" I parrot. "Nothing!" Both my hands slip into my hair and clutch at it.

"Are you jealous?" Her eyes narrow while she fights a small grin.

I snort in disbelief but hell yes, I'm jealous. Jealous that she's smiling at him while she's only giving me those soft eyes. Ones I can't read.

"You're making everyone uncomfortable." Her arms lower, hands curling into fists at her sides.

"Uncomfortable?" I huff. "Uncomfortable would be wearing that dress without your underwear. What's happening here is . . . I don't know what's happening."

"Is that what you want?" She tilts her head. "Do you need me to take off my underwear?" She loses the battle with a flirtatious smile, but I'm too wound up to respond.

"I don't want sex with you, Anna."

The smile melts from her face. Gone is any teasing like an eraser over an old chalkboard.

"That's not what I meant." I sigh.

"We need to talk but now isn't the time," she whispers.

"Time." A bitter laugh fills my throat. "That's all I've been giving is time."

"Time for what?" She tilts her head again.

"Time to grieve. Time to heal. Time to love me." Our eyes lock on each other. "I fucking love you, Anna."

The words rip from my throat. I feel like I've sliced open my chest and tossed my most vital organ at her feet. My heart throbs, hammering so hard I can hardly breathe.

Anna watches me for the longest seconds of my life. "I love you, too."

I don't know who moves first but we're on one another in a heartbeat. Lips on lips. Fingers in her hair. Her hands clutch my shirt. Our bodies are pressed together as if molded for one another. Perfect pieces. Gears that make a machine work. Or puzzle forms that click.

"You're killing me with him," I say as I take her lip and nip her hard.

"I'm not with him." The responding tug of my lip is just as pinching.

"God, I want to lay you out in this room and fuck some sense into both of us."

"Do it." Her command stops us both. Clutching her head between my hands, we stare at one another, breathing hard, chests heaving.

"You don't mean that." While she's been adventurous in bed, she'd never let me have her with a party outside the house.

"Then tonight. In my room." She focuses on my eyes, pinning me in place.

Does she mean it?

"When the party is over. I want you in my bed."

Hot damn. When did my quiet girlfriend become so domineering? And who knew I'd like it so much?

"You better keep those panties intact, sweetheart, because once they're off, you're mine."

"I'm already yours, so stop acting like you want to cut off heads." She does a poor imitation of a Cockney accent, but she's so fucking cute.

Laughter fills my throat and I kiss her once more, long and hard and making my mark. She sheepishly smiles as she pulls away.

"Did we really just say that to one another?" She might need to pinch me again above the elbow.

"We did. And I mean it." She stares up at me while smoothing down my shirt. "I love you."

Chewing on my lower lip, I feel like a giddy teen.

"I love you, too, beautiful."

Chapter 45

1 Month Ago
August

Bedtime

[Anna]

Mason's jealous streak startled me, but I did my best to show him he's the only one I want. When we went to the bonfire, I sat beside him on a blanket. We held hands like a couple. A few raised eyebrows were aimed my way, but I only smiled at the questioning gazes. The position was a bold move, but I was staking my claim.

Mason and I are together. We love one another.

However, one person in particular is watching us. When we eventually return to the house, I want to lead Mason to my bedroom but first I need a moment.

Ruth excused herself earlier from the bonfire, stating she was going to bed. Instead, she sits at the kitchen island. A single light glows down on the countertop where a cup of tea rests before her. Mason presses a kiss to Ruth's head and excuses himself, saying he's going to check on Lynlee's progress getting ready for bed.

"Couldn't sleep?" I ask quietly.

"Sleep is wasted on the young." Ruth laughs. We both know kids need sleep as they grow and to rejuvenate their brains for schoolwork. But I agree with her. It'd be nice to shut off the brain and sleep at night as adults.

"Tea?" she offers, holding up her cup.

"I'll just grab some water." We share a smile and I retrieve a glass from the cabinet. Once I fill it with water, I take a long sip before facing her.

Our eyes meet. I have things I should tell her, but I don't know how to begin. "I miss my mother," I say instead.

Ruth's gray brows lift. "We all miss someone." She gives me a knowing smile. "As your only living elder . . ." She chuckles. "Why don't you tell me what's on your mind?"

"I don't know how," I admit. How do I tell the mother of my late husband that I'm in love with his best friend? Do I need to tell her?

In many ways it feels disrespectful to our relationship not to explain myself.

"Then let me start." Her hands release the teacup, and she sits straighter. "When I lost Frank, I thought the world had ended. A heart attack? Not something we ever suspected even though we were aging. Still, I didn't plan to be alone in my sixties."

Ruth glances down at her teacup. "I can't imagine losing the love of my life in my forties." She pauses. "There's still so much *time* to live."

I nod, agreeing with her as I clutch the glass of water to my chest.

"There are a million sayings about time. Don't waste it. Can't buy it." Ruth waves a hand. "No one can tell you how to spend it, though. That's up to you to decide."

"I know," I whisper, not certain where she's going.

"But if I might offer some advice." She looks up at me again, arching a brow. "Enjoy it. Whatever your decision, make certain that time makes you happy."

I swallow as thickness fills my throat. I'm nodding again without admitting anything.

"You and I are special, dear. We have time. It might feel like a curse. Survivor guilt, I've been told. But there is so much to live for. Your children. Yourself." Ruth exhales. "And love."

I step forward, keeping the island as a barrier between us.

"I didn't plan for it to happen," I say, confessing the truth. I certainly never expected I would feel like this again.

"There are so many things we can't plan in life. Even when we do expect them, like babies and dying. We just never know the joy and sorrow those things will bring to our lives. We can only be grateful for the time we had in between."

Ruth's advice sounds so much like Amelia's though they are decades apart in age.

"Living is where we love. Some never find it, Anna. Some find it once in their life. Others are twice blessed. To have two men love you so strongly, so differently, how could you not love them both."

"You know?" I whisper, keeping my eyes on her.

"One doesn't watch her children without noticing their friends and *noting* when one of them has his eye on a girl." Ruth stares back at me. "You'll always be Ben's. But more importantly, you need to be Anna. And that means, now, you belong to another."

Giving me a warm smile, she adds, "Be careful with this one."

"You don't think he's a good man?" My brows lift, concerned.

Ruth shakes her head, suggesting I've misunderstood. "I think he's a man who needs you more than anyone else. And you need him, too." She winks.

"So I have your permission?" I set the water glass on the countertop.

Ruth's brows raise. Her voice fills with surprise. "Do you need my permission? You're a grown adult. It's your life."

"I'd still like your blessing. Your understanding."

Ruth sighs. Her shoulders relaxing. "No one understands more than me, honey." Compassion fills her smile. "But if you need to hear the words . . . you have all my blessings. For health. For happiness. For love."

"Thank you," I whisper before rounding the counter and pulling her into a hug.

She pats my back and I release her. "Now, you get upstairs to your new man."

"Ruthie," I groan, as if she's read my thoughts. I glance down at my bare feet.

"He's a looker, that one. But he's only been looking at you."

My head snaps up. I can't seem to fight the smile despite my embarrassment.

"Good night, Anna."

"Night."

+ + +

After a final inspection of locks and lights, I climb the stairs. Mason steps into the hallway as I reach the top step.

"Everything okay down there?" His blue eyes soften, cautious. Maybe afraid I've changed my mind but I'm not going backward. My talk with Ruth solidified that Ben is my past.

Mason is my future.

"Everything is perfect." I step up to him and take his hand, leading him toward my bedroom as I walk backward.

"We don't have to do this." His tone gives me an out, but his eyes say he wants in. He wants me.

"We should have done this sooner. You were right." Chewing on my lower lip, wondering if he really has changed his mind, I pause outside my bedroom door. The new room has been a refreshing change while a little bit of a reminder when I was a teenager and only came to Lakeside Cottage for visits.

"Can you say that again?" he teases, stepping closer to me.

I bump into the door at my back. "You were right?" I tip up a brow.

"So glad you agree." He reaches around me and turns the knob, rushing us both inside my bedroom.

I'm spun and my body thuds against the door. Mason locks it while taking my lips in a searing kiss. This man has marked me in so many ways. He's also taught me some things about myself. Like how to demand what I want and take what I need from him. And what I need now is him.

I tug his shirt while he loosens his belt. He smells of campfire and beach air. Once his belt is undone, his fingers are on my dress, tugging the material up over my head and tossing it off to the side.

"You're a fucking vision," he mutters, taking his time to swipe a hand down my chest before cupping one breast. He pulls down the cup of my bra and plumps up the swell before bending down to take me in this mouth. His tongue swirls and I dig my fingers into his hair.

"You have too many clothes on," I tell him.

He only hums before moving to my other breast, sucking and twirling that tongue of his. Then he reaches behind me and pops the clasp on my bra. After it falls to the floor, he takes my hand and walks backward before his knees hit the bed. He sits, keeping me standing before him.

"What we said earlier . . ." He glances down at our joined fingers. Standing before him in only my underwear, I'd feel anxious if I didn't sense his vulnerability. He looks up at me once more. "I just want you to know how much I love you. And I don't want to lose you."

"I think I know," I whisper, combing through his hair and cupping the back of his neck. "And I love you, too."

"This isn't just some wedding thing, right?"

"What do you mean?"

"You . . . we aren't just caught up in your brother and our friend getting married."

I stare at him, understanding what he's saying but not interested in talking. Not yet. "Mason." I smile. "Shut up and kiss me."

"Yes, ma'am." He cups my face and kisses me but the tenderness in his lips hints that tonight is different. It isn't the wedding, but the location tonight. We're in my room and I'm making a statement. I'm ready for us to move forward.

Mason stands and spins us, so I sit on the bed. "Scoot back." He watches me move up the bed while he unbuttons his shirt and tugs it down his arms, giving me a striptease act like none other. I've never been to a male review show, but the guys on a stage taking off their clothes would have nothing on Mason. His socks and shoes were removed on the beach, so he only needs to slip down his pants, taking his boxer briefs with them. He pauses, standing before me a second so I can take in the glory of him.

Then, he drops his knees on the bed and crawls toward me like a predator. Only I'm willing prey, ready to be devoured by him. Somehow, I sense tonight won't be like that. Mason doesn't need to hunt me. He has me and his next kiss proves it.

The kiss is fierce and forces me back to the pillows. His hand coasts down my body, covering every curve and dip while his lips never leave mine. Then his fingers find where I need him most. I moan into his mouth, and he pulls back to glance where he touches me.

"This will never get old. Some days I'm still amazed I'm touching you. Pleasing you."

"You do please me," I assure him.

"I want to do everything for you, anything for you." He lazily looks up at me while scooting his body lower. Those blue eyes spark in the dim light of my room, and he doesn't lose focus as he settles between my thighs. He licks across my slit.

"I love the taste of you."

"I love you," I say to him, combing my fingers through his hair again.

"God, Anna." The phrase is like a switch, turning him into a savage, feasting on me. I have to bite my tongue not to cry out in a house full of people. This is one reason why I've enjoyed sneaking into the apartment bedroom. My children aren't in the other rooms. No guests to hear how much this man drives me wild.

Still, I writhe and groan until stars speckle the ceiling in my vision. Then, he's climbing up over me. His length is hard and throbbing, as he kisses me hard again. The gentleness of his hand on my jaw is in opposition to the kiss.

"You asked me on the boat to make love to you, and I didn't think I knew how." He murmurs at my mouth. "But tonight. I want you to feel how much I love you."

"I do," I whisper. "Every single time." Every time he looks at me, touches me, enters me, I know he feels what I feel.

With his tip at my entrance, he eases in, taking time like he hasn't before. Our coming together is often done in an eager rush and hard thrusts, with time constraints and anxiety that we'll be caught. But there's no fear tonight.

"Fuck. You feel incredible."

With my knees bent, and our hips touching, I wrap my arm around him and hold him to me. "I've never felt anything like this."

I mean it. Mason is different. Or maybe I'm different. Age. Experience. Desire. It has all turned me into this woman. The one beneath him. The one continually surprised at how he makes me feel. That *he's* touching me, tasting me, entering me.

"You feel amazing, too," I whisper to his ear as his head buries in my neck a second. Then, he's pulling back and stroking fingers over my face as his hips rock. Forward and back. Slow and easy. Time ticks in a new beat.

Mason. Mason. Mason.

He fills me up and teases me as he draws back. Suddenly, the tender pace isn't enough, and our bodies react needing more. A little faster. A touch rougher. A bit out of sync as the rush begins. The build climbs.

"Anna." Mason holds one hip, surging forward. In. Out. In. Out.

"I'm right here," I tell him, clutching at his shoulder blades, wrapping a leg over his hip. Begging him with my body to stay connected, to stay as one.

His hand slips between us and he glances down where his fingers stroke me while his thickness enters me.

"God, I love you." His head snaps up, gaze latching onto my eyes. "I fucking love you." He says it like it's a wonder. Like he almost can't believe it. Or maybe he can't believe he's telling me. Opening himself up and giving me all his truths.

"I love you, baby."

His mouth is on mine while his hips take over, moving faster. His length fills me, and the friction of his fingers sets me off. Mouth open but sound stilled, I silently scream as I come undone around him.

"Every time," he mutters. "Fucking gets me every damn time." He stills, digging into my depths as far as he can reach and going off inside me.

Mason gives me his weight only briefly before slipping to my side, taking me with him. We're a tangle of legs and arms, still connected in one important way.

"I don't want you to leave."

Mason pulls his head back, scanning my face. "Your bed?"

"My bed. This house. My life." Earlier fears strain my final thoughts.

He pops up on an elbow. "What are you saying?"

"I don't want you to move to a new house."

"Are you asking me not to leave the apartment?" His expression hardens a bit. A muscle in his jaw ticks.

"I'm asking you not to go anywhere. I'd like you to stay tonight in this bed." I hesitate, suddenly shy about what I want. "And every night after that."

"Anna," he whispers.

"I'm tired of sleeping alone. I'm tired of you being over there and me being in here. I want you with me all the time." I lower my lids, fearing he'll reject that idea. He said he wanted a house of his own. One for Lynlee and him with a yard and a swing set. Maybe he doesn't want more in *this* house.

"Yeah?" His voice croaks around the word.

"Yeah." I meet his eyes and hold, willing him to read the emotion in them. I love him like I've said but there is so much more to what I feel than just three words. "I want to go to bed every night with you and wake up with you and spend days with you and—"

He's kissing me and I sigh against his mouth.

"I want all those things as well. I know some of it isn't much different than what we already do but going to bed each night . . . when you leave my bed . . . I'm always missing you, sweetheart."

"Me too," I admit.

"Ask me to stay and I will." He stares at me, and I'm puzzled a second.

Then it hits me. He'd asked me this once before and I told him to leave. We had reasons then.

"I want you to stay. I want us."

Mason smiles before crushing his mouth to mine once more and rolling so he's on his back and I blanket his body.

"I'm going to love you all the days and all the nights. In this bed. In this house, Anna. Always."

We both know forever isn't guaranteed, but all the days and all the nights equals . . .

"Always."

Chapter 46

1 Month Ago
August

Weddings and Other Rituals

[Mason]

"How is it we're in a bathroom again?" I mutter into her neck, inhaling the warm summery scent of her. Our position is reminiscent of days we snuck into the bathroom at her house, hiding out from the kids. After last night, there will be no more hiding.

In her long dress, exposing her back to me, she's been a tease all evening. Archer and Jenna are officially married, and the reception is in full swing downstairs in the newly renovated dining hall of Bluebird Hollow Inn.

"Because you can't keep your hands off me?" Anna teases, meeting my eyes in the small, rectangular mirror over the tiniest bathroom sink I've ever seen. In fact, this space is hardly large enough for one, let alone two people. No wonder it had water closet labeled on the door.

"If I remember, you're the one who led me up here."

Her eyes twinkle back at me. We're as close as too people can be.

I'm balls deep inside her. Her dress is hiked over her shoulder and my pants are just above my knees. And there is nowhere else I want to be than right here, buried inside her, with her looking at me like she is.

"Fuck, you're beautiful," I whisper.

"You're kind of pretty yourself." She winks.

"I love you," I say to her reflection, loving the playful side of her.

"I love you." Her face turns the sweetest of pink colors and I return to nipping at her neck. She rocks back and the movement shifts me. This angle allows me to feel her in such a different way.

I can't wait to continue to discover all the angles and positions and places with her.

+ + +

Later at night, Anna is on her stomach as I collapse beside her on the bed. On my back, I stare up at the ceiling.

I can't seem to get enough of her.

I'll definitely never have my fill of her telling me she loves me. Or being beside her in bed.

"I'm so tired," she moans, closing her eyes.

"You did so much for them." I turn my head in her direction. Anna really took over as wedding planner for Archer. As she's good at organization and can be a little bossy at times, going into teacher mode, she was a natural at pulling together a wedding in a few months. "Jenna and Archer looked so happy."

Watching Archer exchange vows with Jenna really hit me hard. I've wanted what I saw for so long and didn't think I'd ever come close to having it.

"What's that look for?" Anna quietly asks beside me.

My brows pinch even tighter. "What look?"

"What are you thinking over there?" She rolls to her side and tugs the sheet up over her breasts.

"Just thinking about weddings, I guess." I gaze back at the ceiling.

"I'm not sure if this is the right time to say this . . ."

My head rolls on the pillow again. She's chewing her lip like she's anxious and I open my mouth to speak but she covers my lips with her fingers.

"The answer is yes. If you ever have a question you'd like to ask me. The answer would be yes."

"A question?" I ask, but my heart hammers, blood rushing. Is she saying what I think she's saying? This is more than I ever dreamed happening. Well, I dreamt it. I fantasized it. But the reality of Anna really saying yes to me, that was a thought I couldn't allow myself to consider.

Still, I'm not prepared to ask. Not like this. Not naked and in bed.

This is Anna. She needs special. I need special.

"Would that question be, what kind of pizza you'd like for dinner?" I tease, watching as her eyes light up with laughter.

"That isn't a yes or no question," she playfully frowns.

"How about what position should I take you in next?" I shift to face her, mirroring her.

"Also, not exactly a direct answer question." Her lips slowly curl.

"What about something along the lines of always?" My lungs expand. I hold my breath.

"Yes."

"Hmm." I tease. "Was I asking a question?" I reach for her and tug her closer to me. Her legs tangle with mine as my arm slides over her waist and I cup her nape.

"I don't know. Were you?" She giggles until I lean forward and lick along her neck.

"The only yes I want to hear right now is when I taste you again."

"That's not a question either but the answer is yes please."

I nip the juncture of her shoulder and neck, and she yelps with a laugh in her throat. Then, I'm kissing her.

I do have a question for her.

Soon.

+ + +

We don't necessarily make a two-week vacation around Archer's wedding. We took days off for the celebration, though. As we spend so much time together for both business and pleasure, we didn't see the need to actually gather at Lakeside Cottage.

Hell, we all live in the area now.

I've officially moved into Anna's bedroom. *Our* bedroom as she calls it. Lynlee's things were moved into the room next to Mila. We'll be painting and arranging next weekend.

But first is the night dedicated to our annual bonfire.

The guys and I decided to forgo the tradition of only us. Instead, we keep all the families present deciding our best response to Ben's request

318

would be to show him—if he's watching—how our family of friends has found love and grown.

Logan and Autumn are here with Lorna, two-year old Ben, and little Ruth, the newest addition to their family.

Zack and River along with the twins plus Lake have just announced another baby will be coming soon.

Archer and Jenna are still on their honeymoon, but Archer wasn't ever part of our inner circle. However, they plan to be with us next year as they celebrate their one-year anniversary as Mr. and Mrs. McCaryn.

Anna hopes Amelia can join us as well.

We assemble as living proof that life goes on despite loss. And while our hearts are full of memories of Ben, the present is where we need to live. And learn. And love.

The women in our lives all know about the letters we received. They also know our ritual used to include writing Ben a response.

Instead, we're quiet around the fire, watching the flames flicker and dance in the late evening. The kids have wandered down the beach a little, dancing in their own way with sparklers, lit by Calvin and Bryce. They are both nearly men in their own right, and they understand the meaning of this night. They are giving us a few minutes before marshmallow roasting.

"This is for you," Anna says, leaning into my arm. We're sitting on a blanket while the others fill the Adirondack chairs.

"What's this?" I take the envelope from her, quickly flipping it over to see her name written in Ben's distinct handwriting.

"I found this when I was cleaning out the main bedroom. When I did a final sweep before moving out my things and making the space for Amelia." Anna pauses. "Remember how I'd been so upset that he didn't write me a letter?"

I nod, recalling how she stormed out of the room, angry that she'd been skipped.

"Knowing I'd need something from him at a later date, he intentionally didn't leave me a letter. He knew I'd still be grieving and anything he said then I'd fight."

I twirl the envelope between my fingers. "And?"

"A post-it note was on the outside of that. It said, if you found this, you're ready." She shrugs but her eyes don't leave the small shape between my fingers. "A heart shaped rock was on top of it."

For a moment, I worry that Anna thinks I had something to do with this. Or even that I copied Ben in finding rocks all over this beach for her.

"The rock was perfectly shaped and evenly polished. He'd obviously bought it at a store." She smiles like she knows a secret to his decision and there is a private meaning to that polished stone.

"Read it." She nods at the envelope.

"Are you sure?" I'll admit curiosity has the best of me, but she can keep her thoughts and memories about Ben. She doesn't need to share them all with me.

As she's leaning toward me, she bumps into my shoulder to encourage me. I flip open the flap and slide a single cardstock rectangle out of its holder.

Live every moment, Anna.
Find love. Learn lessons. Accept loss.
Then do it all over again.
Be happy and well, my heart.

"The rock seems symbolic. Ben was polished while you're a little rough around the edges."

My head shoots up and I stare at her over my shoulder. Her smile suggests she's teasing me and doesn't mind the difference.

"Ben was one in a million." Her voice drops but her eyes don't leave mine. "But you're a million in one." Anna licks her lips. "And I'm lucky to have you both love me and to have loved . . . well, currently love . . ." She tips her head. "You both."

I slip the note back in the envelope and hold it out to her. "Thank you for sharing that with me."

Anna tucks it into the back pocket of her shorts and I continue. "You know, you can talk about him with me. Tell me things. Share your feelings. I'm going to listen and understand. Anytime."

"I know." She looks back up at me, giving me another timid smile, before wrapping both her arms around mine and placing her head on my shoulder. "That's one of those million reasons why I love you so much."

I kiss the top of her head and gaze across the fire.

Zack's eyes meet mine first. He smiles, tipping his head. He's been happy for me. For us.

I glance at Logan next, who wiggles his brows while holding his baby girl to his chest. He gives me a thumbs up.

These men are my best friends. The brothers I never had. They are my family along with the woman beside me and our kids.

And together, life goes on.

Epilogue

Present Day
September

On The Beach

[Anna]

"Hey you. What are you doing down here?" I find Mason standing on the beach facing the lake.

It's the first weekend in September. A time when summer ends and fall unofficially begins. A new season is about to start.

Mason's been quiet the past week or so. The night of the bonfire we made love again, similar to the night of Archer's wedding. Something more was happening between us.

Having Mason move into the house permanently and into my bedroom didn't feel as daunting as I thought it would be with the kids.

Resilience. They've had much more of it than me.

Mason seemed like the natural choice to stand by my side. Not replace their father but be my partner.

My lover. My best friend.

With the wedding over and the bonfire more of a party than a memory fest this year, I've been lighter. Happy.

We'll soon settle back into the school year rat race once I return to work. Lynlee will start first grade. Mila will enter eighth grade and an adjustment in her friendship with Lorna will occur as Lorna is a freshman in high school. Bryce will be a senior. Next year at this time, he'll leave as well. One more loss. Only this one is another adventure my children need to make on their own.

Calvin left for college two weeks ago.

I slip up to Mason and wrap my arms around him, hugging him from behind. He didn't answer my earlier question, only peered over his shoulder at me.

"Find any heart-shaped rocks?" He's been running and smells of sweat, sunshine, and man. I squeeze him and place my cheek on his arm as he's too tall for me to reach his shoulder. He rubs a hand over my forearm at his waist.

"A few. In my pocket."

As I'm grabby hands, I slip my fingers into his loose shorts, seeking treasure.

One. Two. Three. Four. It's been a good rock searching day.

But something else is in his pocket and I slip my fingers back inside.

"What's this?" I pull out the item and stare at it as Mason turns in my arms. He takes it from me and holds it up higher.

"Remember that question you asked me about? The one you promised to answer with a yes?"

I tilt my head knowing exactly what he's referring to.

"I'd like to ask it now." As he speaks, he lowers to one knee in the cool sand.

I swallow. Sudden nerves make my heart race. I clutch my fingers together and lift them under my chin, keeping my eyes on him.

"When I found the first heart-shaped rock on the beach, it was only meant to be a reminder that you're strong. You're loved."

His Adam's apple bobs.

"I didn't know you'd enjoy them so much. It became a mission to find new ones and remind you often that you could handle what laid ahead. As difficult as it would be, you were going to go on. Like the battered stones that took the shape of hearts."

I swallow again as tears blur my vision.

"Anna. I've loved you from afar for over twenty-five years. And now, I'd like to love you up close."

"Very close," I whisper, trying to tease him but the words are choked with emotion.

"Days and nights. And all the in betweens."

"Yes," I blurt and Mason chuckles, tipping his head.

"Did I ask a question yet?"

I giggle and cover my lips with my fingers.

"Anna. I'm asking for always. I'd love for you to be my wife. And it would be my honor to be your husband."

I roll my lips and lower my hands. "Is there a question in there?"

Mason shakes his head and good-naturedly huffs. "Yes."

"That's my line." I laugh. Then, I reach down for his face and cup his jaw. "Yes. To days. And nights. All the in betweens."

Mason takes my hand. His trembles while mine is steady as he slips a gorgeous heart shaped diamond on my finger.

Diamonds get their start in the rough.

And while a precious stone is polished and cut in a distinct mold, even the weathered and worn can turn into something beautiful.

Like this man.

"I love you," I tell him.

"I love you, Anna. Always."

Thank you for taking the time to read this book.
Please consider writing a review on major sales channels where ebooks and paperbacks are sold and discussed.

For a bonus scene of Anna and Mason.

Did you start at the beginning of Lakeside Cottage?
Read *LIVING at 40*.

If you like small lake towns, you might also enjoy
THE HEART COLLECTION.

More by L.B. Dunbar

Scrooge-ish
A flirty, over four, silver fox, second chance holiday romance.

Road Trips & Romance
3 sisters. 3 destinations. A second chance at love over 40.
Hauling Ashe
Merging Wright
Rhode Trip

Lakeside Cottage
Four friends. Four summers. Shenanigans and love happen at the lake.
Living at 40
Loving at 40
Learning at 40
Letting Go at 40

The Silver Foxes of Blue Ridge
More sexy silver foxes in the mountain community of Blue Ridge.
Silver Brewer
Silver Player
Silver Mayor
Silver Biker

Sexy Silver Foxes
When sexy silver foxes meet the feisty vixens of their dreams.
After Care
Midlife Crisis
Restored Dreams
Second Chance
Wine&Dine

Collision novellas
A spin-off from After Care – the younger set/rock stars
Collide
Caught

Rom-com standalone for the over 40
The Sex Education of M.E.

The Heart Collection
Small town, big hearts - stories of family and love.
Speak from the Heart
Read with your Heart
Look with your Heart
Fight from the Heart
View with your Heart

A Heart Collection Spin-off
The Heart Remembers

BOOKS IN OTHER AUTHOR WORLDS
Smartypants Romance (an imprint of Penny Reid)
Tales of the Winters sisters set in Green Valley.
Love in Due Time
Love in Deed
Love in a Pickle

The World of True North (an imprint of Sarina Bowen)
Welcome to Vermont! And the Busy Bean Café.
Cowboy
Studfinder

THE EARLY YEARS
The Legendary Rock Star Series
A classic tale with a modern twist of rock star romance and suspense
The Legend of Arturo King
The Story of Lansing Lotte
The Quest of Perkins Vale
The Truth of Tristan Lyons
The Trials of Guinevere DeGrance

Paradise Stories
MMA romance. Two brothers. One fight.
Abel
Cain

L.B. DUNBAR

<u>The Island Duet</u>
Intrigue and suspense. The island knows what you've done.
Redemption Island
Return to the Island

<u>Modern Descendants – writing as elda lore</u>
Magical realism. Modern myths of Greek gods.
Hades
Solis
Heph

About the Author

www.lbdunbar.com

L.B. Dunbar loves sexy silver foxes, second chances, and small towns. If you enjoy older characters in your romance reads, including a hero with a little silver in his scruff and a heroine rediscovering her worth, then welcome to romance for those over 40. L.B. Dunbar's signature works include women and men in their prime taking another turn at love and happily ever. Along with her #sexysilverfox collection, she's made Amazon Top 10 in Later in Life Romance with her Lakeside Cottage and Road Trips & Romance series. She is also a *USA Today Bestseller*. L.B. lives in Chicago with her own sexy silver fox.

To get all the scoop about the self-proclaimed queen of silver fox romance, join her on Facebook at Loving L.B. or receive her monthly newsletter, Love Notes.

+ + +

Connect with L.B. Dunbar

www.ingramcontent.com/pod-product-compliance
Lightning Source LLC
Chambersburg PA
CBHW051436050726

47593CB00005B/1806